Lucy's Legacy

To Margaret.
The Lord bless you
and keep you, and make
his face to shine on you!
Linda Sawley.

Linda Sawley

Published by Burnley Local Authors

Proof reader Barbara Schultz
Cover design by Helen and Philip Creegan

Printed by Nu-Age Print & Copy
289 Padiham Road, Burnley
BB12 0HA
01282 413373

Dedicated to all the excellent teachers I've had in my life, especially Cynthia Ramsay (neé Shaw)

Thank you to all my regular readers, some of whom have supported me from the beginning of my writing journey. Without you, there is no point in writing. Thank you!

Also dedicated to the memory of Debs Foster, an inspirational young woman.

Other books by the same author

Everyone Else's Children (autobiography) 1998

A Ring in Time 2002

The Key
(Mitchell's Modes Saga Book 1) 2004
Changes
(Mitchell's Modes Saga Book 2) 2005
New Century: Changed Lives (Kindle version only)
(Mitchell's Modes Saga Book 3) 2014

The Survivor 2007

Anna 2010

Joshua and the Horrible History Project 2011
(recommended reading age 7 to 13 years, but enjoyed by 5 to 90 years)

Weaving Through the Years 2012

Linda Sawley's Collection of Short Stories 2014 (Kindle version only)

The Rector's Pearl 2016 (Kindle version only)

Pemberley in Waiting 2017

The Quiet Neighbours 2020

1919

Saturday had arrived at long last. The young widow looked round her living room with pride. It had been cleaned thoroughly; not that it needed it as she always kept on top of any dirt, but a special visitor was coming today. His letter said that he would arrive at Whalley station at 1pm, so she could expect him before half-past. He was a former war colleague of her late husband's and he said that he was bringing some of her husband's personal belongings to give to her. She had got up early today, leaving her young daughter asleep in bed, to bake some special treats for their lunch. There were cheese and onion pasties, chicken and mushroom pies, ham and cheese sandwiches, cheese and fruit scones, a Victoria sandwich and butterfly buns. She had baked far more than they could possibly eat at one meal, but she wanted to show her gratefulness that he was coming to visit her. Besides, she loved baking.

Once her daughter arrived downstairs, the mother gave her little jobs to do after her breakfast. The daughter got the best china out, laying it carefully on the large table that was in the centre of the room. The starched cotton napkins were carefully folded and her mother nodded her approval. Later on the little girl asked if she could have something to eat.

'No,' replied her mother, 'wait until the visitor comes. Then we can eat. Why don't you go and play with your toys in the parlour? But don't make a mess. I've tidied up in there.'

'All right, I won't make a mess,' she replied. 'I never do.'

'You are right,' her mother replied. 'You are Mummy's good girl.' However, before anything else could be said, there was a knock at the door and the mother hurried to answer it.

A tall, gaunt-looking man stood on the doorstep, his patched and worn clothes hanging loosely on him as if he'd lost weight. He was still wearing his army greatcoat. Hanging on to his hand was a small boy about two or three years old. On his other arm was a large cardboard box and a square package wrapped in brown paper. She wondered why the man had brought his son with him, but remembered her manners before she said anything.

'Come on in. It's so good of you to come. Come in out of the cold and get warm.' The man and boy stepped over the threshold and she led them to the comfy chairs by the fireplace. She took their coats and put them on the hook on the back door, and the parcels on a chair near the sideboard. Her daughter hung back shyly.

'The food's ready, so unless you need to wash your hands or anything, we can make a start. Come and sit at the table.' The man and boy got up and moved towards the table. She remembered that she still had the high chair her husband had made for their daughter, so she got it out of the parlour for the little boy to sit in. When the teapot was brought to the table, she said grace and then they all tucked in to the food. The man talked about his journey and general matters, but the little boy never spoke; he just sat eating and looking warily about him.

After the food was finished, she suggested that her daughter took the little boy into the parlour so they could play with the toys, whilst more serious adult talk could take place. The little boy was a bit reluctant to go, but was soon persuaded by the man's encouragement and the mention of building bricks.

'My daddy made these building bricks for me out of bits of wood,' she could hear her daughter jabbering away. Satisfied that they could talk in more detail, she left them and returned to the man at the table.

'So, what have you got of my husband's? I got the official letter that all the soldiers were recommended to write before they went to the Front, but that's all I got, and letters from his commanding officer and a doctor he worked with.'

The man went to his coat pocket and pulled out a small package and passed it over to her. On opening it, she saw a lot of her letters that she had written to her husband and her eyes filled with tears. There was also his pocket watch, which was a present she had given him on their wedding day. Finally there was his tiny Bible, which just contained the Gospels and the Psalms.

'Is that all?' she asked, a little disappointed. The man swallowed and looked nervous.

'Yes, apart from the boy.'

'The boy? What do you mean? Isn't he your son?'

'No. It's your husband's son.'

'My husband's son? That's ridiculous! How can that be?' she asked, her whole world falling apart.

'With his last breath your husband asked me to bring the boy to you. He said you'd understand and forgive him.'

Chapter 1
1907

Lucy Coombes knew that she had to say something this Sunday or she may never pluck up the courage again. She had discussed it with her parents so many times before, but they had always said no. This time Lucy had all the facts to hand and a better argument than she had had previously. She had also spoken to William, her elder brother, who, although he thought she was a little touched in her head, agreed that it would be a good thing and he would be on her side. To be honest, Lucy reflected, he probably only said that to shut her up, but she would use anything to get her own way. The only flaw in the plan was that Granny Wall would be there for the day. She was an amazing lady, a real godly woman, but very set on what a woman could or should do. Yes, she might be a problem, even though she loved her granny dearly.

For months now, Lucy had felt that God was leading her to work with children. There seemed to be messages about working with children. There had been sermons on 'Suffer the little children to come unto me', and on the future of the church being the children. The minister emphasised the necessity of teaching and service to others being of paramount importance. Yes, she was sure that was where God was leading her, but could she convince her parents today?

Another reason for choosing to talk to them today was that it was Easter Sunday. They'd been to church this morning and had sung victoriously about Jesus having risen from the dead. After the service, they had all shaken hands, proclaiming that 'Christ is risen' and replying, 'He is risen indeed.' Yes, her father would be in a good mood, especially as her mother had presided over a sumptuous feast, cooked by Mrs Ward and the maid Patsy. They wouldn't have a formal evening meal tonight so that the kitchen staff could have time off with their own families, taking home a large portion of leftovers for their own celebrations. Tonight's meal would be simply sandwiches and the beautiful Easter simnel cake that was waiting in the pantry. By early evening, her father would have had his afternoon nap and would be in the best of moods. There was no evening service on Easter Sundays, so no reason to be hurrying out again as they usually did. Yes, after the simnel cake, she would mention it.

Barely able to contain her excitement, Lucy had only a small sandwich and a sliver of simnel cake, even though she loved it normally. Taking a deep breath, she began her carefully thought out speech.

'Father, I've got some leaflets here from Owen's College, or Manchester University as it is now being called. They train ladies for teaching.'

'Lucy,' her father exploded, 'how many times have I told you that you are not going to train as a teacher! Other girls are quite content to sit at home and learn from their mothers how to run a home until the day they marry. That's what girls were made for.'

'Well, why did God give girls the same brains as men, then?' she asked angrily.

'Lucy, don't give cheek to your father. You know he only has your best interests at heart,' replied her mother Martha.

'I'm just as clever as our William and you don't tell him he can't train for anything.'

'That's different,' interjected her father Edward. 'He's a man. He will need to provide for a wife and children one day.'

'Lots of girls are training now for teaching, so why can't I?'

'You don't need to work. Your father will provide for you until your husband takes over, and then he'll provide for you,' added her mother, not wanting to be left out of the discussion.

'What husband?' asked Lucy. 'I've not seen a queue forming down the street lately. What if I don't marry? What if I want to have a worthwhile career first, or even instead of marriage?'

'There'll be someone special that will want to marry a pretty girl like you,' her father cajoled. 'What about John Bates at church? I know he likes you.'

'He's soppy, Father. I could never marry him.'

'What about Micah Swindlehirst?'

'Never! He has a mean streak in him. He doesn't like animals and he's cruel to his horse.'

'I think you're just a bit picky, Lucy,' complained her mother. 'You're almost 18 now. Time you were thinking of settling down and providing me with some grandchildren to dandle on my knee.'

'I will, Mother, if you let me train as a teacher first. I'll even make a better mother as I'll know how to teach my children their letters. I'll be a good help to my husband, as I will be better educated than most women.'

'Most men wouldn't want you to be too educated, Lucy,' her father replied. 'They would call you a blue-stocking. Shameful!'

'Just look at the leaflets, please?' Lucy pleaded. 'There's special accommodation just for women now, called Ashburne House. The ladies are looked after by a housekeeper, who makes sure they are safe.'

'Where did you get all this information from, I'd like to know?' said her angry father. Lucy knew it was time to play her trump card.

'I got it from Miss Seeney at church.' There was silence in the room and for once Lucy controlled her loquacious tongue.

'Miss Seeney?' asked her father. Lucy nodded, unable to speak. Lucy knew that had got them all thinking. Miss Seeney had arrived at their church two years ago. She had just taken up a post at Lionel Street Infant School and, because Mrs Wills was having another confinement soon, had taken over the running of the Sunday School, much to Mrs Wills' delight, as her increasing brood was making it difficult for her to continue in her role. Recently Miss Seeney had brought another new teacher from the school, Miss Egar, who was also teaching at the Sunday School. Miss Seeney was considered a very resourceful and valued member of the church nowadays, as was Miss Egar.

'Did Miss Seeney train at Manchester?' her mother asked. Lucy nodded.

'Well, it didn't do her any harm. She's an upright young woman and I admire her wholeheartedly,' her mother continued.

Lucy tried another tack. 'Our William thinks it would be good if I trained as a teacher,' she pleaded to everyone in the room.

William laughed. 'Only because I'd get rid of you pestering and asking me to teach you the things that I've been learning at the Mechanics Institute.'

'Well, perhaps we could look into it, if Miss Seeney approves,' said her father slowly. 'I'll talk to her next Sunday.'

'I really feel that God is leading me into this career,' Lucy added. Surely even her father wouldn't argue with God's leading, Lucy hoped and prayed.

'Do I get to give an opinion on this matter?' asked Granny Wall. Lucy's heart sank. Granny would be so damning that her father would change his mind again.

'I think it's more important now that a girl has a career.' Lucy's mouth fell open in disbelief. Had her granny really said that? 'I've been reading about these Suffragists, and they're right. Why shouldn't women have the vote? I'm a woman of property, of independent means and run a business and yet I cannot have a vote, but some people who have the vote abuse it. Lucy is right, too. God did give women brains and they should be allowed to use them. I had long conversations with Miss Seeney at the Faith Supper and I agree with a lot of what she says.'

'Mother, I can't believe you just said all that,' said Lucy's mother.

'I do a lot of thinking when I'm sat on my own, Martha, and, as you know, I like to read the newspapers and keep up with the news. The world is changing, whether you men like it or not,' she said to William and Edward, who both sat with shocked expressions on their faces. Lucy was jubilant with glee and ran towards her granny.

'Granny Wall, thank you so much. You don't know what this means to me.'

'Oh, I think I do. You've talked about nothing else for months. That's why I decided to investigate it,' she added with a chuckle. 'At least we would get some peace if you go.'

'As I said, I'm not promising, but I'll talk to Miss Seeney on Sunday,' her father repeated, as if to remind Granny Wall that he was still the boss in his own house, despite the opinion of his mother-in-law.

The week passed quickly, but too slowly for Lucy, who couldn't wait to see if her plan had worked. It did. Suddenly, the whole house seemed to be in agreement about this next stage of Lucy's life. Her mother reassured herself that Lucy would only be 20 when she finished training and there was still plenty of time for her to get married. Lucy just nodded, but thanked God in her prayers that night that her wish had been granted.

Miss Seeney and Miss Egar helped her to fill in the application form. Lucy grew to highly respect these two ladies, who had made such a difference to her life. Then the exciting letter arrived to say that a place would be available for her to start in September that year. Life became hectic as Lucy and her mother sourced sensible outfits for her to wear. Miss Egar suggested some pinafore-type dresses that could be worn with different blouses or jumpers underneath, depending on the season. Lucy's mother thought it might be a bit early to be buying them, but Miss Egar explained that in the Fielden Demonstration schools, named after the benefactor, Sarah Fielden, Lucy would be teaching quite early on in the course.

At long last, September came round. Lucy's father's groom, Metcalfe, drove the horse and Hansom cab to Manchester, along with her parents

6

and William, who wanted to go along for the ride and to see the city. William got excited every time he saw one of the new horseless carriages and extolled their virtues, but it was falling on deaf ears with his father, as usual. They found the accommodation easily and then wished her well, lifting down all her belongings in a large trunk and a suitcase. Lucy also had a leather satchel to carry her work in daily to her lectures or a teaching session. The people at church had given her little presents: chalks, ink, ink wipers, empty books for taking notes, a ruler, pencils, and coloured pencils. Lucy had been overwhelmed at the final service before her departure. At the end of the service in Bethesda Congregational Church, in the town centre of Burnley, they had brought Lucy to the front of the church, and asked God's blessing on her training and career. Miss Seeney and Miss Egar bought Lucy a beautiful leather-bound Bible, in which they had written a message in the front, wishing her well in her studies. It was all Lucy could do not to cry and she seemed to just keep saying 'thank you' over and over again.

As her parents and William were preparing to leave Manchester, her mother gave Lucy a small package.

'That's from Granny Wall,' she said.

'Thank you, Mother and Father, for letting me do this,' she cried, hugging them both, whilst her father harrumphed at this show of affection in public. They made a striking group: all tall, dark-haired, with the same colour of blue eyes. William and Lucy were both of a slim build, but her mother and father had gained weight as they had got older. Lucy's hair was sensibly braided as befitted her new role of trainee teacher, and she self-consciously smoothed her braids down, even though they hadn't moved an inch since she had fastened them up earlier.

'I suppose you'd better go inside now,' her father said a trifle gruffly, trying to hide the emotion he was feeling.

'Yes, I must,' replied Lucy, and after a last goodbye she walked away into the building, leaving her trunk to be collected by the porter. Even though the teaching course was what she wanted most desperately, as she watched her family drive away, she felt terribly bereft and alone. She would even miss her arguments with William. Still grasping the package from her granny, Lucy turned away from the front door and collided with another girl.

'Oops, sorry, I'm so clumsy,' laughed the girl. She had striking red hair, which was not tied up but flowing behind in a gloriously free way, Lucy noticed. She was only tiny and had an engaging smile and dimples.

'I'm Lucy Coombes. Are you on the training course, too?'

'Yes, I'm Laura Carter.'

'We've got the same initials.'

'So we have. The two LCs we'll have to call ourselves,' but their mutual appreciation society was interrupted by a severe-looking lady approaching them.

'Are you young ladies here for the teaching course?'

'Yes,' they both replied.

'Come this way.' The lady turned round and led them up the stairs, whilst Lucy and Laura grinned at each other behind her back.

'This is your room. You are the last two to arrive. Please put your things away and come downstairs to the Refectory as soon as possible so that you can meet the other students.' With that, she turned and left the room.

Lucy looked round the room. It was the same size as their maid Patsy had at home in the attics. There were two beds, two tiny wardrobes and two small chests of drawers with a candle sconce on each. A small window was at the top of the wall – too high to see out of – with long curtains coming down to the floor. There was a threadbare carpet on the floor and little of any comforts or ornaments; not even a looking-glass.

'It's only the size of our maid's bedroom at home,' Lucy giggled, 'and she has it to herself. Which bed do you want?'

'Can I have the one near the door?' asked Laura. 'I like to be able to get out easily,' she laughed.

'That's fortunate then. I like to be by the window.'

'Good. I can see we're going to get on well, but I suppose we'd better get downstairs to the Refectory.'

Putting her granny's package safely in her drawer, Lucy followed Laura down to the Refectory, locking the door behind her.

Lucy was shocked by the number of people in the Refectory. There were about 100 men and women. That was a surprise too, as she thought that there would only be women in her class. There was no time for further speculation as the severe-looking lady, who turned out to be called Miss Davenport, started giving them instructions and pages of timetables and reading lists.

Fortunately, Miss Seeney had given her a list of suitable books to purchase and also lent Lucy some of her own books to save buying them. They were soon dismissed and after eating a meal that had been provided, Laura and Lucy returned to their bedroom.

'Where do you come from?' asked Lucy, when they had put their belongings away.

'Manchester. And you?'

'Burnley. It's about 25 miles away from here.'

'I'm so excited about the course, aren't you, Lucy?'

'Yes, I had to fight so hard to come here. My mother thought that I should just get married and give her grandchildren.'

Laura giggled. 'My mother told me to come here so that I didn't need to get married.'

'Why not?'

'My parents are poor, Lucy. We don't have a maid. I sleep in a smaller bedroom than this with my two sisters, with a curtain dividing it for my two brothers to sleep in.'

'I'm sorry. I didn't mean to be rude. How did you....', but Lucy stopped. Asking Laura how she'd managed to get on a course like this was even more rude.

'How did I manage to get on this course, were you going to ask?'

Lucy nodded, a little ashamed of herself.

'I was taken from working in the mill to look after the children in the school and teach them their letters, along with a teacher. The teacher said that I showed promise and persuaded the mill owner to pay for my course, on condition that I go back and work there when I qualify.'

'But isn't a mill noisy? How do the children learn there?'

'A mill is noisy, but the school is at the back of the mill, across the road, so it's much quieter there. It's been built by the Borough Council, but the mill owner has promised to pay the teacher's wages as most of the school children work in his mill. Yes, mills are noisy, but then I've known it all my life. My Mum and Dad both work at the mill. Mum's a weaver, and Dad's a tackler. The law says that children who work in the mill can only work part-time and attend school part-time, but they are often too tired to learn after working a shift first. I used to try and make it fun for them, to keep them awake. I always finished the session by reading to

9

them. They loved the books by Mr Dickens that the teacher lent me. Do you love those books, too?'

'I do. I've got them all in the library at home.'

'Library? Are you very rich?'

'No, I don't think so. My father has a manufacturing company and we live in a large house on the outskirts of Burnley. So, I suppose to some people, we appear rich. However, my father gives a lot to charities. He helped fund the local hospital when it was being built and always supports missionaries.'

'Are you an only child?'

'No, I have a brother, William. He's three years older than me.'

'Is he at university?'

'No, he works with my father in the factory, learning the job. He's not very academic, more practical, but he loves the factory and working with my father. William is inclined to be lazy, but father keeps him on his toes,' Lucy laughed.

'What shall we do tomorrow? We don't start lectures until Monday.'

'What do you suggest?' asked Lucy.

'We could go and look round the shops if you like?'

'Yes, I'd like that. You can show me where to go as I've never been to Manchester before.'

'You haven't? Then you're in for a treat. The shops on Deansgate are marvellous, although I only look in the windows as I could never afford anything that they have to sell.'

'Then tomorrow we will go in and look. We don't have to buy anything.'

'Agreed. Now I think we should have an early night if we're going shopping tomorrow.'

The girls blew out their candles, said their prayers, and settled down to sleep, both relieved that they had found each other and were going to be friends during the course. It was only on falling asleep that Lucy remembered the package from her granny. It was too late to look now, so it would have to wait until tomorrow.

Chapter 2

Next morning, Lucy woke early and opened the drawer where she had put the package from Granny Wall. On opening it, she found a letter which she read eagerly.

Dearest Lucy,

I pray that you will use every opportunity that has been given to you on this course. You are a good young woman, although inclined to be impetuous, but I pray that you will allow God to guide you during these next two years. Listen to Him, seek Him, and do not deviate from the teachings of the Bible, and you won't stray from the truth.

I know your father is providing a sum of money for you regularly, but I wanted to give you something so that you can have some little treats that you might not otherwise be able to afford.

I will pray constantly for you.

Your loving Granny.

Inside the package was a small cloth bag. Lucy opened it and was shocked to find 10 guineas. She had never had so much money in her life. Her gasp of surprise woke Laura.

'What's the matter?'

'My granny has given me some money to buy myself some treats.'

'Great. Lucky you. I don't think my granny will do that,' she laughed.

'I'm going to be sensible with it, as I never know when I might need it in the future. My father's going to give me an allowance each month, so I won't really need it.'

'I don't think my father is planning on giving me an allowance. It takes him all his time to feed us all and pay the rent. Although he will be a little better off now he doesn't have to pay for my food. He was delighted when he knew that I'd get all my meals provided.'

'Are you the eldest?'

'Yes, the boys, Albert and Arthur, are only young, so don't earn much yet, being half-timers at school. The girls, Bessie and Agnes, are fourteen and twelve so earn a small wage, which helps, now they've finished with schooling.'

'It must be hard for your father having to feed so many children.'

'There were seven of us, but Henry, who was two years younger than me, died of whooping cough, and the boy between Albert and Arthur died young. He was a bit simple in the head. My mum had a bad time with him; that's what caused it. So, he died young,' Laura added matter-of-factly.

'I'm so sorry. That must have upset your mother, to lose two children?'

'Most families where we live have lost a child or two. It's just the way of things when you're poor.'

Lucy reflected on that and realised just how privileged her upbringing had been, and yet Laura didn't seem bitter about her lot or envious of Lucy's better situation. Lucy wondered if she would have been so gracious if her circumstances had been like Laura's. She didn't like to think about that.

Stopping her morbid train of thoughts, Lucy jumped up. 'Let's go shopping then, Laura,' she said cheerily. 'Perhaps we can have some tea and cake in a café somewhere. Do you know of one?'

'No, I'm not one to go out for tea and cakes,' Laura replied with an attempt at a smile.

'Well, you will be today. I'm going to treat you.'

Laura laughed. 'So much for saving your granny's money.'

'It'll take a lot of tea and cakes to spend granny's money,' replied Lucy, as they put their coats and hats on and ventured outside. They signed out with the doorkeeper, telling him where they were going, that they wouldn't require luncheon that day, and how long they would be, and then set off to the city centre.

The girls eventually arrived in Deansgate and Lucy was overawed by the calibre of shops compared to what was available in Burnley town centre. There was a large department store and Lucy encouraged Laura to go in but she was hesitant.

'This sort of shop is not for the likes of me,' she whispered to Lucy.

'Don't be silly. You are as good as anyone in this shop. We are all equal in God's sight, don't forget.'

'Yes, but some are more equal than others,' quipped Laura. Grasping her arm, Lucy pulled Laura through the door, nodding graciously to the doorman, who had a distinctly disapproving look to him. The ground floor contained furniture and the two girls looked around at what was on offer. Lucy spotted an oval-shaped looking glass on the wall.

'That would be useful in our room, wouldn't it?' Lucy asked.

'It certainly would,' replied Laura, with a longing in her voice.

'Look over there, at the rugs. I think I'd prefer a nice rug by the bedside to cover that old carpet, wouldn't you?'

'Oh, yes,' mimicked Laura, 'one could just see that by the bedside.'

'Never mind, if that's what you think,' said Lucy crossly, not liking to be teased. 'Let's go and look at some other things. There's a sign here. The ladies' department is on the next floor,' and without giving Laura time to reply, Lucy set off up the staircase at a great speed. Laura struggled to keep up with her, but Lucy had already found a navy evening dress trimmed with satin that she was trying against herself in the long mirror. Her former irritation gone, Lucy asked Laura what she thought about the dress.

'Were you thinking of wearing it in the morning or the afternoon class lectures?' Laura asked with a perfectly straight face.

Lucy had to laugh then and replied, 'No, I thought I would wear it for cleaning our rooms on a Saturday morning.'

'Perfect then,' replied Laura, starting to laugh. 'Although I could probably find you something more suitable to wear for the weekly cleaning in our old rag bag at home.'

They watched as some older ladies picked up several garments to try on in the changing rooms, an eager assistant hovering in the background, and commented that they would go to the tearooms afterwards.

'That sounds like a good idea, shall we go to the tearooms now?' asked Lucy.

'If you like,' replied Laura.

'Oh, I do like,' laughed Lucy in return. The two of them went up another two flights of stairs and walked over to the tearooms and were shown to a table.

'Why did we have to be shown to a table? Surely we're capable of walking to a table ourselves?' whispered Laura.

'That's just the way it is. If we were here with a husband or were richer looking, we'd have been shown to a grander table nearer the window, but as he assessed us and decided that we weren't going to be giving a very big tip, we're stuck here, near the door.'

'It's not fair, then, is it?'

'Not really, but that's how it is sometimes.'

'I thought my life was difficult because we have no money,' replied Laura, 'but it's just as bad when you have money. It all depends on how much.'

'That's true,' said Lucy. 'Never mind him. When we're married to rich husbands, we'll demand a window seat.'

'You may perhaps, but I probably won't marry. I have to repay the mill owner for my course fees and then I wouldn't want to be having to kowtow to a man, and having a child every year, like a lot of women do at the mill. If they aren't back at work soon after giving birth, their job is given to someone else. Life is hard in our part of town.' Before Lucy could answer, a neatly dressed waitress came to take their order.

'We'll have afternoon tea for two, please,' said Lucy, in a commanding voice.

'Certainly, Miss,' replied the waitress, who bobbed a brief curtsey and went back to the kitchen. It didn't take long before a three-tiered cake stand appeared. On the bottom tier, there were tiny sandwiches and savouries. On the next tier were scones, with jam and cream, and small cakes and macaroons on the top tier. Laura's eyes widened in disbelief, but she said nothing. Another tray was brought, which contained two delicate china cups and saucers, several small plates with cutlery, and a milk jug and teapot to match.

Lucy poured the tea for them both and told Laura to have a sandwich.

'You first,' replied Laura, and Lucy realised it wasn't out of politeness, more of being afraid where to start. Lucy shook out her napkin and placed it on her lap and Laura followed her lead. Then Lucy took a sandwich and a savoury from the bottom layer, followed by Laura. As they started eating, Laura looked uncomfortable and stopped chewing.

'What's the matter?' whispered Lucy.

'I don't know what I'm eating but it's stringy and awful,' she whispered back. Lucy looked at the sandwich.

'It's smoked salmon. Don't you like it?' Laura shook her head. 'Put your napkin up to your mouth and slip it into the napkin, then put it down on the plate. Try one of the others. This is cucumber,' said Lucy, proffering her another choice. Laura wasn't over enamoured of that either, so Lucy told her to eat the savouries, which she did like, so Lucy ate the sandwiches and left the savouries for Laura. There was no problem with the top two layers of sweet things though. They both munched their way through all the cakes on offer, drinking tea in between. After they had finished, Lucy asked for the bill, which she paid, and then they left the tearoom.

'I'm sorry I didn't like those sandwiches. The cucumber wasn't much better than the smoked salmon,' moaned Laura, 'but I could get used to all those cakes,' she laughed. 'Also, I heard how much that cost you, Lucy. That is so kind of you. That is the same as my mum's weekly wage. I feel guilty that you've spent so much.'

'Don't worry about it. Let's go back to the furnishing department.' Going down the stairs, Lucy led Laura back to the rugs and bought two small brightly coloured rugs, and the looking glass she had commented on previously. Laura said nothing until they got out of the store.

'Why did you buy two rugs?'

'One each. Why?'

'You bought one for me?'

'Yes, why not? You didn't think I'd just have one for myself and leave you without, did you?'

'But I can never repay you.'

'I haven't asked you to. You can clean the room this week if you feel the need to repay me,' grinned Lucy.

'I'll clean it every week in return for this rug. I've never owned anything so lovely. Thank you.'

'It's only a rug, and a pretty basic one, too. You'll need to teach me how to clean anyway. I've never been expected to do it at home. Patsy and the weekly lady do all that.'

'I can teach you to clean. You have to do a lot of cleaning when there's a few of you in the house, and you live near the factories and mines. It's a never-ending struggle. We can start tomorrow.' And so they did. Lucy was exhausted after Laura showed her how to thoroughly clean the room but felt a certain satisfaction in seeing the room sparkle. The new rugs and looking glass seemed to make the room much more homely too and the girls were pleased with their efforts.

Next day being Sunday, the girls attended the service along with all the other students from the college. Church attendance was obligatory, which some of the men complained about, but the girls were pleased. It was a service from the Anglican tradition and quite formal. On the way back, Lucy commented that she preferred her own type of service, where more rousing hymns were sung and there weren't any prescribed spoken responses. Laura agreed. At the Mission where she attended, they often sang Moody and Sankey favourites and long and beseeching prayers were given, rather than the printed prayers they had said today.

'Perhaps we can go to my church next week?' Laura suggested, but Lucy felt that they shouldn't rock the boat so soon into the course and should wait and see for a few weeks. After a large Sunday lunch, the two girls sat quietly during the afternoon, Lucy writing to her family and Laura reading one of the set books for the course which Lucy had lent her. The tea was just sandwiches on Sundays, but Laura laughingly commented that they were better than the ones at the tearooms, as they were cheese and ham with which Laura was more familiar. They also had a large piece of fruit cake each.

Next morning, Laura was struggling to fasten her hair up in a tidy plait, so Lucy offered to help her.

'I'm not used to having my hair done like this,' she complained. 'In the mill, we just tie it up with a piece of string and put a cap on, to save getting our hair stuck in the looms.' Laura started combing the thick luxuriant hair and dampened it slightly from the water jug in their room. That had the desired effect of making the hair go into a seemlier plait, which Lucy tucked underneath with hair grips.

'We haven't time for you to show me how to do that today, but thanks, Lucy. It seemed so easy when you did it.'

'You'll soon get used to it. Now, let's go down to breakfast.' After a large helping of porridge, the two girls made their way to the classroom, finding seats not too near the front but not at the back. They sat together and surveyed the room silently. Out of about 100 people, the largest majority were men. Laura started to comment about one of the other girls in the class, but she was interrupted when a teacher came to the front of the classroom.

'Good morning, ladies and gentlemen. I am Miss Dodd. When I enter a room, I expect you to rise.' The whole class rose and waited for her next utterance. 'That's better; now you may sit, but please remember this in future when I come into the room, or any other teacher for that matter. This is what you should expect from all your pupils, so it's good to get into the habit yourselves now. Respect breeds respect, I always say.' Lucy and Laura looked at each other but remained silent. 'Did you say something, sir?' the teacher asked one of the young men, who blushed furiously at being singled out.

'Er, no, Miss Dodd.'

'Good. "Manners maketh man", I always say. Now let's take the roll call. When I say your name, you reply, "Present, Miss Dodd". Have you understood?' Everybody nodded their heads. 'I didn't hear you. Do you understand?' The pupils caught on quickly.

'Yes, Miss Dodd,' they all chorused back.

'Good. Let us commence.' Miss Dodd read out the list of names and each person replied as instructed. 'Before we start lectures, we will have a short service. This will be required of you at the start of each school day, especially if you aspire to be the headteacher in your establishment.' Lucy and Laura grinned at each other at the thought of being a headteacher, but said nothing. The service was a Bible reading with a very short and simple homily, and a prayer, followed by the Lord's Prayer. Next, the details of the course were given out and a teaching rota pinned up on the wall.

'As you can see, you will start your teaching practice quite early, in the Fielden Demonstration schools. Some of your lectures will be all together, as you are today, but some lectures will be separate depending on whether you are wishing to teach junior or senior children.

'Our first lecture today is a history of education in England. This will take up most of this week's lectures. So, first of all, I want you to discuss with your neighbour why you think education is important and who should receive it.'

Lucy and Laura looked at each other for a moment and then laughed.

'I think everyone should receive it, especially girls, so that they have an alternative to getting married,' said Laura. Lucy agreed and said that God had given them a brain, and they should use it. Miss Dodd was coming near, so they pretended to be writing points down in their notebooks. After some time passed, Miss Dodd stood at the front of the class and asked for answers. No one spoke.

'Come, ladies and gentlemen, surely you have something to say? You were saying plenty to your neighbours.' Still no one spoke. 'Then I shall pick on someone. You, girl, with the red hair, please stand up and say your name and then tell us what you think. You and your neighbour were very industrious when I was walking round.'

Laura rose slowly to her feet, her face as red as her hair. 'Please, Miss Dodd, I'm Miss Laura Carter. I think that everyone should receive education, especially girls.'

'And why is that, Miss Carter?' asked Miss Dodd.

'So that they don't have to get married and have babies.' There was a titter round the class which was soon quelled by a glare from Miss Dodd.

'That is exactly why some people think that women shouldn't be educated as, what is the point if they only marry and have babies?' Miss Dodd asked. Lucy put her hand up. 'Yes, girl, you, what do you have to say?'

'I think that…,' Lucy started nervously.

'Name, girl. Until we all get to know each other, you must say your name.'

'Sorry, Miss Dodd. I'm Miss Lucy Coombes.'

'Then tell us what you have to say, Miss Lucy Coombes.'

'I think that even if a girl does get married as soon as she finishes her education, she will make a better wife to her husband, as she understands more of the world, and will make a better mother, as she can help her children with their learning.'

'Good points. What do the men think about that?' asked Miss Dodd. A lively debate ensued, between some men saying that a wife's place was in the home, not being educated, and others said it was a good thing.

'It's nearly lunchtime now,' said Miss Dodd when she called the debate to an end. 'After luncheon, we will be debating the theory that some of the upper classes have, that universal education will encourage people to rise above their allotted station in life, or even worse, start a rebellion, like they did in France. Mull these issues over during your lunch break and we will reconvene at 1.30pm. Please ensure that you spend some time in the fresh air so that you are not sleepy this afternoon.' With a nod of her head, she swept out of the room, as the students jumped to their feet. Laura let out a sigh of relief.

'Phew! That was intense. I felt awful when they all laughed at what I said.'

'You did very well, Laura. I'm glad she didn't pick on me first.'

'You were quick to make your point, Lucy. I enjoyed the debate though, didn't you?'

'Yes, if all the lessons are like that, we're going to have some fun.' The two girls went to the refectory and queued for their lunch, then took advantage of the warm September day to walk round the grounds, as Miss Dodd had suggested. They realised the benefit of doing that and knew that it was why children always got a playtime between lessons. They both felt ready for the afternoon session.

The week passed quickly and by the end of the week, both girls' heads were spinning with all the facts and figures that they had learned. Dates and Acts of Parliament swirled in their brains and they were glad to have a weekend off to relax. Tired though they were, they couldn't wait to see what the next week would bring.

Chapter 3

The second week of the course was about lesson planning and an overview of different subjects that would be studied. The junior and senior students were kept together, as some schools would take in all age groups and the students needed to know what had been taught at all levels. They were surprised on the last day of the week when a male teacher came into the afternoon session and announced that he was going to teach them eurhythmics. Lucy and Laura had never heard of them, but he further astonished the class by bringing in a wind-up gramophone machine. He explained that the teaching of eurhythmics was very new, but it helped students with physical exercise and was harmonious and pleasing to undertake. He proceeded to demonstrate some simple movements and then wound up the gramophone and started the music.

At first the teacher did the exercises to the music, but then stopped the machine and asked the students to join in with him. There was a lot of hilarity as they all tried this new form of exercise, but eventually most of them got the hang of it, although it had to be said that some would never get a sense of rhythm even if their lives depended on it. By the end of the week both girls were exhausted. Lucy decided on a quiet weekend, but Laura said that she would go home and visit her family.

On the Saturday, Lucy had a walk around the surrounding streets and found a little bakery that made delightful cakes and scones which were very reasonably priced. She bought a cake for after her tea as a treat, and also bought one for Laura for Sunday evening when she came back to college.

After Sunday lunch, Lucy went for a walk round the grounds of the college and sat on a bench by the lawn. Another girl came and sat by her.

'Hello, I'm Mary Watson. You are Lucy, aren't you?'

'Yes, I'm Lucy. Hello Mary.'

'You and your friend are very forthcoming with your opinions.'

'Do you think so? Laura didn't get a chance that first day. Miss Dodd picked on her.'

'You were the second to speak though, totally unsolicited.'

'Is that a problem? She did ask our opinions.'

'Not at all. I was brought up to be quiet until asked to speak. But then your friend obviously hasn't been well brought up. Her accent is terrible. She sounds like she was brought up in the slums. I don't know why you bother with her. She doesn't seem like your sort of class.'

'We share a room,' Lucy said quietly, 'and I'm not bothered about anybody's class. Where they were born wasn't their choice. I admire that she is trying to better herself and have a more educated life than would be her normal lot.'

'Quite the revolutionary, aren't you?'

'Not really, I just stick up for my friends,' Lucy replied, and started to get up.

'Don't go. I'm sorry if I've spoken out of turn about your friend. You just seem a mismatched pair, that's all.'

'Laura has a great desire to be educated and so have I. That is what makes us friends.'

'A great desire to be educated?' Mary laughed. 'That sounds very grand. I just came to see if I could find myself a husband. I didn't like any of the ninnies that my mother paraded before me. I thought that if I came on this course, there were sure to be lots of men from decent backgrounds that I would meet. I was surprised to see so many women here. I thought I'd be one of very few women, and could have my pick of the men, but so far, I can see I'll have competition. You seem to have attracted a lot of interest from the men, and even your common little friend, too.' Lucy stood up this time and walked away without speaking. Even though Mary shouted after her, Lucy ignored her, furious at the snobbish way Mary had referred to Laura.

Arriving back at her room, Lucy wished that Laura were back, but knew she wouldn't be back until tonight. To calm her feelings, she wrote to her mother and told her about the eurhythmics class, suspecting that Granny Wall would be scandalised that they had been cavorting up and down in public. This made Lucy feel better and she decided to forget the ignorant comments that Mary had made and wouldn't mention it to Laura. But in her mind, she remembered what Mary had said about her and Laura attracting a lot of attention from the men. She blushed to remember that. Perhaps she would tell Laura that bit of the conversation, she pondered, and wondered how things would turn out. Perhaps they would also meet the men of their dreams whilst on this course. Lucy fell asleep quite early and never heard Laura come in, so it was a scramble in the morning to get ready for class and they didn't get a chance to talk until lunchtime.

'How is your family?' Lucy asked.

'Noisy as ever,' laughed Laura in reply. 'Oh, and my mum said I'd to ask you to dinner next week. I mean lunch. We call it dinner at home, but I know you lot speak of dinner as something you have in the evening. Anyway, she says for you to come next week for Sunday dinner.'

'That's really kind,' Lucy replied. 'I'd love to come.'

The teaching course began in earnest that week. They were taken into the classroom in the Fielden school to observe lessons in the mornings. In the afternoon they had to discuss the lessons they had heard and prepare their own lesson plan as if they had done the same lesson. Both Laura and Lucy found this hard, as the only teaching experience they had previously was when someone told them what to teach and what to include. Sunday school lessons or teaching in the mill seemed easy compared to what was expected of them. However, after careful thought both girls came up with a suitable lesson plan and had to give them in to Miss Dodd. On the Friday afternoon, Miss Dodd announced that the following Monday Laura was to give the first lesson of the week in the Fielden school. She was to teach a reception class their letters. Mr Richards was picked to teach a class of senior children about rivers in Africa. Lucy heard Mary Watson snigger and whisper something to the girl sat next to her when Laura's name was announced. Lucy ignored it, merely praising Laura for being picked first.

On the Saturday Laura and Lucy cleaned their room and, whilst Laura was working on her lesson plan, Lucy caught up with some reading for the course. The following day after church, the girls set off to Laura's home. It only took them about 20 minutes to walk there, but Lucy noticed that the streets were getting poorer and poorer as they travelled. Small corner shops were everywhere, with the inevitable large sign of the pawnbrokers on one corner. Eventually, Laura turned into a street of terraced houses that were adjacent to a large cotton mill. It had the unimaginative name of Mill Street. Laura stopped halfway down the terrace and opened a door and walked inside, Lucy following. The door opened straight into a small room, which was almost empty. Laura moved through a door into a bigger kitchen with a large black-leaded stove at one side and a big scrubbed table at the other side of the room. All the family were lined up behind the table, all staring at Lucy, and Lucy noticed that although the house was clean, it was very basic. Mrs Carter was looking worried as she saw Lucy looking round the room.

'Hello, Mrs Carter. It's so good of you to invite me. Thank you,' said Lucy. 'I've brought a cake with me; I hope you don't mind.'

'There was no need, but thank you. That's most kind,' replied Mrs Carter. 'Here, sit down, Miss Coombes.'

'I'm Lucy, not Miss Coombes, for all of you,' Lucy smiled back at Mrs Carter, as she sat down. 'Now, will you tell me all your names?'

'I'm Agnes and I'm the eldest now Laura's left home, and when our Bessie's not here,' grinned a laughing smaller image of Laura, her red hair sticking out all over the place. It was quite strange that neither of the parents had red hair, and yet two of the children did. The boys were both fair-haired like their father. Nobody seemed to have dark hair like their mother. 'Our Bessie'll be in shortly. She's working now and only gets to come home on Sunday afternoons,' continued Agnes.

'Yes,' said Laura, 'Bessie has been very fortunate. She has managed to get a job in a dressmaker's shop. At first, she will only be tidying the shop, but she will be taught the trade as she goes along. She will be there for five years in total and has to live in.'

'That's good,' replied Lucy politely, thinking it was a bit young for her to have to live in, but then Patsy was only 14 when she started at her own home. Further comment was interrupted by Mrs Carter putting the food on the table. First there was a large loaf of bread with some white stuff in a dish next to it. Mr Carter carved the loaf into large slices and these were passed round to the children, after serving Lucy first. Then after Mr Carter had said grace, Mrs Carter brought the meal out. Each plate had a tiny portion of meat, one or two small potatoes, and a small portion of vegetables. It was about a quarter of what Lucy would have at home. The children looked delighted and tucked in to their meal, covering the bread with a scraping of the white stuff in the dish. Lucy thought that it looked like the fat that Mrs Ward made pastry with, and politely declined it when it was passed to her, saying that she preferred her bread dry. Now she understood why such a large loaf of bread was provided: the meal itself was very small and the bread would fill them all up. To make it worse, it was probably smaller than usual today, to share it out with her as well, Lucy thought. She felt embarrassed that she was taking some of their meagre share of food and was glad that she'd brought the cake with her.

A large teapot was brought out next and everyone passed their cups, of varying size, shape, and condition over to Mrs Carter. Lucy noticed that the best cup was reserved for her, and she said 'thank you' gratefully when she received the cup of hot sweet tea. After the meal was finished, Laura persuaded Agnes to help her with the washing up, saying that it was a tradition that their mother had a rest on Sunday afternoons. Lucy offered to help but was politely refused. Everyone sat round the fire and chatted, and Lucy noticed that Mrs Carter had fallen asleep. *No wonder*, thought Lucy, *after working all week and having to keep the children clothed and fed and the house clean and tidy.*

Mrs Carter woke up suddenly when the door flew open later in the afternoon.

'Hello, everybody!' shouted a tall, dark-haired young woman as she hurtled through the door, just as Laura often did. She stopped when she saw Lucy.

'Bessie,' said Laura, 'let me introduce you to my good friend Lucy, from college.' Bessie flushed, then dropped a curtsy.

'Hello, Bessie. You don't need to curtsy to me. I'm just one of the girls on Laura's course,' replied Lucy. Bessie's face flushed, just like Laura's did, and she went to sit down near the fire, resting back against her father's legs. Bessie reached into her pocket and slid a shilling into her father's hand.

'Thank you, Bessie,' he said quietly. 'And here's tuppence for you to spend. You're a good girl for bringing your wages home.'

'Thanks, Dad. I'll not spend it. I'm saving it up for as long as I can.'

'What are you saving for, Bessie?' asked Lucy. 'A remnant to make yourself a new dress?'

'No, I get remnants cheap enough from Mrs Smith. I can have all the scraps from the sewing room floor for trimmings, too,' grinned Bessie.

'She made that dress herself,' Mrs Carter added proudly, 'with Mrs Smith's help of course.' Lucy looked at Bessie's basic style of dress that had been enhanced with a bow at the neck, buttons all down the front, and gathered cuffs, to make it less ordinary.

'That's lovely. You are going to be a good dressmaker, I can see,' replied Lucy. 'So, what are you saving for?'

Bessie flushed again and spoke in a very small voice. 'A sewing machine.'

'A sewing machine? That will take you a long time to save for. Can't you use Mrs Smith's?' asked Lucy.

'Yes, but I'd like to have my own when I'm older. Then I can always make things for people and earn some money.'

'That's very good. Do you enjoy sewing, Bessie?' asked Lucy.

'Yes, it's the best thing ever. So much better than the mill. It doesn't make me cough.'

Laura intervened. 'Bessie was having a lot of trouble with a bad cough in the mill, and the teacher recommended that she got a job learning dressmaking as she was the best student in the school for sewing. The teacher even got the place for Bessie. It was her cousin's uncle's wife who owned the shop, or something like that.'

'Well, you'll be set up for life with a chance like that, Bessie. Would you like me to see if we have any pieces of material at home that you could use?' asked Lucy, impressed at the chance this child had to free herself from the mill, like Laura.

'Oh, yes please. It doesn't have to be new material; it can be old clothing, which I can make do and mend.'

'I'll be going home for my brother's birthday in November, so I'll see what I can find.'

'Thank you, Lucy,' replied Bessie, her eyes shining as she snuggled closer to her dad.

'Time for tea,' announced Mrs Carter, as she jumped up and pulled the kettle on to the fire. 'Lucy has brought us some cake to have with our tea; isn't that kind?'

'Cake?' shouted Arthur. 'Yippee!' And everyone laughed.

Tea was just more bread with a thin scraping of the lard, covered with an even thinner layer of jam. After everyone had eaten some of the bread - Lucy glad that there was jam on to cover the taste of the lard - the cake was brought out and Mrs Carter cut it into slices, whilst everyone looked on in silence. Mr Carter was served first, then Lucy, and then the children, who all ate it slowly, without speaking, and carefully relishing every morsel.

'Can you come again next week, Lucy?' asked Albert innocently.

'Albert, don't be so rude,' reproved Mrs Carter, but everyone else laughed.

'I think it's time that we were getting back to college,' Laura said.

'Yes, you are right. Thank you for having me. I've had a lovely time and am glad to have met you all,' said Lucy as she stood up. Albert went to get their coats and soon they were out in the dark, cold streets.

'Did I embarrass your mother by bringing a cake?' asked Lucy, as soon as they were clear of the street.

'No, but you don't need to bring anything when you are invited. It makes it look like we can't afford treats.'

'I'm sorry, I have so much to learn. I was just trying to help.'

'That's the way Mum took it. She wasn't offended. Arthur and Albert certainly weren't,' Laura laughed.

'That's right,' agreed Lucy. 'I made them happy.'

'As all of us were,' added Laura. 'We loved your cake.'

Once back in their room, Lucy and Laura checked over Laura's lesson plan for the next morning.

'Your lesson plan is really different, Laura. I'm sure everyone's going to enjoy it.'

'I hope so. You don't think it's too outrageous?'

'Not at all. Come on, let's get an early night. Tomorrow is going to be interesting!'

The two girls were soon settled in bed, and although Lucy fell asleep straight away, Laura was a little worried that she had to be the first to teach in front of the others. Eventually tiredness overtook her and she too slept until dawn.

Chapter 4

There was a buzz in the classroom next morning, as the student teachers waited for the children to arrive. Their class teacher came in first and said good morning to all the student teachers, and then the children filed in. The children all said 'good morning' to their teacher and then said a collective 'good morning ladies and gentlemen' to the visiting teachers. A short assembly commenced and then the register was taken.

'Could Miss Carter come to the front, please?' asked Miss Williams, the class teacher.

Laura stood up slowly, collected her notes, and made her way to the front of the class. Lucy gave her an encouraging smile.

'This is Miss Carter, children. She is going to teach you this morning. What do we say to Miss Carter, children?'

'Good morning, Miss Carter,' droned the children.

'Good morning, children,' Laura replied. 'Today we're going to learn our letters, or the alphabet as it is called. Can you all say that word? Alphabet?'

'Alphabet,' the children repeated.

'Good. Now, the alphabet is made up of 26 letters. That's a lot of letters, nearly as many as there are children in the class. Every word we use is made up of different letters.' Laura put up a picture with all the letters of the alphabet on a stand next to the blackboard. She had painstakingly made this picture over the last week.

'Now I want you to copy each letter onto your slates as I write it on the blackboard.' Laura wrote the letter 'a' on the blackboard. 'This is the letter "a". Apple starts with the letter "a", so all copy it on to your slate, please.' Laura walked round the classroom, watching the children make their laborious attempts to copy the letter, correcting some children who seemed to have no idea how to draw anything, and encouraging children to use their right hand rather than their left, and to grip their chalk correctly. As she went round the classroom, she quietly spoke to each child, asking their names as she did.

'Now draw an apple next to your letter "a", so that you'll remember that apple begins with a letter "a",' Laura instructed, and the children quietly followed her instructions.

Next, she progressed to the letter 'b' and so on until they got to the letter 'e', adding a drawing to represent each letter.

'Let's see how much you can remember already,' said Laura. She pointed to a letter on the board and asked, 'What is this letter?' After many random guesses, one child correctly said the letter. 'How did you know it was a "b"?' asked Laura.

'Cos "b" is a boat, like my picture,' said the small child.

'Well done, Tommy, isn't it?'

'Yes, Miss.'

'That's very good because you are already working out that letters can make words. Shall we make a song of it?' Laura proceeded to sing, 'a is for apple and b is for boat, c is for cab and d is for dog and e is for elephant.' At this, the children all laughed.

'Does anyone know what an elephant is? It's a funny word. Elephant,' she enunciated slowly, but no one answered. 'It's a great big animal with a long trunk,' Laura waved her arm in front of her, like an elephant's trunk, 'and it's got big ears,' so Laura flapped her ears with her hands to make them look bigger, 'and it's got big tusks.' Laura held two pencils up to her mouth to look like tusks. 'Next time I see you, I'll bring a picture of a real elephant for you to look at.'

'Please, Miss,' said little Dora, 'my big sister's got an animal book at home.'

'Perhaps you could bring it in tomorrow and show everyone and Miss Williams could look to see if there is a picture of an elephant in it,' said Laura, looking sideways at Miss Williams for approval.

'Yes, that's a good idea, Miss Carter. Carry on,' replied Miss Williams.

'Now, before we go on to the next letters, I'm going to show you another way to learn the different letters. Martha, can you come out here, please?'

Martha, one of the bigger children in the class came out to the front and stood beside Laura.

'I want you to see if you can make a letter "a".' Martha proceeded to wave a roughly 'a' shaped movement with her arm. 'Now try making it with your own body. Can you bend your body into an "a" shape?' There was a titter from the back of the class, and Lucy realised that it was Mary Watson. It was soon stopped by a glare from Miss Williams, whilst Laura blushed but carried on. Little Martha contorted her body into an 'a' shape and Laura praised her.

'Well done, Martha. Now I want you all to stand up and do the same,' she instructed, and all the children got up out of their seats and began twisting and turning into 'a' shapes. There was a lot of hilarity, but eventually most children could make an 'a' shape.

'And what does "a" make?' asked Laura. A sea of hands was raised, everyone wanting to answer. Laura asked Margaret for the answer.

'Apple, Miss,' lisped Margaret.

'Very good. That is correct. Now let's try making a letter "b". Who wants to help me?' Again, the sea of hands was raised and Laura picked a boy from the back of the class called Harry, who soon worked out how to make a 'b', after Laura reminded him which one was a 'b'. Once they'd all mastered the letters as far as 'e', Laura picked three children out and asked them to make the letters 'c', 'a', and 'b'. Whilst they were stood there, she taught the children that those three letters together made the word 'cab' and made sure that they knew what a cab was. Little Jimmy waved his hand agitatedly at Laura. 'Yes, Jimmy, what do you want?'

'My dad drives a cab,' he said proudly.

'Does he? That is a very hard job as you have to know how to drive it, but also have to care for the horses.'

'He lets me stroke the horses if I'm good,' Jimmy persisted, keen to tell his whole story.

'You are a lucky boy. Do any of you other children get to stroke horses?' Only two put their hands up. The bell rang then for playtime, after the children had a drink of milk. The student teachers hurried to the refectory for a drink after being dismissed by Miss Williams. Lucy was complimenting Laura on her lesson as they sat down at the table together. Mary Watson was at the next table with her friends and some of the men, speaking loudly so that everyone could hear.

'Well, I can't imagine what Miss Dodd is going to say about that lesson, it was appalling,' she laughed. 'But what can you expect from a mill girl. That's probably how they teach the slum kids, but it won't do for us more refined types,' she sniggered.

Laura flushed a bright shade of red, but Lucy touched her hand and whispered to Laura not to respond. Lucy took hold of both drinks and moved to another table at the far side of the refectory, but it was soon time to go back into the classroom.

'Take no notice of her.' Lucy urged, 'You were very good.' Laura carried on with the lesson. Soon the children were dismissed for their lunches and

Laura was free. Lucy and Laura ate their own lunch very quickly then walked outside, away from the others.

In the afternoon, the student teachers sat in on Miss Williams' class. She was teaching them simple numbers in the afternoon and the student teachers all watched and made careful notes on her technique. When the children had gone home for the day, then it was the turn of Miss Dodd and Miss Williams to give feedback, which was done in front of the whole class of student teachers.

Miss Dodd spoke first. 'Miss Watson, I noticed you were making depreciative sounds when Miss Carter was teaching. Would you like to explain?'

'I thought that would have been obvious, Miss Dodd. I've never seen such an appalling method of teaching. Getting the children up and excited in class, there was no discipline whatsoever.'

'I see. Does anyone agree with this opinion?' Miss Dodd asked icily. Mary's brave companions were all silent, seeing the look in Miss Dodd's eyes, even though two of them had agreed with Mary.

'Does anyone else have an opinion before I ask Miss Williams to comment?' Miss Dodd asked.

A hand went up before Lucy could speak. It was Cynthia Shaw, a quiet young lady who hadn't spoken up in class before.

'Please, Miss Dodd, I don't agree with Miss Watson. I thought that was an excellent lesson.' Then she promptly sat down. Lucy heaved a sigh of relief.

'Please expand, Miss Shaw?' Miss Dodd asked.

'Er, well, it made the children think about shape as well as letters. It used different ways of teaching them in one lesson, to keep their interest.'

'Very good, Miss Shaw. Relevant comments. Anyone else?' No one spoke.

'Right, Miss Williams. Can you tell us what you think?'

'Of course. Yes, I agree with Miss Shaw. It was an innovative lesson and certainly kept the children's interest. When they were playing out after their lunch, they were all making the shapes together and citing the letters. I've never seen so much play around their lessons ever before – certainly not from my lessons. I think I'll be using this next year with the new intake of little ones. Well done, Miss Carter. You seem to be a natural teacher. You managed to use whatever the children said to further incorporate them into the lesson, like the animal book.' Laura glowed with happiness.

'I agree,' added Miss Dodd. 'Now, Miss Carter, would you like to explain how you came up with these unique ideas?'

Laura rose to her feet. 'Oh, Miss Dodd, I claim no glory for this lesson. It was what I was taught at the school I worked in before I came here. The children were half-timers – they worked in the mill for half a day and had lessons for the other half of the day. They were often so tired, especially the afternoon classes where the children had already worked since 6am. It was very hard to keep their interest in the lessons, so the teacher in charge made learning into fun. So, I copied her.'

'Let's hope the day soon comes when they will be allowed to go to school full time and not work until they are at least 12 or 14 years old. You must have worked for a very innovative mill owner that encouraged teaching,' said Miss Dodd.

'He's realised that children who can read and write are better weavers and workers, as they can read instructions and keep a tally of the work pieces they have completed. It makes life easier all round. I think it's more about profit than allowing children to learn for the sake of it,' replied Laura, which raised a laugh in the classroom.

Very pleased by the success of the day, Laura and Lucy made their way to the refectory for their tea and when they sat down, Cynthia Shaw asked if she could join them. They welcomed her to their table. She was a petite girl, with blonde curly hair framing her face.

'Thank you for speaking up for me,' started Laura.

'I didn't like what Mary Watson was saying. I've heard her a few times, picking on you both or name-calling behind your backs. I tried to stick up for you, but she got nasty with me, so now I just keep out of her sight, which is awkward as my room is on the same corridor.'

'Sit with us anytime,' said Lucy.

'Thank you, I will.'

'Where do you come from, Cynthia?' asked Lucy.

'Bolton. My dad's an architect and we belong to a Methodist church near our home. There are several businessmen in the church and, although we have a large Sunday school hall, they have all committed to building a proper school with three or four classrooms for the different age groups. My dad's designed the school at no cost to the church, and the other businessmen are all sending workmen to do the building. They're building the school next to the church and eventually they'll build a house for the headmaster. The church members want me to be a teacher at the school, too.'

'That sounds good,' replied Lucy. 'You're sure of a job when you finish, like Laura is.'

'Yes, as long as I want it,' said Cynthia.

'We're going out for afternoon tea on Saturday. Would you like to come too?' asked Lucy.

'Yes please. Where are you going? Kendals?'

'No,' laughed Laura, 'we went there last time. Bit too fancy for me. We've found another quieter tearoom down a side street, so we're going to try that this week.'

'Well, let it be my treat,' said Cynthia. 'I've not really made any friends here yet. I've been too aware of Mary sneering at me.'

'Sounds good to me. I'm all for someone else paying,' Laura laughed. 'I don't have an allowance from my father like Lucy does, and I bet you do too.'

'Yes, that's right,' admitted Cynthia.

'By the way, don't take any notice of Mary. She's just here to find a husband,' said Lucy.

'Really?' said Cynthia. 'How do you know?'

'She told me. Doesn't want to teach at all. Thinks it's boring and made fun of me and Laura for being too keen.'

'Well, let's hope she finds a man soon and leaves the course,' said Cynthia.

'Oh, Cynthia, that was a bit harsh,' said Lucy.

'She just irritates me. Take no notice of me. When is it your turn to teach, Lucy?' she asked, trying to change the subject.

'Not until mid-November. When is yours?'

'The week after next, but Mary is teaching next week, so we can see what she makes of being in a classroom she doesn't want to be in.' Ironically, or perhaps intentionally on her part, they didn't see Mary teach as she reported sick the day before. The three girls looked at each other without saying anything when it was announced and one of the male students was asked to stand in at short notice. He did amazingly well and the girls were quick to heap praise on him in the refectory afterwards, causing him to blush.

32

For the next few weeks, when Laura went home at weekends, Lucy and Cynthia would spend time together. However, soon it was Lucy who was going home for the weekend. It was William's birthday on November 6th and as he would be 21, they were having a family party for him at church. Lucy was spending all her spare time finishing a thick sweater for him as her present. It was in leaf green and had a cable tree pattern on the front, as William loved trees. His birthday was on the Wednesday, so Lucy was going home on the Friday following. William was coming to collect her. Lucy faithfully finished the jumper and even had time to make a hat and gloves to match. Laura and Cynthia were going out to the shops that weekend and were looking forward to it. Lucy was thinking only of the party and couldn't wait.

Chapter 5

Friday soon came round and eventually William arrived. Lucy was looking out onto the street, searching for the Hansom cab, when a shiny black motor car roared up the street and screeched to a halt outside the college. Lucy stared when the driver got out of the motor car. It was William!

'How do you like her? It's my birthday present from Mother and Father. Aren't I lucky? I never thought they'd let me have one for years yet, but 21 is a special age, isn't it?'

'No, I didn't think you'd get one. Father seemed so against them.'

'They kept asking me what I wanted and I said nothing as I couldn't have what I wanted. Then they said, "well, what do you want?" Father paled when I said a motor car. He didn't say yes straight away, but then took me to the motor car showrooms in Blackburn last week, as we haven't got a garage in Burnley yet. I've called her Topsy. What do you think of that name?'

'Topsy? Why do motor cars need names? And why female? Shouldn't motor cars be male, as women will never drive them.'

'No, they should be female as we men spend a lot of time looking after them, like we do a woman.'

'Huh! Pity the woman who gets you. You'll be awful as a husband.'

'Why?' asked William, looking affronted.

'Well, you're not a very good brother, are you? Always arguing and getting the best because you are eldest and the son and heir. Anyway, even though you don't deserve it, here's your birthday present. I didn't finish it in time to send via the Post Office. You can open it....', but her instruction was too late, as the wrappings were already off.

'That's perfect, and it's got trees on it. Just right for wearing in my motor car.' He took off his coat and put jumper, gloves, and hat on, then put his coat back on. 'Come along then, hop in,' he chivvied.

'Me? Get in that motor car?'

'Well, it's a long way to walk home if you don't get in,' laughed William. 'Here, tie this scarf on over your bonnet to keep yourself warm. The blanket on the back seat is to go round your legs. Put your suitcase on the back seat. See what a caring brother I am,' he laughed. Lucy had barely got in the motor car before William jumped out to crank the engine starter. Eventually, it fired up and they were off, Lucy clinging for dear life on to the side of the car.

'Slow down, slow down,' Lucy shrieked, but he just ignored her and carried on. Lucy shut her eyes and prayed – very hard. Once they got out of town he seemed to go even faster and he shouted over the noise of the engine that the speed limit was now 14 miles per hour out of town. To Lucy, it felt more like they were doing 100 miles per hour, but she said nothing. Eventually they arrived back home and Lucy heaved a sigh of relief when the motor car stopped outside their house, along with a prayer of untold gratitude to her Creator for arriving safely. She slowly got out of the car, feeling as if her whole body had been shaken up and she wouldn't be able to walk. But walk she did, albeit slowly. Her mother rushed to the door and held her close.

'I'm so glad you've got home safely.'

'So am I!' quipped Lucy.

'There's a light supper for you and then we can talk tomorrow. You must be exhausted.' Lucy nodded, slipping her coat and hat off.

'We wouldn't have been home for hours yet if I'd brought the Hansom cab,' crowed William, and Lucy had to agree, however uncomfortable it had been. She went straight upstairs and Patsy brought her a hot drink and some sandwiches. Although she drank the tea, she couldn't face the sandwiches as her stomach felt that it was still in the motor car. At least she fell asleep quickly that night.

Next morning, Lucy and her mum had a leisurely breakfast, remaining to drink extra tea after the men had gone to the factory to work.

'What's happening then?' asked Lucy. 'What sort of party is there tonight?'

'We've hired the church hall and have ordered caterers in so that our staff can come to the party instead of having to work even longer hours than they do now.'

'That's very thoughtful, Mother. Who's coming?'

'The entire church and everyone we know or are related to, I think,' she laughed. 'Some of your father's business colleagues as well. It should be a lively evening. We've ordered a string quartet to come and play music.'

'I'm glad I bought a new dress then,' laughed Lucy.

'Have you? That's good. Where did you buy it?'

'Actually, I've had it made. My friend Laura has a younger sister who works for a dressmaker and I went there, in Manchester. It was far cheaper than the dressmaker here in Burnley. Oh, talking of dressmaking, do you have any old clothes that Laura's sister, Bessie, can reuse to practise her sewing on?'

'I'm sure I can find something,' Martha replied.

'I'm sure you can, Mother, as you never throw anything away. I'll look through my wardrobe as well. I bet I've got a lot of dresses that don't fit now or are impractical to wear. I don't quite have the social life in Manchester as I do at home. Going out for afternoon tea is about the limit of my dressing up nowadays, apart from church. What time is the party starting tonight?'

'7pm.'

'I think I'll have my bath this afternoon then. I can wash my hair and put my curling rags in. That'll leave plenty of time for Father and William to get ready after work.'

'Good. Mrs Ward has made some sandwiches for lunch and then I've told them all to go home so that they can get ready. We can make our own cups of tea before we go. I'll have my bath straight after lunch then, before you. It will give the water time to heat up again for the men. I suppose they'll be last minute as usual,' Martha laughed.

'Is William going to Turf Moor to watch the football this afternoon?' asked Lucy.

'Have you ever known him miss?' asked her mother in reply.

'No!'

'He'll probably walk down though, or go straight from the factory, as he won't want his beautiful new motor car getting scratched,' laughed Martha.

'I should think not! At least I won't be wanting a motor car for my 21st birthday present, you can rest assured there.'

'Oh, I don't know. The Mayoress has got her own motor car. Where will it end?'

'Has she really? I wouldn't want one. They're far too fast for me.'

'It depends on who the driver is. The Mayoress doesn't drive fast; she crawls round the town, most of the time,' laughed Martha. 'Right, I think I'll go upstairs and start sorting out some old things for you.'

'Good idea; so will I,' and the two ladies headed upstairs together, separating into their own bedrooms, to sort through a large amount of clothing, most of which was hardly worn.

Lucy glanced over to her new dress which was hanging over her wardrobe door. It was in pale blue wild silk and wasn't an evening gown, as she felt that it would be too fancy for a party at church, but it was smarter than what she would wear as an afternoon tea gown. It had a square neckline, edged in darker blue velvet, and was nipped in tightly just above the waist, as was the fashion, with a flowing A-line skirt below, reaching almost to her feet. A broader thick velvet band was fastened above her waist and then lengths of velvet draped loosely from the side of her waist to the bottom of the dress. The sleeves were fussy and full at the top, but then tighter on the rest of her arms, finishing with a blue velvet bow at the wrist. Lucy had managed to purchase some dark blue velvet slippers to complete the outfit and Bessie had made her a little bag to match the dress, out of scraps of material left over. Perhaps it was a little grand for a church party, but Lucy loved it and she could wear it for other events, she was sure.

Having found quite a pile of clothes that she could bear to part with, she also found some gowns that she could give to Laura, who didn't have many. In fact, Laura only had one best dress, for church and going out. Nobody would know that they were Lucy's as she hadn't worn them in Manchester. It was a good job that the girls were a similar size, although Lucy was taller, but Laura could always shorten the dresses to make them the right length or, if she were being daring, she could wear the dress at the new slightly shorter length which some girls were wearing, showing off their shoes and ankles. Once she finished sorting out her clothes, Lucy got on with the more important job of getting bathed and dressed, ready for the party.

Eventually the whole household was ready and they all got into William's motor car, despite Martha fussing about not liking being in it, but the Hansom cab was needed to take all the staff to the party. As it was, it would have to make several trips, as the staff were taking their families as well.

On entering the church hall, Lucy felt a buzz of excitement as she saw many people gathered there, sitting or standing in groups, animatedly talking together and the quartet playing softly in the background. When William entered, after he had parked the motor car on the side street, somebody set up a cheer and began singing 'Happy Birthday to you'. William grinned at everyone, then thanked them for coming and also for singing. At a sign from Mrs Coombes, the caterers brought out all the food and, after the minister had said grace, the children rushed to the long trestle tables, debating whether to have hotpot, meat and potato pie, or cheese and onion pie, all served with peas, of course. The adults waited until the children were served, then they all joined the queue as well, taking their heaped plates of food back to the small tables that their children had reserved. Many of the people had seconds. When the children saw the pudding being brought in there were whoops of delight. There were large dishes of jelly with fruit in and jugs of cream, and, as if that weren't enough, plates of cakes were brought in. When everybody had had their fill, the caterers brought out a large birthday cake with 21 candles, all lit and glistening like fireworks. There was loud cheering and they had to sing 'Happy Birthday' again to William, who grinned all the time, before he blew out all the candles in one blow, amidst more cheering. Mrs Coombes went forward to cut up the cake so that everyone could have a small piece and, although many of the adults said they were quite full, nobody actually refused the cake, Mrs Coombes noticed.

Lucy watched all that was going on, totally happy for the fuss that William was getting for his special birthday. She watched as all the young ladies in the room seemed to be trying to get noticed by William that night. William was merrily smiling at every young lady who approached him, to Lucy's amusement. Perhaps he would choose one of these girls for his wife, Lucy idly wondered, looking at the press of girls around William. *Well, it had better not be Agnes Riley*, thought Lucy bitterly. She still hadn't forgiven her for spoiling her new white kid shoes about five years ago. Agnes said it was an accident, but she knew that Agnes was always jealous when she got anything new, as her parents were less well off than Lucy's. Lucy believed it was deliberate, even though her own mother had told her off about it and agreed with Agnes that it was an accident. She was still cross with her mother for siding with Agnes, but of course, she wouldn't dare say so.

Suddenly, she didn't want to watch William making a fool of himself with all these girls, especially Agnes Riley, so she went to the other side of the room where she couldn't see him, and talked to Miss Egar and Miss Seeney. They had a lovely chat about the course she was on and she thanked them again for all their help and support. Lucy told them of Laura's innovative way of teaching letters and had them both laughing and saying that it was an idea they might use as well. Lucy couldn't wait to tell Laura what they had said.

When all the food had been cleared away, they started playing games such as Musical Chairs, Charades, Hunt the Thimble, and guessing games. Eventually, the children were getting tired after running round wildly and some were sitting on their mothers' knees, falling asleep. The younger families started to drift away and that seemed to trigger the breakup of the party. The minister stood up and thanked the family for letting them share in William's coming of age and suggested that they all sing the Doxology before they left for home. Everyone stood and the age-old words filled the room:

Praise God from whom all blessings flow
Praise Him ye creatures here below
Praise Him above ye Heavenly Hosts
Praise Father, Son and Holy Ghost.

With this fitting end to the party, the room soon emptied and Lucy's father slipped the caretaker some money for the extra work he would have to do tonight to remove all traces of the party before church tomorrow morning, telling him to take home the food that was left, except for the birthday cake, of course, which they were taking home.

In the motor car going home, Lucy teased William about the impact he had made on all the young girls in the room.

'I think quite a few of them were thinking they would like to be Mrs Coombes Junior.'

'One of them might well be,' laughed William. 'They all seemed to have grown up overnight. Or have I not been looking? I didn't think I was ready for marriage, but I think I might have changed my mind now. Maggie Pilling and Agnes Riley were looking especially sweet tonight.'

'Agnes Riley?' asked Lucy with disgust.

'Yes, why not Agnes Riley? She's of age and is not spoken for,' replied William.

'I thought you liked Miriam Bates?' countered Lucy.

'I did, but she's keen on Freddie Wilson now. I missed the boat there.'

'Well, I prefer Maggie Pilling to Agnes Riley,' said Lucy.

'I hope you're still not holding that old grudge against Agnes,' said her mother sharply.

'No, of course not,' replied Lucy, but thinking differently in her heart. After that, they were all silent as they were driven home, too tired to continue the discussion.

When Lucy got into bed that night, she started saying her prayers, giving thanks for the lovely party they had had for William. But all too soon, her mind wandered off to Agnes Riley again and the old hurt came back. She knew that she should forgive her properly, but somehow, she found some things very hard to forgive. Softly, the thought came into her mind that when she had asked Jesus to come into her life, He had forgiven all her sins. All of them. Lucy asked forgiveness from God for being unforgiving and said she would try harder, but begged God not to let William marry Agnes, if He could manage it, and promptly fell asleep.

Chapter 6

Everybody overslept next morning and it was a scramble to get to church on time. It was only because of the motor car that they arrived before the service started, and Lucy and William's parents reluctantly agreed that the motor car had a place in the future of this modern world and new century. The day passed quickly and it was soon time for Lucy to go back to college. William wanted to get back without having to drive both ways in the dark.

Lucy was glad to be back at Manchester and found Cynthia in hers and Laura's room.

'Have you brought back all your possessions?' Cynthia laughed, looking at the bags full of clothes that Lucy had brought.

'Oh, no, they're for Bessie, Laura's sister. She wants to start making clothes herself, so I said I'd see if I could find anything at home. I asked Mother as well.'

'Have you anything left in the wardrobes?' asked Laura dryly.

'Oh, yes, plenty,' replied Lucy, in all seriousness.

'I wish I'd known,' said Cynthia, 'I could look through my wardrobes too. I've far too many clothes – so has Mother and my sisters. Next time I go home, I'll sort some out for you, Laura.'

'Thank you,' said Laura.

'Never mind the clothes. Tell us about the party,' grinned Cynthia. 'Did he get lots of presents?'

'Oh, no, he told everyone he didn't want presents. He put a box in the entrance hall and if anyone wanted to, they could make a donation towards a new wing that they want to build in the local hospital.'

'That's very commendable,' said Laura.

'Yes, I think I'd have preferred presents,' giggled Lucy. 'Never mind the presents or the clothes; I've brought cake home for you.'

'Even better,' added Laura. Lucy got the cake out and they all ate their slice. After they had finished, Lucy told them about her brother's surprise present of a motor car from their parents. Both girls were suitably impressed.

'Did you get a ride in it?' asked Cynthia.

'Did I? He came to collect me in it on Friday night. I was freezing cold and frightened to death, but they are so much quicker than the horse and cab that I think I could get used to them. It didn't seem as bad on the journey back here.'

'My young brother Albert is very keen on motor cars. He runs after them all the time and if one comes near the mill, he asks the owner if he may look after it for them, like it's a horse that might run away,' Laura laughed. 'Wait until I tell him that you've been for a ride in one. He'll be green with envy.'

'Well, I think it's time I went to my room,' said Cynthia. 'Thanks for a lovely evening, both of you. Good night.' Both girls chorused 'good night' back and then after Cynthia had gone, Lucy and Laura looked at the clothes.

'There's a couple of dresses here that might fit you, Laura. I've never worn them in Manchester, so no one will know that they haven't always been yours. Your Bessie could trim them or shorten them to make them new.'

'That's so kind of you, Lucy. Bessie will be very excited. How can I ever repay you?'

'Just continue being my friend,' Lucy replied. 'Oh, and by the way, Mother asked if you would please come and stay at our house for a week at Christmas. Would your parents allow that, do you think?'

'Stay at your house? Really? I'd love that! But won't I be too shabby and not good enough for the likes of you?'

'Rubbish. I've told you, we're all equal in God's sight. Will you come?'

'I'll have to ask my parents, but if they say yes, then of course I'll come, if you're sure you want me?'

'Of course I want you to come. You can help me annoy my brother. It's my chief delight! You should have seen all the girls swarming round him at the party. All simpering and smiling at him. I can't think why. How anybody could be able to love my brother, I'll never know.'

'I can't believe it. Going to your house for Christmas! I'll go and ask my parents tomorrow after class finishes.'

'There's no need to rush.'

'I want to go home to take all these clothes round to Bessie anyway. She'll be so excited.'

'There's a lot to carry. Shall I come with you?'

'Yes please.' And so they did. Both girls staggered into Laura's home the next evening with the clothes, showing them to Laura's mother, who was suitably impressed by them all. After taking out the dresses that were for Laura herself, and one for Mrs Carter, they walked round to where Bessie lived and were glad they had done when they saw how her face lit up. Laura was also delighted that her mother had made no objection to her going to Burnley for Christmas either. Lucy said that she would write to her mother tomorrow to confirm it.

Soon it was Cynthia's turn to teach the children. Her class were seven-year-olds who were in their third year of schooling. She had to teach them the use of adjectives, which Lucy thought was a difficult subject, but Cynthia rose to the occasion and, to her relief, was given a good report.

The week after it was Lucy's turn. Lucy's task was to teach the second year children their 3 times table. The children were soon competent at singing the rhyme accompanying the 3 times table, but Lucy wasn't convinced that they understood the concept properly. She got the children to stand in groups of three, which took some time as they all fussed about who was going to stand with whom. Eventually, they were all sorted out into threes and Lucy got each little group to move to the other side of the classroom. When they had run out of children at 'ten threes are thirty', Lucy encouraged the first six children to run to the other side of the classroom to make up the whole table.

The children seemed to really enjoy the activity and grasped what she was trying to teach them. Lucy received a very favourable comment from both the class teacher and Miss Dodd, and also from the other students. All three girls were glad they had done their first session with the children and wouldn't be as frightened the next time they had to teach. Slowly, the rest of the term was completed and all the student teachers had taken their turn in class.

There were only three young men in the class who were taking the younger age group; most of the male students were training for working with older children. Very often at mealtimes, the three young men would come and sit with Lucy, Cynthia and Laura. The young men's names were Jacob Atherton, Huw Roberts and David Wood. The girls felt very cosmopolitan at having male friends, which would never have been allowed at home. Despite disparaging loud remarks from Mary Watson, the friendship continued, and sometimes they walked round the grounds together in the lunch break or evenings. Lucy knew that Jacob was keen on her, but it wasn't reciprocated. Cynthia and Huw, however, were another story. Huw always managed to dawdle behind the others when he was talking to Cynthia, and the other four laughed at his antics, which he thought weren't obvious.

As it got nearer to Christmas, the students had to help with a Nativity play that the children would be performing for their families. Because

Cynthia was the best piano player of all the students, she was selected to play for the carols, and when Huw offered to be the page turner for the music, it was difficult for the others not to laugh. The children worked very hard to learn their lines and retell the ageless story of the birth of Jesus. After the Nativity play, the children were given a party, which involved lots of sandwiches, cakes, jelly and, as a great treat, each child got a tangerine, some of whom had never seen one before. Then the children were given a small book each as they left the school for the holidays. After a great deal of tidying up, the children and staff were glad that they were having a holiday as well.

As Christmas Day was on a Wednesday that year and it was Laura's 19th birthday on Saturday, 21st December, Laura's mum invited Lucy to go round on the Saturday for tea. They decided to make it a Christmas meal as Laura wouldn't be with them on Christmas Day. That gave Lucy the excuse to buy them all Christmas presents, as a thank you for letting Laura go home with her to Burnley over the holiday.

For Laura, she bought a dress. It was made of soft wool and was a day dress and Lucy knew that it would be perfect for Laura to wear over Christmas. It was in pale green wool with darker green trimmings and fitted her perfectly. For Laura's father, there was a packet of his favourite tobacco and a new pipe. For Laura's mother, Lucy bought a soft cashmere shawl, which she loved immediately and wore it all day as soon as she opened the parcel. For the young boys, there was a collection of Charles Dickens' books and some building bricks, which they both loved. Agnes received a red jumper which Lucy had knitted (red being Agnes' favourite colour) but there was a skirt of red tartan to go with it. Agnes was ecstatic. Bessie had been allowed home for the party but she was speechless at her present. Lucy had bought her a second-hand sewing machine that she'd spotted in the pawnbrokers on her way home from Laura's house a few weeks before.

Mrs Carter remonstrated with Lucy and said that she had spent too much on them all, but Lucy argued that they had made her so welcome and she wanted to give something back. As it was getting late, Lucy and Laura decided that they had better be getting back to college, and Laura went upstairs to get their coats, when there was a knock on the door. Agnes went to answer it but didn't bring the person in.

'Who is it, Agnes?' shouted her father.

'It's a gentleman,' she replied.

'Well, bring him in,' her father replied.

'William, what are you doing here?' gasped Lucy, as her brother entered.

'Thought I'd come a day earlier for you,' William replied sheepishly. 'Sorry to intrude, Mr Carter,' he apologised.

'That's all right,' replied Mr Carter, 'come in and sit down.'

'I actually heard from my sister that there were two young boys that live near here somewhere that wanted a ride in my motor car,' he grinned.

'That's me!' shouted Albert.

'And me!' added Arthur, not to be done out of a treat by his elder brother.

'Can I come too?' asked Agnes, looking hopeful.

'You can all come if that's all right with your parents?' replied William. Mr Carter nodded. 'Come on then. You, young lady, can sit in the front and the boys can go in the back. You'll need warm coats and hats.' Quicker than Lucy had ever seen them move before, the children got their coats and hats on and were out of the door before Laura had come downstairs. Mrs Carter went upstairs to tell Laura what had happened and told her to get her belongings ready, as they were going a day early.

The children were soon back, their eyes aglow with excitement. Then William insisted on Mr and Mrs Carter and Bessie going for a short ride too. As they arrived back, Laura was just coming down the stairs with her bags packed. As she entered the room, William stood stock still and stared at her, speechless for once.

'William,' cried Lucy, 'where are your manners? This is my friend, Laura Carter. Aren't you going to greet her properly?'

'Er, yes, er, how do you do, Miss Carter?' stuttered William, whilst Lucy looked on with disbelief.

'Pleased to meet you, Mr Coombes,' replied Laura, laughing at the look on his face. 'I've heard so much about you from Lucy.' That seemed to break his reverie.

'Oh, don't believe anything Lucy tells you about me. She exaggerates.'

'I do not!' Lucy replied, but everyone in the room began laughing. 'I suppose we'd better be setting off as we'll need to get my things from college before we go home,' said Lucy, when she could be heard.

Within minutes, both girls were settled in the motor car with Laura's belongings. As William cranked the motor car to set off again, many of the curtains twitched on Mill Street, as the motor car drew away from the curb, with all the family waving them off.

Whilst Lucy got her things together, Laura ran down to Cynthia's room to tell her about the change in plans, and to give Cynthia Christmas presents from herself and Lucy. Lucy returned to the communal lounge where visitors were allowed to wait and sat with William.

'You didn't tell me how pretty your friend was,' said William as soon as Lucy sat down.

'You didn't ask,' replied Lucy cheekily.

'Is she betrothed?'

'Of course not.'

'Good.'

'I hope you're not getting any silly ideas, William. She's not interested in men.'

'We'll have to see,' he replied, but the conversation ceased as Laura returned to the room.

They were soon ready to go and William tried to manoeuvre Laura into the front of the motor car, but she insisted on being in the back seat, as she was a little nervous of riding in a motor car. The miles passed and Lucy was glad that William was taking his time as it was a dark night, there being no moon. She tried to keep the conversation going with Laura as she knew she was nervous, but it was difficult and, for once, William was silent, but was probably concentrating on driving in the dark, Lucy reflected.

It was very late when they arrived in Burnley, but all the lights were on in the house, and Patsy was at the door to let them in.

'Come along in, Miss Lucy. I've got the kettle boiling ready to make you a drink. You go and sit in the lounge; the fire's still lit. Your parents have already gone to bed, as they didn't know Mr William was going for you tonight.'

'Thank you, Patsy. This is my friend, Laura.'

'Welcome, Miss Laura. Do you need a snack?'

'No, thank you, Patsy. We've had a large meal at my house,' replied Laura. Lucy led her into the lounge and sat her by the fire, whilst William brought in all their bags and took them upstairs to Lucy's bedroom. After they'd drunk their tea, William came into the room and helped himself to a cup of tea.

'I've put all your bags in your room, Lucy. Is Laura sharing? Mother was suggesting that Laura might prefer a separate room,' said William.

'I'd rather share Lucy's room,' said Laura. 'That's if you don't mind, Lucy?'

'That's what I told Mother. We're used to sharing, aren't we Laura? I don't know about you, but I'm tired. Shall we go to bed, Laura?'

'Yes, please; it's been quite an exciting day.'

'It certainly has,' added William, with an inane grin on his face. The two girls said goodnight and left William by the fire, ignoring his comments.

As soon as they got in the bedroom, Lucy laughed at Laura.

'I think you've made quite an impression on my brother. I don't think I've ever seen him like that before.'

'What do you mean?' asked Laura.

'Grinning and smiling at you. He was speechless when he first saw you. That's a first.'

'I'm not interested, Lucy. I've got a course to complete.'

'I know. That's what I told him.'

'You told him? Why?'

'He asked if you were betrothed and I said no, and that you weren't interested in men.'

Laura blushed, but agreed with Lucy. 'That's right. I'm too busy for men.'

'I'll show you where the bathroom is and then we can both get to sleep. We'll have to be up early for church in the morning.' After Laura marvelled at the bathroom – they didn't have them in Mill Street, but just a shared outdoor privy and a tin bath hung up in the scullery – the two girls were soon in bed and fast asleep.

Next morning, as the girls descended the staircase for breakfast, Lucy could hear her mother shouting at William, but the voices soon stopped when the girls entered the breakfast room. Mrs Coombes jumped up and came over to Laura and apologised for not being there to greet them last night. Mr Coombes added his apologies too, then sat down, reading the newspaper throughout breakfast, as he usually did.

'This foolish son of mine took it into his head to go and fetch you last night without telling us. I'm so embarrassed that you arrived after we had retired for the night. I've taken Patsy to task about it. She should have woken us up. Come and sit down here next to me, Laura.'

'Don't worry about it, Mrs Coombes. Patsy looked after us beautifully and told us that you weren't aware that William had decided to pick us up early.'

'That's a lovely dress you're wearing, my dear,' said Mrs Coombes, admiring the pale green dress that Lucy had bought for Laura's birthday.

'Thank you,' replied Laura. 'Lucy kindly had this made for me.'

'Just the right shade. It suits your colouring.'

'Thank you.'

'Laura's sister Bessie is training to be a dressmaker and helped her employer make the dress,' said Lucy.

'Is that the same person who made the dress you wore for William's birthday party?' asked her mother.

'Yes. Mrs Brenda Smith.'

'I can see that she is an excellent dressmaker. Perhaps she could make me a gown or two?' asked Mrs Coombes.

'I'm sure she could,' replied Laura.

'What about your own dressmaker, Mrs Miller? You've been going to her for years.'

'Oh, haven't you heard? She's retired now.'

'No, well that's convenient,' laughed Lucy. 'We can go to Mrs Smith now, although it's quite a long way to go for fittings.'

'A good excuse to do some shopping in Manchester as well. Especially now we've got the motor car,' she looked indulgently at William when she said this, who'd been silent throughout breakfast.

'Talking of which,' William spoke at last, 'I'd better get the motor car ready for church. I'll see you shortly.'

Soon they were all ready and got into the car and motored into Burnley centre. After the service, Lucy made a beeline for Miss Egar and Miss Seeney, to introduce Laura to them, and they had a long chat over coffee.

After a sumptuous lunch, during which Granny Wall asked Laura a lot of questions, Lucy and Laura decided to go for a walk. William offered to accompany them but they declined, saying they wanted to talk about girls' things and didn't want a boy with them. This deflated William, being called a boy, much to Lucy's delight.

They walked down to Queen's Park and took a stroll round the grounds there. It was the first public park in the town, and the land had been donated by a local landowner, Sir John Thursby, in 1893. He called it Queen's Park in honour of the Queen's Golden Jubilee a few years before. Laura was very impressed as there were no such parks near her house.

'Your house is very grand,' said Laura wistfully.

'I suppose so. When you've always lived there, you don't think so. It's not as grand as some of the houses further up the road. Oakleigh is the nicest and is very large. It has a beautiful sweeping staircase, with a stained-glass window at the curve of the stairs. My parents were invited to a party there once when old Mr Altham lived there. He was a great philanthropist in the town.'

'Your parents are lovely, too, and your grandmother.'

'Yes, I'm very fortunate.'

'You really are, but you don't let it go to your head. That's what I like about you. You are not a snob at all.'

'I'm glad you think so. My parents have always drummed into us that we are there but by the grace of God, and we should never take anything for granted.'

'That's a very sensible attitude. Even though compared to you, I have nothing, yet I'm grateful, because I have a loving family and enough to eat and a roof over my head, and I've got the chance of taking this course, so I can improve my lot in life.'

'Precisely. We both can. I wonder what life holds for us both?'

'Only God knows. It's like that new hymn we sang this morning. "God holds the key of all unknown and I am glad." I liked it. I've never heard it before.'

'Yes, it is a new one, but I like it too,' agreed Lucy.

'Perhaps we'll be famous teachers or something like that,' suggested Laura.

'Maybe. Or we may just marry and have children.'

Laura pulled a face. 'Not for me. I have to finish the course and work for the school for two years before I can think about marriage and children.'

'We'll just have to trust God and see what happens. What shall we do tomorrow?' asked Lucy.

Chapter 7

On the Monday morning, the girls were up early and Lucy decided to take Laura to Burnley town centre to shop. Laura was impressed that such a small town could have so many shops of all different types and they enjoyed strolling round the town, looking at all the festive window dressings. Finding a café, they went inside for a hot chocolate, which they both loved. After that, Lucy took Laura to her father's factory to show her round. Laura was impressed by the safety measures that were in place, as large buckets of sand and hose reels were everywhere. Lucy reminded her that the factory made matchsticks, so there had to be strict observance of safety because of the flammable nature of the product.

Just as they were about to leave, William came hurrying into the office, pulling his jacket on as he came in.

'Hello, I've only just heard that you were here. You should have let me know you were coming. Do you want a tour round the factory?'

'No, thanks. We've already had one. Father took us round,' replied Lucy.

'Oh,' said William, somewhat crestfallen. 'Have you had lunch yet?'

'No, we're thinking of catching the omnibus home for lunch.'

'Let me take you to the Cross Keys Hotel, which is fairly new. They have a small parlour where it is acceptable for ladies to visit,' William suggested.

'That's not like you, William. You've never offered to take me out for lunch before during the working day. What would Father say?' Lucy teased, but kept a straight face.

'Oh, I'm sure Father won't mind. I'll go and ask him,' and William was out of the door before Lucy could respond. He returned with Mr Coombes.

'Now, what's all this about Lucy? Trying to take your brother away from his work?'

'It was his idea, Father, not mine,' scowled Lucy, who got a glare back from William.

'Well, I suppose we have to entertain Miss Carter whilst she is here, so go, run along all of you, but be back before two, William. The traveller is coming and you need to deal with him.'

'Thank you. I'll be back,' William promised, grabbing his overcoat and hat. He led the girls out of the factory and down the long main street to the new hotel. They were taken into the small parlour and served a very creditable meal, during which William constantly asked Laura questions about herself.

'Give her time to eat her food, William. You've never stopped since we sat down.'

'Sorry. It's just so much more interesting talking to a new person than talking to you, sister dear.'

'So I noticed,' said Lucy grinning. 'Anyway, it's almost two o'clock. Didn't you have to be back by then?'

'Oh, no, I must go,' William said reluctantly. 'See you tonight,' and he dashed out of the door before the girls could even say goodbye. Both girls looked at each other and burst out laughing.

'I'm exhausted,' Laura said. 'I've never been asked so many questions at the same time before.'

'I've never known William talk for so long or ask so many questions either!' Lucy laughed. 'I think you've made a great impact on him.' They made their way out of the hotel and back to the main shopping street. After a few more purchases, they went to the omnibus station and back to Lucy's home, chatting on the journey as Lucy pointed out places of interest.

That evening, the Christmas tree was set up and Lucy and Laura spent the next afternoon putting decorations on the tree, with candles, tinsel, and little chocolate gifts. It suddenly felt that Christmas was close. Lucy got out the Nativity scene and arranged it on the mantelpiece in the lounge, just to remind everyone of the true meaning of Christmas, despite the trappings of tradition like the Christmas tree. There was also another Nativity scene which was put on the hall table, so that it was the first thing that everybody saw when they arrived at the house.

It was soon Christmas Day. After a small breakfast, the whole family and servants went to church and enjoyed singing the special carols about the Saviour's birth. After the service, along with the usual cups of tea, mince pies were served, much to the delight of Lucy who loved them and could never eat enough. Although the turkey had been in the oven most of the morning whilst they had been at church, the rest of the Christmas meal was prepared after church. Everybody helped, as was their usual tradition. The large extensions to the dining table were fixed in place by William and Metcalfe, the groom, and the special Christmas tablecloths laid on top. Extra chairs were brought in from the breakfast room and kitchen. Mrs Coombes then got out the pretty table decorations that were packed away in the attics each year and arranged them on the table. The best china was also put out, together with special embroidered serviettes that were only used at Christmas. Lucy and Laura were helping Mrs Ward and Patsy in the kitchen, preparing vegetables – Laura much more used to this kind of task than Lucy was – but everyone helped. Even Granny Wall was helping set the cutlery out.

Laura couldn't understand why there were so many chairs round the table but didn't say anything. When it was time to sit down, she realised just what was happening. All the staff were to sit down to eat with the family, and all their families too. There was Mr Ward, Mrs Metcalfe and their two boys, and Patsy's mum and dad and their four other children. The room was crowded when everyone sat down, but there was no room for Mr and Mrs Coombes to sit down. Laura tried to offer her chair, but Lucy told her to wait. Laura understood when Mr and Mrs Coombes came in and served all the staff, after giving thanks for the season as well as the food that was about to be eaten.

'They do this every year,' explained Lucy to Laura, after they'd eaten the main course. 'Because the staff serve us all year, we serve them at Christmas to remind them how much we appreciate them, but also to show that we are all equal before God.'

'That is very special. I couldn't imagine our mill owners doing that,' chuckled Laura.

'Wait 'til afterwards. You won't be as pleased then. After the present session, we have to wash up. Then we all sit round together playing games…,' but they were prevented from any further conversation as Mr Coombes came in carrying the Christmas pudding which was set alight, to the wonderment of the children, and Laura. After the pudding, when everyone insisted that they could not eat another thing, they all went into the lounge and sat down. Lucy went to the piano and played some Christmas carols, with which everyone joined in, except Mr and Mrs Coombes, who were eating their meal.

Then it was time for the present giving. Mrs Ward, Patsy, and Metcalfe simply received an envelope, with a monetary gift inside, but the rest of their families got presents. Mrs Metcalfe received a warm wool skirt length and Mr Ward received leather gloves and a hat. Patsy's parents received a clock and some scented soap, but the children each got a stocking which contained nuts, sweets, a tangerine, and small toys. The boys got soldiers and model motor cars and the girls got skipping ropes and spinning tops. The children all received a little Bible story book too. Once all the staff had received their presents, Lucy jumped up and told William it was time to wash up and he pulled a face. Laura offered to help and suddenly William agreed.

'That's the first time he's ever willingly offered to help me wash up. I usually have to drag him into the kitchen,' laughed Lucy. Despite the massive pile of dishes, cutlery, and pans, the three of them made light work of it, ensuring the remains of the food were put away into cupboards, tins and the meat-safe.

When they got back into the lounge, games were in progress: Hunt the Thimble, Charades, musical chairs and guessing games. At around seven o'clock, Mrs Coombes went back into the kitchen and brought fresh tea to drink, together with thick wedges of Christmas cake, slices of chocolate log, and mince pies. Although nobody thought they could eat anything, everybody managed one or all of the delicacies that had been produced. After this small repast, Patsy's parents said it was time for them to be getting the children home, and this seemed to break the party up. Everybody drifted home, saying thank you and taking their presents with them. The staff would all have Boxing Day and the day after at home without working, and the Coombes would fend for themselves. Soon, just the family, Granny Wall, and Laura remained.

'Time for our presents now,' shouted William with glee. He went under the Christmas tree and brought out lots of presents. 'I'll give mine out first. Granny Wall, this is for you.' He proffered a large ungainly package that wasn't very well wrapped. Wrapping presents had never been William's forte, Lucy reflected. He was too impatient.

'What can this be?' pondered Granny Wall, but was amazed when she opened it. William had bought her a set of leather gloves, goggles, and a hat for travelling in the motor car. 'Oh William, when am I ever going to go in a motor car?'

'Tonight,' replied William with a twinkle, 'when I take you home. Look, I've got the same for everyone,' and he promptly handed round identical presents for all the people in the room. Laura was amazed.

'You've bought a present for me?'

'Yes, why not? You are our guest for Christmas. I couldn't leave you out.'

'But I could ask the same question as Mrs Wall. When will I ever go in a motor car?'

'Well, I'll give you the same answer. When I take you home, but not tonight of course,' he laughed. Laura just blushed and said nothing. Everybody else opened their presents and admired them, leaving William suitably pleased with his purchases.

Granny Wall was next and had bought everyone a woollen jumper, including Laura, who again was overwhelmed. Next it was Martha and Edward's turn. Martha had chosen different presents for them all. For Granny Wall, there were beautiful thick towels, which were richly embroidered.

'Granny wants those every year as she loves them, but we never see them in use in her bathroom,' Lucy whispered to Laura. 'I think she just likes to see them in her drawer, but they are handy in case important visitors come.'

'Stop whispering, girls; you know I don't like it,' rebuked Martha. 'Here are your presents, but perhaps I should make you wait until last now.' Despite saying that, she handed both girls identical small packages. Inside were gold crosses and chains for each girl. Both girls were pleased and immediately fastened them round their necks, admiring each other's present. William was given a pocket watch, with which he was very pleased. Next, Lucy brought out her presents. For her parents, Lucy had bought a china tureen with gravy jugs that matched their best dinner service, which pleased them both. For Granny Wall, Lucy had bought a crystal vase which she loved. For William there was a new fountain pen, and for Laura, a leather-bound Bible, just like the one she received from Miss Seeney and Miss Egar, but in a different colour, so that they didn't get mixed up in their room at college. Laura was pleased with it and admitted that she had never actually owned one herself, having to share a Bible with her family.

'I've only bought you small presents, and none of them will compare with what you have given me. It is so kind of you all. I can never thank you enough,' Laura began, but Mrs Coombes told her not to worry, that they weren't expecting any presents from Laura as she was the guest this year. Laura had bought a large box of chocolates for Mr and Mrs Coombes, some scented soap for Granny Wall, a new skirt for Lucy, which her sister had made, and she had knitted a long scarf and gloves for William. Exclaiming that he loved them, William wore them straightaway, even though it was very warm in the room.

Once all the presents were opened, Lucy jumped up and shouted, 'Christmas Wishes.'

'Oh, yes,' said Granny Wall, 'we'd better get the Christmas cake back in.' Laura looked puzzled.

'We always have another slice of cake and then tell each other what our Christmas wishes are for the following year,' explained Lucy. William came back with the Christmas cake, along with small cake plates and forks and some slices of Lancashire cheese, a traditional delicacy that always enhanced the Christmas cake. Once they all had a plate each, Mr Coombes started the ball rolling.

'My Christmas wish is that I can build a canteen for my workers, so that they can have somewhere nice to go instead of eating near their benches. What about you, Granny Wall?'

'My Christmas wish is that I can give more to the poor and needy, although I quite like the idea of a workers' canteen, Edward. I'll discuss that with you another time, but in the meantime, I'll talk to my mill manager about it and see what he thinks. Your turn now, Lucy.'

'My Christmas wish is that I can learn to be a good teacher. What about you, Laura?'

'Mine's exactly the same. I want to be a good teacher.'

'What about you, Mother? What is your wish?' asked Lucy.

'Well, now, I thought this year I might wish for grandchildren, but I can see that isn't going to happen yet, so I suppose I'd better think again.' Lucy and William looked at each other and raised their eyebrows. 'Now, let me see,' she said thoughtfully. 'Yes, I suppose I wish for you all to be happy and healthy this year. Now it's your turn, William.'

'Oh, I don't know what to say. I do have two wishes, but it's far too soon to mention either of them at the moment,' he said evasively.

'No, William, that will not do,' cried Lucy. 'You're not allowed to be so mysterious. You have to tell us one wish.'

'Well, all right then, but you probably won't like it; Father especially.'

'Me?' said Mr Coombes. 'What's it to do with me?'

'My Christmas wish is that I could open a motor car salesroom and employ a mechanic to help with mending the engines.' There was a stunned silence in the room as everybody digested what William had said. Mr Coombes was the first to react.

'What's brought this on, my lad? Aren't you happy at the mill?'

'We should never have bought him that motor car for his birthday,' Mrs Coombes interjected. 'It's gone to his head.'

'Yes, no,' replied a confused William.

'You'd better explain yourself then,' Mr Coombes replied.

'I do like working with you, Father, but I see the future of motor cars being much bigger, not just a fad, like you think it is. There is nowhere in Burnley that sells motor cars and certainly no one with the skills to keep them in good repair.'

'So, how would you go about it?' asked Mr Coombes.

'I'd rent or buy a large warehouse and fit it out with special equipment. Then I'd find someone who had the skill to mend the machines and we could sell the motor cars or even rent them out to people who need to be taken to an event or to go on holiday, but didn't want to buy their own vehicle.'

'And how do you think you were going to fund all this business? Were you still thinking of working at the mill as well?'

'I haven't thought that far, Father.'

'No, I thought you hadn't. Well, come and see me when you've got the money to waste on this foolish business and then we'll talk.'

'How much do you think it would take to set all this up, William?' asked Granny Wall.

'I'm not sure; I haven't done final costings yet,' muttered William.

'Would £1000 be enough?' she asked.

'Mother? What are you saying?' gasped Martha.

'Leave this to me, our Martha. When William was born, being the first grandchild, my Jack set up a trust fund for him to come to fruition when he was 21 years old. The paperwork has just arrived so the money is available for you now, William. Your Grandfather thought that it would probably buy you a nice house so that you could live an independent life, but there are no instructions on how you should spend the money. Well, would it be enough?'

'More than enough, Granny. I can't begin to thank you,' started William, but she interrupted him.

'Don't thank me; it was your Grandfather's idea. He didn't expect you to set up a business with it, but if it makes you happy, then so be it. At least you'll still have a job if it all goes wrong,' she laughed.

'It won't go wrong. It is the future,' William insisted.

'We'll talk about this tomorrow,' Mr Coombes said, with a voice that brooked no opposition.

'I'm tired now,' yawned Lucy. 'I think I'll go to bed.'

'Shall I take you home then, Granny?' asked William.

'No. If you don't mind, Martha, can I stay here tonight? I think all the excitement has tired me out.'

'Of course you can, Mother. I'll just go and put a hot water bottle in the spare room.' Mrs Coombes bustled out of the room and Lucy and Laura said goodnight and went upstairs.

When they got to their bedroom, Lucy said, 'Well, I never. That was a total surprise. He's never said a thing to me.'

'Your father didn't look too happy,' said Laura.

'No, he's not one for change really. I was surprised that he wants to make changes at the factory. Something must have made him want to make a workers' canteen. Perhaps he got it from someone at the Chamber of Commerce. They often like to keep up with what each other is doing,' Lucy laughed. 'I'm so tired, I'm going straight to bed now. We'll talk tomorrow. I wonder what the second wish was that William had? Bet we'll never get to know now. After that reaction, he might never reveal his feelings ever again.' However, in that she was totally wrong. Lucy yawned as she got into bed. It had been a perfect day.

Chapter 8

Boxing Day dawned and the family had a large, leisurely breakfast that would last them until teatime. William insisted that everyone went out for a walk but he couldn't persuade his grandmother to go, as she preferred to go home instead. Undaunted, William got out hats and gloves and strong boots and told Lucy to find a pair for Laura. Soon, they were all wrapped up against the bitter cold day, and they set off out of Burnley down Barden Lane, then up Greenhead Lane until they got to the village of Fence. Mr and Mrs Coombes were quite out of breath by the time they got to Fence and were glad to sit on a wall for a while and drink some cold tea that they had brought with them. Eventually, they made the return journey and arrived home to an empty house.

'I'm glad we banked up the fire before we went,' Martha commented as they went in the house. 'It feels lovely and warm. Shall we have a cup of tea before Lucy and I start making the tea?' Everyone agreed, so Martha went into the kitchen and whilst waiting for the kettle to boil, she put the soup on the stove to start warming up. Lucy joined her, followed by Laura, who asked if there was anything that she could do to help. Martha declined Laura's offer and said that she quite enjoyed being in the kitchen as she hadn't been used to servants when she was first married.

Lucy busied herself getting things out of the pantry ready for their tea. There was a large raised pork pie, jars of pickles, and she got the bread and butter from the scullery, and the cold turkey out of the meat-safe, ready to make the sandwiches. Next, she got out the Christmas cake and some buns that had been left over from Christmas Eve. Covering everything over with a tablecloth, and turning the soup down to simmer, Lucy helped her mother carry the tea trays back into the lounge and they all had a cup of tea.

Later, the three women went into the kitchen and finished preparing the tea which was met with delight by the men. Insisting that the men had to do the washing up, Laura was amazed when they did. She knew her father would never wash up at their house! Afterwards they had songs round the piano and all decided to have an early night – the fresh air had quite worn them out. The day after Boxing Day was spent quietly by the ladies, the men going back into work leaving the women on their own. The following day, the staff returned to work, so the house felt restored to its usual bustling self, after the quiet of the last two days. On Saturday afternoon after William had finished work, he had promised he would take Laura home so that she could spend time with her own family. Lucy knew that he would have preferred to take her home on his own, but he was aware that it wouldn't be allowed for propriety's sake, but somehow, he managed to manoeuvre Laura into the front seat next to him, leaving Lucy to sit behind. Laura tried to object but to no avail, so a very pleased William got his wish. He chattered constantly to Laura all the way home and insisted on taking her right to the door and going inside the house. Albert and Arthur were delighted and William ended up having to give them a short ride round the neighbourhood along with four of their friends, who thought it was the best Christmas present they had ever had, and were impressed at Albert and Arthur's posh friends.

Eventually, Lucy insisted that it was time for them to go home, but not before having a cup of tea and a mince pie. On the journey home, William allowed Lucy to sit in the front seat with him and extolled Laura's charms all the way home.

'You're wasting your time, William. Laura has no intention of getting seriously involved with you or anyone else. She is dedicated to learning to be a teacher, as I am, and nothing will stop in her way.'

'I can wait. I can't stop thinking about her, Lucy. I've never felt like this before.'

'Oh, change the subject, William, you're beginning to bore me.'

'Wait until you fall in love with someone, you'll be the same and then I'll laugh,' William said.

'Tell me about the motor car business. I was quite surprised when you said it was what you wanted.'

'Well, I couldn't say the other wish that I wanted.'

'Why not?'

'Because it was that I want to marry Laura.'

'Marry? You've only known her for a week. Anyway, I've just told you, I don't want to hear about Laura anymore tonight. Tell me about the motor car business.'

So he did, but Lucy was only half listening. She could foresee trouble ahead if William put pressure on Laura. Lucy only hoped that it didn't affect her friendship with Laura or she wouldn't be best pleased. After getting home, Lucy feigned a headache and, after her mother fussing over her and insisting she took a cooling powder for her head, Lucy went to bed to sit and think about what William had told her. Whilst it would be excellent to have Laura as a sister-in-law, Lucy didn't think it could ever happen. Poor William, he was in for heartache before long, Lucy sighed as she settled down to sleep.

On New Year's Eve, the family all went to the church hall for a social event with supper which ended at 11.30pm and then everyone moved into the church itself for a Watch-Night service. The old year was reviewed and promises made to be better in the New Year of 1908, by recommitting their lives afresh to God. Lucy promised to work hard at her studies and show that she was a capable teacher and worthy of her parents trusting her to go to Manchester for training. She didn't dare think about what William was promising and she didn't ask him.

On the Saturday, William took her back to Manchester ready for the new term but she refused to allow him to go to Laura's house on the way. Laura would make her own way back, Lucy insisted, and William had to return home, without seeing the object of his desires and dreams, but not before telling Lucy that she was a hard-hearted woman!

Classes restarted on the Monday and it was lovely catching up with Cynthia and the other trainee teachers in their class, but the work seemed to have become more relentless and their work schedule was hectic, with increased teaching time with the children, which all needed a lot of preparation. Cynthia had brought a pile of old clothes for Bessie, which Laura and Bessie were delighted with.

The term continued with a vengeance and teaching skills were honed regularly. At the beginning of February, Lucy got a letter from William – a fairly rare event – but he was full of his business plans. It arrived just as they were going into class, so Lucy put it in her pocket and waited until lunchtime to read it. They were sat together with Cynthia, and joined by their three male friends, Huw, Jacob and David. Lucy started reading the letter.

'Laura, would you believe it, William has opened his motor car business already,' said an excited Lucy.

'A motor car business?' asked David. 'Where is that? I thought your brother worked in the family business?'

'He does, but he astounded us all at Christmas by saying that his Christmas wish was to open a motor car business. It seems he's already done it. Shall I read you the letter?'

'Yes please,' Laura and David replied, so Lucy read the letter out loud.

Hello Lucy,

Would you believe it? I've opened my business. Do you remember the old warehouse that Father bought, next door to our factory? He did intend to expand at some stage but never got round to it. Well, he's let me use the building, at a peppercorn rent of course, to open a motor car garage. Just think, it'll be the first in Burnley. The whole of the downstairs will be divided into two with the front half having great glass windows and doors large enough to move the motor cars in and out. There will be a desk for me and chairs for the customers. At the back of the building, there will be a workshop with a separate entrance so that the motor cars can be mended or serviced.

I've managed to get young Freddie from the factory to come and work for me. He's the young man who worked in the factory steam engine shed and was always mending machines. I've already sent him to work at the Blackburn garage for four weeks to learn all he could. We'll be able to learn together now how these motor cars work. Also, Freddie can already drive a motor car - he's a fast learner – and he and I are going to offer to drive people around, especially those who don't want to drive or would only need a motor car occasionally, so that will bring income in before the motor car sales grow, as I know they will.

The first booking is for Saturday, February 29ᵗʰ, and I'm to take Mrs Barber and her daughter Clare to Manchester shopping. I'll have to wait around all day so I thought I could visit you and take you out for a meal? Perhaps Miss Carter could come too? Do let me know.

Your loving brother,
William.

'I say, lucky chap,' said Jacob, when Lucy had finished reading.

'I agree,' said Huw. 'Do you think he would let us all have a ride in his motor car when he comes?'

'I'm sure he would,' replied Lucy, 'he loves to show it off.'

'No, I meant lucky chap for getting to go out for a meal with Miss Carter and Miss Coombes,' Jacob laughed. 'I'd rather go out with them than a ride in a motor car.'

'I'd like both,' laughed Huw. 'A ride out and a meal too, as long as Miss Shaw could come as well.'

'Why not?' said Lucy, 'that would be great fun if all of us could go out for a meal together. Shall I write and ask him?' The friends all agreed and so Lucy wrote to William suggesting that his offer of a meal out had grown into a group of seven, including William; the men all insisting they would pay their share. William wrote back by return of post – an unheard of occurrence from him – and he offered to book a table for them all.

The 29th February soon came round and William arrived about 11.30 am, and Lucy made all the introductions. First William took the three men a ride around the college area and then dropped them off in town, near to the restaurant where Lucy and Laura had had afternoon tea on their first visit into town together. Then he came back for the three ladies, manoeuvring Laura into the front seat again.

The waiter showed them to a large table near the window, Laura noticed. 'What a difference having men with us has made,' she whispered to Lucy, who grinned back. The conversation was very male-dominated whilst waiting for their meal and the talk was all about the future of motor cars. They all agreed that William was making a very sound business opportunity and applauded him for it. David was asking if William could accommodate his elder brother who was very keen on having a motor car and William agreed to demonstrate one for him at a suitably convenient date. The girls, meanwhile, had been talking about things close to their hearts, and it did not include motor cars! Eventually the talk became more general and was enjoyed by all.

Huw was a younger son with two elder brothers, so no chance of inheriting the family castle and estate. That was why he was training as a teacher, he explained to them all. David was the son of a headmaster and was following in a long line of teachers in his family. Jacob hated everything to do with the cotton mill that his family owned and had proved pretty useless at working there, so his exasperated father had allowed him to train as a teacher, which he saw as a whimsical calling, so Jacob felt that he had to prove his worth as a teacher, or go back into a life of misery in the mill.

Jacob was keen to bring Lucy into the conversation all the time, but she wasn't very interested in him. He was a nice young man, but that was all. She didn't actually dislike him, but didn't want to get to know him any better. He was just a friend, albeit a male. Her teaching course was more important first.

Eventually, it was time for them all to go so the four men split the bill between them, despite the girls being independent modern Misses and offering to pay their share. William offered to drive the girls home, but they decided to walk back to college as they would have the men as chaperones. William tried one last time.

'Are you going home instead, Miss Carter? I could drive you there, and I know your brothers would love to have a ride in my motor car,' he pleaded.

'Sorry, my parents are away visiting my grandparents in Salford. There'll be no one at home. I'm going straight back to college, but thank you for asking. I'll tell the boys they missed out on a treat.' William looked crestfallen but took his leave of everyone, saying how much he had enjoyed the day and they must repeat it soon.

'Good idea,' said Jacob, 'let's meet again before we break up for the summer,' and everyone agreed.

The term continued up until Easter, which was late in 1908; Easter Sunday not being until April 20th. Despite an invite from Martha, Laura declined to visit Lucy's house at Easter. William was bitterly disappointed and urged Lucy to change Laura's mind but to no avail. Laura was adamant that she would not go to Burnley, but would celebrate Easter with her own family at the Mission church.

In Burnley, after the sombre service on Good Friday meditating on the crucifixion of Jesus, it was a joyous celebration service on Easter Sunday. The minister spoke about the role of women in Jesus' life and how the women were the first to see the risen Jesus. Lucy reflected on the last year in her life and how it had changed so much after that fateful conversation last Easter Sunday. She beamed to herself when she remembered Granny Wall sticking up for her and encouraging her father to think again about her career as a teacher. She must remember to give Granny Wall an extra big hug today, she reflected.

When William took Lucy back to college, he managed to hang around long enough to see Laura arrive back from home. William had suggested that they go and pick her up but Lucy refused. He stayed as long as he could, chatting to the two young women but eventually, he had to leave, so that he could get home, much to Laura's relief.

'William was really disappointed that you didn't come and stay with us in Burnley for Easter. He wanted to go and pick you up today to save you walking back to college.'

'I'm glad you didn't come. I don't want him getting any ideas about me,' replied Laura.

'Oh, Laura, it's too late for that.'

'What do you mean?'

'He's already besotted by you.'

Laura blushed and was silent for a moment and then said, 'Well, he's wasting his time.'

'Why? Do you not like him at all, Laura?'

'I do like him, but he's above my station and I've no time for romance. I have a course to finish and a commitment to the teaching job.'

'Above your station? That's ridiculous. We're only three generations from mill workers ourselves. Besides, I think you know that my family are not snobbish and they really like you.'

'They like me as your friend, but it would be a different matter if William was serious about me.'

'No, they wouldn't mind at all. He is serious about you, you know.'

'I don't wish to know. Please don't talk about it, it only upsets me. I want to get ready for class tomorrow and read up about the topic I'm teaching, so please leave me alone.'

'If that's how you feel, I'll read my new book,' replied Lucy, a little huffily.

'Don't be angry with me, Lucy. I need to concentrate on my course for now. Besides, I think Jacob Atherton was trying to get your attention quite a lot today at tea time.'

'Was he?' asked Lucy, looking thoughtful.

'Yes, now leave me in peace,' replied Laura, but laughed to herself when Lucy became very quiet and reflective and didn't read any of her new book at all.

Chapter 9

The summer term rushed by with extra teaching sessions expected of each student and end of term examinations looming. Eventually they reached the last week of term, all congratulating each other in having survived the first year of the course. Just before the end of term, the seven returned to the restaurant for a meal. Mary Watson overheard them planning it and tried to join the group and was quite nasty to Lucy when she refused. Mary had been watching William with his motor car earlier when he was waiting to see Laura, and although Mary had tried to push herself forward for an introduction, Lucy took William for a walk round the gardens to avoid it.

However, on entering the restaurant, the first person that Lucy saw was Mary Watson, sat on the table next to theirs with two of her friends. Mary came over and asked to be introduced to William, pushing herself onto the seat next to him, making simpering noises and excluding all the girls from the conversation. The head waiter came over and offered to join the tables together. Lucy declined, but Mary thanked the waiter, flashing him one of her big smiles, and extra seats were set round the table. Throughout the meal, Laura, Cynthia, and Lucy hardly spoke, as Mary flirted with William, ignoring the girls she had brought with her too. Jacob Atherton kept trying to get Lucy talking, but she couldn't bring herself to chat about trivial things when she felt so miserable. It was a subdued meal and Lucy was glad when it was all over.

Mary asked if William would give her and her friends a lift in his motor car, but he valiantly refused, saying that he had promised to take Lucy, Laura, and Cynthia home. Mary pouted but knew she was beaten, so the three other men offered to walk home with Mary and her friends. Mary had to agree with that, even though Lucy could see that she wasn't happy.

The following morning, Mary sought out Lucy after church and started asking her lots of questions all about William and his business. Lucy replied with as little information as she could, whilst still remaining civil, even though she didn't think Mary deserved civility. Her next question astounded Lucy.

'May I come over and stay with you during the summer holidays, Lucy? I'd love to see where you live and meet your family.'

'I don't think so, Mary. I'll be busy doing voluntary work with my mother over the summer. Besides, we're not particular friends, are we?'

'That's your fault, Lucy. I've tried to befriend you on many occasions.'

'I hadn't noticed,' replied Lucy wryly. 'Anyway, I heard you telling people you were going to Italy with your family this summer, so why would you want to come to Burnley?'

'Just to be a better friend to you.'

A likely story, thought Lucy, but she smiled sweetly and declined the offer, hurrying away before Mary could think up any more lies as to why she wanted to come to Lucy's home, when Lucy knew that she blatantly wanted to inveigle her way into William's life. Lucy knew that there was no hope for Mary as William was totally in love with Laura. However, she wasn't going to tell Mary that or she would probably use it against Laura and Lucy wouldn't let anything hurt her dearest friend, certainly not Mary Watson.

'What did Mary Watson want?' Laura asked later when they were in Cynthia's room together.

'Don't ask!' replied Lucy.

'Why not?' asked Cynthia.

'You'd not believe her audacity.'

'Try me,' said Cynthia.

'She asked if she could come and stay at my house in Burnley over the summer holidays.'

'Whatever for?' asked Laura. 'I thought she was going to Italy? We've heard nothing else all month.'

'I know. Mary says she wants to be friends with me and that she has been trying to be my friend for some time,' said Lucy, but Laura and Cynthia both laughed.

'I can't believe how stupid she is,' said Cynthia. 'Mary has been no friend to you, or any of us for that matter. Her behaviour was awful at the restaurant on Saturday. Look how she completely monopolised your William.'

'I think that is her plan. I think she sees him as an ideal husband,' replied Lucy, 'but it couldn't be further from the truth. William is already in love and wouldn't entertain Mary at any cost.'

'He is?' asked Cynthia. 'How exciting. With whom?'

Lucy hesitated before answering and glanced at Laura.

'What? Come on, what are you hiding, Lucy?' asked Cynthia.

'He's in love with Laura, but she won't entertain him,' Lucy replied quietly. There was silence for a while, then Laura spoke.

'I can't be involved with anyone. I have to work at the school for two years as payback for my course here,' Laura said quietly.

'Do you have feelings for him?' persisted Cynthia.

'I can't.'

'That's not answering my question, Laura. Do you have feelings for him?' There was a long silence and then Laura quietly said, 'Yes.'

'Yippee!' said Lucy. 'Laura will be my sister one day.'

'I doubt it,' Laura replied, with a sad voice.

'Never say never, Laura. God moves in mysterious ways. If it is His will, it will work out,' Cynthia said.

'I can't see how it could work out, so it'll have to be a secret for now, please,' said Laura.

'I hope it does work out. I never want Mary Watson to be my sister, that's for sure!' Both girls laughed at this and the tension was broken.

'Well,' said Cynthia, 'if we are talking secrets, I must tell you about mine. Huw has told me that he has feelings for me.'

'I knew it!' exclaimed Lucy. 'I've seen the way he always takes your side in arguments and wants to walk with you when we walk out together.'

'How do you feel Cynthia? Do you have feelings for him?' asked Laura.

'I do,' admitted a blushing Cynthia. 'He has spoken to my parents, but they say we can have a formal courtship arrangement but no engagement until I've finished the course. They've invited Huw to come over in the college holidays, and he has offered to stay and work on the building of our school.'

'That's so special. I'm very pleased for you, Cynthia,' said Lucy.

'So am I,' added Laura wistfully.

'Your turn will come, Laura, when the time is right,' replied Cynthia.

'And we'll all be bridesmaids for each other!' added Lucy.

'Definitely!' said Cynthia. 'Now I must finish my packing. My father's groom is coming to pick us up in an hour.' Laura and Lucy jumped up and, after saying goodbye to Cynthia, went back to their own room, discussing the news they had just heard.

The next day, Laura and Lucy were also going home. William had persuaded Laura to have a lift home with all her belongings and she had agreed. When William arrived, he was full of ideas for the summer holidays. In early July, all the mills in Burnley closed at the same time to give the workers a holiday. It was called Wakes Weeks in some cotton towns, but in

Burnley it was always called Burnley Fair, as it coincided with the annual visit of a fair of exciting rides, hooplas and food stalls. A Pot Fair came to town as well, selling every conceivable piece of pottery, glassware, or china that a woman could want. Many brides-to-be would save up all year to buy things from the Pot Fair for their 'bottom drawer'. If anybody could afford a holiday, they would go on the train to Blackpool for a week, staying at a bed and breakfast establishment. The town was often quiet!

William and Freddie had decided to close the showroom for the two weeks, but offer to take people on holiday to Blackpool or Southport. However, his offer to Laura completely stunned her.

'I want to take all your family for a day trip to Blackpool during the holidays,' said William. 'Please let me. I know your brothers would love it. Have you ever been to Blackpool?'

'No, we haven't,' replied Laura. 'There's never enough money left for holidays.'

'But you'll let me take you, with Lucy as well, of course?'

'How can you take all of us at once?' asked Laura.

'I'll take you, Lucy, Agnes, and Bessie in my car and Freddie can take your dad, your mum, and Albert and Arthur,' replied William.

'You've got it all worked out,' said Laura.

'Yes, Lucy thought that you'd never been to Blackpool, but Freddie and I realised that it could be a good source of income for us, when everybody else's business is closed. So the idea of frequent daily trips to Blackpool started. Do say you'll come.'

'I'll have to ask my parents of course, but as you are taking me home now, you can ask them.' Laura replied, a quiet smile on her face, which contrasted greatly with the enormous grin on William's face. The girls got their belongings together and William loaded them into the motor car and drove round to Mill Street.

Within five minutes of their arrival, the whole family were excited about the proposed trip, even though Mr Carter hadn't been too sure at first, but the desperate pleas of his young children persuaded him. It was decided to go on the Tuesday following, which was when William and Freddie had no other engagements. Then Lucy and William left to return home.

'You've made one family very happy,' Lucy commented on the way home.

'I'll do anything that will make me seem helpful to Laura's family and improve their lives.'

'I think you're doing that all right,' Lucy laughed. 'I thought Arthur was going to burst, he was so excited.'

'Another thing I want to do when we're at home is to teach you to drive, Lucy.'

'No! what would I want to learn to drive for?'

'Because you're a modern woman and you should grasp every opportunity you can. It would make it much easier on a Sunday if we could take two motor cars to church.'

'I'm not sure. It seems to go so fast; I don't know how I'd manage.'

'You go slow until you are confident,' laughed William. 'I'll teach you slowly and carefully, you know I will. Besides, you know how Mother and Father have always insisted on treating us equally. I'm sure they'll want to buy you a motor car for your 21st birthday.'

'Why would I want a motor car?'

'If you are teaching in some other town, it will come in very handy,' William suggested.

'Yes, I suppose you are right. Who knows what the future will bring or where I'll be in two years' time. All right, you win. I am a modern woman, and you can teach me to drive,' Lucy laughed. And so he did, but first they had the day trip to Blackpool which was thoroughly enjoyed by all the Carter family. They came home full of delight, not to mention food, and grateful to William for this unexpected treat, which would stay in their memories for many months to come. William also pulled off a remarkable achievement at the end of the day. He persuaded Laura to come and stay in Burnley for a few days, which she agreed to do.

Martha and Edward Coombes welcomed Laura back to their house and she soon settled in with Lucy, glad to be back in Burnley. The girls enjoyed going shopping during the week whilst the men were working. Lucy and her mother also took Laura to the Pot Fair and insisted on buying her a teapot to start her 'bottom drawer', despite Laura trying to refuse.

In the evenings, William started teaching Lucy to drive, but insisted that Laura sit in the back seat to watch. One day when they were out driving, they stopped for a short walk and then William insisted on Laura having a go at driving. She objected fiercely, but William gave the same arguments that he had given to Lucy and, for once, Lucy agreed with him and encouraged Laura to try her hand at driving. Laura took to it even better than Lucy did and was soon competent behind the steering wheel, although she laughed and said that she would never be able to own a motor car in her life. However, William just replied that she didn't know the future but would be ready to face it as a modern woman, like Lucy, which caused her to laugh.

During the few days they had together, Lucy watched Laura and realised that she was thawing and beginning to respond to William's overtures. Lucy was delighted and knew that, although Laura thought their romance was impossible, William thrived on impossibilities and would get his own way if he could. After Laura had gone home again, it started making Lucy think about her own life. Laura was beginning to love William, and Huw and Cynthia were falling in love, but she was being left behind. Was there a special person for her, she wondered? Perhaps she could develop feelings for Jacob Atherton, but much as she tried, he didn't make her feel special like William did to Laura, and Huw did to Cynthia. Perhaps love wasn't for her and she was destined to be a teacher for all of her life and be a good aunt to William's and Laura's children. Then she laughed at her fancifulness. She was only 19, not exactly on the shelf yet. She left it all in God's hands. If He wanted her to marry, He would find a helpmeet for her.

The holidays soon passed and Lucy was eagerly waiting her examination results. They had been told that they would receive them towards the end of August and, as the time got nearer, Lucy started to worry. Perhaps she hadn't done enough revision? Had she misinterpreted any of the questions? Was her teaching practice good enough? Would she be told not to return to the course? By the time the letter arrived, Lucy had worked herself into such a state that when Patsy brought an official looking letter to her, Lucy froze and was unable to open it. She put it in her pocket and walked outside in the garden for a few minutes, trying to be calm and reminding herself that whatever the result, it would be God's will for her life. Suddenly she couldn't bear the thought of not being a teacher. Soon, soon she would open it, she promised herself.

Chapter 10

Lucy was drawn back into the house when Mrs Ward shouted that there was a telephone call for her. Lucy hurried inside to answer the call and it was Cynthia on the telephone.

'Well? Have you passed?'

'Passed? I don't know,' Lucy stuttered.

'Haven't you had your letter yet? Hasn't your postman been?'

'Er, yes, but I haven't opened it yet.'

'How could you not open it? Open it now!'

'Just a minute, whilst I put the handset down,' said Lucy, her hands trembling as she opened the envelope. She scanned the letter and gave a sigh of relief. 'Yes, I've passed, Cynthia. Have you?'

'Of course I have. I wouldn't be ringing you if I hadn't,' Cynthia laughed. 'Isn't it great, we're halfway there to being qualified teachers. Huw's passed, too; he's just telephoned me. Isn't that great? I hope all of our friends have passed.'

'So do I. I had better go and tell my parents. I've been unbearable these last few days. I got it into my head that I might have failed,' Lucy admitted.

'I was a bit the same. I suppose when something is so important to you, you want it all to go smoothly.'

'How did Huw get on with your parents?'

'Famously. They really like him, but you go and tell your parents. We can chat another day. Now go!'

'I will, and thank you Cynthia, and congratulations too.'

'See you next term,' laughed Cynthia, as she hung up the telephone.

Lucy ran through the house shouting, 'Mother, Father,' but no one replied. She went into the kitchen, desperate to tell someone her news. Only Mrs Ward was in the kitchen.

'Do you know where my parents are?' she asked Mrs Ward.

'Your father has gone back to work and your mother is up in the linen room with Patsy, sorting out the bedding.'

'Thanks,' said Lucy, as she flew out of the kitchen and up two flights of stairs to the linen room, dragging the door open. 'Mother, I've passed the examination. I can't believe it!'

'I never doubted you,' replied her mother, hugging her close.

'I doubted myself, especially these last few days, knowing the results would be out soon.'

'Yes, we had noticed,' laughed her mother to Patsy, who smothered a giggle.

'Congratulations, Miss Lucy,' said Patsy. 'Shall I ask Mrs Ward to make your favourite meal for tea?'

'That's a lovely thought, Patsy, but I'd happily eat anything today, I'm so relieved. May I ring Father at work, Mother? Or should I wait until he comes home?'

'I think he'll be pleased if you ring him.'

'Thanks, Mother,' and Lucy was off downstairs, only pausing to tell Mrs Ward before she went to the telephone. As expected, her father was delighted and praised her hard work.

Only one week left, Lucy thought to herself *and then she would be in her final year of the course. It was so exciting.* William was late home that night, but had to listen to Lucy's excitement. His first thought was for Laura.

'Has Laura passed?'

'I've no idea. She hasn't got a telephone, so I wouldn't know.'

'I'm taking Mrs Barber and Miss Clare shopping again to Manchester tomorrow. They're getting quite a taste for it! Do you want to come with me and we'll call at Laura's?'

'Oh, yes, that would be lovely. You're not a bad brother sometimes, although I know it's only because you want to see Laura.'

'Guilty as charged,' William laughed.

'What time are you going?'

'I'm picking them up at nine am. We'll need to be ready by about half past eight. Can you manage that?'

'What a cheek! I'm always up much earlier than that at college.'

'Yes, but you've had two months of laziness since then, so I thought I'd check. It will be so good to see Laura. I've missed her.'

'So have I.'

They were both up early next morning and were waiting to pick the Barbers up. Clare was her own age and, although Lucy sat in the front seat, she chatted to Clare about her course and the friends she had made. She could see that Clare was envious of the freedom that Lucy enjoyed, but didn't feel she wanted to do anything so extreme as to have a career. It was marriage and children for her, she said.

Lucy replied that she was not ruling those out, but would wait until getting her teaching qualification, which made Clare laugh. After the mother and daughter had been dropped off near the shops, Lucy suggested going to get some lunch somewhere, but William was adamant that they should go to Laura's first. They were in luck. Laura was at home and was surprised to see William and Lucy, until they explained about William's job as a chauffeur that day.

'Have you passed the examination?' Lucy asked excitedly.

'Yes, I have. Have you?' Laura replied, with a glow on her face.

'I have. Aren't we just clever girls?' Lucy replied.

'Can I take you both out for lunch?' William asked. 'I really feel I need to congratulate you for being so clever.'

'Oh, yes, that would be great, William. Do say you can come, Laura.'

'I'll just consult my diary, Lucy,' Laura replied seriously, looking in a book that was on the table. 'Ah, it appears I am free for luncheon today,' Laura added in a pompous voice, but then collapsed into fits of giggles.

'Great, let's go before you change your minds and want to go shopping,' said William.

'Oh, shopping in Manchester?' said Lucy thoughtfully. 'Laura, shall we ditch William and just go shopping?' However, the murderous look on William's face made her say that she was only teasing, and he whisked them out of the door before they could change their minds. Just as they were getting in the motor car, Bessie arrived home for her half day.

'We're just going out to lunch, Bessie. Do you want to come?' asked Lucy.

'Yes, please. Have you time to let me change my clothes?'

'Ten minutes, that's all,' said William sternly, knowing how long young women take to get ready, but Bessie was back out of the house again in five minutes and they set off together. Lucy was glad to hear all about Bessie's learning at Brenda Smith's shop. Bessie was very enthusiastic about all the dresses she was being allowed to work on now, and Lucy praised how much she had improved in the year they had known each other. It left Laura and William free to talk to each other, and Lucy wasn't sure who had the biggest smile on their face.

After lunch, the girls said that they would like to look round the shops. William groaned, but said that he would accompany them, so that they were safe. A weak excuse, thought Lucy, knowing it was a ploy to stay closer to Laura, but she said nothing. William put up with going round the haberdashery shops, which delighted all three girls, especially Bessie, but drew the line when Lucy told him that they were going into the underwear department. He tactfully but reluctantly withdrew as he didn't want to waste a minute of this precious time with Laura. They arranged to meet back at the large department store where they had previously had afternoon tea.

On arrival at the store, Lucy noticed that William had parcels, but said nothing. They went up to the restaurant and ordered tea and cakes – they were too full after lunch to have the large afternoon tea. Bessie was in her element, looking at all the ladies' dresses and making comments to Lucy, as William and Laura were once again engrossed in a private conversation. When they got back to the motor car, William gave presents to Lucy and Laura for passing their examination. They were leather-bound note books with pencils attached.

'I thought they looked very suitable for school teachers,' he explained.

'They are lovely, but you shouldn't have bought me one,' said Laura.

'I couldn't leave you out when I was buying Lucy one, because you passed the same examination. I haven't left Bessie out either,' and he handed her a parcel.

'I haven't passed any examinations,' Bessie said, but clinging on to her present.

'No, but you've worked just as hard, I'm sure,' replied William. Bessie ripped off the brown paper and gave a loud sigh of pleasure. William had been back to the haberdashery shop and bought Bessie a pair of pinking shears that she had longingly admired when they were shopping.

'Oh, thank you, Mr Coombes. I couldn't have wished for anything better; you are very kind,' she said.

'Just call me William. I'm used to having to buy nice presents with a sister like Lucy,' he teased.

'I must admit,' said Lucy, 'he has improved in that department. He used to buy terrible presents when he was younger, until I took him in hand.'

'I hate to say it, Lucy, but if we are to take Laura and Bessie home, we need to be going soon. I said I would pick Mrs Barber and Miss Clare up at 4pm and it's nearly that now.'

'We can walk home on our own,' offered Laura, but William was having none of it. He insisted on taking them right home and then had to hurry to meet the Barbers. There was plenty of chatter on the way home and William was silent – not being able to get a word in edgeways when women were talking about shopping – but he had a happy smile on his face and Lucy was glad that the day had worked out so well. She decided that she liked this new William that had developed because of him being in love. It made him a much softer, thoughtful person, and it was obvious that Laura was softening towards him, too. It augured well for the future.

It was soon time to be packing to go back to college and Lucy couldn't wait. She was eager to be getting on with her course. Her last full weekend at home was spent visiting friends and relatives. Lucy had a lovely day with her Granny Wall as they had lunch in a new tea shop in Burnley town centre on Saturday. Granny Wall was telling her about the improvements that she was making at her cotton mill. Although Grandpa Wall had been dead for some time and they had no sons to carry it on, Granny Wall still ran the mill with the help of a manager. In the past she had tried to get William interested in running the mill, but he was even less interested in cotton than he was in making matches. Lucy's father's idea had sparked Granny Wall to have a new canteen built for her workers, and Granny Wall was going into great detail about the workman who was doing the renovations.

'He's a very pleasant man; in fact he's staying at my house whilst he's doing the work at my mill. He did your father's canteen, and I was so impressed that I asked him to stay on and do mine. His lodgings owner was unable to keep him, so I suggested he came to live with me.'

'Oh Granny, isn't that risky? Having an unknown workman living in your house when you live on your own? You don't know who he is.'

'Live on my own? Yes, I suppose I do, apart from my four servants, you mean?' Granny Wall laughed.

'Yes, but he could be a wanted criminal for all you know. What do you know about him?'

'He's worked for your father for the last four months, without disaster, fire, flood, or theft.'

'Has he?' asked Lucy frowning, trying to remember if her father had mentioned this. She knew her father had a workman in to improve the canteen for his staff, but beyond that, she hadn't really taken any notice. 'Where did my father find him then?'

'You know the Mens' Breakfasts he goes to with other Congregational churches in Lancashire?'

'Yes.'

'Well, this man is a member of the Congregational church in Clitheroe.'

'Oh. Well, I don't think Father told me that. So, how come I didn't know he was living with you, Granny?'

'I tend to come to your house, rather than you coming to mine, and the man tends to go home at weekends anyway. And you are away most of the time nowadays. Are you looking forward to going back to college?' Granny Wall asked, changing the subject.

'Oh yes, I can't believe I'm halfway through the course. It's gone so quickly.'

'Have you any idea where you'll be working when you finish?'

'I'd like to stay in Burnley. There are so many schools nowadays so I'm hoping there'll be a vacancy locally.'

'Good. I'm glad you're not going far away. I'd miss you if you lived away.'

'And I'd miss you, too, Granny. Shall I get the bill?'

'Certainly not. I'm going to treat you. That's what Grannies' are for.'

Lucy giggled. 'That's all right, Granny, I'll let you. We poor students have to conserve our money.'

'Are you short of money, Lucy? You have only to ask.'

'Oh, no, Granny. You and father are always generous.'

'Well, now you've mentioned it, I do have something for you to take back to college with you.' Granny Wall delved into her handbag and brought out a small new purse.

'I was going to give you this tomorrow when I come to lunch after church, but you might as well have it now.' She passed the purse over to Lucy, who could tell by the feel of it that were lots of coins in it.

'You don't have to give me any money, Granny. Father gives me an allowance.'

'I know that. This is for fripperies and desires of your heart. Who else do I have to spoil, if not my only granddaughter and grandson?'

'Thank you so much. You are very generous. Let me pay for our lunch out of this purse.'

'Certainly not. That is for when you are at college.' They both stood up and went to the desk to pay for the meal and then left the café.

'Do you want to go home now, Granny?' asked Lucy.

'Yes, I think I will. I've got an idea; shall we go round to your brother's garage and he can give us a lift home?'

'Excellent idea, Granny,' and the pair of them walked leisurely through the town to Yorkshire Street where both her father's factory and brother's garage were situated. They walked through the large open doors at the front of the garage. William jumped up when he saw who it was.

'Granny, what a joy to see you! Hello, Lucy.'

'Oh, so it's not a joy to see me, then, William?' Lucy teased.

'I see enough of you at home,' William laughed in return.

'We've just been out for lunch and decided that you could take us home now,' Granny said.

'I'm really sorry, Granny, I would love to, but I have an appointment any minute.'

'Oh, yes? Is your appointment at Turf Moor to watch your beloved Clarets football team?'

'No,' said William, pretending to be affronted. 'Of course not, this is a business appointment. In fact, I think this is them just arriving.' Lucy turned to look to the door and there was David Wood from her college course, with another man.

'David,' she called, 'how lovely to see you.'

'Hello, Lucy, I wondered if I'd see you today. This is my brother Richard. Miss Lucy Coombes, her brother William, and this is?' David gestured towards Granny.

'This is my Granny Wall,' Lucy replied, and they all greeted each other.

'Richard has come to purchase a motor car today,' said David.

'Good. Perhaps we'll leave you to it and go,' Lucy suggested.

'I'll get Freddie to drive you home if you like?' William offered.

'That would be excellent,' replied Granny Wall. 'Nice to have met you young people. Goodbye.'

'Goodbye, Mrs Wall,' said David. 'Goodbye Lucy. I'll see you at college next week.'

'You will. I can't wait to get back.' William went into the workshop to ask Freddie to take the ladies home, and they all soon left. In the motor car on the way home Granny Wall was full of questions.

'Is David a particular friend of yours? His brother seemed nice, too.'

'No, we are good friends, but he's not a particular friend, Granny,' Lucy laughed.

'Are you sure about that, Lucy? He seemed pleased to see you.'

'Laura, Cynthia, and I are friends with three young men and David is one of them. We just go for walks together and eat our meals together. We all went out for a meal in Manchester with William and that's how he knew that William sold motor cars.'

'So, no romance?'

'No, Granny! You are worse than Mother. She would have much preferred me to get married than train as a teacher.'

'You and Laura are such pretty girls, as I'm sure Cynthia is, so I'm surprised that the men aren't interested in you.'

'There is a little romance going on, but it's between Cynthia and Huw, one of our three men friends.'

'I see. But what about you and Laura?' Lucy hesitated too long before answering and Granny Wall noticed it. 'Well, come on Lucy. What is going on?'

'Someone is in love with Laura, but she won't entertain him because she has to work for the mill owner who paid her course fees after she qualifies.'

'And who's the lucky man?'

'I can't really say, Granny.'

'Why not? I'm not going to say anything, am I?'

'It's difficult. I don't think I should say anything as it's not my affair.'

'You can tell your Granny. I promise not to tell.'

'You may not be able to keep silent if I tell you.'

'Why on earth not? Now you must tell me. You've made it so mysterious, I'll never sleep tonight.'

'All right. I'll tell you, but you mustn't say anything. It's William.'

'What's William? You're not making sense, girl.'

'It's William who's in love with Laura.'

'Our William? Your brother?' Lucy nodded. 'Why does that have to be a secret?' asked Granny.

'I don't think William has said anything to our parents. Besides, Laura is adamant she can't have a serious courtship, but William is equally adamant that he will marry her,' said Lucy, bowing her head, but soon lifting it when she heard the sound of laughing. 'Granny, what are you laughing at?'

'Just the thought of William not getting his own way for once. It must be very irksome for him. He won't like that at all. He's used to getting his own way.'

'Don't I know it!' Lucy replied with feeling.

'I'm glad,' said Granny Wall.

'About William not getting his own way for once? So am I!'

'No, I'm pleased about Laura. I think she's a lovely girl and will make a fine wife for William. I do hope it comes to pass. I love a good wedding.'

'I think you'll have a long time to wait, Granny.'

'Here we are at home. Do you want to come in for a cup of tea?'

'No thanks, Granny, I'll get home to finish my packing, if you don't mind?'

'That's fine by me. I'll see you at your house tomorrow for lunch.'

'Looking forward to it. Goodbye, Granny.'

Freddie set off again, and Lucy thanked him for taking her home.

'Nice to have a trip out. We had no bookings today, Miss Lucy.'

'How do you like working for my brother?'

'I love it. I love working with the engines and finding out how they work.'

'I can't believe that my brother isn't going to watch the football today.'

'He is as soon as the customers leave,' chuckled Freddie. 'We're both going, hopefully.'

'Not you as well?'

''Fraid so. I love football. Mr Wood is only picking his motor car up this afternoon, so it won't be a long appointment. Apparently, he's a teacher and he's got a new job in another town, so wants the motor car before the new term starts.'

'Yes, his younger brother is on the same course as me at Manchester. His whole family are teachers, I believe. Thanks for bringing me home, Freddie. You'd better get back to the garage now. You wouldn't want to miss the kick off,' Lucy chuckled.

'Thanks, Miss Lucy,' said Freddie grinning, and set off back to the garage.

Lucy went up to her room and put the small purse from Granny Wall in her trunk, after checking its contents. There were another ten guineas. Lucy reminded herself to thank Granny Wall next day for such a large gift.

After church on Sunday morning, Lucy went upstairs to put her coat and hat away and wash her hands before lunch. She picked up one of her books and started reading and lost track of time, until Patsy knocked on the door and asked Lucy to come downstairs as lunch was ready. Lucy agreed, putting the book down, and Patsy scurried off, to help serve the meal, Lucy suspected.

Lucy walked along the upstairs corridor and was just about to go downstairs, when she noticed a young man in the hallway. He was stood in front of the hall table, his head cocked to one side, and he was feeling the grain of the wood on the table. Lucy stopped where she was, not willing to alert this man to her presence. He spent a long time stroking the wood and it was all Lucy could do not to laugh out loud. Suddenly, Patsy came into the hallway and ushered the man into the dining room, so Lucy hurried downstairs before Patsy was sent to look for her too.

Chapter 11

'There you are, Lucy. Where have you been?' her mother's voice rang out.

'I was just reading….' Lucy started, but her mother interrupted.

'Come and sit down, we're waiting to start. Come, Mr Marsden, sit here next to me.' The young man went to sit next to Mrs Coombes whilst Lucy had a surreptitious glance at him. She wasn't sure who he was but he seemed very nice. He had blonde hair and was of a slim build, his jaw was firm and he had large blue eyes and was smiling politely at her mother. Her mother's voice drew Lucy out of her reverie.

'Lucy, wake up. What is the matter with you today? I'm trying to introduce you to Mr Marsden.'

'Yes, Lucy, this is the young man who is staying with me at the moment,' added Granny Wall, with an impish grin on her face.

'Er, hello, Mr Marsden,' Lucy said tentatively.

'Please call me Harry. I've heard so much about you.'

'You have?' gulped Lucy.

'Yes, from Mrs Wall. She tells me you are training to be a teacher. That is very commendable.'

'Yes,' was all Lucy could manage, mesmerised by this lovely young man who was smiling at her so beautifully. His smile was crooked on one side, she noticed, showing his even white teeth.

'Well, Harry, you must come again,' roared William. 'I've never seen my sister so quiet,' which made Lucy come out of her reverie enough to glare at William. She managed to regain her composure.

'Do you approve of women having careers, Harry?' Lucy asked.

'I certainly do. God gave women brains as well as men.'

'That's just what I think,' replied Lucy, with a big smile on her face.

'How's the work coming on at Mother's mill, Harry?' asked Martha Coombes.

'I'll be finished in about four weeks, then it's back to Clitheroe for my next job,' replied Harry. Suddenly Lucy felt like the sun had gone down. He was leaving in four weeks, but she was going away again this evening, straight after tea, just when she wanted to get to know him better. It was just her luck that the first time she had been attracted to a man she would never see him again. It was so unfair.

'What's your next job?' Mr Coombes asked.

'I'm making a set of furniture for a couple at church. They want a new table and chairs and a dresser.'

'And then what?' asked William.

'Then I'm at Brierfield Mills, making a canteen for the workers there. It seems to be the fashion at the moment. Unless they're all copying you here in Burnley,' he laughed.

'That is probably because I was telling the owner about your work when we were at the Chamber of Commerce meeting,' said Mr Coombes.

'Well, it's certainly keeping my orders flowing in, so I can't complain, and thank you for recommending me.'

'Any time. I will always give you a reference if you need one, too.'

'Thank you.'

'What's your favourite work, if you could choose,' Lucy found herself asking.

'Definitely furniture. I love creating something that is going to last for years and be part of that family's life.' As he was speaking, Lucy noticed that he was stroking the grain of the table as he spoke. He definitely loved wood; she could see.

'So, you don't like making canteens then?' Granny Wall said, with a smile on her face.

'Oh, yes. I like making anything in wood, but what I like about the canteens is that you care for your workforce. That shows what good people you are. Not just out to make a profit like many mill or factory owners are.'

'A happy workforce is a good workforce, I always find,' commented Mr Coombes. 'Certainly, productivity has gone up since the canteen was installed, especially when I employed a cook to make cheap nutritious meals. It saves the women a lot of time so they are very grateful. I've even heard about some women buying portions to take home for their husbands' teas to save them having to start cooking at night,' he added with a laugh.

'I don't blame them,' said Lucy. 'There must be nothing worse than having to start making a meal after you've just done a hard day at work.'

'That's just the way it is though,' said Granny Wall. 'Even though the woman may have worked as hard as her husband, she will be expected to start making a meal, whilst the husband sits down with the paper and is waited on.'

'Mother, I can't remember the last time you had to start making a meal after a hard day's work,' teased Mrs Coombes.

'No, that's true, but I hear some of my women workers talking about life and that is one of their chief complaints.'

'If everyone's finished their meal, let's go into the lounge for tea and coffee now,' Mrs Coombes announced, and everyone moved away from the table.

'When are you going back to college, Miss Coombes?' Harry asked.

'Oh, please call me Lucy. I go back this evening.'

'So soon?'

'Yes, William is taking me back.'

'Why don't you come with us, Harry? You said you wanted a drive in a motor car. We could chat on the way home after we've dropped Lucy off. We won't get chance on the way there, as Lucy will chatter all the way non-stop.' Lucy could have hit William for saying that, but forgave him quickly for inviting Harry to go with them. They would have a little longer together. She held her breath until Harry answered.

'Yes, I'd love that, William. It would make my life much easier if I had a motorised vehicle of some sort. Especially as I seem to be getting orders from farther afield nowadays. The horse and cart take too long.'

'I could source what types of commercial vehicles are available for you, if you like, and get some costings?'

'William, please will you remember that it is the Sabbath. Do not talk business in my lounge,' his mother reproved.

'Sorry, Mother. We'll talk another day, Harry,' William promised, not one to lose the chance of a sale.

'Are all your things ready, Lucy?' Mrs Coombes asked.

'Yes, Mother. I think I'll just have a walk in the garden. I feel too hot in here, even though the windows are open.'

'Why don't we go for a walk?' William suggested.

'Good idea,' said Harry.

'We could walk down to the playing fields and back. That will give us an appetite for tea,' laughed William.

'Or we could set off back to Manchester early and take sandwiches,' Lucy suggested. 'We could pick Laura up then. It would be easier for her than having to carry her belongings back on foot.' Lucy couldn't help but smile as she said that, as she knew what the answer would be.

'That's a good idea, Lucy. Mother, would you mind if we set off back early? We could take sandwiches, as Lucy suggested, and have a picnic on the way and show Harry some of the sights.'

'Go and ask Mrs Ward if it is all right. I don't want to make it difficult for her, but you'll have to take Granny Wall home first. Metcalfe is not on duty to take her home in the carriage tonight.'

'Of course I'll take Granny Wall home first. I'll just go and see if it is convenient for Mrs Ward,' and he left the room. Lucy smiled. Nothing William could request would ever be inconvenient for Mrs Ward; she worshipped the ground he walked on.

William soon came back smiling. 'The picnic will be ready in 15 minutes. Lucy, is your trunk ready?'

'Yes.'

'Good. I'll go and bring it downstairs.'

'Can I help you?' asked Harry.

'Yes please. She takes so much stuff to Manchester, you wouldn't believe it. She's so vain, that's probably why,' he laughed.

'I am not vain,' Lucy retorted.

'I'll let Harry be the judge of that when he feels how heavy your trunk is,' William replied.

'A lot of the weight is books,' Lucy said.

'If you say so, sister dear,' William replied, which made Lucy even more angry. How could he make her look such a weakling in front of Harry? On reflection though, Lucy had to remind herself that she had only met Harry today and wasn't going to see him again, so why did it matter? But somehow, it did matter what he thought of her. The two men left the room and the trunk was soon downstairs, but William was alone with it in the hall.

'Harry is poorly; he's never carried such a heavy trunk,' William teased, but Lucy refused to be drawn. Although she did wonder where Harry was, only to find out that he had been to the bathroom and William was just being his usual annoying self.

Eventually, they were all ready. Granny Wall was sat in the front of the motor car and Harry and Lucy and her trunk had to squash into the rear seat. William had put the trunk by the side so Harry and Lucy were very close together on the back seat. Lucy could feel the heat rising through her body at the nearness of him. They took Granny Wall to her home and made sure she was settled in. William told Harry to sit in the front seat so they could talk, and Lucy was instantly disappointed. She liked the feeling of his body next to hers, but then blushed at the thoughts she was having. They set off to Manchester, but stopped at Clowbridge reservoir to have a picnic. Mrs Ward had made enough sandwiches to feed a family of eight, which was her usual way, not just a snack for three people who had had a substantial lunch. There were also cake and scones, and bottles of home-made lemonade.

The two men tucked into the feast, but Lucy wasn't really hungry. During the picnic, Harry was telling them both about his work with the Red Cross. He was a firm believer that everyone should learn how to do simple first aid, and he was now an instructor, going round to clubs and groups to encourage people to learn.

'The more people who are aware of first aid will improve safety in the workplace and the home,' he said.

'Perhaps I should learn first aid,' Lucy suggested. 'As a teacher, it would be useful in the classroom.'

'Exactly,' replied Harry. 'I think every teaching course should include first aid.'

'How would I learn?' asked Lucy.

'There are classes in Burnley, but I'm sure that there will be classes in a place as big as Manchester. I could find out and drop you a line if you like?'

'Yes, please,' replied Lucy, just a little too eagerly. 'I'll write my address down,' which she did immediately before he changed his mind. 'I'll mention it to my tutors as well. I think this is something that the college might take on board.'

'The more the better,' Harry said, smiling at her. Although Lucy knew she had a silly grin on her face, she couldn't help it, so hurriedly picked up a piece of cake which she didn't really want. Soon after, they set off again, going straight to Laura's house to collect her. They were also able to leave most of the picnic for Laura's family, and the boys fell on it with delight.

Saying goodbye to her family, Laura got into the back of the motor car with Lucy. Lucy could tell she was longing to ask who Harry was, but William had just introduced him as a family friend. They were soon at the college and the men took the girls' trunks into the porch, ready for the porter to take up to their room. Even brothers were not allowed anywhere near the girls' dormitory corridor, and only in the communal lounge.

'Hello, William, how delightful to meet you again,' a female voice trilled out. Lucy's heart sank. It was Mary Watson. She had hoped that Mary would have given up the course or even failed, as she did very little work at all. 'And who's your friend? I'm Mary Watson, and you are?'

'I'm Harry Marsden,' Harry said, and made a small bow.

'Manners as well. I like a man with manners.'

'She likes any man,' said Laura in a quiet voice to Lucy, who laughed out loud.

'Oh, hello, Lucy. I see you're back to your usual mean ways, laughing at people behind their backs.' She didn't even speak to Laura. Lucy was fuming that Mary could belittle her and make her look bad in front of Harry, but also that she had slighted Laura.

'I'm surprised to see you back, Mary. I thought you'd have married a rich man during the holidays,' Lucy said with unusual venom.

'Not yet, but I'm still looking,' she said with a provocative look at William and then Harry.

'That rules us two out, then,' said Harry, and Lucy was delighted he'd said that. 'We're just poor working men,' he added.

Fortunately at that point, the porter arrived to take Mary's trunk up to her room, so they were rid of her presence.

'I'm so sorry you had to meet Mary, Harry. She is a troublemaker. She never even spoke to Laura.'

'Don't let it worry you, Lucy; I don't,' replied Laura. 'She's just a snob.'

'A mean snob,' added Lucy viciously.

'Lucy, you don't sound like the person your grandmother talks about,' said Harry.

William made it worse by saying, 'Oh, she can have her moments, but overall, she's not too bad.'

'Do you mind not discussing me as if I weren't here,' Lucy replied.

'Sorry, Sis, you know I love to tease you. Mary is a nasty piece of work, though. I wouldn't trust her as far as I could throw her,' William added.

At that point, Cynthia and Huw arrived at the door, so even more introductions had to be made. The porter then arrived to take the girls' trunks upstairs, so William, Harry, and Huw said that they would have to leave. As they were all saying goodbye, Harry leaned over to Lucy.

'I'll write to you shortly, Lucy.'

'Thank you,' said Lucy, wishing she could stop the blush on her cheeks. Soon they were all gone and the girls were back in their own rooms. They had only been there a few minutes when there was a knock on the door.

'I hope that's not Mary Watson,' said Laura, but it wasn't. It was Cynthia.

'Who was that lovely man who is promising to write to you, Lucy? What have you been up to on your holiday?'

'You beat me to it, Cynthia. I was just about to ask the same myself,' said Laura.

'Oh, er, he's just a carpenter who has been working at my Father's and Granny's factories. I only met him today.'

'Today? You looked very cosy together, and he's already promising to write to you. What is going on?' asked Cynthia.

'He is very keen on everybody learning first aid and he's going to find out where the nearest place is round here to learn. He thinks that everyone should learn the basics of first aid in case of accidents.'

'And you're going to learn first aid?' asked Laura.

'Yes, why not? If a child had an accident in the playground or the classroom, it would come in useful, don't you think?'

'Oh, definitely, especially if Harry is teaching you,' laughed Laura.

'Precisely,' added Cynthia. 'I think you are smitten, despite only meeting him today,' she teased.

'Don't be silly,' replied Lucy, but her blush belied the truth.

'We'll wait and see,' said Laura, laughing at Cynthia.

Chapter 12

The next day college work began with a vengeance. A new intake of students had commenced and the girls laughed as they watched Mary weighing up all the new men.

'I wonder which one will take her fancy?' said Laura.

'The one with the biggest bank balance, I suspect,' replied Lucy.

'If only we knew who it is, then we could warn him to leave now, whilst his bank balance is intact,' added Cynthia, but further discussion was stopped as Miss Davenport swept into the classroom.

'Silence!' she roared. 'You sound like the infant class. You are senior students now and should know better. Sit down.' The class did so quickly, wondering why Miss Davenport was with them, as she was universally not liked. They were soon to find out.

'I'll be your lead tutor for this second year and you will meet other new tutors as well. If this is the sort of behaviour I'm going to have to put up with, I think I'd better warn the other tutors,' said Miss Davenport. Lucy's heart sank. Miss Dodd had been so pleasant, fair, and encouraging, even though she was strict. She wished she could say the same for Miss Davenport. However, there would be other tutors and perhaps they would be better, Lucy hoped.

'This year, you will teach across all age groups, even if you have signed up for only one age group. Do you understand? There is no point being a teacher if you can't stand in for colleagues at short notice. You need to have a comprehensive knowledge of many subjects. Here are your teaching schedules.' Miss Davenport passed out papers for each student, allowing them some time to absorb the new schedules, as she paced the class watching the students intently.

'Right. Put those away now. You can study them in your own time. Lesson planning will also be different this year. Instead of planning a short one-hour lesson, the other tutors and I will require a full term's lesson planning, with indications where each lesson fits into the theme and also relates to the other material being taught.'

Laura and Lucy exchanged raised eyebrows, but it was intercepted by Miss Davenport.

'You, girl, Clarke or something. Red hair. What was that remark you were making to your neighbour?'

Laura flushed to the roots of her hair, but stood up slowly. 'I didn't speak, Miss Davenport.'

'Don't be impertinent, girl. You raised your eyebrows, which is making a remark, even if you didn't speak. Well, what were you implying? And what was your friend thinking, too. Stand up Miss, Miss, er, whatever your name is!'

Lucy stood slowly to her feet. 'It's Miss Coombes, Miss Davenport. We were just thinking that we're going to have to spend a lot more time on lesson planning this term, compared with last term.'

'That's right. You will. So don't forget that fact. You may all go for a break now and we'll start in earnest when you get back.' With that, Miss Davenport marched out of the classroom, leaving the whole class stunned.

David Wood was the first to recover his tongue. 'Goodness, she can be a bit sharp,' he said.

'That's putting it mildly,' replied Lucy. 'I think we'd better go to the refectory now or else she'll complain we've been too long.' Quickly, the students went to the refectory and got themselves a drink and some got food as well. The six friends sat together, but looked round the room to see if anybody from their year had not returned. There were only three people missing as far as they could gather. A very timid girl who was homesick all year and wouldn't join in with anyone, despite many people trying to befriend her, had not returned, at which no one was surprised. But two of the men who were very good were missing, too, but no one knew why they hadn't come back.

Lucy noticed that Mary Watson wasn't with their year group, but was talking to a young man from the new first year group.

'Oh dear,' said Cynthia, 'do you think Mary has found her prey?'

'I know him,' Jacob said. 'He's the Honourable Simon St John-Forbes. He comes from just outside Rochdale.'

'The Honourable? That explains everything,' said Lucy laughing, 'but is he rich, Jacob?'

'Rich compared with us, but he hasn't a great deal of prospects. He has a cousin who is due to inherit a large estate and title, but he's next in line if the cousin doesn't produce an heir. The cousin's over 40 now, so it's looking less likely. So I suppose 'The Honourable' is getting more hopeful as each year passes.'

'I feel sorry for him if Mary gets her clutches into him. She'll probably poison the cousin to make sure she gets a title,' said Laura. The six friends all laughed so loud that Mary looked round to see what they were laughing at, which made them calm down and decide that it was time to go back to the classroom. The lessons went on relentlessly and they were all so tired by teatime they didn't even go for a walk that night. The more intensive lesson plans took up a great deal of their spare time, and nerves were getting frayed as the term continued. Laura disliked teaching the older children, but Huw found he preferred the older children to the younger group. However, they all did their best attempt and grudgingly had to admit that Miss Davenport was right. They should be able to stand in with any group, and lessons should be planned as a whole, not just an individual hour here or there.

The first week of term Lucy had kept a watch for the post being delivered, but was disappointed. Laura teased her and said that Harry had probably forgotten all about his promise to write, but Lucy prayed that was not the truth. She couldn't stop thinking about him and even when she tried desperately to concentrate on her studies or lesson plans, his face kept appearing in her head. She thought about the way he put his head on one side when he was thinking, the way he stroked any wooden surface he came into contact with, his lop-sided smile, and on it went.

Finally on the second week of term, as they were going into class, there was a letter in her pigeonhole and Cynthia spotted it.

'Ooh, looks like you've got a letter, Lucy. I wonder if it's from your mother?' she asked with a grin. Lucy snatched the letter out of the pigeonhole and knew she was blushing.

'Aren't you going to open it?' asked Laura. 'We're all ears!'

'That is exactly why I'm not going to open it until I'm on my own,' replied Lucy, pushing the letter deep into her pocket, but keeping her hand on it, just in case it should fall out and be lost before she'd read it. She couldn't wait for the lesson to finish and, during the break, said that she needed to go back to her room for something, trying to look nonchalant, but Laura and Cynthia laughed as she fled from them. Lucy sat on her bed and drew the letter out of her pocket as fast as her trembling fingers would allow. It was a good quality piece of paper she noted as she opened it. It was written on headed notepaper, with his Clitheroe address. Lucy's heart leapt. She now knew where he lived.

Dear Lucy,

It was so good to meet you at your house. I hope your studies are going well. I am pleased you are keen to learn first aid. There is a course that runs in Salford, which is not too far from your college. It's held in the Parish church hall, which the Red Cross rents from them. Or there is the Girls' Friendly Society who help young women to get into good employment; they often run classes to help girls who want to go into nursing work.

The Burnley branch of Red Cross meets every Thursday at the Mechanics Institute, but I know it would not be possible to attend classes in Burnley whilst you are at college, although you could complete a course when your teaching studies are finished. I teach a course at Clitheroe, but that is too far for you to attend, of course.

Did you manage to ask your tutors if they were interested in incorporating first aid lessons into your curriculum? Perhaps you could let me know.

I do hope you find a course near you.

Yours sincerely,
Harry Marsden.

Lucy let out a long breath when she'd finished reading it, realising that she'd held her breath all the way through. He'd sent his address and asked her to write back to him. Her heart was racing as she read it time and time again. She even smelled the paper to see if she could smell him, to no avail. He taught a course in Clitheroe, so Lucy was feverishly thinking how she could get to Clitheroe each week for the course, just to see more of him, but knew it was impossible. Unless she could get a teaching post in Clitheroe when she qualified, but that was a year off and she couldn't wait that long. But at least she knew that if she studied first aid, it would be a link to him, so she resolved to find the nearest course and enrol immediately.

The door opening made Lucy look up and push the letter into her pocket quickly. It was Laura.

'Are you all right, Lucy? We were worried that you didn't come back to class.'

'What time is it?'

'Lunchtime. We told Miss Davenport you were feeling sick, so you'd better make something up. Cynthia said you were lovesick.'

'To Miss Davenport?'

'No, silly. To me. Well, what did he have to say?'

'Just some information as to where I could train in first aid,' Lucy said, trying to sound nonchalant.

'It took you a long time to read a bit of information, then.'

'Well, I had to be sure of what he was saying.'

'Of course you did,' Laura replied, trying not to smile. 'I'll tell Miss Davenport that you've got a headache.'

'I don't want you to lie for me, Laura. Just tell her….'

'I'll tell her you are lovesick but miss out the word love. Will that do? I'll just say you are sick. That's not a lie. You are sick of Miss Davenport picking on us and being horrible.'

'All right, but I hope she won't want me to report to the sick bay.'

'I doubt she'd do that; she'd have to have a heart first,' Laura laughed, and went back to join the others in the refectory. Cynthia asked her how Lucy was and laughed when Laura told her she'd spent the whole lesson reading Harry's letter.

'I think she's got it bad,' said Laura. 'She didn't even want me to bring her something to eat, and Lucy never misses a meal. Definitely lovesick!'

Lucy spent the whole afternoon composing a reply to Harry and tearing up the sheets as she couldn't find the right way of saying what she wanted to say. In the end, she merely thanked him for his letter and the information he'd sent. She hadn't had time to talk to her tutors, but she would soon and would let him know the result, and also when she had enrolled on a course. In that way, she would have a reason to write him another letter, she decided. Carefully sealing the envelope, Lucy decided that she would post it as soon as possible. She felt like getting some fresh air as she had developed a headache now. That served her right for almost lying about one. Popping the envelope in her pocket, Lucy left the room and went out across the grounds towards the post office, but a voice shouted to her. It was Miss Davenport, of all people.

'Recovered, have you? That was quick.'

'I've got a bit of a headache now, Miss Davenport, so I thought if I got some fresh air, it would make me feel better and clear my head.'

'Very sensible, and make sure you get a good meal inside you. I can't abide these girls who don't eat enough.'

'I will, Miss Davenport, and I'll see you in class tomorrow.'

'Good,' and she strode off before Lucy could make another comment.

Letting out a sigh of relief, Lucy hurried to the post office and put her precious letter into the post box, adding a prayer for the recipient as she did. Arriving at the refectory, she found her other friends just finishing their evening meal, so joined them to eat her tea. The men were genuinely concerned for her, not knowing about the letter or the importance of it to Lucy, so she reassured them that she felt much better.

Next morning Lucy was worried as she went into class that Miss Davenport might make a fuss, but she said nothing, for which Lucy thanked God.

The term seemed to fly, but Lucy was living for the next letter from Harry. She had talked to her tutors about the first aid course, and they were interested in the concept and wished to talk to Harry about it, so Lucy gave them his address. That left her daydreaming that perhaps he might have to come to Manchester. Lucy also signed up for a first aid course in a church hall near to the college and was pleased when Cynthia, Huw, and Laura came with her. That was an excuse to write another letter to Harry, she thought gleefully. One letter she didn't expect was from her brother as he wasn't the best correspondent but Lucy knew it would have something to do with Laura. She was not wrong. For his birthday in November, he wanted to take Lucy, Laura, Bessie, and Agnes out for afternoon tea on the Saturday, as Agnes had frequently mentioned that it wasn't fair that they hadn't taken her out last time. Lucy wrote straight back to say yes, they'd all be delighted to accept. Burnley must be playing away from home that day or he would never have missed the match if he could help it, but if he felt about Laura like she felt about Harry, then she understood it.

William said he would pick Bessie and Agnes up and then come for Lucy and Laura but they said they wanted to go shopping first, so would meet William at the restaurant with the younger girls.

Laura and Lucy were laughing together when they entered the top-floor restaurant and walked towards William and the girls, but Lucy stopped dead in her tracks when she saw who else was there. It was Harry.

Chapter 13

Lucy's heart seemed to stop momentarily, but she took a deep breath and joined them at the table. Harry stood immediately, which pleased Lucy, although William didn't bother; he was too busy talking to Laura.

'This is a surprise, Harry,' she managed to say. 'We weren't expecting you.'

'Hello, Lucy, Laura,' he nodded to them both. 'I hope you don't mind my gate-crashing your tea party.'

'Not at all,' Lucy replied, a little too eagerly.

'It was William's idea. He's managed to find a firm in Manchester that supplies commercial motor vehicles, so we've come today to pick one up. So, it made sense to combine the two events and save William having to come specially another day.'

'That makes great sense,' replied Lucy, thinking she would hug William later if the opportunity arose.

'Are you two going to sit down and order what you want, or are we going to be here all night?' William asked.

'Sorry,' said Lucy, blushing. 'I'll just have the afternoon tea, please.'

'Me too,' added Harry, pulling the chair out for Lucy to sit down. It just happened that because they were the last to sit down, they were sat next to each other, for which Lucy was grateful.

'Well, to say it's my birthday today, I've not even been wished "Happy Birthday" from my only sister yet. Seems she has other things on her mind,' William teased.

'Sorry, William. Happy Birthday and many more. Here's your present.' Lucy drew out a package and a card from her large handbag. William opened them eagerly and thanked Lucy for the leather wallet she had bought him. Then Laura produced a package as well and handed it to William.

'I hope you don't think it's forward of me to give you a present, but it is from my whole family, who can never thank you enough for the day trip to Blackpool in the summer. We thought this would look well on your desk at the garage. It was Albert's idea.'

'Nothing you could do for me would make me think you were forward,' replied William, looking longingly at Laura.

'Are you going to open it or just look at it?' asked Lucy.

'Oh, yes,' said William. It was a pen holder, but it had a small model motor car on top. 'This is perfect and just what I need. Thank you, Laura. Oh, and thank all your family, too,' he added. Bessie also gave him a little package and it was a pen-wiper which she had made herself, with his initials in the corner. 'That's perfect, Bessie. I'm always making a mess with the ink, so this will be a great help.'

'Yes, we had noticed your fingers are always inky,' laughed Bessie, which made everyone else laugh too.

'So how are you getting on with your first aid course, Lucy?' asked Harry.

'I'm enjoying it, thank you.'

'You said Laura was coming too, I think?'

'Yes, and Cynthia and Huw, who are on our course.'

'Excellent. The more, the better. I'm trying to persuade William to go to classes as well.'

'Good idea.'

'Mother suggested that I take you back with me tonight, Lucy, as it is my birthday celebration?' said William, trying to change the subject. 'I'd bring you back tomorrow night.'

'Er, I don't know. I have a lot of work to do,' said Lucy.

'Oh, go on,' prompted Laura. 'You've worked so hard you deserve a treat and it is William's birthday.'

'Actually, Mother said why don't I bring Laura as well,' William said, with a pleading look in his eye.

'Really? That is very kind,' said Laura, 'but I don't think I should intrude.'

'You won't be intruding. Mother considers you as part of the family now. Anyway, it's my birthday, so I should be allowed to invite who I want.'

'Why don't you go, Laura? It'll make more tea for us tomorrow if you aren't there,' said Agnes, and everybody burst out laughing.

'Agnes, you are so rude,' Laura chastised, but everyone else was still laughing.

'So do you agree? Will you both come?' William asked.

Lucy and Laura looked at each other and then nodded.

'Yes, we'll come, William, seeing as it is your birthday,' said Lucy, and was rewarded with a beaming smile from William.

'I'll have to call at my house to tell my parents, as I was going there tomorrow,' said Laura, 'but I'm sure they won't mind. I can go next weekend instead.'

'Good. Now has everyone had enough to eat?' William asked.

Everyone nodded in the affirmative, so William went to pay the bill, whilst the others got on their coats, hats, and scarves. He came back with a box and gave it to Bessie, saying that it was for their tea tomorrow night. It was a selection of cakes similar to what they had just eaten. Bessie's and Agnes' faces lit up with joy, but they remembered their manners and thanked William.

'If I take Laura and her sisters home, could you take Lucy back to college, Harry, and then I'll bring Laura back and we can go home? That's if you are not too proud to be driven in a commercial vehicle, Lucy?'

'Certainly not,' replied Lucy, thinking she would go on a bicycle if it meant spending more time with Harry alone. 'Shall I pack a bag for you as well, Laura?' asked Lucy.

'Thanks, that would be useful and save time.'

'I just need to make a telephone call,' said William, 'and then we can go. I'll ask the waiter if I can use their telephone.' Lucy and Laura decided that they would go to the ladies' room, and on the way Lucy said that she could bet that William was ringing their mother to tell her that they were coming.

'Do you think your mother didn't really ask him to bring us?' asked Laura.

'Knowing William, I think he just thought it up on the spur of the moment.'

'Perhaps I'd better not come.'

'No, you must come. Can't disappoint the birthday boy, can we?'

'Well, if you are sure? It will be nice to see your parents again.'

'As well as being with William?'

Laura hesitated, but then said, 'Perhaps I shouldn't. We have no future, so it'll only make it worse.'

'Nonsense. You can make your future whatever you want it to be. You are halfway to being a trained teacher. Did you ever think you would be in this position two years ago?'

'No.'

'Come on then, or they'll think we've had an accident, we've been so long!' and Lucy was pleased to see that Laura was laughing.

Joining the others, they all went down to find the vehicles. William's and Harry's motor cars were parked next to each other near the shop. Harry helped Lucy into his vehicle and William set off with the other girls. Harry's motor vehicle looked like a motor car at the front but instead of a back seat it had an area without seats, where he could carry his tools.

'I'm afraid you'll have to wait in your motor vehicle. You won't be allowed in the college.'

'Don't worry. I'll be fine. I've got a book in my pocket. Take your time.'

Lucy, although loathe to leave him, hurried upstairs and packed a small case for both herself and Laura. Arriving back outside, she got in the motor car and found Harry engrossed in his book.

'What are you reading?' she asked.

'*The Imitation of Christ.*'

'I've not heard of it. Who is it by?'

'Thomas à Kempis. He was a monk who lived in the 15th Century, and saw the ordinary things of life, such as making meals, as service to God.'

'Sounds interesting. Perhaps I could borrow it when you've finished it?' Lucy was a bit dismayed at herself. It did sound a good book but her first thought was that it was something else to keep her in contact with Harry. He said he would let her borrow it, without further comment.

Eventually, Laura and William arrived.

'You might as well drive home with Harry, Lucy. You look quite settled there,' said William. Lucy saw through his guile. He wanted Laura to himself so she agreed but hoped her excited heart would calm down at the thought of being alone with Harry or she might be sick. With William being a much more experienced driver than Harry, they were soon out of sight. Harry drove much slower, which Lucy was grateful for.

The journey passed quickly as Lucy kept asking Harry questions.

'Where are you working now?'

'Another mill in Brierfield. I'm staying at Mrs Wall's again.'

'At Granny's? That's convenient for you.'

'She offered and I was glad to accept. Much more comfortable than living in lodging houses. Makes it feel more home-like.'

'Don't your parents miss you?'

'Probably not. They could never find me at meal times and I was usually in the shed outside, working with wood.'

'What about the rest of your family?'

'I've got two sisters and a younger brother.'

'Are you the eldest?'

'No, my sisters are both older than me - quite a bit older. They had the two girls close together, then a gap, and then two boys.'

'What are they all called?'

'The eldest sister is Betsy, then the younger one is Lizzy, then my brother is John. Is there just you and William?'

'Yes. I'd have liked a sister, though.'

'You probably wouldn't. Betsy and Lizzy were always falling out. It was a relief when Betsy got married.'

'Has Betsy any children?'

'Yes. She's always having children.'

'How many?'

'Six. There's Edward first, after my father....'

'Oh, my father is called Edward!' Lucy interrupted.

'I believe so. Next there's Maud, after my Mother, then Lizzie, after her aunt, then Alice, then Elsie, then Matthew, after his father.'

'Is Lizzie married?'

'Yes, but she's only managed two children so far. She was a long time before the first one came along and had given up hope really. It made it worse when Betsy seemed to have children so easily.'

'It must have done.'

'John isn't married yet; he's too young!' laughed Harry.

'What children does Lizzie have?'

'Two boys, Lionel and Stanley.'

'So you've got eight nieces and nephews?'

'That's right, at the last count,' he laughed. 'It costs me a fortune at Christmas. The boys are easy; I just make them toys such as soldiers or forts or trains. The girls are trickier, although they were very pleased when I gave them a large dolls' house as a communal present four years ago. Even Maud loves playing with it, although she pretends she is too grown up now for dolls.'

'What does your father do?'

'Goodness, is this an inquisition?' Harry laughed.

'Sorry, I'm so nosy. I just like to hear about other people and families and compare them with my own. I won't ask any more questions now.'

'I was teasing, Lucy. My father is a doctor and my mother was a nurse. That's how they met.'

'Ah, so that's where the interest in first aid comes from. Didn't you want to be a doctor?'

'No, thanks. We hardly ever saw my father when we were growing up.'

'So how did you become interested in woodwork?'

'My godfather worked with wood and I loved to spend time in his workshop, so that's how it started. When he died, he bequeathed me all his woodworking tools, which I still have. I think my parents were quite disappointed that I wasn't going to be a doctor, but they indulged me. My father wanted me to take over his practice when he retired, but my sisters have both married doctors, so the practice is safe, and I can concentrate on woodwork,' he laughed.

'Both of them married to doctors? That's unusual.'

'Not really. There were always student doctors coming to stay to learn about general practice, so I suppose it was inevitable.'

'Yes, I suppose so.'

'What about you? Where do you want to teach when you finish?'

'Anywhere there's a post, really. I'm not bothered, but near home would be handy for travelling.'

'Unless you got a motor car. William tells me he's been teaching you to drive.'

'He has. That might be an option, but I'm not keen on having my own motor car for a long time yet. So was your grandfather a doctor?'

'No, he was a builder and owned many properties. He was very disappointed when my father wanted to be a doctor, but became proud of what he achieved. My grandmother owns lots of properties now which she rents out, and has a team of builders who maintain them for her, now grandfather has passed away.'

'I'm sorry about that.'

'Granny said, "he died as he lived" - he fell off a roof he was repairing and broke his neck. He wouldn't have felt anything, my father said.'

'That's so sad.'

'He would have hated to be an invalid. He was a very fit and active man, who thought nothing of walking 15 miles at a time.'

'Our grannies are so similar. Both married to successful businessmen, who carried on their husbands' businesses after they passed away.'

'That's true. We have even more in common,' replied Harry, smiling at Lucy.

There was a companionable silence between them for the rest of the journey, as Lucy felt that she had asked enough questions. Soon they were having to go slowly as Harry drove down the steep hill that took them into Burnley. After going through Burnley centre, they drove up Colne Road towards Lucy's house. Harry pulled up outside and was just saying that he had enjoyed the journey when Mrs Coombes came and stood on the doorstep, with her arms folded.

'Oh, you're here at last. Lucy, go straight to your room.' Lucy stared at her aghast. What was the matter with her mother? She soon found out.

'Mr Marsden. I can't believe that you had the audacity to take my young daughter, without chaperone, on a journey lasting several hours. I don't know how you behave in Clitheroe, but in Burnley young women do not go unescorted with young men, nor do they allow their friends to do the same. I just hope that nobody who knows us in Burnley saw you driving together. What would they think?'

'Mrs Coombes, surely I was the chaperone for Lucy?' said Harry, trying to defend his actions. 'I would never harm her, and I have taken great care of her.'

'You should never have compromised her in the first place. A decent gentleman would not have entertained it.'

'But Mother, it was our William....'

'Lucy, what are you still doing here listening to private conversations? Upstairs to your room at once, at once I say!' Lucy went into the house, but as she did, she heard her mother tell Harry that he was not welcome in their house again.

Bursting into tears, Lucy ran upstairs into her room to find an equally woebegone Laura sat on her bed.

'Oh, Lucy! Thank goodness you are home. It's been awful. I was sent straight up here and not allowed to talk to William or say anything. Your parents and William have been having an awful row. I wish we hadn't come, but William was so keen, I didn't want to disappoint him on his birthday.'

'Mother's just torn Harry off a strip, but he was a gentleman and didn't blame William for arranging us to be together. But she's told Harry that he's not welcome in the house anymore. Oh, what am I going to do, Laura?' said Lucy, as she burst into tears afresh.

'She'll come round, won't she? My mother has a shout now and again, but is soon laughing again.'

'I don't know. I've never seen her so angry before. She's usually fairly placid. What will I do if I never see Harry again?'

'So, that's it? It's Harry you're more worried about.' Lucy stopped crying, but replaced it with loud sniffs instead and said, 'He's such a marvellous man, the first one that has ever interested me, and now it's all gone wrong.'

'It won't be as bad in the morning. Your mother may have calmed down.'

'I hope so,' but their hopes were dashed when the door opened and Mrs Coombes marched into the bedroom.

'I'm very disappointed in you, Lucy. You have put us all in a very difficult position. What would Mrs Carter say if she found out that we had put Laura at risk of ruining her reputation? I could never look her in the face again. Mrs Carter entrusted Laura to our care and you and your brother had a blatant disregard for what is right and proper. Why on earth did you separate and travel in different motor cars? Is this the way we have brought you up? I don't know what Granny Wall is going to say about this. I'm uneasy about her having that young man in her house now, if he is unreliable.'

'But, Mother....'

'Don't interrupt me, girl. You can have your say soon enough, although nothing you can say would make any difference. What possessed you to ask your brother if you could come home tonight? That wasn't planned at all. Why couldn't you have stayed at college? I don't know what that college is teaching you, but I'm dismayed at your new kind of behaviour. I shall reconsider you being on that course if anything else like this happens. It is not befitting a Coombes, or a Christian young woman.' Her mother stopped for breath, so Lucy jumped in quickly.

'But, Mother, we didn't ask if we could come home. It was William. He said you'd asked him to ask us.'

'A likely story. Why would William want to bring you both back, knowing he would have to take you back tomorrow? It doesn't make sense.'

'You'd better ask him,' Lucy retorted.

'I will, don't you worry. I still don't see how you came to be in separate motor cars.'

'William took Laura and her sisters home to ask if Laura could come here, and I went back with Harry to collect our overnight things.'

'Oh, Harry is it? Since when did you become so familiar with this man we know nothing about?'

'He's worked with Father for four months and lived with Granny Wall most of this year, without any problems.'

'Don't be impertinent, my girl. That still doesn't explain why you stayed in his motor car instead of sharing with William and Laura?'

'When William came back with Laura, he just waved and set off, so we had to follow.'

'I will have words with William later. For now, you two girls will stay in your room and I'll get Patsy to send you up a light snack. I'm sorry you have been dragged into this, Laura, and had to listen to all I've said. I hope your mother will forgive us. Now you'd both better say your prayers and ask for forgiveness.' Not giving Laura chance to respond, Mrs Coombes swept out of the room and banged the door behind her. The girls were silent for a while, just looking down at the ground.

'I hope William admits that it was his idea to invite us, or we'll be branded liars as well,' said Lucy forlornly.

Chapter 14

A knock on the door made the girls sit up, wondering who would be coming in this time. It was Patsy, with a large tea tray.

'Hello, Miss Lucy, Miss Laura. I've brought you some sandwiches and cake and a pot of tea. Is there anything special I can get for you both?'

'No thanks, Patsy, that's very kind of you. There will be enough here. I don't think either of us are very hungry,' said Lucy.

'Right, Miss. Just leave your tray outside your room when you've finished with it and I'll collect it later. Then I don't have to disturb you.'

'Thanks, Patsy.' Lucy waited until Patsy had left the room before she asked Laura if she wanted a cup of tea.

'Yes, please. I've been longing for one ever since we got here, but with all the trouble, I didn't dare ask.'

'You should have gone down to the kitchen and found Patsy. She would have looked after you.'

'I was too frightened. I didn't want to meet your mother again.'

'I don't blame you,' Lucy laughed at last. 'She was really upset, wasn't she?'

'If Harry's banned from the house, the same might go for me as well.'

'I doubt it. Mother doesn't see that you did any wrong, fortunately, but were manipulated by me and William.'

'Let's hope so, as I love coming here to stay with you.'

'And William, of course.'

Laura flushed. 'Yes, and William.' The two girls picked desultorily at the sandwiches and cake, then after another cup of tea, decided to go to sleep, not forgetting their prayers asking for forgiveness for all the trouble they had caused. But Lucy also added a prayer that her mother would forgive Harry and see that he was not to blame for the faux pas. She lived in hope, but wasn't confident as to what the answer would be. Despite it being early, the girls were soon asleep.

Next morning, the girls were up early and cautiously went downstairs to the dining room. It was empty, so they helped themselves to the breakfast set out on the hot cupboard. As they were finishing, William came in and said hello.

'Why did you tell Mother that I'd asked you to come home?' he asked Lucy angrily.

'Because you did ask us,' Lucy replied, with a glare.

'I told Mother that you had asked to come home,' said William, calming down a little.

'I know, and I got into trouble for saying it. It was your idea, William, and it's your fault that we're in trouble. You asked us to come, then you set off with Laura before Harry or I could say anything. I think that was your ploy all along, just to get some time on your own with Laura.'

'It wasn't....' but William got no further because their mother walked into the room.

'You'd better hurry up, or we're going to be late for church. After church we will have lunch and then you will go straight back to college, Lucy and Laura. I've arranged for Freddie to take you both back.'

'Freddie?' said William. 'Why Freddie? He's supposed to be taking Mr and Mrs Dawson to see their daughter and new grandchild.'

'Is he William? Well, now you are taking Mr and Mrs Dawson, and Freddie is taking the girls to Manchester. Understood?' Mrs Coombes said with a glint in her eye.

'Yes, Mother,' William replied sullenly. Lucy and Laura said nothing but kept their heads down. When Mrs Coombes left the room nobody spoke, but they all got their coats and hats on and piled into the motor car. Mr Coombes had gone down earlier in the cab as he was on door duty at the church, welcoming the congregation. There was silence in the car, too, and as soon as they got to church, Lucy dragged Laura across to sit with Miss Egar and Miss Seeney, rather than sit with her mother in the family pew.

The sermon made Lucy squirm. She almost suspected that her mother had requested such a text today. The reading had been from the book of Ephesians, chapter 5, but the minister said that he wanted to concentrate on just two of the verses: one and fifteen. He re-read the verses for them.

'Verse one says, "Be ye followers of God as dear children" and verse fifteen says, "See then, that you walk circumspectly, not as fools, but as wise". I want to talk about our Christian walk with God today. Another word for followers is to be imitators. We should try and imitate Christ in our daily walk.' Lucy looked downward. The word 'imitate' reminded her of the book Harry was reading. She must shut him from her mind this morning, she thought, as she tried to concentrate on what the minister was saying.

The minister continued. 'When we tell people that we are Christians, they watch us. They want to see how we live our lives. Whether we tell lies, are dishonest or cheating, whether we oppress people. Everything is under scrutiny. We must be extremely careful in all our dealings so that no one can point a finger of blame or suspicion on our lives. If we do wrong, then it brings dishonour to the name of Christ.' The sermon seemed to Lucy to last forever, as the minister enlarged on his theme.

In the motor car on the way home, Mrs Coombes said how much she had enjoyed the sermon today and hoped that, as it was very relevant to all concerned, they would take it on board and examine their consciences. Lucy and William squirmed in their seats but said nothing.

Lunch was a sombre affair. Granny Wall arrived; she had been to the parish church where she was a member and told everyone that Harry had attended with her that morning, as he didn't want to go to the Congregational church. Mrs Coombes gave her mother a disgusted look.

'Don't mention that young man's name in this house again,' she said sternly.

'Yes, Martha, I heard that you tore him off a strip last night. What was that all about?'

'He knows what he did and that's all I'm going to say about it.' Granny Wall looked at Lucy, but she shook her head slightly and Granny Wall took the hint.

After that, Mr Coombes tried to make light conversation, but nobody made much of a response. Lucy and Laura were glad to go upstairs to collect their belongings. When Freddie arrived, Laura thanked Mrs Coombes for her hospitality and the pair left.

Freddie was quite chatty in the motor car. He thought taking the girls back to Manchester was far more exciting than going to visit a new baby. The girls were quiet, but Lucy did notice that Freddie was sporting a black eye and she asked him what had happened.

'I had a bit of a disagreement with my stepfather,' he admitted. 'I don't think I can stand it for much longer. He's all right until he starts drinking. I just used to hide away, but I won't now. I stand up to him as I'm frightened he might hurt my mother.'

'Do you think he will?'

'I don't know. My mum says he's better when I'm not there.'

'Have you mentioned this to William?'

'Not really. It's my problem.'

'William is your boss and he'll help you if he can. Please tell him.'

'I'll have to tell him now I've got this black eye!'

'Good. I'm sure William will think of something.'

'Such as? Getting my stepfather sent to Australia?' Freddie laughed bitterly.

'I've no idea, but I'm sure he will help if he can.'

'All right, I will tell him tomorrow. I just hope my eye doesn't close up any more or I won't be able to see what I'm doing with the motor cars, let alone drive.'

'Let's hope not,' replied Lucy. The two girls talked quietly for the rest of the journey and were soon back in Manchester. They went straight to their room, and before long Cynthia arrived.

'Hello, did you have a lovely weekend?' she said gaily. Lucy and Laura looked at each other. 'What? Has something happened? Tell me all. Weren't you going to the restaurant with William for his birthday?'

Lucy told Cynthia the whole sorry saga from beginning to end, with Laura chipping in with extra information.

'Well, I don't know what to say,' said Cynthia at the end. 'So do you think you'll not see Harry again?'

'I doubt it,' said Lucy. 'When Granny Wall addressed it with my mother next day, she shouted at Granny Wall. I've never heard my mother do that before.'

'What did your mother say to Harry exactly?'

'That he was not welcome in this house anymore. That's obvious enough, isn't it? Doesn't leave any room for doubt.'

'What a mess. I'm so sorry for you both,' said Cynthia.

'Mother wouldn't even let William drive us back today. She sent William off on a driving engagement which Freddie should have been doing, and made Freddie bring us back.'

'Who's Freddie?' asked Cynthia.

'He's the engineer who works with my brother. He mends the engines and takes people to where they want to go.'

'Mind you,' said Laura, 'Lucy was too busy trying to sort out Freddie's affairs on the way here to worry about what was going on at home.'

'What do you mean, Laura?'

'Freddie had a black eye and Lucy found out that his stepfather had given it to him, so Lucy was telling him to discuss it with William as soon as possible,' replied Laura.

'Typical of Lucy. Sort out the world, even though her own world is in tatters,' replied Cynthia, and Laura nodded her agreement.

'How's your weekend been, Cynthia?' asked Lucy, wanting to change the subject.

'I've been working on my lesson plans, as I'm teaching the older group this week.'

'I wish we'd done that,' said Lucy ruefully.

'So, is Laura still welcome at your house?' asked Cynthia.

'Oh, yes, Mother was so apologetic about Laura being dragged into it. She kept saying Laura's mother would never forgive her if anything had happened to Laura. As if William would ever let anything happen to Laura! It was because he wanted to spend more time with Laura that the whole episode started.'

'Well, well, what an experience! I'm glad I stayed doing my lesson plans,' laughed Cynthia. 'I hope it turns out all right for you both. I'll get back to my room now; I want an early night.'

'Night, Cynthia,' said Lucy and Laura together.

'I think I could do with an early night as well, Laura. I'm quite worn out. What do you think?'

'Yes, that's a good idea. I keep thinking that perhaps your mother might not want our friendship to continue and then I won't be able to see William ever again.'

'So, would that bother you?'

'Yes. He's been so kind to me and my family.'

'Kind? Is that all you feel, Laura?'

There was a long silence before Laura spoke. 'No, that's not all. The more I see him, the more I love him. We talked the whole way home on Saturday. It was a very precious time. I couldn't bear that this episode will affect our relationship. Especially after what your mother said about the sermon. I felt terrible.'

'So did I. Perhaps we should commit our situations to God. Confess where we went wrong, promise to behave better in the future. and pray that God will sort William and Harry out for us.'

'That's a lot to ask,' said Laura.

'But He's a big God, isn't He?'

'True,' replied Laura. The girls were a long time at their prayers that night.

Next morning, the girls were up and out to the classroom, after having breakfast. Cynthia was a little nervous about her lesson, so they tried to reassure her and give her encouragement.

'I really appreciate your support,' said Cynthia.

'Do you think that will count as being true followers of God, Lucy?' Laura asked.

'I hope so,' said Lucy, then seeing that Cynthia had a puzzled look, they explained about the sermon and Mrs Coombes' comments.

'We can only try our best,' said Cynthia, 'and that's what I intend to do this morning. I just wish it weren't Miss Davenport taking us. She makes me nervous before she even speaks.'

'We'll pray for you,' said Laura sincerely, but was unprepared for the major miracle that occurred. Mr Banks came in to take the class. He said Miss Davenport was indisposed.

'That's an answer to prayer,' Lucy whispered to Laura.

'Although we'll have to be careful not to be too glad about it, or we'll be judged as not being true followers!' Laura laughed in return. Further conversation was stopped as Mr Banks led the short assembly, and then Cynthia commenced her morning of teaching.

The session was excellent, as the girls expected, and Mr Banks was fulsome in his praise of Cynthia, as well. Lucy watched as she turned slightly so that she could smile at Huw – that secret smile between two who love each other – making Lucy think about Harry all over again. At least she hadn't thought about him for a whole hour this morning, whilst Cynthia was teaching, but she worried about whether she would ever see him again.

The following day, Lucy received a letter and trembled when she saw that it was Harry's writing on the envelope. Was this going to be a final letter to end what friendship had been beginning? Was he cross at her for getting him into trouble? Had William finally admitted guilt for the whole affair? She was unable to wait until break time, so tore it open in the refectory. Reading the contents, she breathed a sigh of relief. He was not angry.

Dear Lucy,

I'm sorry about the débâcle on Saturday night. I never wished to cause you any trouble or upset your mother. It all happened so quickly with William setting off with just Laura, leaving you with me. I know that William did this because he wants to spend as much time with Laura as possible, but it put us in an untenable position. We had no option, especially as William drove so fast that I couldn't have caught up with him, even if I'd wanted to.

For now, I must respect your mother's position and not attempt to visit you or your house. I have written to her to offer my apologies for what happened and reiterated that you were in no danger at any time, whilst alone with me. I hope that will suffice and soften her heart towards me.

In the meantime, perhaps you will allow me to write to you at college occasionally, to keep in touch? Although I will understand if you feel this would be insensitive.

I remain,
Your friend,
Harry.

Lucy's heart was pounding when she finished reading the letter. She was so pleased that he had written and wanted to continue writing, but the thought of not being able to see him again still hurt.

'Well?' said Laura.

'He wants to keep writing to me and has also written to apologise to my mother, even though it was all William's fault.'

'Is that what he said to your mother? That it was all William's fault?'

'No, he's too much of a gentleman, but it was William's fault and we got the brunt of it.'

'True, but at least he wants to write. I'm so pleased. That will have to suffice for now.'

'Yes, I'll just live for his letters. I'll reply in the lunch break so that I can get it in the last post tonight.' Lucy smiled as she walked towards the classroom, as if a great weight had been lifted off her. She thanked God for the letter and the hope that it had within it.

The letters continued coming, about two every week, and they were a real lifeline for Lucy as the weeks flew by towards Christmas and all the extra activities in the school classrooms. When she and Laura were out shopping one day, she bought a large leather box which had a lock and key so that she could keep all the letters together. It had a tray that lifted out and she put the letters underneath, but put some jewellery on the top tray, so that it looked just like a jewellery box if anyone looked at it.

There was no invite for Laura to come to Burnley for Christmas this year; indeed, there had been no communication from her mother since William's birthday. On Laura's birthday just before Christmas, however, William drove over to visit and take them out for tea. Lucy looked round longingly, but there was no sign of Harry this time, and William said that he had not seen him either. Their mother thought William was at the football match!

William produced two identical packages from his pocket. They were gold bracelets to match the crosses that Lucy's mother had given her and Laura last Christmas. The bracelets had little crosses all the way round as well. Laura said that she couldn't accept such a gift from William, so he said it was from Lucy as well, and Laura relented. William told Lucy that the bracelet was her Christmas present as well, so don't expect much on Christmas Day! As it happened, Lucy had bought Laura a jewellery box for her birthday present and a brooch for Christmas, so it all fitted together well.

Watching Laura and William together made missing Harry even worse, so with a large sigh, Lucy took a book out of her handbag and read for a while to give the other two time to talk. It just compounded her loneliness and longing for Harry. For the first time ever, Lucy was not particularly looking forward to Christmas.

Chapter 15

Even though Lucy wasn't looking forward to Christmas, it didn't stop her going to see Bessie at Mrs Smith's shop and have a new dress made. Whilst she hadn't fully forgiven her mother for being so horrible to her, nevertheless, as a dutiful daughter, Lucy bought her mother a new dress, too. Lucy's was in a soft pale grey material, whereas her mother's was in her favourite shade of brown. She also bought a warm skirt and matching shawl for Granny Wall.

For her father and William, she bought new overcoats of a shorter length, that were more practical when riding in motor cars. She had certainly given Mrs Brenda Smith a lot of her allowance this Christmas.

Christmas Day was much as last year's had been. There was the usual visit to church, lots of food, presents, games, and singing; Mr and Mrs Coombes waiting on everyone else; and William and Lucy doing the washing up. The servants all seemed to thoroughly enjoy the day and went home happy, with their piles of presents and lots of food. Lucy's thoughts, however, kept turning to Harry and wondering what he was doing today. Was he at home with his family? Was he at one of his sisters' houses? Was he thinking about her?

When Granny Wall was going home, she took Lucy to one side and gave her a small package. 'Put this away quickly; it's a little extra Christmas present for you.' Lucy did as she was told and when she got upstairs, she opened the package. Inside was a large envelope containing a book. It was a copy of 'The Imitation of Christ'. Lucy was thrilled as she'd never got round to reading the book that Harry had recommended, but when she opened the flyleaf, two pages fell out. On the first page were the words:

To Lucy
From Harry
Christmas 1908

On the second page were more words:

Dear Lucy,
I wish that I could be with you to give you this book in person as I know you want to read it. I enjoy reading your letters, but would much prefer to meet you, although I know that is not possible at present. Your Granny Wall knows what happened and agreed to give you this book for me. The

111

inscription on the other page is what I would have written in the book for you, if I thought it wouldn't cause you any further trouble.

Take care, and have a lovely Christmas.

Yours sincerely,
Harry.

Suddenly, thought Lucy, this was the best Christmas ever! She ran upstairs and hid the pages from Harry in her locked box and came downstairs holding the book in her hands as she couldn't bear to part with it.

'What's that book you've got there, Lucy?' her mother asked.

'It's a book that was recommended in Manchester, and I mentioned it to Granny Wall, so she's just given me a copy.'

'May I look?'

'Certainly, Mother.' Her mother looked at it and then passed it back.

'An excellent book. I'm pleased to see you are reading serious, life-giving books as well as secular ones, Lucy.'

'Yes, Mother, I think this is going to be my favourite book now,' Lucy said, smiling sweetly, without giving a hint of who had really given it to her.

'Good.'

Lucy curled up on the settee, reading her book, whilst her mother started some needlepoint, glancing at her daughter occasionally with softening glances. There had been a distinct atmosphere since she'd arrived back home. Her mother had been cool and distant, but Lucy thought that this might be a turning point in their relationship, bringing it back to their usual happy footing. *If only she knew*, thought Lucy, but would never tell her.

On Boxing Day Lucy and William went for a walk on their own, going beyond Fence and as far as Barley village, in the shadow of Pendle Hill. It was exhilarating but also difficult walking back up the steep hill on the way home. However, by the time they reached Greenhead Lane, most of it was downhill. A lazy day was spent at home for Lucy and Mrs Coombes on the following day, but it was back to work for William and Mr Coombes.

The day before Lucy was due to go back to college, she announced at breakfast that she was going into town, if anyone wanted anything collecting.

'Why don't you come and visit me at work?' William suggested.

'Why would I want to do that? Don't I see enough of you at home?'

'I could show you the improvements that I'm making at the garage.'

'Very exciting, I'm sure. Now if you were going to invite me for lunch, that would be a different matter.'

'All right then, if you insist, I'll take you for lunch.'

'Seriously?' Lucy couldn't believe her ears. William was offering to take her out for lunch, without it involving a ploy to see Laura. Suddenly, the day looked a little bit more exciting, but she could only suspect that he had another motive for this unusually generous offer.

After completing her purchases, Lucy went round to the garage and found William sat at his desk in the showroom, with no customers in sight.

'Quiet day?'

'Not really, I've already sold two motor cars this morning. Plus five people have been in to book the motor car for an outing. Business is booming. I told you it would.'

'Good. Did you manage to sort Freddie out?'

'Yes, I'm glad you made him tell me what was going on. He's moved into the garage now and things have improved for his mother at home.'

'Moved into the garage? Does he sleep in a motor car and nip in the canal for a wash?'

'Of course not. We're having the whole top floor converted into offices and making him a bedroom, kitchen, living room, and bathroom. We've actually got two bedrooms up there. They're almost finished.'

'Why do you need two? Are you thinking of moving in here?'

'No, but that's a good idea. Do you want to go up and have a look?'

'Won't Freddie mind?'

'No, he's out on a job; besides, I still own the rooms.'

'Or Father does,' Lucy reminded him.

'Father did, but he signed them over to me for a joint Christmas and birthday present, so I own the place now. Anyway, go on up there, before Freddie comes back,' William said, with a smile on his face. So Lucy set off upstairs and went first into an office, which was obviously where William kept all his paperwork. It was rather untidy, unlike the neat showroom. She heard a noise in the next room and was a bit embarrassed in case Freddie had come back early, but as she was hurriedly bypassing that room, Harry came out.

'Harry! What are you doing here?' she gasped.

'Working. What do you think?'

'Working?' she repeated.

'Yes, I'm working for William, converting his upstairs floor.'

'Oh!' replied Lucy, a little lost for words, which was ironic when she had often thought about what she would say to him if she ever saw him again.

'Didn't he tell you?'

'No.'

'It's good to see you again.'

'Yes, and you. Oh, and thank you for the book,' she added.

'It was the only thing I could think of to send you that wouldn't arouse suspicion, especially after Mrs Wall offered to help.'

'She did?'

'Oh, yes, she was very keen to help. She knows our side of the story.'

'She does? How?'

'Because I told her. I wanted a chance to be heard with my side of events and your mother wasn't going to let me, so I went to Mrs Wall. Now, let me show you round the flat. This is the first bedroom, which is Freddie's. Next door is another bedroom, which is the same size. Then this is the kitchen and the living room next to it, and down this little corridor is the bathroom. If Freddie weren't living here, I'd be tempted to rent it myself, although I've got to say, I'm very comfortable living at your granny's.'

'You're living there now?'

'Yes, didn't William tell you?'

'No, or I'd have been down to visit, I can assure you.'

'Didn't he tell you I was here today?'

'No, he just invited me for lunch. I must admit, I was surprised that he'd invited me when there was no chance of seeing Laura. I thought he'd turned over a new leaf.'

'He did it for me. I asked him if he could manage to lure you here so that I could see you. It's me that wants to take you to lunch.'

'Oh, we couldn't do that. What if someone sees us and mentions it to Mother?'

'No one will see us. Come back into the lounge.' She followed him into the lounge and he gestured for her to sit down at the small table. He disappeared for a few minutes then came back with a picnic basket and a flask of tea, with two cups.

'What if Freddie comes back?'

'Freddie won't. He's gone on a long journey today.'

'What if William comes upstairs?'

'William won't. I've threatened him. Just relax and enjoy this time together. It might not happen again for some time.' So Lucy did relax, and let Harry serve her the small sandwiches and fruit pies that he had bought. They were all her favourite foods: cheese and pickle, and ham sandwiches, and bilberry pie with cream.

'These are my favourite things for a picnic,' Lucy said.

'I know,' replied Harry, looking rather smug. 'I asked Mrs Wall what your favourites were.'

'Granny knows we're here? What if she tells Mother?'

'She won't. It was her idea.'

'Granny suggested we had a picnic here?'

'Yes.' Lucy had to stop eating to think that over, but decided the time was too precious to waste worrying about who knew what. They spent a delicious hour together talking about lots of things and getting to know each other better. Eventually Harry said that he had better go back to work, or his boss might sack him. Lucy said she would forbid it and would like Harry to work for her brother forever, if it meant they could meet.

In a dream-like state, Lucy went back downstairs to find William with a big grin on his face.

'Did you like your surprise lunch?'

'I did. I can't believe it was Granny Wall who suggested it.'

'Oh, I can. Granny Wall is a good friend to Harry. She thinks the world of him. So do I. We've become firm friends since my birthday, even though I had to apologise to him at the time. I do get obsessed with trying to see Laura, so I don't always think things through.'

'You certainly don't. But I'll forgive you as you really thought this through for me.'

'I recognised how Harry was feeling as I know how it feels, too, so I wanted to help. We'll stay with the picnic theme at home, though. I don't want mother to find out I was in on the plot.'

'Your secret is safe with me, or is it my secret? Whatever, I'll be saying nothing at home and thank you for giving me such a lovely picnic, with all my favourite food,' Lucy grinned.

'Any time,' replied William. 'You've gone along with so much for me so that I could see Laura. It was only fair that I did the same for you.'

'Yes, it's about time I got something back from you,' she laughed.

'Do you want a lift home?'

'No, it's a mild day; I think I'll walk. I might even pop in to see Granny Wall at the mill on the way home – just to say thank you to her, as well.'

'That's fine. I'll see you at teatime.'

There was a tricky moment at teatime when Mrs Coombes asked where William had taken her for lunch, but Lucy managed to make out that William had made a big adventure and provided a picnic of all her favourite foods, telling them that he was a caring brother. Fortunately, Mrs Coombes didn't intercept the look of complicity that passed between Lucy and William.

The following day, William took Lucy back to college, picking Laura up on the way. Lucy felt it was only fair that he should have some time with Laura, after he'd organised her meeting with Harry. As soon as the girls got back to their room, Lucy couldn't wait to tell Laura all that had happened over the Christmas holiday. She had just finished her story when Cynthia arrived and the story had to be repeated. However Lucy was happy about that, as she was talking about Harry, her favourite subject of the moment.

The college work resumed two days later and the new term was gruelling, with lots of teaching being undertaken by all of them. Nobody was surprised that Mary Watson hadn't returned, but they were quite shocked when they heard why she hadn't resumed the course. After the Christmas holidays, she had returned a day early but was caught coming out of the men's dormitories by no less than Miss Davenport. Mary protested her innocence and said that she had only been returning a book that she had borrowed, but to no avail. She was dismissed from the course instantly. It was Jacob Atherton who gave them all the details, as it had happened outside his room.

'Whose room had she been to?' asked Laura, unable to resist.

'No prizes for guessing,' replied Jacob. 'It was The Honourable's room.'

'And has he been asked to leave the course as well?' asked Lucy.

'No, he protested his innocence as well, but they believed him, where they didn't believe her. The power of the man as usual – or his rank.'

'The woman is always to blame, as it ever has been since time began with Adam and Eve,' said Laura mournfully.

'Mary will be no loss to the teaching profession, but I think if she was dismissed, then he should have been too,' added Cynthia, and they all nodded their agreement.

Soon after returning to college, Lucy received a letter from Harry saying how much he had enjoyed their time together and he hoped it could be repeated very soon. Lucy wrote back in the same vein, but she didn't hold out much hope that there would be any opportunities. But her resourceful brother came up trumps again. In the middle of February, he wrote to say that he and Harry would be coming over to take them out to tea on the Saturday. They would come early and then there was time for a walk in the park, before going for a meal. Lucy and Laura were both ecstatic and couldn't wait for the day to arrive. By arrangement with William, Cynthia and Huw came along too, as they struggled to get any time together. They set off for a walk at half-past ten, but quickly separated into the three couples, although keeping the others in sight for propriety's sake. It was hard for them to leave and go to the restaurant, but they all enjoyed the entire day. Far too soon, in Lucy's opinion, Harry and William had to leave. William wished that they had arranged to stay overnight in a hotel, so that they could see the girls again on the Sunday, but hadn't mentioned that at home, and thought it might cause trouble if he rang up now to suggest it. Besides, Harry had only recently been allowed back into the Coombes' family home, so didn't want to rock the boat again. It was only by William's insistence that Harry was his friend, that he had been allowed back in, but Mrs Coombes was keeping a close eye on him, he told Lucy.

Lucy said her goodbyes to Harry and he and William left with Laura. Harry offered to stay in the motor car whilst William went in Laura's house, but Laura insisted on him coming in and meeting her family. Laura was staying with her family overnight and going back to college late Sunday evening.

Left on her own for the evening, Lucy read and re-read Harry's letters and went over every piece of conversation that they had had during the day. Perhaps it was something in the Coombes' family blood that made them fall in love so quickly and deeply, Lucy pondered. Eventually she fell asleep, only to dream about Harry.

Chapter 16

It was soon Easter. Many of the course members were already applying for posts to commence in September. Laura watched their furious activity, worrying about whether they would get an interview, and smiled to herself, knowing that she had no need of application forms or interviews. Lucy was one of those seeking a job. She had applied to three schools, two in Burnley and one in Brierfield, the next small town up the road from where she lived. Only the Brierfield one wrote back, inviting her for an interview. It was on the first day back after the Easter holidays, so Lucy had to get permission from Miss Davenport to be late for the first day of the final term. Surprisingly, Miss Davenport happily agreed, as she said that it was important that all the students went for interviews, because they had a good chance of obtaining posts as Owen's College already had a prestigious reputation for producing good teachers.

Feeling very nervous, Lucy put on her best two-piece suit, which was a sober navy twill with plain white, high-necked blouse, to attend her interview. Her hair was scraped up into a bun at the top of her head under her navy hat. The questions were being put to her by the headmaster, who was an older gentleman, and a younger man who was from the Parish council, who owned the school. The local vicar was also in attendance.

Lucy felt that she had managed to answer all their questions adequately, but as they only said 'I see' after each answer, she couldn't gauge how she was performing. They spent a long time reading her references from Miss Davenport and Miss Dodd, and Lucy wondered what they had put in them as she hadn't been allowed to read them. After the interview concluded, the headmaster said he would let her know, and Lucy was dismissed. She got the distinct impression that the headmaster wasn't keen on women teachers, and he'd even asked her if she was engaged. The vicar had also asked her why she didn't attend the Parish church, but she was quick to point out that she had a strong Christian faith and attended church regularly, but preferred the Congregationalists' way of worshipping. That would probably lose her the job, she thought to herself, which was silly as they were all worshipping the same God at the end of the day, and it wasn't even a church school. Lucy was a bundle of nerves all day afterwards and kept going over and over in her mind what they had asked, and what she had replied, and wondering if there was a better way. Eventually she decided it was too late to worry. They would already have made their decision.

Arriving back at college late that night, Lucy found Cynthia in their room, full of her news. Huw had been to stay at her house over Easter and met the elders of the church and had been appointed to one of the teaching posts at the new school, teaching the older children. Also, Cynthia had been given a post teaching the younger class. They were both ecstatic, she told them. But that wasn't all Cynthia's news. Huw had proposed to her and talked with her father and, although they couldn't announce it and she couldn't wear her ring for college, they were engaged. She produced a solitaire diamond on a necklace, which she was wearing under her blouse, so that no one saw it. Cynthia put the ring on for Lucy and Laura and they both congratulated her and admired the ring.

'When are you going to get married?' asked Lucy.

'August.'

'This year?' said Laura.

'Yes, it's so exciting, isn't it? I want you both to be bridesmaids as well. You were so kind to me when I started the course, and we've all become such good friends.'

'What about your sisters? Aren't you having them as bridesmaids?' asked Lucy.

'Yes, there'll be five of you altogether. I must get back to my room now I've told you my news.'

'Going to do your lesson plans?' asked Laura.

'Certainly not! I'm writing my guest list and my wedding present list. Oh, and we're being allowed to stay in the headmaster's house, as he owns a property on the next street to the school and doesn't want to live in the school house. Just think, a brand new house to live in as well.'

'You certainly look as if things are going well,' said Laura, just a trifle enviously.

'I'm sure everything will work out well for you two, I hope it does. Night-night.'

Lucy and Laura looked at each other. They didn't have Cynthia's confidence that all would be well for them, but they could only hope and pray.

The final examinations were stiff and the teaching programme relentless. Harry's letters kept Lucy sane, but another letter also brought her great joy. It was from the school at Brierfield, offering her the post to teach the youngest children in the school, on a one year's probationary contract. Lucy was ecstatic and couldn't wait to write to Harry and tell him. At long last the final day of college arrived. William came to pick Lucy and Laura up, as she was coming to their house for two weeks. Mrs Coombes had graciously said that they would take Laura on holiday with them during the second week of Burnley Fair. Laura didn't have to report to the school until the first Monday of September. Lucy was annoyed at William because he was late, but he said that he'd been doing some business that took him longer than he anticipated. The thought of leaving college soon dispelled any annoyance. Clutching her certificate to say she was a trained teacher in her hand, Lucy got in the motor car – in the back of course - William had made Laura sit in the front as usual.

At the end of the first week of Burnley Fair, they set off to go to Scarborough for a week. They'd booked in at the Grand Hotel. Mr and Mrs Coombes were too tired after travelling to go anywhere the first night, so, after dinner, William and the girls set off for a walk along the cliff top. William purposely walked quicker with Laura, leaving Lucy behind. She didn't mind. She just daydreamed along, thinking about Harry and wishing she could walk out like this with him.

Suddenly, Lucy realised that William and Laura had stopped and William was looking at Laura intently and Laura seemed to be shaking her head. Eventually, Lucy caught up with them. Laura looked distressed.

'What's the matter?' Lucy asked.

'I've just proposed to Laura and she says she can't marry me,' William said forlornly.

'You know why I can't,' Laura repeated.

'You didn't let me finish though. You said you couldn't marry me because you are committed to working at the school. You only have to work there until Christmas to meet your obligations.'

'What do you mean?' asked Laura.

'I've been to see your mill boss and he's agreed to release you after three months, instead of two years. That way, you'll get experience teaching for the future, but you'll be free to leave and get married.'

'How did you manage that?'

'It took some negotiating, but I managed it. I have to find him a teacher who will take over from you when you leave at Christmas.'

'How are you going to do that?' Teachers don't usually leave during the year.'

'I've already done it.'

'What do you mean?' asked Lucy.

'Jacob Atherton is taking the post after Christmas. He wants to stay in Manchester and was very keen when he heard that it was a mill owner who would be paying his wages, as he comes from a mill owning background himself. He said that he intended working with poorer children and Laura's school would suit him down to the ground. However, it hasn't suited his father, who all along had hoped that his son would return to the mill, despite his lack of passion for the business.'

'Well, that's surprising. You have been busy,' said Laura.

'It's not surprising that Jacob wants to stay locally. He's got his eye on a girl in the first year group who lives in Manchester,' laughed Lucy.

'I can't believe you've managed to convince the mill owner to release me after three months. He paid for my training.'

'I know. I'm having to pay for another teacher to be trained to get your release.'

'You can't do that for me, William,' Laura said.

'I've already done it. Well, I've signed an agreement. But it's not the only man I've managed to convince recently.'

'What do you mean?' asked Lucy.

'I've managed to convince Mr Carter that I may ask Laura to marry me.'

'What did he say?' asked Laura.

'He said "Yes please," fortunately,' laughed William. 'So now, will you be my wife, Laura?'

'Oh, do say yes, Laura. I can't stand the suspense!' Lucy cried.

'Yes, I'll marry you, William. I can't believe how much effort you have gone to, to make it possible to marry me, and expense for that matter.'

'You are worth every penny,' William said, holding her close.

Lucy turned away from this sensitive moment and started walking back to the hotel. They needed to be alone at this special time. She would wait for them near the hotel, so that they all arrived back together. If only she and Harry could spend time together like this, she thought, until her heart ached with longing.

When they all arrived back at the hotel, their parents had gone up to bed, so the three of them sat in the lounge, talking about the engagement. William had not bought a ring, preferring Laura to choose her own. William planned to take her into Scarborough town to choose one on Monday.

Next morning, over breakfast, William told his parents that he was the happiest man alive and that Laura had consented to be his bride. Both parents were delighted, Lucy was pleased to see, and they said they would discuss details after visiting the local church. After the service, the family had lunch, then retired to the lounge to talk.

Mrs Coombes asked when they were going to marry. Laura replied 'Next year,' but William said he couldn't wait that long. If Laura was finishing school on Friday 17th December, when her contract ended, they could get married the week after, on her birthday, the 21st.

'Can you organise your wedding from Friday to Tuesday, my love?' he asked with pleading in his eyes.

'I suppose so, if I plan carefully. But why that date?'

'It's the day I first met you, two years ago, as well as being your birthday. What better date? At least I won't forget your wedding anniversary, like most men, my Father being the prime candidate.'

'I only forgot once,' Mr Coombes defended himself, laughing, 'but I'm never allowed to forget it.'

'A winter wedding! Will there be any suitable flowers?' asked Mrs Coombes, practical as ever.

'There'll be holly and ivy and Christmas roses,' said Laura, 'What else could I want?'

'Mistletoe?' said William hopefully.

'Oh, yes,' replied Laura, 'lots of mistletoe.'

'Where will you marry, my dear?' asked Mrs Coombes.

'At the Mission, I suppose. It's been my church for all of my life. All my friends and family live near there, too.'

'Is it a large hall? Is there a Sunday school attached?'

'No, it's one big building, but with no fixed seats, so that it can be used for various activities.'

'So, you could have a reception there?' pressed Mrs Coombes.

'I suppose so,' replied Laura, but Lucy could see strain appearing in Laura's eyes and knew she was already worrying about the cost.

'I know you'll have to discuss it with your parents, but please could we pay for the reception as our wedding present to you both? We would bring caterers in to save all the bother for your mother. Would she be happy with that?' added Mrs Coombes.

'I'm sure she would. It is very generous of you. Thank you,' replied Laura.

Lucy sat quietly as the arrangements were being made and discussed. She reflected that her two closest friends were to be married before the year was out, leaving only her unmarried. Would she ever marry? She certainly hoped so. Time would tell. The rest of the week flew by. William and Laura went to buy a ring during the week. Laura chose an unusual ring which had a large ruby in the centre, with a diamond on each side. Red to match her hair, she told William, laughing.

Although plans for the wedding were being put into place, first there was Cynthia's wedding to attend. As promised, Cynthia wanted Lucy and Laura to be bridesmaids, along with her own sisters. The wedding was set for August 14th, so that they would have time for a little honeymoon and be able to settle into their new home together before the school term started.

The church had been happy for Cynthia to have a teaching post when she was married, because she was one of their own congregation. Most ladies had to give up teaching on marrying, which Cynthia thought was unnecessary and had told the church members so. Fortunately, they had agreed with her. They were both excited that the headmaster didn't want the school house as it meant they didn't have to search for somewhere to live.

William took Laura and Lucy over to Cynthia's house the night before the wedding so that they could get ready there and help Cynthia with her final preparations. Next day he would bring all the family over in his new charabanc. It was a Daimler, and it could hold 20 people at a time. William had invested in it before the July holidays so that he could take whole families, or even streets, on holiday or for day trips all at the same time, saving lots of money on repeated trips. Charabancs were becoming very fashionable everywhere. Already Freddie was taking trips out each Saturday and Sunday afternoons, which were proving very popular. So much so, that William was thinking of hiring another driver to allow Freddie to concentrate on his engines.

When William bought the charabanc, it was open to wind and rain, but he and Freddie had managed to make a frame with canvas sheeting to keep off most of the bad weather. However, it was not needed for Cynthia's wedding. The sun shone brilliantly all day. The charabanc wasn't as fast as a motor car, so William had to set off very early from Burnley, with his parents, and then go to Manchester to collect Mr and Mrs Carter and the four children. Albert and Arthur were beside themselves when it arrived to pick them up, although William had to leave the charabanc in the mill yard as he couldn't reverse in the small street. The boys made sure all their friends were watching anyway.

They finally arrived at the Bolton church in plenty of time for the wedding and for William to top up the radiator and find a petrol station to fill the tank again before the return journey.

The bride arrived, walking proudly on her father's arm, smiling shyly at all the wedding guests. She was followed down the aisle by five radiant bridesmaids, all wearing matching summer dresses of pale blue organza, with puffy sleeves. Cynthia's gown was simple, but classically beautiful. Her sleeves were plain and not fussy at all, some of the guests thought. She wore a diamond necklace that her father had bought for her, which set off the square neckline of the dress, showing the necklace to perfection. Cynthia wore flowers in her hair, matching the flowers in her bouquet, and had a long veil that had been her mother's and her grandmother's before her.

As Cynthia approached Huw at the altar, Lucy watched as Huw's face lit up at the sight of his bride. If only it was Harry there, looking at her. Harry had not been invited to the wedding due to the difficulties with her parents, so Lucy felt all the more on her own, especially as she had seen Laura and William talking together, with love shining on their faces. Lucy had to content herself with the thought that Harry was now allowed back in her house, so hopefully things could develop the way Lucy would like them to do.

After the wedding ceremony, the guests were all taken to a large hotel in Bolton town centre. William was comparing notes with the drivers of two other charabancs who had been hired for the occasion. *Typical*, thought Lucy. *William talking business even at a wedding.* The wedding breakfast was sumptuous, the speeches witty but short, and the toasts were made to the happy couple. Viewing of the presents then took place before the bride and groom left for their honeymoon trip, having borrowed one of Huw's father's motor cars. They were staying the first night at a hotel in Chester, and then driving down to Wales to visit with Huw's family for the rest of their honeymoon. Cynthia had only met them once before so she was quite nervous, but her worry was unfounded as they loved her as if she were a daughter, and she thoroughly enjoyed her honeymoon.

It was soon time for the new school term to start and the three young women were becoming nervous about their roles as qualified teachers. They wouldn't have the support of their colleagues or their teachers to help them but would be on their own with a classroom full of children, who were depending on them for their education.

Lucy made many plans for her lessons, but as she didn't know what the children had already been taught, if anything, it was difficult. She thanked God for all the meticulous lesson plans that she had been made to prepare, as it made life easier for her now. As the first day of term drew near, Lucy was getting more and more anxious. What if she was a failure? What if the children wouldn't listen to her? What if they were unruly? What if they didn't understand what she was teaching them? She tried talking to her mother, but she was unsympathetic, saying that Lucy had wanted a career in teaching, so what was the problem? At the Wednesday evening Bible study group, she had talked to Miss Egar, who was much more reassuring and said everybody felt nervous at first, but it soon became much easier. Lucy was not convinced and got herself into a state the day before she was due to commence teaching. But after the Sunday lunch at home, she went into her room and opened her Bible. She turned to the Book of Psalms. She had learned early that whatever her problem was, there was always an answer in the book of Psalms, and it didn't fail her this time. Her eye fell on Psalm 37, but it was verse five that stood out.

'Commit thy way unto the Lord, trust also in Him; and He shall bring it to pass.'

Lucy read the verse through several times and then started to feel a peace stealing over her. It was so easy, why couldn't she just trust her God? He hadn't led her into this career for nothing. He would bring it to pass. Suddenly she remembered that Granny Wall had given her an envelope this afternoon, as she was leaving. Perhaps Granny Wall had some words of wisdom for her. But if Granny Wall had any words of wisdom, she kept them to herself. The letter was in Harry's handwriting.

Chapter 17

Lucy tore the envelope open eagerly and drew out the single sheet of paper.

My dear Lucy,

I know that you will be feeling nervous today, as I know that you always like to get things right and you will be worrying. You have no need to worry; you will make a marvellous teacher. I am so proud of you. Write to me and tell me how your first day was.

Your devoted friend,
Harry.

Lucy knew that what he was saying was right and it just confirmed what the Bible passage had said. She would be all right. She re-read the letter and noticed that he had called her 'My' dear Lucy for the first time, and called himself your 'devoted' friend. If only she could say 'my' Harry to him. Picking up her pen, she wrote a reply immediately and bravely addressed him as 'my' dear Harry. Addressing the envelope to his Clitheroe address, she hid the letter in her school bag. She would post it on her way to work tomorrow. Work! That felt such a special word. This was the start of a new phase in her life, and at long last, she was calm and ready for it.

Next morning, Lucy forced herself to have a good breakfast, even though her tummy had butterflies. Collecting her lunch from the kitchen, she set off walking, as Walter Street School was less than a mile from her house. Walking up to the school entrance, Lucy recited the Psalm she had read the previous afternoon and found renewed strength coursing through her. She found her way to the headmaster's office and knocked on the door.

'Come in,' said a deep voice.

'Good morning. Miss Coombes, Sir.'

'Ah, good morning, Miss Coombes; nice and early I see. I like people who are early.' *Phew*, thought Lucy, *that's a good start. Glad I came early.*

'You will be with the infant class, as I think we told you in your letter of confirmation.'

'That's correct. Although I'm competent to teach all ages, I find the smallest children the most rewarding.'

'Good. Now let's see if you are as good as Miss Davenport says you are.'

'I beg your pardon, Sir?'

'Miss Davenport was very fulsome in her praise of you, and please call me Mr Treadwell.'

'She was, Sir? I mean, Mr Treadwell?'

'Most fulsome. It was because of her reference that you got the position. You sound surprised.'

'Miss Davenport was, er, rather serious, and not forthcoming with praise.'

'Well, she's obviously a woman who knows her own mind. Now, I'll show you where your classroom is and you can hang your coat up before the children come in. I will ring the school bell in the yard, and then the children will file inside class by class. Your first job is to make a register of attendance, then we will all go to the hall for assembly. I'm going to let Tommy Earnshaw stay in your class today. He is in the next class really, but he's a bright boy and will be able to catch up quickly when he returns to his own class. He can stay all week if you prefer. He'll guide you into the way we work.'

'Thank you, Mr Treadwell. That sounds really helpful.'

Mr Treadwell got up and took Lucy down the corridor to her classroom. It had lots of small desks and tables crowded together, but there were large windows with plenty of light coming in. In the front of the classroom, there was a large fire stove which wasn't lit, being summer, but looked as if it would be very warm for the winter. There were gas lights at several places in the room, so Lucy was very pleased.

Putting her coat, bag and lunch in the small cupboard, Lucy smoothed her hair back and took a deep breath. There was a large book on her desk with the word 'Register' on the front. She opened it and found that someone had already written all the children's names in it, so that would save her time this morning. Hearing the bell ring outside, Lucy braced herself to meet the children. Soon, a trickle of children arrived in the classroom and each found a seat, looking up in awe at their teacher. Some were sniffling, probably because they didn't want to come to school. Others were chatting to their neighbours, obviously friends from before they came to school.

'Good morning, children. I am Miss Coombes. When I say, "good morning, children", you must say to me "good morning, Miss Coombes". Do you understand?'

'Yes, Miss Coombes,' some of the children replied.

'Now all of you, please.'

'Yes, Miss Coombes,' they all replied this time. *Goodness, I sound like Miss Dodd, Lucy thought.*

'Now I need to take a register, so that I will get to know your names and know who is present today. When I say your name, please put your hand up so that I will know who you are.'

Lucy read through the register, hoping she would soon learn the individual children's names. She had barely finished when there was a knock on the door and one of the older children came in and asked Lucy to take her class to the hall for assembly. Asking the children to line up by the door, Lucy asked Tommy Earnshaw to lead the line to the hall, and she followed at the rear.

The children went and sat at the front of the hall, Lucy wasn't sure where to sit, but then noticed a chair next to her line of children and that other teachers were sitting by their classes. She sat down quickly, and Tommy nodded his approval. Everybody seemed to be waiting in expectant silence, and then Mr Treadwell marched into the room and took his place at the front.

'Good morning, children,' he boomed.

'Good morning, Mr Treadwell,' they chorused back.

He started the assembly, which was a hymn, a prayer, and a little talk, mainly about being good children and doing your lessons. Then he announced that there was a new teacher today and bid them say welcome to Miss Coombes. A hundred pairs of eyes swivelled to Lucy and said, 'Welcome, Miss Coombes.'

'Good morning, children,' Lucy replied.

'You are dismissed,' Mr Treadwell said, and for an awful moment, Lucy thought he was speaking to her. Then, as she watched all the children stand up, she realised that he had dismissed the children back to class. Her children left first, so she followed them back to class and waited until they all settled down.

'Please, Miss, shall I give the chalk boards out?' young Tommy Earnshaw asked.

'Yes, you may, Tommy. Is this your second year at school?'

'Yes, Miss Coombes,' he replied. 'I'm here to help you.'

'And I'm sure you'll be a great help to me, Tommy. Now, children, I'm going to put some letters up on the board, and I want you to copy them down.' Whilst the children were working, Lucy walked round the classroom, helping and advising the children on her way, and reassuring the ones who looked on the verge of tears, that they would be all right. It was soon playtime, and the children quickly filed out into the playground. Tommy held back from the other children.

'You go to the staff room for a cup of tea now, Miss, whilst we're playing out.'

'Thank you, Tommy. It's so different from where I've worked before. I'm grateful for your help.'

'Right, Miss. Staff room is down the corridor, last room on the left.'

'Thanks, Tommy. You go out and play now.'

'Yes, Miss,' and he was off. Lucy found her way to the staff room and stopped as she walked in and three pairs of eyes stared at her.

'Hello,' she said shyly. 'Miss Lucy Coombes.'

The three gentlemen stood up until Lucy had sat down. One was a portly, older man, with a red face. 'I'm Mr Johnny Bridges. I teach the oldest children.'

'Mr Matthew Brown, at your service,' said a dapper middle-aged man.

'I'm Mr Edwin Procter. I teach the group above yours,' said a young man with dark hair.

'Is this your first teaching post?' Mr Bridges asked, bringing Lucy a cup of tea.

'Oh, thank you. Yes, it's all new to me yet.'

'We all know what it's like,' said Mr Procter. 'I used to take the youngest class, but as we're now offering schooling until twelve years for all children, Mr Treadwell has divided us into four classes, so I moved up. If you have any problems, just ask me. I understand the new entrants to a school,' he laughed.

'Thank you. I'm very grateful,' Lucy added.

'Where do you live?' asked Mr Procter.

'Just down the road, on the outskirts of Burnley.'

'That's handy,' he replied. 'You'll be able to get here in the snow.'

'Take no notice of him, Miss Coombes,' said Mr Bridges. 'He's just complaining about me because I couldn't make it into school one day last year. I live at Lane Bottoms and we were snowed in. Six foot-high drifts. He never stops on about it.'

The bell rang in the playground then and the staff all jumped up.

'Ah, well, back to work, educating the masses,' laughed Mr Procter, and they all went back to their respective classrooms.

The first day went well. Lucy shamelessly pinched Laura's ideas about getting the children to make the shapes with their bodies and had them all laughing. Even Tommy joined in and said that he wished Miss Coombes were teaching him this year.

'Mr Procter didn't do anything like this,' Tommy laughed.

'Did you learn your lessons, Tommy?'

'Yes, Miss.'

'Then Mr Procter taught you well. There are always different ways to teach the same thing.'

''Spose so, Miss, but you are more fun.'

'Let's get on with the next lesson, then,' Lucy said, hiding a smile, but secretly feeling pleased with this critical analysis from a six-year-old.

Guided by Tommy, the day flew by. She learned that the school provided meals for the children and she could purchase a meal if she wished. Lucy decided to do this each day, as it would save Mrs Ward or Patsy having to prepare her something, and her having to carry it to school each day.

At the end of the day, she thanked Tommy for all his help and gave him an apple that she hadn't eaten from her lunch box.

'Thanks, Miss. I'll see you tomorrow,' he grinned.

As she was getting her coat on, Mr Procter popped into the classroom.

'How did your first day go?'

'Better than I expected; they are lovely children.'

'Yes, the majority are from poor backgrounds, but are grateful for the learning that we give them and that they don't have to go to work full time yet. They also love the school meals!'

'Do the children get them free?'

'We ask for a contribution, but no child is refused a meal if his parents haven't paid. For many children, it's the best meal they'll have today, and for some it's the only meal.'

'Really? That's sad.'

'Yes, there are some very poor families and also large families here.'

'Thank you for your help today.'

'I'll help you any time, Miss Coombes. May I say, it's a delight to have a female teacher join us. Much better than just having men around. You make the place more interesting.' Lucy smiled but didn't respond. She wasn't sure whether Mr Procter was being too familiar with her or not, so she collected her things and said, 'Goodbye.'

Leaving the school, Lucy felt exhilarated. She set off walking at a brisk pace and, when she got near to Reedley Road, she noticed a commercial vehicle that looked a little like Harry's. As she drew nearer, she could see someone waving at her. It was Harry! She walked over to him and he looked through the window.

'I couldn't resist coming. How did your first day go?'

'It was amazing. Mr Treadwell – he's the headmaster – let me have a boy from the class above to guide me for the first day. It made everything so much easier. He told me where to go and when. But what are you doing here?'

'I've run out of screws, so I'm going into Burnley to buy some.'

'Can't you buy them in Brierfield?'

'Yes, but I wouldn't have seen you then. Now I have, I might go back to Brierfield to buy them. You'd better go. I don't want anyone seeing us together and it getting back to your mother.'

'Definitely not! Thank you so much; I can't believe you came to see me.'

'I'd go a lot further than this to see you anytime if I could. But quickly, go. I've got a surprise for you on Sunday.'

'Oh, what is it?'

'Won't be a surprise if I tell you. You'll have to wait until Sunday.' Hurrying off, Lucy couldn't imagine what it could be, but she almost skipped home. A perfect end to the first day of her teaching career. As she walked home, though, she knew that she should commit this burgeoning relationship to God. Lucy didn't want to get deeply involved if it wasn't what God wanted for her life. She resolved to pray about it that night before anything else.

On arriving home, Lucy looked for her mother to tell her how her day had gone. However, Patsy said that she was out at the Ladies Circle at church and wouldn't be home until late, as they were having an afternoon tea to raise money for a village school in Africa.

Bursting to tell someone, Lucy decided to telephone Cynthia to see how she had fared with her first day at school. Cynthia's sisters had joined together to have a telephone put in the new school house as a wedding present, as they said they couldn't bear not to be able to talk to their sister. Lucy rang through to the exchange and asked to be connected to the Bolton number. She was soon connected, but it was Huw who answered.

'Hello, Bolton 614, Mr Roberts speaking,' he said.

'Huw, hello. It's Lucy Coombes. How did you and Cynthia get on with your first day at school?'

'It was good. Would you like to speak to Cynthia?'

'Yes, please.'

'I'll just get her.' Lucy waited, but could hear Huw shouting for Cynthia, who came to the telephone.

'Lucy, how good to hear from you. How was your day?'

'I had a lovely day. But you'll never guess what? Harry was waiting for me after school, just down the road.'

'Wasn't that a bit risky?'

'Yes, I kept looking around to see if anyone I knew was coming, but I think we were all right. He said that he's got a surprise for me on Sunday but wouldn't tell me what. I can't wait, or even imagine what it is.'

'You'll just have to be patient then. It's only six days to Sunday.'

'That's such a long time off,' moaned Lucy, but Cynthia only laughed.

'I'm surprised you're speaking out loud about this. What if your mother hears?'

'My mother's out for tea. I knew it was the only time that I could tell you.'

'You really like Harry, don't you?'

'Yes. I've never been interested in men before and I feel that I don't want to be interested in men ever again. If I can't have Harry, I don't want anybody else.'

'You have got it bad,' Cynthia laughed. 'I'll have to pray that all will be well for you both.'

'Yes, please, along with my prayers, too. I really have to try and concentrate on other things in my prayers now. They keep drifting to Harry.'

'You should try the "Jesus" prayer.'

'What's that?' asked Lucy.

'It's what the Desert Fathers used many years ago when trying to meditate. Every time their thoughts wandered, they would pray, "Lord Jesus

Christ, Son of God, have mercy on me, a sinner", and it would concentrate their thoughts again. The quicker version is "Jesus, have mercy".'

'I shall definitely have to try that,' Lucy said.

'I'd better go now, as I was making the tea.'

'Oh yes, how are the domestic skills coming along? How is it with no servants at your beck and call?'

'It'll take time,' laughed Cynthia in reply. 'Goodbye.'

'Goodbye,' replied Lucy, hanging up the receiver. She wandered into the kitchen and helped herself to a cup of tea from the pot which Mrs Ward always kept on the go. Lucy sat down in the chair by the fire and told Mrs Ward and Patsy about her day, and that she wouldn't need any lunches in the future.

Lucy went to her bedroom and sorted out her work for the next day, then lay on her bed remembering her meeting with Harry and wondering what the surprise would be.

Chapter 18

The first week of school went surprisingly well, apart from having to virtually shout at Tommy Earnshaw to go to his own class, as he wanted to stay with her longer than was necessary. Lucy gave him an old copy of Oliver Twist by Charles Dickens as a reward for all his hard labour. He was very pleased with the book and wanted to go back to his own class to show off his new acquisition.

Lucy was exhausted by the end of the week and was growing more feverish as the week went on, wondering what Harry's surprise could be. On Friday evening and Saturday morning, she prepared all her next weeks lessons and had finished them by 11am. Feeling restless, Lucy decided to go for a walk to Queen's Park, and decided to call on Granny Wall, who lived nearby on Queen's Park Road in a detached house, in an elevated position overlooking the park.

After a brisk walk round the park, admiring the beautiful flower beds that were always kept in immaculate condition by the gardeners, Lucy called in at her Granny's. Her maid opened the door, and welcomed her in, but said that Mrs Wall was out for the day and would she like a cup of tea? Lucy was surprised at that; her granny didn't usually work Saturdays, but she accepted the cup of tea. On arrival in the lounge, the maid left Lucy whilst she made the tea, which she brought in shortly afterwards, along with a slice of cake, which she knew was a favourite of Lucy's.

'Is there no one else in?' Lucy asked innocently, but desperately hoping that she would say that Harry was in.

'No, Miss, only Cook and me. Mr Marsden has gone home again now.'

'Oh, when did he go home?'

'He went to work on Wednesday, but as he was finishing his job at Brierfield that day, he went straight home from work Wednesday night.'

'Thank you.'

'I'll leave you to enjoy your tea, Miss.'

Lucy smiled and longed to ask if Harry was coming back but didn't dare. It would be too obvious a question, especially as she had turned up when Granny was out. It was all very mysterious and annoying. After she had finished her tea and cake, Lucy asked if she might use the bathroom, and then returned home. Her walk had not made her any less unsettled.

Sunday dawned and there was the usual household hurry to get to church. The sermon was on the topic of 'Be still, my soul.' Lucy knew that it was just for her. She had found it very hard to be calm and still all week.

On arrival home, after taking her hat and coat off, Lucy stayed in her room until Patsy called her into the dining room. As she walked in, the first person she saw was Harry, sat next to her mother, who was smiling away at him. He stood up instantly.

'Good afternoon, Miss Coombes,' he said.

'Oh, you may call her Lucy,' her mother said.

'Thank you. Lucy it is then,' Harry replied, with a light bow of his head.

'Harry has become such a good friend of William's,' her mother went on. 'He's brought William lots of orders for motor cars from every job he does. They see him arrive in the commercial vehicle he drives and want to know more. William is even thinking of giving him commission on each sale he recommends,' her mother laughed.

'Goodness!' replied Lucy. It was all she could manage, as her heart was still beating too fast and she couldn't think sensibly.

'Where is William?' asked Mr Coombes.

'Taking Miss Seeney and Miss Egar to their friend's house at Colne. Then he's going to collect them this evening,' his wife replied.

'Working on the Sabbath?' Mr Coombes asked.

'More a question of helping some dear friends, although he seems to be having to work many Sundays now, I'm afraid, with all these day trips. Freddie can't manage them all.' Whilst this conversation was going on, Lucy kept glancing at Harry and he returned her smiles, making sure her mother wasn't aware.

'Why couldn't he take them yesterday afternoon?' Edward Coombes asked.

'He went to the football match, and Freddie was busy with Granny Wall,' replied his wife.

'Yes, what was your mother up to yesterday?' said Edward. 'She just said she wanted a day out when I asked her.'

'That's all she said to me as well. She must be up to something.'

'I called round to see her yesterday after my walk in the park and she wasn't in, but the maid didn't say where she was,' said Lucy, coming out of her reverie.

Further discussion about Granny Wall was interrupted by William arriving home, so the lunch commenced. After eating, they all retired to the lounge for tea and coffee, and the chat was general. Mrs Coombes went upstairs, probably for a sleep, thought Lucy, and Mr Coombes was reading the paper, so William suggested that they went a walk. The three young people went out, but instead of a walk, they got in William's motor car and drove to Scott Park, which was at the other end of Burnley, up Manchester Road. Harry had never been there before, so was interested to see it, but in truth, he was just as excited about being with Lucy as she was about him. William decided to sit on a bench, whilst they wandered off on their own.

'Did you like my surprise?'

'I did! The best surprise I've had for a long time. How did you manage to get round my mother?'

'William finally told her the truth about his birthday, but it took her a long time to invite me round again. It was only when William kept telling her about the business deals he was doing because of me, that she completely thawed, but it's the first time I've been invited for Sunday lunch.'

'I'm so pleased.'

'Not as pleased as you'll be about what else I have to tell you. I've asked your father if I may court you.'

'You have? What did he say?'

'I started by saying that we had all got off on the wrong foot on William's birthday and although there was no idea of impropriety on my part, the longer I'd spent time with you on the journey home, the more I liked you, and that I wanted it to be more open before I said anything to you.'

'Did he object?'

'No, he agreed, but only if you wanted it. He didn't want me to force myself on you. He said that when you tell him that you are interested in me, then we can consider ourselves to be walking out together.'

'Oh, Harry, I want to go home now!'

'Now? Don't you want to spend time with me alone here, well, almost alone, apart from William, who's conveniently left us?'

'Yes, now. I want to go and tell my father that I want to be walking out with you officially. I've never wanted anything more in my life! William, William, we need to go home!' Lucy shouted.

'Whatever's the matter. Has something happened?'

'Yes, Father has agreed that I may walk out with Harry. Isn't that wonderful?'

'It's a relief, that's for sure, but why the rush?'

'He won't let Harry court me until I tell him that I'm happy about it. I need to tell him now. Come on, William, hurry up.'

Laughing, William pretended to dawdle back to the motor car, but Lucy was having none of it and dragged him along with her. As soon as they got in the house, Lucy ran up to her father, threw his paper to one side, hugged him and cried, 'Yes, yes, Father. I'm happy for Harry to court me.'

'Are you sure, Lucy? I don't want you to be unhappy or rush things.'

'I'm very sure, Father. Harry is the only man that I have ever been interested in, and I met many at college.'

'Good. You'd better go and tell your mother,' but before he'd finished the sentence, Lucy was off out of the door and upstairs to tell her mother, having to repeat how she felt about Harry.

'I'm really sorry, Lucy, but I'm going to have to go now,' said Harry. 'I have an early start tomorrow as I'm working in Yorkshire. My fame is spreading,' he laughed. Lucy was crestfallen but recovered quickly and said that she would walk him to the door.

'With your permission, Mr Coombes, may I take Lucy to visit my family next week? I've told them so much about her. I'm happy for William to come as well if you prefer.'

'Yes, I think for the first few times, it would be better if William came with you.'

'Thank you, Sir, goodnight.'

At the front door, Harry took hold of Lucy's hands, gazing into her eyes, then drew her forward, kissing her cheek lightly. Lucy shivered with delight and said a gentle goodbye. He promised to write to her from Yorkshire and would see her next Sunday, when she would meet his family in Clitheroe.

In the end, it wasn't William that accompanied her, it was Granny Wall. William had to help Freddie with a large group that wanted a trip out and Granny Wall wanted to meet Harry's family, with him having lived with her so many times. Lucy tried to find out where Granny Wall had been with Freddie, whilst they were on their way to Clitheroe, but she wouldn't tell. She said it was something to do with a work matter and it involved another person so she couldn't comment. Lucy was even more puzzled but knew she would get no further information from her granny, who could be stubborn when she wanted.

Lucy felt very nervous driving over to Clitheroe. It was the furthest she had ever driven on her own, but they arrived safely at Harry's house. Harry met her at the door and gave her a light kiss on the cheek, but then did the same to Granny Wall, who was as delighted as Lucy.

The house was a large detached one with a small side building, which was the surgery where the patients visited. Apart from the surgery, it looked quite like Granny Wall's house, Lucy thought. Lucy and Granny Wall went into the large hallway and Mrs Marsden came out to meet them.

'Miss Coombes, Mrs Wall, it is such a delight to meet you at last. Harry has talked about nothing else but you two ladies for months. Come into the lounge. Lunch won't be long, but Edward has had to go and visit a child with croup. He and Matthew take alternate weekends on duty. Much better than when he was on his own. He was never off duty,' she laughed. 'Do you need the bathroom? I know motoring can shake your bones up, or just a cup of tea whilst we wait?'

'Both,' said Granny Wall, so they were directed to the bathroom, whilst the maid went to bring the tea. They had only just finished their tea when Dr Marsden arrived back.

'Hello, hello, sorry I wasn't here to greet you, but croup's a tricky thing. You need to get steam into the child to relieve the spasm,' he explained.

'Oh, Edward, save the medical details for another time,' his wife chided.

'You'll get used to it, Lucy. Father discusses everything round the lunch table. Just be grateful it was croup today and not a bowel ailment,' said Harry laughing.

'I believe you are a teacher, Miss Coombes?'

'Oh, please call me Lucy. Yes, I trained at Owen's College in Manchester; they're calling it Manchester University now. My parents weren't keen at first, but Granny Wall talked them round.'

'I had to almost run away to train as a nurse because of my parents, but I'm glad I did, or I wouldn't have met my husband,' said Mrs Marsden. 'I believe you run a cotton mill, Mrs Wall? You are an enterprising family.'

'Yes, I took over the running of the mill when my husband died, but I had been helping him ever since Lucy's mother had gone to school, so it wasn't an out and out shock. I knew what was going on, fortunately.'

'Your father is in business, too, isn't he Lucy?' asked Dr Marsden.

'He has a matchstick factory and my brother used to work there, but he's opened a garage in Burnley, next door to my father's factory.'

'I've met your father at the Mens' Breakfasts at church, but we never really had time to talk, and because of my job, I wasn't a regular attender. Harry went more than me.'

'What about having a motor car, Father? Have you thought any more about it yet?' asked Harry.

'No, I like my pony and trap. It's been good enough for me all these years.'

'I wish he'd buy one; sometimes he gets drenched in the trap,' said Mrs Marsden. 'Matthew Fletcher, our son-in-law, is thinking of buying one, but we haven't a garage in Clitheroe yet, so he's going to go and see your brother soon.'

'The other doctor in the town has one, so I hope you both get one,' said Harry. 'You'd be much safer, and quicker getting to your patients for that matter.'

'I'm too old to learn how to drive,' Dr Marsden groaned. 'Leave me be, Harry,' and Harry took the hint and changed the subject.

After the meal, they spent time chatting and getting to know each other and eventually, although she didn't want to leave Harry, Lucy said that she must be getting home, as she wasn't confident driving in the dark yet. Harry suggested that they come again when Granny Marsden was there, but Granny Wall intervened.

'I've a better idea. Why don't you bring Granny Marsden over to my house next Sunday, Harry, and Lucy can come too and we can all meet?'

'Yes, I can do that. Granny Marsden will like a trip out, I'm sure. What time shall we come?'

'Come straight after church. We'll eat about two pm, if that's satisfactory?'

'That'll be perfect,' said Harry. 'Until next Sunday, then.' He gave Lucy a peck on the cheek, but Granny Wall proffered her cheek as well.

'Don't leave me out; I don't often get a kiss nowadays,' she laughed.

'Oh, Granny, I often kiss you,' said Lucy.

'I mean from a handsome young man, Lucy; you are family,' she chuckled. 'Come on, then, let's be going.' As they were getting in the motor car, Dr Marsden was also getting his coat on; another case had been rung through from Clitheroe workhouse. Mrs Marsden stood on the doorstep, waving them all off, saying to Harry how much she approved of Lucy.

'I told you that you'd like her, but I'm glad you do. I couldn't stand it if the two most important women in my life didn't get on.'

'Only two most important women in your life? Don't let Granny Marsden hear you say that,' Mrs Marsden chuckled, as they went inside.

Chapter 19

The weeks up to Christmas went quickly for Lucy and William, as his wedding was getting closer. They went for a few trips over to Manchester to see Laura and for fittings for wedding finery. Lucy was concerned that Laura's parents wouldn't be able to afford new clothes for all the family, so she gave Mrs Carter one of the little purses that Granny Wall had given her, still with the ten guineas intact. Mrs Carter tried to refuse, but Lucy insisted. If there was any money left, it would help towards them all having to have a day off on a work day, for which they would receive no pay.

Lucy, Cynthia, Bessie, and Agnes were all due to be bridesmaids, and Harry was to be the best man, which Lucy was grateful for as it meant that he would be at the wedding, unlike for Cynthia's wedding. Bessie was making Laura's wedding dress under Brenda Smith's instruction, and also making all the bridesmaids' dresses and Mrs Carter's outfit. On one trip to Manchester, Mrs Coombes came along and met the rest of the Carter family, whilst going for a fitting for her new outfit, which was being made with the others at Mrs Smith's dress shop. At the same time, she booked the catering for the wedding breakfast.

After a hectic week of Nativity plays and carol concerts at school and at church, Lucy was ready for the wedding, and glad to have two weeks' holiday from school, as she was exhausted. The Coombes family, Granny Wall, Harry, and all the servants from both the Coombes' and Wall's households, went over in the Daimler charabanc to Manchester the night before the wedding. They were staying overnight to make it easier to get ready for the wedding. Freddie was bringing Miss Seeney and Miss Egar over in the morning in Harry's motor car, so that the newly-weds could go away on honeymoon in it. The two teacher friends would return with the rest of the family in the charabanc.

In the end, after looking at the Mission Hall, Mrs Coombes realised that it would be very hard to prepare food and serve it in the same room as the wedding was taking place, as there would be nowhere for the guests to go whilst they were setting the tables to change it from a church to a dining hall. So she had hired the local St John's Parish church hall for the meal.

Finally, everybody was ready, and looking resplendent in all their wedding finery. Both Mr Carter and the boys had new suits, and Mrs Carter had a smart two-piece with a long jacket that would last her for years for Sunday best, she told her husband. William and Mrs Coombes had new outfits, but Harry and Mr Coombes just wore their best suits with smart new cravats. All the men wore top hats, although Mr Carter took his off at the earliest opportunity, as he felt uncomfortable. Children from the school where Laura had been teaching were lined up outside to wish their teacher a happy wedding day.

The church organist started playing the Wedding March and Mr Carter led Laura down the aisle made between the chairs. Her dress was unusual. Bessie had copied it from a journal that Mrs Smith had received from London. The gown was in fitted white satin, with a frill round the bottom, and it had a small white cape, edged with swans down round the neck to wear over it, with it being a winter wedding. She wore no veil, but just a circlet of silk flowers surrounding her head, which looked very effective, her hair being neatly braided for the occasion. Mrs Coombes was pleased to notice that she wore her little cross and chain that they had bought her that very first Christmas. The bridesmaids wore fine woollen dresses in varying colours, also with ruffles round the bottom, with long puffed sleeves and matching bonnets.

Mr Carter said that he gave his daughter to be married, and sat back with Mrs Carter. Nobody objected to their union, so the minister performed the marriage ceremony and gave a homily based on 1 Corinthians chapter 13, on the theme of love. They were pronounced man and wife and everybody cheered. After the register was signed, the families and friends walked over to the Parish church hall, ready for the meal. The caterers had decorated the whole building. There were sprigs of holly and ivy, candles burning on each table and window sill, and even a Christmas tree twinkling in the corner, full of tinsel, baubles, and candles.

Because of the time of year, Mrs Coombes had opted for a full Christmas dinner for the wedding breakfast, even down to a flaming Christmas pudding. It was also Laura's 21st birthday, so there was a birthday cake as well, and Laura was made to blow the candles out, whilst everybody sang to her and gave her good wishes. As soon as the food was cleared away and the wedding cake cut, everyone received a box containing a piece of birthday cake, a piece of wedding cake, a tangerine, and a mince pie, just in case they were hungry when they got home!

Before everybody left, Granny Wall said that she wanted to make an announcement that affected most people in the room. She asked for Mr Carter to come and stand beside her. Lucy was mystified.

'My chief tackler is retiring this week, and I've persuaded Mr Carter to come and move his whole family to Burnley and for him to be my new tackler.' There was a stunned silence, whilst everybody digested this surprising news, and then Albert broke the silence.

'Does that mean I can leave school and go and work with Laura's new husband in his garage? After all, I am twelve now.'

'Come and see me later, young man. I think you're a bit young yet, but maybe soon,' William promised.

'Did you know about this?' Lucy asked Laura.

'Not until Monday morning, when no one went to work.'

'I was worried about the whole family having to lose a day's pay for the wedding, but William insisted on marrying on your birthday.'

'Your granny has paid my father from yesterday, even though he won't start work until the day after Boxing Day, so he was able to give his notice and finish last Friday. They're moving tomorrow, as the house belongs to the mill.'

'Well, I never, that is a surprise. We knew Granny Wall had been up to something connected with work, but nobody seemed to know what. I'm so glad your family will be coming to live near you.'

'Yes, and mum has got a job in the mill as a weaver, too.'

'Where will they live?'

'Apparently, your granny has found them a house on Albion Street, which isn't far from the mill.'

'Good. She has been busy behind our backs!'

'Where's my wife?' shouted William, interrupting the chat that Lucy and Laura were having. 'It's time we were going. We've a long way to go today.' All was in a flurry then as each person wanted to thank the bride and groom and wish them well, but eventually the bridal couple managed to get away. They were staying in Harrogate that night, but then going to the hotel where they had all stayed in the summer, in Scarborough, for two weeks.

Freddie was chivvying all the Burnley contingent to get into the charabanc, as it was already dark and snow was threatened. Fortunately, there was no snow and they all got home safely. In the darkness of the charabanc, Harry held Lucy's hand all the way home, bringing it to his lips several times. Lucy thought she could never be more happy.

It had been decided that William and Laura would start their married life living with his parents, until they decided where to buy a house. The day after the wedding, Lucy got Freddie to take her and Patsy up to Albion Street, the Carters' new house, where they lit the range fire and took a large pan of broth and dumplings that Mrs Ward had made, along with a rich fruit cake, two loaves of soft bread, some butter, and a large cheese, to set them up until they found their bearings, Mrs Ward said. Mrs Coombes had sent a bouquet of flowers, already in a vase, and some soap and lavender sachets, to welcome the family. Freddie had gone to pick them up in the charabanc, so that all their furniture could be brought as well. Lucy waited until the family had arrived and the furniture was all inside, before she and Patsy got a lift home with Freddie.

Later in the day, Lucy and her mother rearranged William's bedroom ready for the newly-weds' return in the New Year. Several of the wedding presents had been bed linen and towels, so these were put ready for use. By teatime, Lucy was exhausted but happy, and went to bed early that night.

Granny Wall came round for dinner the next evening. Mrs Coombes chided her mother for keeping the secret about the Carters coming to Burnley.

'I couldn't say anything as he was very unsure what to do. It means a lot to uproot a whole family, and there was Bessie to consider.'

'Yes, what's happening with Bessie?' Mrs Coombes asked.

'She's staying at the dress shop. On her days off, she will go to either her Granny Carter's or her Granny Whittaker's. Or she could catch the train to Burnley if she had longer than a day off. She's coming over to Burnley for Christmas.'

'It'll seem funny without William on Christmas Day even though Freddie is coming to have Christmas Dinner with us,' Lucy said, 'and the Carters will be in a new house, without Laura, so it will be strange for them, too. Why don't we invite them all over to have Christmas Dinner with us?'

'I'm not sure Mrs Ward would like it,' started Mrs Coombes.

'Nonsense,' said Granny Wall. 'She'll relish it!' And so she did! It was a little crowded round the table, even with the extensions, and in the end all the children had to be seated at a smaller table, but everyone thoroughly enjoyed themselves. Lucy especially enjoyed her task of going and buying extra presents for the Carters, and she spent a lovely day in town shopping, with occasional stops for hot chocolate. Her only sadness was that Harry didn't arrive until the evening of Christmas Day, as he wanted to spend the lunch time with all his nieces and nephews, but it was worth the wait she told him. Little did she realise that she had just made the biggest understatement of her life.

They were sat in the lounge and the servants, Freddie and the Carters had all gone home. Mrs Coombes brought in the Christmas cake and a pot of tea and announced it was Christmas Wishes time. Lucy explained to Harry what that meant, but he just grinned at her.

They went round the room saying what their Christmas Wish was and Harry was the last person to say anything. He stood up, walked over to Lucy, pulled her to her feet, and said, 'My Christmas Wish is that Miss Lucy Coombes would do me the honour of becoming my wife.' Lucy gasped and stared first at Harry, then her parents, but they both seemed to be beaming.

'Yes, oh yes! I'd love to be your wife,' Lucy eventually managed to say.

'Hurrah, at long last!' said Granny Wall, and everybody laughed.

'How did you know about the Christmas Wishes, Harry?'

'When I asked your father if I may marry you, and that I wanted to propose to you on Christmas Day, he suggested that I made it my Christmas Wish and told me of your tradition. I do have a ring with me. It was my granny's, but her arthritis is too bad for her to wear rings now. She wanted you to have it, but if you prefer a more modern setting, I can buy one for you as soon as the shops are open again.' He reached in his pocket and drew out a small box, opening it to show to Lucy. It was a hooped band of five diamonds. Lucy tried it on and it fitted perfectly. 'I love this ring; it looks lovely, and I also love it because it was your granny's,' she said, twisting her hand so that the diamonds sparkled in the light. 'Please thank your granny for me. No, I will write her a note and you can take it.'

Just then, the telephone rang. Mr Coombes went to answer it, muttering about who it could be on Christmas Day? But he came back with a smile on his face. It was William and Laura, ringing up to wish everyone Happy Christmas, but also to tell what their Christmas Wishes were. William's was to be the best husband ever and Laura's was to be the best wife ever. Lucy ran to the telephone.

'Laura, guess what Harry's Christmas Wish is? To marry me!'

'Congratulations! I didn't think it would be long before you were married. Have you set a date?'

'Hardly, I've only been engaged ten minutes!' she laughed. 'Don't worry, you'll be the first to know.'

'Well, I can't be a bridesmaid for you.'

'Why ever not?'

'Because I'm married now, so I'll have to be a Dame of Honour, like Cynthia.'

'Oh, of course. As long as you're with me, that's all that matters,' replied Lucy. Lucy turned to find Granny Wall at her elbow. 'Do you want me, Granny?'

'No, I want to speak to your brother or his wife.' Lucy handed the receiver over to Granny Wall, whilst Laura handed their receiver over to William.

'Well now, grandson,' she said, 'do you remember two years ago when we did Christmas Wishes and you said that you wanted to start a garage, but you had another wish which you couldn't talk about?'

'Yes, I do. It was that I wanted to marry Laura, even though I'd only just met her.'

'I know that. Well, I've just done the same. For my Christmas Wish, I said that I would give more to charity. But I also had another one which I couldn't talk about.'

'Oh, Granny,' said William, 'you've not fallen in love like I did, have you? You're not going to get married again, are you?'

'Certainly not! I've decided to move house.'

'That's lovely. Where to?'

'I've got my eye on a new house up Manchester Road. It'll be nearer to the mill.'

'So that's your secret wish this Christmas?'

'No. I'm giving my house to you and Laura. That's my secret Christmas wish.'

William was silent for a while, then said, 'You can't just give us a house, Granny. That's too much.'

'Why not? You'll get it one day when I'm gone, and the mill, but you probably don't want that. I told you that I'd give you your wedding present after Christmas and this is it. My house.'

'What about Lucy? It isn't fair on her.'

'Don't you worry about Lucy. She'll want for nothing.'

'Well, what can I say, Granny? "Thank you" seems so small a word at a time like this.'

'It'll be easier to start married life in your own home; I've always believed that.'

'Granny, Laura wants to speak to you, although she is crying.'

'Granny Wall, thank you so much,' said a tearful Laura. 'I will cherish your house. What a day it has been. Lucy and Harry getting engaged and now this. Oh, William wants to speak again. Thank you.'

'When are you thinking of moving, Granny?'

'Give me chance, lad. I haven't bought anywhere yet. You can move in with me if you want to, but I'd prefer you to wait until I've moved!'

'Yes, we'll wait. Just take your time,' said William. 'Oh, we have to go now. The hotel manager has been letting us use his telephone and he needs it now. Goodbye, everyone!', and he rang off. Lucy and Granny looked at each other, smiled, and then went back into the lounge, to tell everybody what had just happened. *It was a perfect ending to a perfect day*, Lucy said sleepily as she went to bed, admiring her ring, to dream of Harry, yet again.

Chapter 20

On Boxing Day, normally it would be a very quiet day with no servants, but Harry's parents had asked that the Coombes went over to visit them and have lunch, so that they could all meet. Harry came to collect Lucy, her parents, and Granny Wall, and after introductions had been made, a massive buffet lunch was spread out in the dining room. After they had all partaken of the festive food, they sat down and talked about the wedding plans.

'I don't want a long engagement; I want to get married soon,' Harry said, which made Lucy blush, but he continued. 'I know that it is important for Lucy to complete her full year as a teacher so I suggest we get married as soon as the school term is over. Will that be early July, Lucy? Does Brierfield have the same Burnley Fair holidays?'

'Yes. I'll be finished on Friday the first of July.'

'Shall we get married on the second of July then?'

'Oh, no, please,' said Mrs Coombes. 'Give us a week to get ready. What about the ninth of July, or maybe even the sixteenth?'

'The ninth will be fine,' Harry said. 'No later.'

'The ninth it is,' said Lucy, grinning. *Who would have believed that all three girls would be married within a year*, Lucy thought to herself. *When they had started the course, marriage was the last thing on their minds.*

'We'll find a house somewhere to rent for the time being,' Harry said. 'Do you mind where we live, Lucy?'

'No, not at all. I presume we'll be living in Clitheroe? It's usual for the bride to go to the groom's town when she marries, isn't it? I suppose it will depend on the best place for your work.'

'I can live anywhere, as long as I have an out-building where I can do my carpentry.'

'What about the old farmhouse at Barrow?' asked Granny Marsden.

'What about it?' asked Harry.

'Would that do for your first home?'

'What about the tenants?'

'They've just left, but I thought it would make a good first home for you and Lucy.'

'Where's Barrow?' asked Lucy.

'It's on the road between Whalley and Clitheroe,' replied Harry. 'The farm belonged to my granny's grandparents, who were farmers. Most of the farmland was sold to a builder when none of the family wanted to continue farming, and he built all the terraced houses further up the road. It would be perfect, as there are still lots of out-buildings, barns and the like, so I'd have plenty of room for my woodworking tools.'

'What do you think, Lucy?' asked Granny Marsden.

'It sounds lovely. How big is it?'

'It's nowhere as big as this house,' Dr Marsden laughed.

'Good,' said Lucy. 'I wouldn't want a big house.'

'It's a good size,' Harry said. It's got four bedrooms, plus two attics, a large kitchen, a scullery and walk-in pantry, a large parlour, and a small breakfast room.'

'I also put a bathroom in just before the last tenants moved in,' Granny Marsden added.

'So would we be able to rent it from you, Granny Marsden?' Harry asked.

'Rent it? Certainly not! You can have it. Blame your Granny, Lucy. It was her that gave me the idea.'

'My Granny? Granny Wall?'

'Yes, me,' said Granny Wall, laughing. 'I was telling Harry's grandmother what my secret plans were for William and Laura to have my house, and she said that was a good idea, and she'd do the same for Harry when the time came.'

'But you've got four grandchildren, Mrs Marsden, not just two, like Granny Wall. It wouldn't be fair to the others,' said Lucy.

'Oh, Lucy, don't worry your pretty little head about the others. They'll all be well catered for,' said Granny Marsden. 'I've plenty more properties in my possession. Besides, it's already been decided that Betsy and Matthew will inherit this house, when the time comes.'

'Trying to get rid of me, Mother?' said Dr Marsden.

'Not at all, and I wish you a long life, Son,' she replied. 'Harry, why don't you and Lucy drive out and take a look before it goes dark? I haven't got the bunch of keys with me, but you could look through the windows and the out-houses will probably be unlocked.'

'Good idea, Granny. Come on then, Lucy.'

'Can I come?' asked Granny Wall, never one to miss out on an occasion.

'And I,' added Mrs Coombes. 'I'd love to see where Lucy might be living.'

So, in the end, Harry took Lucy, Granny Wall, and Lucy's parents, all squashed up together, in Harry's commercial vehicle, which had no seats in the back. Lucy loved the house. It was facing the main road and directly opposite a school and church, which just happened to belong to the Congregational church.

'Oh, look,' said Mrs Coombes, 'a church and school right opposite. The children won't have far to go to school, when they come along,' which made both Harry and Lucy blush!

Lucy looked at the house; it was very symmetrical and had large windows, with a roof that was in a good condition. She peered through the windows and, although the rooms were empty of furniture, Lucy could see that they were of large proportions. Harry was more interested in the out-buildings and earmarked which ones he would use for his workshop.

'Look, there's even a chicken run, Lucy,' Harry said excitedly. 'We could have our own eggs!' At this, everybody laughed, but as it was growing dark, they decided to get back to Harry's house.

After a lot of conversation about the house, Lucy, Granny Wall, and her parents went home, but not before Mrs Marsden had pressed another meal on to them. Thanking her for a lovely day, Mrs Coombes said that they must come round to Burnley for a meal in the New Year, which they promised to do.

After dropping Granny Wall off at home, Harry took Lucy and her parents home. She invited him to stay for hot chocolate, but he wanted to get back home to his family. Lucy still had her coat on, so she walked to the door with him. As he was leaving, he pulled Lucy towards him and held her close, then kissed her on her lips. Just a gentle one at first, but the second was deep and lingering. Lucy moved away, breathless, unable to understand the sensations that were going on in her body. Her body seemed to be yearning for something, but she didn't know what. Now she could understand why Harry didn't want to wait to get married. Neither did she!

'I think I'd better go,' said Harry, in a husky voice, 'or I might forget myself.'

'I think you'd better,' said Lucy, 'or I might let you forget yourself,' at which he laughed, and left her quickly, promising to telephone on the next day.

Laura and William returned from Scarborough full of joy and appeared very happy together. They had lots of plans for their new home and still couldn't believe Granny Wall's generosity, but William told Lucy privately that he was relieved about Harry's granny having offered them a home too, as it made him feel less guilty.

'I don't know why you worry, William. Everything goes to the son, that's just the way it is, but it works both ways, and Harry's granny wants us to be happy too in our own home. So, don't worry; I'm not going to be out on the streets just yet,' Lucy laughed.

Granny Wall bought a house just above the Railway station on Manchester Road. It was smaller than her old house, and had a much smaller garden, but she was very happy with it. The double move took place in mid-February. Granny Wall had taken her staff with her, except for Mitchell, the gardener, so Laura and William just employed a young woman who was a maid of all work, although they had someone coming in once a week for cleaning and laundry. They kept Mitchell on, as William said he didn't want to spend his time off looking after the garden. William loved looking at all the trees across the road in Queens Park too, besides the ones in their own garden. Laura quite liked making meals for them sometimes when young Edie was off duty. Laura had always had to cook if she was home first, so it was no trouble.

The same couldn't be said for Lucy. She had never made a meal in her life and knew even less about running a home or directing servants. During the following months, she spent hours with Mrs Ward in the kitchen, learning to cook. Patsy couldn't help but laugh at Lucy's disasters, but Lucy was determined to succeed. They weren't intending to have any servants when they married, apart from a cleaner, so she needed to be able to do most of the jobs in a house. Her mother was proud of her attempts and the fact that she was following the proper pathway for a young woman, she kept insisting, which in Mrs Coombes' eyes, was still marriage and children.

Over the next few months, Harry and Lucy weren't able to spend a lot of time together – he was busy with his work and she was busy teaching – but they spent time on the telephone when they couldn't meet, and also wrote letters, which Lucy stored in her special locked box.

Lucy had been honest with Mr Treadwell and told him that she was engaged and would be leaving at the end of summer term. He didn't express surprise and Lucy knew that he would probably replace her with a man, who wouldn't have to leave if he married.

Easter was early that year, Easter Sunday being on March 27th, so it was colder than usual, but it didn't detract from the enjoyment. It was a special time for both Harry's and Lucy's families as they rejoiced that Jesus had risen from the dead, and they partook of traditions special to that time. Harry had never seen egg-rolling, so he was especially excited with that, and was like a child himself, wanting to join in, much to Lucy's delight.

Lucy spent a lot of time with Laura, especially when William was at the football match or working on a Saturday, and they loved to walk into town and shop and go for a meal together. One Saturday at the end of May, they got Freddie to drive them over to Cynthia's house in Bolton, as Lucy and Laura weren't keen to drive so far.

Cynthia was delighted to see them and showed them round the house proudly. Huw was out on a cycling trip, so it was a good day to come, Cynthia had told them, laughing.

'William is working,' Laura laughed. 'That's why we could have a day out.'

It was just like old times and the three girls chatted about everything under the sun, laughing and joking. As they were almost ready to go, Cynthia said that she had something to tell them before they went. Lucy and Laura sat down again, to listen to what Cynthia had to say.

'I'm expecting a baby,' she said shyly.

'How wonderful!' said Lucy. 'When is it due?'

'It will be due at Christmas,' Cynthia laughed.

'You'll have to call it Christabel or Noel, then,' Lucy quipped. 'I hope you'll still fit in your Dame of Honour dress,' she added.

'I should be all right. That's why I was relieved when you suggested that our dresses were gathered under the bust. It will hide my secret,' said Cynthia.

'So when will you give up teaching?' Lucy asked.

'At the end of term. I don't want to be still teaching when it's obvious and the children start asking questions!'

'Well, we'd better be going,' Laura said. 'I have to get William's tea tonight. Edie is going to meet her new in-laws-to-be, but, knowing Edie, she'll have left a casserole ready in the oven.' The girls chatted happily all the way home and when Freddie had dropped Laura off, he took Lucy home. As they were driving, Lucy thought about Cynthia's news. Laura had gone very quiet when it was announced, and Lucy wondered if perhaps Laura was

151

possibly expecting but it was too soon to know. That led to thoughts that by this time next year, she might also be having a baby. It was a scary thought. A lot had to happen before then, but now she was home, all thoughts of babies had to be forgotten for a time as her life took over. However, she did buy some white baby wool and started knitting a fine two-ply circular shawl for Cynthia's baby, for the christening.

During May, the country was saddened when they learnt of the death of King Edward VII, and he was deeply mourned. The new King, George V, wasn't having his Coronation until the following year, so Lucy was glad that it wouldn't interfere with the date of her wedding. She didn't want to share her day, but then felt guilty about her selfishness.

The wedding drew nearer and many preparations were being put into place, but before the wedding it was Lucy's 21st birthday on Sunday, June 12th. With it being so near the wedding, the family had decided that they wouldn't hold a party as they had done for William, as the same people would be coming to the wedding. Instead they had a meal in the private rooms of the Cross Keys Hotel. They invited all their family and the Carters, and Harry's family, plus close friends from church, so they were a large party. As it was so near her wedding, Lucy told everyone not to buy her any presents. However, some people did buy them, especially her parents. As she was about to set off for church prior to the birthday lunch, she noticed a small new motor car outside the house that hadn't been there the night before.

'Happy 21st Birthday, Lucy,' said her father. 'This is your motor car.'

'For me? I didn't expect you to buy me a motor car. You have all the expense of the wedding.'

'You didn't expect me to treat my children differently, did you?' he asked gently. 'Besides, you'll need a motor car when you are married so that you can come and visit us when Harry is working.'

'I much prefer this model to William's motor car. It's much smaller and I like that there are proper doors and a top so that I don't get wet or cold! Thank you, Father and Mother. You are so kind.'

'You are welcome. Are you going to drive it to church?'

'No, I think I'll wait until we are going to the hotel and let Harry drive with me for the first time,' she laughed. They waited for William to arrive to drive them down to church, and Lucy thanked William for his choice of motor car for her.

As soon as Harry arrived, she showed him the motor car and together they drove slowly down to the hotel, to let Lucy get used to driving her own motor car. The meal was a success, and it was only when they got home that Harry gave her a present. It was a necklace with a single diamond, which she put on immediately.

'I thought you could wear this on our wedding day,' he said softly.

'I will wear it now, and on our wedding day, and forever more,' she promised.

'Well, only until I buy you another necklace. Then you'll have to take it off.'

'Harry, I don't want lots of necklaces. I just want you. So this necklace is enough for ever.'

'I think you must be the only woman in Christendom that has actually uttered those words,' Harry said. 'Not wanting jewellery? I knew I'd found a good wife when I first met you, but I didn't know how good then,' he teased.

'So that's why Laura and William bought me a large jewellery box for my birthday? They're pre-empting all the jewellery you are going to buy me,' laughed Lucy.

'Correct. We colluded, I'm afraid. There are some other things I have got you, but you'll have to come to the house to see them.'

'Oh, what are they?'

'You'll have to wait and see,' Harry laughed, as he got in his motor vehicle and left for home.

It was two weeks before she had a chance to find out what else Harry had got for her. They were going to Harry's parents for tea and called at the house on their way. Harry let them in with the key and Lucy gasped as she saw that there was a lot of furniture in the house. There was a large oak table and six chairs in the parlour, and another large table for the kitchen, but in pine this time, with matching chairs. There were sideboards also in the kitchen and the breakfast room.

'Come upstairs,' he urged.

'Harry, we're not married yet!'

'Don't worry, I'm not about to ravish you. I want to show you the bedroom furniture.' He led her upstairs and Lucy looked first at the large wardrobe that he had made, but then her glance went to the large bed which dominated the bedroom they had chosen. The headboard had been intricately carved and included their two sets of initials, intertwined. He must have spent hours working on it, Lucy thought.

Harry came up behind her, taking hold of her and said gently, 'Not long now until I make you my own. I can't wait.'

'Neither can I,' replied Lucy, in an even quieter voice. They kissed passionately but drew apart quickly when they heard a voice downstairs.

'Hello, Harry? Are you here? I saw your vehicle.'

It was Matthew Fletcher, Harry's brother-in-law. Lucy and Harry laughed and ran downstairs together, holding hands. Matthew looked at them a little suspiciously.

'You can take that look of your face, Matthew. It's not what you are thinking. I was just showing Lucy all the furniture I've made for our house.'

'And do you approve, Lucy?' asked Matthew.

'I do. I don't know how he's had time to earn a living with all this work.'

'Oh, I can tell you how he does it. He just dumps his special customers and leaves them high and dry to concentrate on your furniture.'

'Really?' said Lucy, her eyes wide.

'Take no notice of Matthew,' said Harry. 'He's just being sarcastic. He's asked me to make some new shelves for the boys' bedrooms, and I haven't got round to doing them yet. Now I've finished all this furniture, I'll make a start this week, I promise.'

'I won't hold my breath,' laughed Matthew. 'You'll probably think of something else that you just have to make for Lucy.'

'There's nothing else I want, thank you,' said Lucy primly, and the two men laughed.

'We'd better be getting home or Mother will send the search party out,' Harry said.

'Yes, and I'd better get on with my visit. The sick won't wait. See you at the wedding, Lucy. Not long now.'

'No, not long now,' Lucy breathed deeply as she said it. It was perhaps as well that the wedding was soon, because if Matthew hadn't disturbed them, she didn't know what would have happened. Well, perhaps she did know what might have happened, even if she wasn't quite sure of the exact details, and that scared her. How could she have lived with herself if she had pre-empted her wedding vows? Thank God Matthew came!

They were soon at Harry's house and with only two weeks to go, discussions about the wedding were the main topic of conversation. Lucy had to tear herself away from Harry that day, but knew she would be kept busy with finishing the school term, and the days to her wedding would fly by.

On her last day at school, the children all said 'goodbye' and the staff gave her a cut glass vase as a wedding present, for which she thanked them. Mr Treadwell told her that he had employed another lady for her class.

'Another lady? I thought you'd have preferred a man?' she replied.

'No, I was against lady teachers – I won't pretend otherwise – but you have shown me that with the youngest children, a lady can bring out the best in them. As good a teacher as Mr Procter is, the children have responded better to you, I think because they have been used to being at home with their mothers. So, you have changed my mind.'

'I'm glad about that. I have really enjoyed my time working here and thank you for the opportunity.'

'If at any time you need a reference in the future, please don't hesitate to use my name.'

'That's very kind of you, Mr Treadwell, but I don't think I'm likely to teach again. It's marriage and motherhood for me now, as my mother would say. Besides, married teachers aren't allowed to stay in post or I would have done.'

'That is true, but someday things might change. I said I would never employ a lady teacher and I've just appointed a second one. The times are changing, Miss Coombes.'

'They certainly are. Thank you and goodbye,' said Lucy, as she left the school, feeling a little sad to be leaving her teaching career behind her, but so very excited about her new role as a wife. It was only one more week!

Chapter 21

Bessie had taken a week's holiday from her work so that she could attend the wedding and finish any last minute preparations for the wedding clothes, and help to dress the bride and bridesmaids. She was also looking forward to staying with her family for a week. Laura collected her the morning of the wedding and took her to Lucy's house.

Lucy had peered out of the window on the morning of the wedding and it was pouring with rain. Her heart sank but she knew that traditionally, at Burnley Fair weeks, it often rained the whole fortnight. Going to the bathroom at the start of her special day, Lucy could only pray that it stopped raining later.

Patsy arrived with a cup of tea and a slice of toast.

'Oh, Patsy, I couldn't eat a thing; I'm too nervous.'

'Well, Miss, your mother said that you'd say that but I was to insist, as you'll need your strength to get through the day, and she doesn't want you fainting at the altar.'

'All right, I'll try my best,' replied Lucy, nibbling at the toast. 'The weather's not good.'

'No, Miss, but it might brighten up later.'

'I certainly hope so. I think I'll have my bath now, but keep my dressing gown on.'

'Right you are, Miss. Shall I help you?'

'No thanks, Patsy. I'm going to have to get used to fending for myself, aren't I? I won't be having servants at my new house.'

'However will you manage?'

'Like many other women before me have managed. I'll just get on with it. It'll give me something to do now, as I won't be teaching.'

'That's true. I bet you'll miss those little ones at the school, but never mind, you'll soon be having some little ones of your own,' said Patsy.

'Not too soon, I hope,' Lucy replied. 'I'd like to enjoy being married first.'

'We don't have a choice, though, do we?' Patsy said.

'Not really. Now, I must have my bath.' Patsy left the room and Lucy sank into the deep bath of hot water, to which she'd added some special bath salts, luxuriating in this last bath at her parents' home. For the last few days, everything she did was 'the last time', and she had become quite maudlin.

Even though she couldn't wait to marry Harry, it was still sad to be leaving her parents, and all that was familiar to her.

When Bessie and Laura arrived, they came straight into Lucy's bedroom. Bessie had Lucy's dress ready to help dress her, together with Laura. Lucy had surprised everybody by not having a brand new dress but asked if she could wear her mother's wedding dress. Lucy had always admired the dress on the formal photograph of her parents' wedding, that was at the top of the staircase. Her mother had been delighted. Although it was a little old-fashioned, being made of lace rather than satin or velvet, it suited Lucy perfectly. Bessie had made only a few alterations, making it a little more modern looking, with the addition of trimmings and a shorter hemline, in line with current fashion. The dress had a high neck which showed Harry's necklace off perfectly. Lucy wore the same veil and headdress as her mother too, wearing her hair up off her face in a bun.

Lucy's mother came into the room when they had all finished.

'You look radiant, Lucy,' Mrs Coombes said, with a tear in her eye.

'Thank you, Mother. Has Cynthia arrived?'

'Yes, she's just getting changed in William's old bedroom.'

'Good. And Harry's nieces?'

'Yes, all four of them are in my bedroom. Stop worrying; everything is well organised,' her mother chided. 'I'm going to go to church now with the bridesmaids. Your father is waiting for you downstairs.'

'Thank you, Mother. Thank you for everything. I'll see you at the church.' When they'd all left the room, Lucy let out a deep sigh. This was it then. She was getting married. Unable to kneel down, due to her wedding finery, Lucy closed her eyes and said a simple prayer.

'Father God, thank you that this is my wedding day and you have led me to Harry. I pray that I will be a good wife and that I will do everything that is full of grace and honesty, according to your will. Bless me, Lord, today and every day in the future. Amen.'

Opening her eyes, Lucy took a deep breath, opened the door, and started to descend the staircase to meet her father, who was standing near the front door. She paused to look at the photograph of her parents on their wedding day and then went towards her father.

'You look beautiful. Just like your mother did on our wedding day,' he said, with a gentle expression on his face that Lucy rarely saw.

'Thank you. Is it still raining?'

'Yes and no,' he replied. 'It's not raining just at this moment, but it has been on and off for the last hour. Let's get going whilst it is still fine.'

They walked outside together and it was obvious that it had only just stopped raining. Droplets of rain were glistening everywhere on the trees and grass. Lucy had decided to go to her wedding in the old Hansom cab, rather than a motorised vehicle. As she was getting into the Hansom cab, she looked up and exclaimed.

'There's a rainbow! How lovely. God is reminding me that he won't forget me.'

'He certainly is,' said her father, as he helped her into the carriage. The journey into Burnley centre went without a hitch and they were soon at the church.

Mr Coombes led Lucy up the steps and into the entrance to the church. The bridesmaids and Dames of Honour were all waiting. Laura and Cynthia were watching over Harry's excited nieces, Maud, Lizzie, Alice, and Elsie. Their brothers, young Edward and Matthew, had proudly shown all the guests to their places, and John, Harry's brother, was acting as the best man. The bride's attendants were all dressed in the same style, but each had a different colour of dress.

'I've just seen a rainbow on my way here,' Lucy said excitedly, 'and you look like my own private rainbow in your lovely dresses!' The wedding music changed and it was time to walk down the aisle. Lucy and her father went first, followed by the girls. Lucy let go of her father's arm and turned to look at Harry. Her heart missed a beat as he gave her an intense look, and then the service started.

'Dearly beloved, we are gathered here today, to witness....' the minister read the words of the wedding service and Lucy could hardly remember them afterwards. But eventually, they were declared man and wife, and Harry was given permission to kiss the bride. It was a chaste kiss, Lucy reflected, which was just as well in front of all her family and the whole church congregation. She remembered their recent searing kisses and blushed at the thought of it. After signing the register, the couple went outside, so that photographs could be taken, and the children could throw rice at the happy couple. A sudden outburst of rain stopped the photographer, so everybody ran back inside to complete the photographs. When they were finished, people started to drift downstairs, to the church hall, where the reception was to take place.

A five-course meal was served, consisting of soup, a fish course, a roast dinner, a choice of puddings, then tea and small hand-made chocolates. Most people had to take the chocolates home as they were too full. When everybody had finished eating, the food was cleared away so that people could talk a little longer. The caterers cut the wedding cake, wrapped it in paper napkins and distributed it to every guest.

Soon it was time for Lucy and Harry to go on honeymoon. She had no idea where they were going, except Harry had asked if they could go in her motor car, rather than his commercial vehicle. As she was leaving, Lucy tossed her bouquet over her shoulder, and Bessie caught it, amidst a lot of speculation in the crowd as to whom she would marry, which caused Bessie to go scarlet. More than one man in the church congregation had been interested in talking to her that day, and at 17 years old, she had developed into quite a beauty.

Waving goodbye to their guests, Lucy and Harry went back to Lucy's home to get changed for the wedding journey. Harry was delighted when Lucy gave him a pocket watch as a wedding present, which he attached to his waistcoat immediately, saying he loved it. Lucy's case was all packed, so she changed into a matching lightweight dress and coat as her going-away outfit. They slipped away quietly before the family and servants got home again. For the first night, they weren't travelling far. Harry had booked them into a small hotel on the outskirts of Preston, so Lucy still had no idea where they would go after tomorrow. Not needing any more food to eat, they went straight to the bedroom, hanging their coats up in the wardrobe.

'I'll just go for a walk round, whilst you get ready,' Harry said nervously.

'Thank you,' said Lucy, and watched him go out of the door. She, too, was nervous about what was to happen. Her mother had been very vague when she asked questions, and all Laura said was that it would be all right and just enjoy it. But what if she wasn't able to enjoy it? Or to please Harry? What if she couldn't do what she was expected to do? After getting her new broderie anglaise nightdress on, she climbed into bed, but blew the candle out before Harry got back.

Chapter 22

The first thing Harry did when he got back was to light the candle.

'What are you doing in the dark, Lucy?' he asked, laughing.

'Er, just waiting.'

She watched Harry as he undressed but averted her eyes when he got down to his underclothes. When she looked again, he had his nightshirt on.

'Don't you think we ought to pray first? I think it's important that a couple pray together,' said Harry, stood by the bed.

'Oh, yes,' said Lucy, jumping out of bed and kneeling down. Harry came and joined her, but took hold of her hand as they prayed together. Lucy loved it that Harry asked God to bless their marriage always, then squeezed her hand as they got up off the floor. He held her tight and kissed her slowly, then gently pulled her onto the bed. His kisses became deeper and he started stroking Lucy, becoming more intimate moment by moment. Lucy couldn't believe what was happening to her body, but she didn't care as long as Harry didn't stop what he was doing. Afterwards, they lay holding each other close. Lucy stared at Harry; she couldn't quite believe what she had experienced.

'Did I hurt you?'

'Only a little,' said Lucy, 'but it was worth it,' she laughed, cuddling closer to him, and they soon fell asleep, close together, both happy.

At the breakfast table next morning, Lucy couldn't stop smiling at Harry throughout the meal. She was so happy! Now she knew why Laura had said 'just enjoy it'. It took her all her time to eat her breakfast and she giggled when Harry urged her to eat up, as she would need all her strength for tonight. As it was a Sunday, Harry and Laura found a local church and attended the service, then set off for the rest of their journey. Lucy still didn't know where they were going; it was all a big mystery.

They ended up at Lake Windermere in the Lake District, part of Cumberland. Harry had booked a hotel right on the edge of the lake, and their bedroom faced out on to the lake. During their days there, they would go on walks or take a trip on the new paddle steamer that was on the lake. Other days, they explored further afield in the Lake District. After nearly two weeks, Harry said they had to go home, as he couldn't afford to have any more time off work, now he had a wife to maintain. They took their time going home, and when they arrived back at Barrow, the house was ready for them. Harry's parents' staff had been in and filled the larder with all the foodstuff they would need and, although it was summer, they had lit the black fire range which heated the water as well.

Lucy decided to have a bath, and after a light snack they went to bed. They would sort the house out tomorrow. Next morning, which was a Saturday, Lucy got up and found that Harry had already raked the fire to keep it going and had brought some eggs in from the hen house.

'Look at this,' he said. 'Our hens have laid eggs for us, for our first breakfast together in our own home.'

'Poached, fried, or scrambled?' Lucy asked, very pleased that she knew how to make all three now, thanks to Mrs Ward's tuition.

'Poached, with two slices of toast,' replied Harry. 'Do we have any marmalade? I love marmalade.'

'Yes, I did notice. We had to ask for extra marmalade every breakfast time on holiday,' giggled Lucy.

Harry was rooting in the cupboard under the dresser.

'Yes, here it is. I thought Mrs Watkins would have got me some. She knows I can't start the day without it. Oh, here's a note from Mother. I didn't notice it last night.' Harry read the letter. 'They want us to go to their house for lunch tomorrow. That's good. It'll save you having to cook a Sunday lunch.'

'That is good. My roast dinners aren't up to much yet,' Lucy laughed. 'Looking through the cupboards, I think we have enough food to last us until Monday, and then I can go to the shops and buy in. I'll make a list today. That's if you are going to work Monday?'

'Yes, but I'm only working locally this week, so I'll be home at nights. Some days, it won't be worth me coming home when I'm working further afield, even though I'd want nothing better.'

'I won't like being on my own and I'll miss you, but it'll make it all the better when you do get home!' she grinned wickedly.

'That's my girl,' said Harry, laughing. 'Now, what shall we do today?'

'Can we walk round the village so that I can get my bearings?'

'Good idea. We'll go after breakfast.' After washing the few pots, Lucy and Harry set off round the village, Harry pointing out the local houses and businesses.

'This house is called The Tithe Barn, but it's the summer stopping place for cyclists. There can be groups of 20 or 30 cyclists going through at a time. It's quite spectacular.'

'I'd like to have a bicycle here, as it's so flat. It was too hilly in Burnley.'

'Good idea. We'll both get one and then we can go cycling on Saturdays or even on summer evenings, and you can explore the area. We'll leave the motor cars at home for when we have to go on longer journeys. Now, this is the print works. Many of the local people work here, or on the land, although some work on the railways as well, and some of the wives are in service to the larger houses. The terraced houses were built originally to accommodate the print work staff.' They walked back into the village. 'There's a Methodist chapel just down this lane; can you see it?'

'Oh, yes, the village is well off for chapels then, with the Congregational one opposite our house.'

'Yes, so you could choose where to go,' Harry laughed.

'I'll stick with the Congregational one, I think,' said Lucy.

'Good, that's what I hoped you'd say.'

So, next morning, they breakfasted early and walked across the road to their new church. They were welcomed warmly by everyone and introduced to many of the families from the village. The headmaster of the school, Bill Hunter, and his wife Liz, were especially interested in hearing that Lucy was a trained teacher.

'Do you have children?' Bill asked, probably wondering if he was going to get any extra pupils.

'Not yet,' said Harry. 'We've only been married two weeks, but we're working on it.' Lucy nudged Harry to shut him up, and Bill laughed at his mistake.

'Well, if ever any of my teachers are off sick, I'll know where to come,' Bill said.

'You must come round for a cup of tea one morning,' Liz said to Lucy.

'I'd like that,' replied Lucy. The Hunters were older than Lucy and Harry, probably about 40, Lucy reckoned, but it would be good to have a friend in the village, as she couldn't keep going back to Burnley to visit Laura. She needed to make friends here.

Soon it was time to go and visit Harry's parents, who wanted to talk about how much they had enjoyed the wedding, and asked after the honeymoon.

'We had an excellent time,' replied Harry, with a big grin, making Lucy blush. Whilst they were at Harry's parents, they collected all their wedding presents, which the Marsdens had taken home from Lucy's house so that they were nearer, ready for them moving into the house. Harry and Lucy had an enjoyable time unwrapping all their gifts and making a list of who had bought what, so that they could send thank you letters.

Next morning, after Harry had gone to work, Lucy made a list of all the things that she might need. The first thing on her list was notepaper. She decided that it would be better to go into Clitheroe so that she could buy a good quality paper and envelopes, and also order some headed notepaper for the future. She was soon ready and parked on Castle Street, the main street in Clitheroe.

The first shop she noticed was called Mitchell's Modes. It was a large department store that sold almost anything a woman could want. She decided to do her necessary shopping first, then come back to Mitchell's Modes. Walking further down Castle Street, on York Street she found the stationers, Borough Printing, that Harry had told her about. Finding a good quality of paper and envelopes, she bought more than enough to send as thank you letters. Afterwards, she ordered some headed notepaper and felt great delight that the notepaper would have Mr and Mrs Harry Marsden at the top, followed by their address and telephone number.

After ordering the paper, Lucy decided to visit Mitchell's Modes. It was a delightful shop, and she met the owner's daughter Rachel whilst she was there. Apparently, Rachel's mother Jenny had inherited a small shop when she was 18, which specialised in ladies' clothes and weddings at first, and had expanded into the big store it was today. Lucy didn't buy much that first visit, apart from an embroidered tablecloth that took her fancy, but she knew it was a shop she would visit frequently in the years to come. Rachel mentioned that they had a café a few doors away, so Lucy decided that she might as well go to the café and have her lunch; it would save making it when she got home. The café was run by Rachel's cousins, Lydia and Hannah, and the décor and ambience were excellent. Lucy felt very comfortable there, even though she was on her own, but she could see that the café was very popular with ladies who were catching up with each other. She would have to bring Laura here, soon.

After buying fresh fruit and vegetables, Lucy went to the butcher's shop and got some meat for tea. She was going to make a mince cobbler and hoped it would turn out as well as Mrs Ward's did. Lucy couldn't believe how quickly the day passed and it was soon time for Harry to return from work.

He was very impressed by Lucy's attempts at cooking, as he knew how little experience she had. Lucy was pleased with his praise, but secretly thought that the cobbler was nowhere near as good as Mrs Ward's, but time could only improve her culinary skills she hoped.

Laura didn't get over to visit Lucy for a few weeks, but when she did, she thoroughly enjoyed going in Mitchell's Modes, not to mention the café. They were glad to catch up with each other and compare notes about married life. Now Lucy was much more confident driving, they planned a visit to Cynthia before the baby was born in December, or the dark nights drew in.

They eventually went in the middle of October and couldn't believe how big Cynthia was.

'Good job I didn't have to postpone my wedding,' Lucy said. 'You'd never fit in the dress now.'

'I don't fit in anything now,' moaned Cynthia.

'I've taken Laura to a shop near me in Clitheroe, and they specialise in making dresses for ladies who are expecting. Shall I send you a catalogue? They will post clothes out to you.'

'Oh, yes please. We're quite a way from the shops here and, as I don't have a motor car like you fortunate ladies, I'm tired now by the time I've walked home or taken a tram.'

'I'll send one for you this week,' promised Lucy.

All too soon, Laura and Lucy had to leave, but promised to visit again as soon as possible. As they were leaving, Lucy handed over the baby shawl that she had knitted for Cynthia, who greatly appreciated it.

Just before Christmas, Lucy received a letter through the post from her Granny Wall. It also contained a bank book.

Dear Lucy,

You will remember when William wanted to start up his garage, I gave him a legacy from his Granddad Wall that had just matured after his 21st birthday. I'm pleased to say your Granddad also gave you a legacy, which I have now received. I have taken the liberty of opening a building society account for you and put the money in it. I looked around the local building societies and thought that this one was the most appropriate!

Your loving granny.

Lucy looked at the bank book. The name of the building society was called Marsden Building Society. *What an excellent name,* thought Lucy. She immediately rang her granny to thank her, but also to share the joke about the name of the building society being the same as hers. She would save the money in case she ever needed it. It was certainly a lot of money.

Life went on for all three girls, Lucy and Laura adjusting to married life and the new rhythm of their days, and Cynthia anticipating her new arrival. Christmas came and went, and with it the arrival of Master Stephen Huw Roberts, on December 26th, St Stephen's day, weighing six pounds and seven ounces. Mother and baby were both well, the letter stated, so Lucy and Laura sent congratulations to the new family with a promise to visit as soon as the weather improved.

As it happened, Master Stephen was three months old before Lucy and Laura were able to visit. Much fuss was made of Stephen by the two friends, and Cynthia smiled at them both, from the superior position of motherhood, and said that it would soon be their turn.

'I do hope so,' said Lucy, but Laura merely smiled.

Chapter 23

The next time Laura came over to Barrow to visit, they went to Mitchell's Modes again and then to the café. Lucy noticed that Laura was very quiet, so she asked her what was wrong.

'I don't seem to be able to have babies,' Laura whispered.

'Nonsense! You've only been married six months longer than me, and I haven't got any yet. It just takes time,' said Lucy. 'Why do you think you can't have them?'

'I keep thinking I'm expecting but then after about three months, my monthlies come and are usually very heavy, probably because I haven't had one for three months.'

'Have you been to see the doctor?'

'No. I don't want anyone to know about it. It's bad enough that Granny Wall and my mum are watching me like a hawk all the time, or asking me if I've got anything to tell them,' Laura said sadly. 'I feel such a failure.' Lucy could see that Laura was near to tears, so she paid the bill and got Laura back in to the motor car and started driving.

'Where are we going?' Laura asked.

'To my father-in-law's. He'll probably know what the matter is.'

'Oh, I couldn't see him.'

'Why not? At least your mother and Granny Wall won't know, and he might be able to help you.' They had already arrived at the house, so Laura reluctantly agreed to go in. Mrs Marsden welcomed them, getting the maid to bring tea, and Lucy quietly told her of Laura's problem. Unfortunately, Dr Marsden was out on a case, but Matthew was seeing a patient in the little surgery. When the patient had gone, Mrs Marsden went in and explained things to Matthew, who asked Laura and Lucy to come into the surgery.

'Now, what seems to be the problem, Mrs Coombes?' he gently asked, and, haltingly at first, Laura explained the cycle she was having. It appeared she might be having a baby for a few weeks, but then she wasn't, she explained.

'I'll have to examine you to be sure, I'm afraid,' Matthew said, 'but Lucy can stay with you, of course.' Laura nodded her agreement, even though extremely embarrassed. After his examination, Matthew asked Laura how long it was since her last monthlies.

'It was just last week,' she replied.

'I thought as much. How many episodes have you had like this?'

'Three, maybe four,' said Laura.

'I think you are having early miscarriages. When I examined you, the neck of your womb seemed slightly open like you had just given birth. Was there more blood when you had missed your monthlies?'

'Yes, but I thought that was because I hadn't had them for three months. Does this mean I can't carry babies?'

'Not necessarily, but it may take you longer and you will have to be patient. It appears that the neck of your womb opens too easily, letting the babies miscarry. There is no treatment for this at present. The only thing I can recommend is that as soon as your monthlies don't appear, you should go straight to bed and stay there. It will be tedious, but it is the only way that you will have a chance of having a baby.'

'Do you know anybody who has been like me, but had a baby?'

'Yes, but they had to be patient. And it seems that once they have managed to have a baby, it often doesn't happen with further babies. So, it will be worth the wait. At least you seem to be able to conceive quite easily, so that is good.'

'Thank you, Doctor, I can't thank you enough. You have given me hope again.'

'Another word of advice which you won't welcome, Mrs Coombes.'

'Yes?'

'Refrain from marital relations until you are past the fifth month. That will help.' Laura blushed, but nodded her head and they left the surgery, going back to see Mrs Marsden.

'Now, I bet you need another cup of tea, girls?'

'Yes, please,' they both said together. Mrs Marsden, long trained to silence in medical matters, asked no questions, so they chatted about the weather and other inconsequential stuff for half an hour and then left. They went back to Lucy's house, where Laura had left her motor car.

'I feel so much better now, Lucy. I'm glad you made me go. I've been so worried and downhearted. I've kept reading the Bible story about Hannah pleading for a child and promising to give it back to the Lord if she had a baby. I've been praying the same, although I'm not sure I could give it back, like Hannah,' Laura added miserably.

'God might not ask for it back. He might want you to keep the child and bring him or her up as a good Christian instead.'

'I suppose so.'

'Now, you must tell William everything tonight, and you need to tell your staff because next time it happens, you need to go straight to bed and stay there. No coming to visit me, I'll come to visit you. No going in Mitchell's Modes café either for a while,' Lucy teased.

'It'll be so hard to stay in bed, but if I end up carrying a child to nine months, it'll all have been worthwhile.'

'Yes, it's about time I had a nephew or niece to fuss over,' grinned Lucy, and they hugged each other tightly.

'I'll go home now. I think I'll tell William to come home early and then I can tell him everything.'

'Yes, do. Why don't you tell your mother as well? Oh, and Granny Wall. She won't like it if she doesn't get told,' Lucy laughed.

'Very true. I'll tell your parents as well, tomorrow, after I've told William.'

'Good. I'll send you lots of books to read to keep you in bed.'

'Thank you, Lucy. You are a true friend.'

'So are you because I know you would do the same for me.'

When Harry got home that night, Lucy told him all that had happened, and they both prayed together that night that Laura would carry a baby.

Two months later, Lucy got a message from William to say that Laura had taken to her bed. Lucy sprang into action and collected knitting wool and needles, books, magazines, and some Florentines that she had bought specially from Mitchell's Modes café, which were particular favourites of Laura's.

Lucy stayed with Laura for over two hours, chatting about everything under the sun, and daring to discuss what might be in nine months' time. The maid, Edie, brought a tray of tea and cakes, but they decided to eat the Florentines instead. Lucy was glad to see that the staff were taking their duties seriously and protecting Laura.

Before she left, Lucy whispered that she suspected that there might be another baby coming too, but it was a little too early to know for certain yet. Laura was delighted and said that would sustain her over the next few months, if she knew Lucy was having a child too.

Lucy still couldn't believe that she might also be having a baby, but a month later, it was confirmed by her father-in-law. Harry was ecstatic. After the initial sickness in the first few weeks, there was no stopping Lucy as she was so full of energy. Besides knitting and sewing little baby garments, she spent long times sitting with Laura, who was still expecting, due to following Matthew's advice, but was extremely fed up and frustrated.

Harry carved a beautiful wooden cradle and it was ready five months before Lucy's baby was due, which was in mid-April of the following year. He then started on making another cradle, which worried Lucy.

'Do you think I'm having twins?' she asked. 'Has your father said something?'

'No, of course not,' Harry laughed. 'I'm making it for our baby's cousin.'

'Oh, thank you! Laura and William will be so pleased.'

'I made one each for Betsy and for Lizzie for my nieces and nephews, so I thought I'd better start a Coombes tradition as well.'

'No good having a carpenter in the family if we can't have bespoke cradles made,' laughed Lucy.

The Christmas of 1911 was spent quietly. Harry and Lucy went to Harry's parents that year, but didn't stay long as they wanted to get back to their own home, although they visited Laura, William, and Lucy's parents on Boxing Day for a short time.

News came on March 4th that Laura had given birth, three weeks early, to a healthy boy. Lucy rang Mitchell's Modes and asked them to send some baby boy's outfits to Laura, rather than going to the shop herself, as it was getting a little bit difficult to sit behind the steering-wheel nowadays. Harry drove her over to visit Laura that weekend. Lucy went up to the bedroom to see Laura and the baby.

'Thank you for the outfits. They arrived today and are beautiful.'

'That was quick. I'm glad you like them.'

'I'm calling him Samuel Henry,' Laura said, and Lucy knew why. In the Bible, Hannah had called her long-awaited child Samuel, and Henry was the name of Laura's brother who had died young.

Lucy jumped, sitting in her chair.

'Are you all right, Lucy?' asked Laura.

'Yes, just my baby kicking. I think this one is going to be a footballer, with all the kicks I keep getting.'

'It will be so good to have them a similar age. They can play together,' said Laura.

169

'Yes, it's just a shame we don't live nearer each other.'

'We are so blessed, though, in having a motor car each. We're more fortunate than a lot of young mothers that we know.'

'I count my blessings every time I turn the crank shaft,' laughed Lucy, 'although I'm having trouble fitting behind the steering wheel now,' which set Laura off laughing.

'Yes, I count my blessings, and especially for this little one, which I never thought I would have,' Laura said softly, smiling down at little Samuel. Harry came in at that point and said that it was time for them to go to her parents, where they were going for tea. Lucy cradled little Samuel Coombes in her arms then gave him back to his mother, with a smile on her face.

'Soon be your turn,' said Laura softly, and then in a more jocular voice, she added, 'and your turn for sleepless nights!'

'I can't wait,' said Lucy, with not much delight in her voice.

It was good to see her parents and be back in her childhood home. Mrs Coombes was marvelling about little Samuel and saying that she couldn't believe that soon she would have two grandchildren. She didn't have long to wait. On April 15th, at 2.20 am precisely, Lucy gave birth to her first child, after a protracted labour, which left her exhausted. But it wasn't the birth of her child that was on everybody's lips that day. The news had arrived that the RMS Titanic had sunk, with the loss of many lives, even though it was deemed unsinkable. It was the exact same time that Lucy was giving birth.

Lucy lay back exhausted in the bed, totally unaware of the events going on in the world around her. She just wanted to go to sleep, but the baby wouldn't let her. Harry came upstairs as soon as he heard the wailing of the newborn, running towards Lucy and kissing her tenderly.

'How are you my love?' he said gently.

'Tired and sore, and we haven't got a footballer. We've got a girl.'

'Even better,' said Harry. 'A miniature Lucy. She's got good lungs, hasn't she?'

'Yes, the midwife wants me to feed her now, so hopefully that should quieten her down a bit.' The midwife let Harry stay and he watched, fascinated as the little baby latched on to her mother's breast and seemed to know what to do straight away.

When the baby was satiated, Harry was encouraged to go downstairs and make a cup of tea, if he knew how, the midwife added, whilst she sorted mother and baby out. The baby was soon asleep and Harry brought up a cup of tea for both Lucy and the midwife, but Lucy was asleep too. Leaving the cup on her bedside table in case she wakened, Harry went downstairs with a smile on his face, only sorry it was still the middle of the night, and it was too early to telephone anyone.

As the rest of the world was reeling with the news of the sinking of the Titanic, Harry and Lucy were in a little bubble of love in their home. Baby Grace was beautiful, both parents agreed. She looked like Lucy, but had Harry's fair hair. They often just sat looking at her asleep in her cot, amazed by this wonder that had been created from their love for each other. The midwife had been recommended by Harry's father and was living in the house for the first month, to help Lucy. It was a good arrangement. She slept in the bedroom next to Lucy and Harry and kept the cradle in with her, only disturbing Lucy when Grace needed feeding.

They decided to call the baby Grace because, as Lucy said to Harry, God had shown great grace to them both, and they hadn't had the problems in having a baby that William and Laura had experienced. They added the middle name of Laura, after her aunty.

Chapter 24

In the end, Mrs Snowden the midwife stayed for three months because young Grace Laura Marsden liked being awake at night-time and fed better during the night, leaving Lucy exhausted. Eventually though, between the two women, they managed to get Grace into a better pattern of sleeping through the night. It was a worrying time for the first week after Mrs Snowden had left, but Lucy quickly became more confident, especially as she had a family full of doctors to call on if necessary. Also, Liz Hunter, the schoolteacher's wife, popped round regularly to check whether Lucy needed any groceries or help. Lucy was very grateful and vowed that as soon as she was able, she would take Liz to Mitchell's Modes café for a treat. There wasn't a schoolteacher's house attached to the school, so Liz and Bill had bought a terraced house in the village. Their two sons, Thomas and Martin, were 15 and 16 respectively, and both attended Clitheroe Grammar School.

It also helped Lucy cope as they started going on alternate weeks to Harry's parents or Burnley for Sunday lunch again. It meant less cooking for Lucy, for which she was always grateful. On the week they went to Burnley, sometimes they would go to Lucy's parents, sometimes to William and Laura's, and sometimes to Granny Wall's.

One Sunday in October they had gone to William and Laura's house and Laura told Lucy that she had hired a nanny.

'A nanny? How many girls from Mill Street have a nanny?' Lucy teased.

'I know. It does sound pretentious, but wait until you see who it is,' replied Laura. No sooner had she said those words, than Mrs Carter walked through the door.

'Hello, Mrs Carter, how lovely to see you. Are you well?' asked Lucy, respectfully.

'Better than I was, Lucy. How are you, and little Grace?'

'We're both fine, thank you, now she's got the hang of which is day and which is night. The first three months were hard work,' Lucy laughed.

'Our Albert was like that. Born in the night, so always wrong way round.'

'Yes, Grace was born in the night; that must be it.'

'May I introduce you to my new nanny?' Laura asked. Lucy looked round the room, but there was no one else there.

'Whom do you mean?' asked Lucy.

'My Mum. She's my new nanny.'

'Really? What a good idea. How did that happen?'

Mrs Carter took up the story.

'Well, I was having more and more trouble with my chest and the doctor said that I would be better leaving the mill, so Laura's dad said we could afford for me to give up work now. He gets a better wage from the mill as chief tackler, and there's only Agnes and Arthur at home now, so life is a lot easier. Albert's living over your brother's garage now he's working there, and Agnes is leaving home soon anyway.'

'Oh? Where's Agnes going?'

'She's going to a young ladies' college in Manchester so that she can train as a teacher when she's 18. She'll live with her Granny Carter. It'll be nice for Granny Carter as she's a widow now, and it'll be good for Bessie to have young company again.'

'Is she going to Owen's College like we did? Or should I say, Manchester University.'

'She's hoping to. Fancy, two of my daughters being teachers; it beggars belief.'

'We could give her a lot of text books, couldn't we, Lucy?' said Laura.

'We certainly could, and a lot of advice, too. So, how did you become the nanny then, Mrs Carter?'

'Well, I kept coming up to help at first, really to see my grandson and, although I was glad to leave the mill, I missed being busy and useful. It started as a joke, really. I was here at teatime one day when William came home and he said, "Oh, is the nanny still here?" as a joke, but that started Laura thinking. They tried to pay me a wage, but I won't have it.'

'We get round it in other ways, though,' Laura said. 'William is paying for my Mum and Dad to go to Blackpool for two whole weeks at Burnley Fair, and is taking them there as well, along with Bessie, Agnes, and the boys. He says that's meagre wages for what she does.'

'But you also give me meals to take home so that I don't have to start cooking at night,' said Mrs Carter, 'and I bring my washing here instead of boiling it in the tub at home. Laura has got one of those fancy new washing machines now, and young Edie or Martha does my washing for me. Fancy me having somebody doing my laundry and making my meals. I feel like the gentry sometimes! That's better than any wages.'

'You deserve it, Mum. You've worked hard to bring up all us children as well as working full-time.' Laura turned to Lucy. 'The best part is she gets to see her grandchild almost every day,' added Laura.

'It's perhaps as well with things being the way they are,' said Mrs Carter darkly.

'What do you mean?' asked Lucy.

'I'm expecting again,' said Laura. 'I went to the doctors because I kept feeling poorly and he told me I was with child. I couldn't believe it. I'm five months and been running around after Samuel every day, but kept this one inside at the same time. It's a miracle.'

'It certainly is,' said Lucy, but privately thinking that she couldn't cope with another baby just yet. 'How old will Samuel be when the new baby comes?'

'Just under a year.'

'You will need a nanny!' said Lucy, which made all three women laugh.

Christmas Day was a riot that year. Harry, Lucy, and Grace spent it at William and Laura's and had great fun watching Samuel and Grace playing together, or rather, fighting over the same toys. All Laura's family were there too, and Lucy's parents, and Granny Wall, so they were a large crowd. Both Lucy's and Laura's Christmas Wishes that year were that they would be the best of mothers to their children.

Boxing Day was no less riotous, as Lucy and Harry went to his family home, where six of the eight nieces and nephews were there, all fighting to entertain Grace. Lizzie and her family hadn't visited this year, as Lizzie's husband Edgar was on call, and they lived near Sheffield, which was a long drive, even with the most up-to-date motor cars available.

Laura managed to go to full-term with this second baby, and he was born on February 4th, just a month before little Samuel's first birthday. Life became very hectic in the household, and Laura thanked God every day that she had her mother to help her. Whereas Samuel had been dark like his father, little baby Edward William had a head full of red hair, like his mother. They had called him Edward after his grandfather Coombes, but also the other boy that was lost in childhood to Mr and Mrs Carter.

Lucy was a frequent visitor with Grace, and the cousins spent time together whilst the mothers caught up with each other. Often they would take the children round Queen's Park in their perambulators, enjoying the fresh air, and Samuel, once he found his feet, would run round and round until he was dizzy. Of course, this led to Grace copying him at the first opportunity that she got, and Lucy and Laura loved to see the children playing and running round freely. It was so different to Laura's upbringing, as she had been minded by another lady when she was young, whilst her mother went back to work. There were no parks near Mill Street, so Laura was so grateful that her boys were being brought up near a park.

Back at home, Lucy and Harry continued to thrive in their relationship and were doting parents to Grace. Harry always had a full book of orders of people who wanted furniture. His favourite part was to make furniture, but he would accept any commissions that involved woodworking. Sometimes he had to stay away from home if he was working far away, but this only made the reunion even sweeter when he returned. Some days he worked at home in his outhouse, making bespoke furniture, and Lucy loved it when he worked at home. Grace worshipped her father, and her first word was 'da-da', much to Lucy's disgust, who had been trying to get her to say 'ma-ma' for weeks. Harry made Grace a small chair with long legs so that she could sit up to the table when they were having meals. He also made her a lovely stool on which he inscribed her name. Grace would sit on the stool and say, 'Grace's stool', and pat it with her chubby little hands. Grace was cross one day when Lucy stood on it to get something down from a top shelf of the dresser.

'No, Mama, Grace's stool,' so Lucy had to get down quickly and give the stool back to Grace.

Harry came home one night with a three-seater bicycle for them to go out on. Saturdays were spent spinning around the country roads, Harry or Lucy pedalling furiously, and Grace, tightly strapped in, laughing as they went faster. Lucy was happy in her world with husband and child, and both of their families, and needed nothing else.

There were many other friends, too, from the church across from the house. Their life was complete. Lucy had also developed an interest in gardening. With the help of Scott, a local gardener, she had planted vegetables and fruit bushes. Scott had also pruned all the fruit trees in the small orchard and they were beginning to give healthy fruit, which Lucy was able to incorporate into her cooking, but also prepared a lot of preserves for the winter, with Liz Hunter's help. Lucy's pantry was full of chutneys, sauces, bottled fruits, jam, and lots of marmalade, that would keep her going all winter through, when fresh fruit and vegetables were difficult to obtain. It also meant that she always had something on hand if there was a sale of work at the church, along with knitted garments that she made.

Lucy couldn't believe how much she enjoyed being a housewife, as she had never done anything to help at home, relying on Mrs Ward and Patsy. In Barrow, Lucy employed a lady from the village to come in and clean once or twice a week and help with the changing of beds and the laundry. Mrs Jackson was worth her weight in gold, Lucy maintained. Mrs Jackson was glad of the job, as her four children were all at the school so it meant she could work round school hours to fit in. During school holidays, Lucy encouraged her to bring the children, and they were happy to take Grace with them when they played out in the garden.

Harry was busy in the house too, building beds and wardrobes in all the spare rooms. In fact, at Christmas 1913, Lizzie, Edgar and their boys, Lionel and Stanley, had stayed at Barrow, to save congestion on Harry's parents' house. Grace loved having her two big cousins there and followed them round all week.

When Grace was two years old, they had a little birthday party for her, attended by all the grandparents, great-grandmothers, aunties and uncles and cousins. Harry complained that they had better buy a bigger house if there were any more children in the family, as the house was full that day! Lucy had even made a birthday cake for Grace, and Liz had helped her ice it, as that was a skill far beyond Lucy's capabilities, even though she was good at baking now.

Lucy had little interest in politics, but Harry took a keen interest and was worried about the tensions in Europe that were building up between different nations. It came to a head in the June of that year when Archduke Ferdinand was assassinated in Europe. At first, the majority of people in England thought it of no consequence, but gradually the realisation came that England was becoming politically drawn towards war with Germany, who had been massively increasing their navy and army. Lucy couldn't believe that the two kings of the nations, who were cousins after all, just like Grace and Samuel, could declare war on each other.

'It could tear the Royal families apart,' Lucy told Harry when he explained it to her.

Harry replied, 'It will tear many families apart before it is finished.' His words were a grim prophecy of the future. In August, England declared war on Germany. Young men were cheerfully joining up, saying that they would soon sort out the Hun and it would all be over by Christmas. Lucy watched the young men marching through Clitheroe town centre, and Grace learned a new word in her vocabulary – soldiers.

Liz Hunter came round in tears one morning. Martin, who was barely eighteen years old, had joined up and was going the next day to training camp in Yorkshire. Lucy comforted her as best she could, but nothing she could say would cheer Liz up. Instead they just committed Martin to God and prayed for his safety.

At first, it didn't appear that the war would indeed be a long one, as nothing much happened, but by September, there was news of heavy casualties, and the lists of men who had died started to appear in newspapers. Harry read the newspaper with deepening silences, and Lucy knew that he was worried about the way the war was going. However, nothing prepared her for when he returned home one night, with a guilty look on his face. Lucy had just put Grace to bed.

'I've joined up,' he said, his head bowed.

'Joined up? What do you mean?' Lucy asked, her heart pounding.

'I've joined the army. I was reading that they need men with first aid experience. I couldn't stay at home any longer and live with my conscience.'

'I thought married men weren't needed yet. Conscription is only for single men,' Lucy cried frantically. 'You can't go; we need you.'

'I feel I have to go, Lucy. Believe me, I haven't done this lightly. I need to serve my country and make sure that the enemy doesn't come to England. Besides, I won't be in the front line like the other poor men. I'll be in a hospital, helping injured soldiers. I'll have a better chance of surviving than most, won't I?'

'I don't want you to go. Doesn't that count for anything?'

'I don't want to go, but believe me, I must. I have prayed so hard about this decision, yet I feel I must go.'

'What will your parents say?' Lucy said, trying another tack.

'Father is too busy working out how to manage without Matthew. He has volunteered too.'

'Matthew? With all those children?'

'Yes, he feels as I do, that he can help soldiers who are injured.'

'You are decided, aren't you?'

'Yes, I go on the 15th of October.'

'But that's next week!'

'I know, but there is a great need for anyone who has my experience.'

'I can't bear it. I can't bear to be without you here with me and Grace.'

'It's how many men and women feel at the moment, but we've got to stop this war as soon as possible. Be brave, Lucy. I'll be back before you know it and we can resume our life and have more children and grow old together.'

'Promise?' asked Lucy.

'Promise,' said Harry. They held each other closely, until Lucy's sobs had ceased.

'I'll try and be brave. I'll do my best to bring Grace up without you, and perhaps there'll be things that we women can do whilst you men are away fighting.'

'That's my girl,' said Harry. 'Now, let's have a cup of tea together,' so Lucy put the kettle on the stove.

October 15th came all too soon for both of them. Harry finished off his commissions and explained to his other customers that he wouldn't be able to honour his commitment, but all of them praised Harry for joining up and said they could wait until he came back. The night before he went, Harry and Lucy clung to each other in bed, knowing that it would the last time they would be together for some months or possibly years. As he was getting dressed next day, Lucy gave him a small Bible which contained the New Testament and the Psalms to keep in his pocket. On the flyleaf she had written the Jewish blessing, from the Old Testament:

'The Lord bless thee and keep thee, the Lord make His face to shine upon thee and be gracious unto thee. The Lord lift up his countenance upon thee and give thee peace. Numbers chapter 6 vv 24 -26.'

Grace didn't understand what was going on but kept saying 'Daddy, soldier', which made them both laugh. Lucy dropped him off at Clitheroe railway station, where many more men were waiting. Harry was going into a different regiment from some of his friends from Clitheroe, as he was going straight into a medical corps, as was Matthew.

Lucy threw herself into being busy in the house and trying to find things she could do for the war effort. Contacting the leader of the Red Cross, she found that all the young men had volunteered, like Harry, and they were short of teachers, so Lucy started teaching first aid to young people and quite a lot of women joined too, eager to learn how to care for themselves with their husbands away. Many brought their children with them, and books were collected so that the older children could read to the little ones whilst their mothers were learning.

At first, Lucy thought that she might be expecting a baby when Harry had gone and was thrilled that they would have a second child together, to add to their family, but it turned out to be a false alarm and Lucy was heartbroken. She was just glad that she hadn't told Harry of her suspicions, as it would have been harder to tell him that there was no baby.

Mrs Marsden persuaded Lucy to join her fund-raising committee to buy small Christmas presents for the men who were serving in the trenches. Knitting became a furious pastime, too, as mitts, scarves, and hats were in short supply for the soldiers.

Harry's first letter brought great delight to Lucy. She read it and re-read it until the paper was nearly worn through. He wasn't allowed to tell her much, but he was still in the North of England doing intensive training before he went abroad. Just before Christmas, he was allowed a weekend at home. Lucy was delighted, until she learnt it was because he was going to France the following Monday.

Chapter 25

It was a long wait before Lucy received a letter from Harry once he'd gone abroad. Lucy was keeping them all locked in her box, which she'd had since before they were married. Harry said he was well, but very busy. They worked long hours and it was relentless. He was working closely with a surgeon, who increasingly was giving him more responsibility as the days passed. He had made good friends but often, when they had time off, they only wanted to sleep rather than go anywhere.

Christmas was a bleak affair that year, with no Harry or Matthew. Even Harry's younger brother, John, had joined up, much to Mrs Marsden's distress, as he was only just 18, and was supposed to be going to university. To make matters worse for Lucy and Laura, William had joined up. He had offered himself to the army as a driver, as very few people coming through the ranks had that skill. Freddie was going to stay behind and run the motor car business. He'd been refused entry into the army as his vision in his left eye was damaged. The doctor thought it was due to the blow he had from his stepfather, resulting in a black eye, but it kept him out of the army. With young Albert coming on board, Freddie was teaching him all about the mending and maintenance of engines. Also, William had found a retired army captain who was used to motor cars and was happy to keep the sales side of the business going.

When Lucy was visiting Laura one day, they rang Cynthia up to see how she was.

'Well, I have good news and bad news,' she said.

'Let's have the good news first,' said Laura.

'I'm expecting another baby.'

'Oh, that is good news.' Laura turned to tell Lucy.

'So what's the bad news, then?'

'Huw has joined up. His timing wasn't brilliant as I'd just found out I was expecting.'

'Poor you,' said Laura.

'But that's not all the bad news. I have to leave the house, because Huw's replacement is coming from away and has nowhere to live, so I'm going back to live with my parents for the duration.'

'That's probably better as you won't be on your own when the new baby comes.'

'That's true. We'll wait to buy our own house until Huw gets back. They've said they'll hold the job open for him. The man who is coming had just retired but is returning to work for the war effort. His wife will help teach as well.'

'That's a shame you have to move, though.'

'I don't mind. We knew it was only temporary. Let me tell you about David and Jacob. David has joined the navy and Jacob has joined the army. So, that's all our friends from college and our husbands. We are women bereft,' said Cynthia.

'We certainly are,' replied Laura, 'but hopefully it won't be long before it's all over. Although my father-in-law thinks it might be a long job.'

'We'll just have to pray it's over soon, then,' said Cynthia, to which the girls agreed.

The war wasn't over soon. It dragged on. In the late summer of 1915, Harry managed to have a week's leave at home. When he arrived home, Lucy flew towards him, but he stopped her and said he was going into his workshop to get rid of his clothes, which probably still had fleas on them. He asked Lucy to throw him a dressing gown, and stripped off completely, going straight for a bath before he let Lucy near him. Grace was in bed for a nap, but when she saw Harry, she was a little wary of him; a year was a long time for her to remember her daddy. Lucy longed for the evening when she could share her bed with Harry and be reunited with him in love, but when she returned from the bathroom, he had fallen asleep and slept for 24 hours. When he woke the next night, he was sorry for sleeping so long, but Lucy said that he must have needed it.

The rest of the week was spent in gentle walks, playing with Grace, who got used to her daddy again, and gentle lovemaking at night. Lucy had washed and steamed his uniform so that it was free of fleas once more. She tried to get Harry to talk more about his life in France, but he didn't say much. Although he did say that he was assisting the surgeon as if he was a junior doctor now. When the doctor operated, Harry would stitch the wound, or even stitch some simple wounds without the surgeon seeing the patient first; such was his trust in Harry's work. Indeed, he'd been trying to persuade Harry to go in for medicine after the war. Harry had declined, saying there were enough doctors in the family and he preferred wood. Harry mentioned a friend he had made called Archie Alderson, who was another medical orderly from Blackburn.

Eventually, the day came when Harry had to return. He left early, leaving his two girls still in bed, kissing them gently before leaving. Lucy held him tight and he had to pull himself away from her, saying, 'I'll be back before you know it.' Grace just stirred, then fell back to sleep. Lucy thought this second leaving was worse than the first, as she knew it could be another year before she saw him again.

Once Grace was up and breakfasted, Lucy suggested that they go out, as she didn't want to stay at home today. They went across to Liz and Bill's house and had a cup of tea and a scone from a batch that Liz had just made. Chatting with Liz brightened her day. At lunch time, Bill arrived home for his lunch.

'We'll be going now,' Lucy said, not wanting to disturb Bill's lunch break.

'Don't go Lucy. I was going to come and see you tonight anyway. My colleague joined up yesterday. It's left me in rather a mess. I was wondering if you could come and teach at the school for a while?'

'Me? What will I do with Grace?'

'You could either bring her with you, or perhaps you could get someone to look after her?'

'I'll have to think about it,' Lucy said.

'Please do,' Bill said, as Lucy left.

As soon as she got home, Lucy rang Laura to tell her what had happened.

'You can bring Grace over here every week. The boys would love to see her more often. So would your parents and Granny Wall.'

'I'm not sure yet. It'll mean leaving her a lot of the time.'

'She'll be going to school herself next year. So, why not give her some freedom before she goes to school?'

'I'll think about it,' Lucy promised. Next, she rang Mrs Marsden and explained the situation to her.

'Why don't you come and have Sunday lunch with us each week, then leave Grace here, and pick her up later in the week? I'd love to have her,' suggested Mrs Marsden. The more she thought about it, the more Lucy liked the idea of going back to teaching. It would while away the time and stop her thinking of what might be happening in France. It could be her own war effort, she decided. In the end, Lucy had a plan. When she put it to Grace, the little girl laughed with glee to think that she would be a big girl and go on her holidays to Granny Marsden's and Aunty Laura's every week. So, a new phase of Lucy's life started. It was good to be back in the classroom, and Grace was happy about the arrangements. On a Sunday after church, they would either go to Laura's or Mrs Marsden's for lunch, then Grace would stay until the Tuesday night, when Lucy would pick her up. Each evening they would say their prayers together on the telephone before Grace went to bed. On Tuesday nights, Lucy would pick Grace up and take her home and on Wednesdays, her cleaner Mrs Jackson would look after her for the day. She was also very pleased about the arrangement as it was extra money for her. Then on Wednesday nights, she would go to the other relative and stay until Friday night, when Lucy would pick her up, and they would have a lovely weekend together.

Harry was very approving of this new arrangement, once Lucy reassured him that Grace was happy with it. He said he was proud of his wife helping out at the school, and he imagined her back in class when he was writing his letters to her.

In early January of 1916, came the sad news that Huw had been killed in the trenches. Cynthia was distraught and it was so difficult not to be able to go over and comfort her in person. However, what with teaching and looking after Grace, and Laura having the two boys at home, and not wanting to use too much petrol, they were unable to visit.

Although they were sad for Cynthia, who had given birth to a little girl called Elizabeth, Lucy and Laura were glad that their husbands weren't in the trenches and were in safer jobs. William had been fuming at first, when he'd been assigned to driving the top military personnel round London and to meetings all over the country, but at least he was safe. He'd have preferred to be in the trenches with the other men, he had moaned, whilst Laura was delighted that his work was only in England. Harry just spent his time patching up the results of war, not fighting himself, Lucy reassured herself.

The war dragged on and Lucy read the 'Clitheroe Advertiser' each week and saw the increasing number of deaths of young men from the area. Six men from their little church had joined up, including Liz and Bill's son. One young man had died quite early on in the war, but the others were all still out there fighting.

One day during assembly in the school hall, Lucy noticed the telegram boy coming towards the school. She didn't really understand what he was

183

doing, as nobody lived at the school, but she thought she'd better go to meet him.

'Sorry to trouble you, Miss. I'm looking for Mr Hunter. Is he here? There's no answer at the house, so I thought I'd better come over.'

Lucy's heart sank. 'Yes, shall I give him the telegram? He's just taking assembly.'

'Thanks, Miss, that would be helpful. I've another to deliver in the village today, unfortunately.'

Lucy almost asked who that was for, but then remembered that he wouldn't be allowed to say, so just took the telegram and went inside. She hid the telegram in her pocket until assembly was finished, then telling all the children to go into her classroom and start reading, she gave the telegram to Bill, staying with him.

His face drained when he saw what it was and opened it quickly.

'Martin's dead, Lucy. "Killed in action", it says,' Bill said, and then his face crumpled. 'How will I tell Liz?'

'I think she must be out because the telegram boy said he went to your house first.'

'Perhaps she's at the shop. She didn't say she was going anywhere today.'

'You go home, Bill. I'll take the children today. Go on, go and find Liz.'

Looking suddenly years older, Bill nodded, and then left the school. After he had gone, Lucy took a deep breath and went into her classroom. She decided to tell the children what had happened. Unfortunately, the children were used to death and dying nowadays and were almost matter of fact about it. She quietly told the children and then asked one of the older boys to go to her house, where Mrs Jackson would be working and ask her to come here. Thank God she was working on a Thursday this week instead of her usual Wednesday and Grace was at her Granny Marsden's.

Mrs Jackson arrived in a hurry, asking what was wrong with her children, so Lucy had to tell her that her children were fine, but she gave her the sad news about Martin Hunter.

'What I'd like you to do for today is sit with the little ones and do their reading with them. Can you do that?'

'Yes, just tell me who to read with.' Lucy explained her reading rota and set the rest of her class some work to do, whilst she addressed the older children, and sorted out some work for them. She was suddenly very glad of all those times she had been made to teach the older students at Owen's College. Between them, Lucy and Mrs Jackson muddled through the day, but they were both glad when the school day ended. Mrs Jackson sat in Lucy's chair and said, 'Goodness, I'd no idea how exhausting being a teacher was!'

'You were marvellous, Mrs Jackson. I can't thank you enough for coming and helping. Do you think you could do the same tomorrow as well? I'm sure Mr Hunter won't be up to teaching tomorrow. I'll pay you as if you were working for me, if that's all right?'

'You don't have to pay me, Mrs Marsden. I'd do it just to help out.'

'I would rather pay you. You might not be able to undertake any other work so you would lose money.'

'Thank you. That's very kind of you, and my name's Annie.'

'No, it's thanks to you, Annie, and I'm Lucy, but not when the children are around,' she laughed.

Finding a casserole in her oven that Annie must have prepared before Lucy sent for her, Lucy put half of it in a dish and took it round to Liz and Bill's house. She knocked on the door, then shouted 'Hello' and walked into the kitchen.

'I know you won't want company, but I've just brought you something to eat,' Lucy said. Liz was sat huddled in a chair, her eyes red with weeping, but she looked up when Lucy spoke.

'Thank you, Lucy. I don't think we feel much like eating.'

'I know, but you need to keep your strength up.' Liz opened her arms towards Lucy and Lucy ran to her and cradled her in her arms.

'I'm so sorry, Liz. He was such a lovely young man. I wish there were something that I could do to help.'

'You've already helped. You've come and even brought us food, and I know you'll be praying for us, because that is your nature.'

'I'm sorry I deserted you this morning,' Bill said, with a heavy voice. 'How did you manage?'

'I managed fine. I told all the children, so that you don't have to when you come back. The other thing I did was recruit Mrs Jackson to be a temporary teacher. She was marvellous. I hope I did the right thing?' Lucy asked.

'Mrs Jackson? What made you think of her?'

'I knew where she was and I know she loves reading, so she was my only option really. She read with the little ones and helped them with their set work, whilst I taught the older ones.'

'I'll be back tomorrow,' Bill promised.

'No, you won't. I've arranged for Mrs Jackson to come in again, so you'll have tomorrow and the weekend to grieve together. Then we'll think about it again next week.'

'Thank you, Lucy. You are most kind.'

'I'll leave you alone now, but I just wanted to let you know I was here if you needed anything.'

'He was only 19,' said Liz, sadly.

'I know. Taken too young, but he laid down his life for others, like the Lord Jesus did. No one can do more than that.'

Bill and Liz said 'goodbye', and Lucy went home, where she wept for some time. *This war was so cruel. How many more people were going to die before it all ended? Nobody knew*, she reflected mournfully. She was a long time getting to sleep that night and she hadn't got Grace to distract her.

Lucy and Annie muddled through the school day on the Friday, and then Lucy went to pick up Grace from Mrs Marsden's, hugging her tight and glad that she was a girl and she would never have to go to war. *If only this war would end soon*, Lucy cried to herself.

Chapter 26

Bill was back in school on the Monday and life returned slowly to the little community, who had lost two of their two sons on the same day, the other young man being a member of the Methodist church down the road, and unknown to Lucy.

The year flew by for Lucy, between teaching and running backwards and forwards picking up Grace. In the summer, she went to stay at Laura's for two weeks instead of a holiday. It was lovely for them to catch up and they laughed at how Samuel lorded it over Grace and Edward. Both Samuel and Grace were going to school after the summer holidays, which would make it much easier for Lucy not to be having to run about everywhere to drop off Grace.

They did manage to leave the children with Mrs Carter one day and escaped to go and see Cynthia on their own, although taking lots of pictures with them to show Cynthia. They went to Cynthia's parents' house. For the time being, Cynthia had decided to stay there, rather than buy a house, as it was easier with the two small children than being on her own. They had a lovely time together, recalling their student days, but Cynthia said that now Huw was dead, she didn't hear about the other boys they had been friendly with, as he had always kept in touch. On leaving, the young women promised to meet again, when they would bring all the children, probably causing havoc!

The big day arrived and Grace was looking forward to being a schoolgirl. She practised calling her mummy 'Mrs Marsden' as she would have to do in school. Normally, a teacher wouldn't teach her own child, but there was no option. It was too far to take her into Whalley or Clitheroe to school and also be at work at the same time. Bill was happy with the arrangement and said it was only for a few years anyway, until she went into his class.

Harry was thrilled when Grace wrote her first letter to her daddy. It was brief.

'helo daddy I miss yu and mummy dus cum home soon xxx'

Lucy knew that Harry would treasure this letter and he wouldn't know the sad fact that Grace could hardly remember her daddy; he'd been gone so long.

Harry's letters were fairly predictable. He couldn't say much because of the censors and he was loathe to pour out his feelings on paper, he said, but assured Lucy and Grace of his love. 'My lovely girls', he called them.

187

Lucy longed for him to come home again, but all he said was that he would be home soon, but he never came. Leave was always cancelled because of a big push going on.

Christmas 1916 was a much scaled-down affair. Grace and Lucy just went to Laura's for Christmas Dinner, but didn't stay overnight. They came home again, as they were going to the Marsdens' on Boxing Day. Nobody made Christmas Wishes that year either. People generally were fed up with the war, and rations were being introduced to ensure that everyone got fair shares of the available food. Lucy was luckier than most as she had her hens and vegetable and fruit gardens.

Grace loved to work in the garden with her, so it provided many a shared activity for the two of them and also put extra food on the table. Liz Hunter found working in Lucy's garden helped her, and she was able to supplement their own table. Their younger son, Thomas, had joined up, but he had been assigned to the Royal Flying Corps. He was placed as an aircraft mechanic because he had done one year at university of an engineering degree. Liz was glad this younger son of hers was not in danger, like Martin had been. But the death toll kept rising inexorably for other families, nevertheless.

During the Easter school holidays, Lucy and Laura took all the children to visit Cynthia. The children had great fun and all played well together. Cynthia's parents' home had large grounds, so as it was a fine mild day, the children played out most of the time, only coming in for food, or to sort out disputes. With Laura and Cynthia both having two children, it made Lucy feel sad again that she only had one child and longed for the day when Harry was home and she would have a second child.

For the school summer holidays, Laura and Lucy decided to take the children to Scarborough for a holiday. They went to the hotel where they had been when William and Laura got engaged and later spent their honeymoon. As a surprise, William was working in the area, having to take some Generals to a week-long meeting in Yorkshire, so he was allowed leave and joined them in Scarborough. Lucy was delighted to see her brother and also pleased that Laura and he could be together. However, it only highlighted that Harry had not been home for two years now, although she knew from what William was saying, that many of the men hadn't been home at all. But it didn't stop Lucy from longing for Harry, especially when she saw Laura and William so happy together.

Young Edward, Laura's second boy, was very keen to tell everybody in the hotel that he was going to school after the holidays. He was a natural comic and entertained a lot of the old ladies who were there alone. That was until Laura found out that they were all giving him money, so Laura had to stop it.

When the new school term started, there were three boys and girls in the school who had lost their fathers in the holidays. Lucy thought back to her blissful weeks in Scarborough and thanked God that Harry was in a safe job, like William. In October, Laura telephoned Lucy to tell her that she was expecting again. Lucy suggested that it must have been the sea air in Scarborough, or something, to which Laura laughed, and said, 'or something.' There had been a little scare in the early stages, so Laura was taking life very easy again, keeping Mrs Carter busier than ever. Lucy started knitting in the long winter evenings, to while away the time. She was even teaching Grace to knit, but didn't think the knitting would be good enough for Laura's new baby; there were too many dropped stitches yet.

After Bonfire Night, the children started preparing for Christmas, beginning with the real meaning of Christmas in their lessons. Lucy was allowing the children to write a Nativity play, which they would perform for their parents in the last week of term.

On a Saturday morning, the first of December, Lucy and Grace were having a lazy breakfast of eggs on toast, when there was a knocking on the door. Thinking it might be Liz, Lucy went to the door, smiling in anticipation. Her smile soon faded when she saw it was a telegram boy, proffering her an envelope. Thinking there must be some mistake, Lucy read the envelope to check who it was for. It was addressed to her. Her first thought was that Harry might be coming home on leave and this was to tell her when to expect him, so she then opened it eagerly.

Regret to inform you that Lance Corporal Harry Marsden was killed in action

Lucy heard someone screaming but didn't realise that it was herself until Grace came to the door, looking worried.

'What's the matter, Mummy? Have you got a pain?'

'Sorry, sweetheart, yes, I've got a pain, a bad pain.'

'Shall I kiss it better?'

'Yes please.' Grace kissed her mother on her forehead, just the same as

189

Lucy did to Grace when she had a pain. 'That's better now, darling. Please could you go and feed the hens?' Grace nodded and went out into the garden.

Lucy was trying to absorb what the telegram was saying. It said 'killed in action,' but how could that be? He didn't go into action. Perhaps they've sent the telegram to the wrong person – yes – that must be it, Lucy's fevered thoughts went on. There was another knocking at the door. *Thank goodness,* Lucy thought. *This will be a second telegram telling me they had made a mistake.* It was Liz.

'I saw the telegram boy. Are you all right?'

'I think it's a dreadful mistake,' Lucy started. 'It says Harry was killed in action, but he doesn't go into action,' Lucy cried. Liz took the telegram.

'No, Lucy. It definitely says Harry was killed in action. I'm so sorry.'

'How can he? I don't understand it.'

'I've no idea, but perhaps they were going to another place and were attacked. I'm sure that somebody will tell you later. When Martin died, I got a letter shortly after he died from the Commanding Officer, who explained how he died and that he didn't suffer.'

'I'll wait for the letter then,' said Lucy. 'Then I'll believe it.'

'Don't you think you need to tell Harry's parents though?'

'No, it might be a mistake.'

'I've never heard about anyone getting a telegram by mistake,' Liz said gently, knowing that Lucy was desperately holding on to any hope.

'You haven't?'

'No.'

'Oh, Liz, what am I going to do?'

'The same as I did. You'll look to God, from whence comes your help. Only He can get you through it. Besides your friends, of course. That's what helped me. You being ready to help at any time. Knowing I could talk to you about how I was feeling and talk about Martin at any time. You've got a good family, too. They'll help you.'

'I can't live without him, Liz.'

'Yes, you can. You have to, now. At least you have Grace to remember him by. Does Grace know?'

'No, I couldn't tell her.'

'Do you want me to tell her?'

'Yes. Oh, no. It should be me, and then I'll ring his parents.'

As if on cue, Grace came through the door with her little basket, with the eggs.

'Look, Mummy, we've got three eggs.'

'Well done, Grace. Now come and sit with me, as I need to tell you something.'

'I'll go,' Liz said, 'but come round anytime. Don't forget?'

'Thank you, Liz.' Lucy watched her go through the door before she started talking to Grace. *Just how do you tell a five-year-old that her father has died, she asked herself.* She took a deep breath.

'Do you remember Mummy getting a letter from the postman this morning?'

'Yes, and then you got a pain.'

'That's right. Well, the pain was because the letter had some bad news in it. The army have written to tell us that daddy has died and gone to live with Jesus in Heaven.'

'Will he be staying there?'

'Yes, I'm afraid so.'

'So he won't be coming home soon?'

'No.'

'Can we go and visit him?'

'I'm afraid not.'

'Oh. I'd like to go and visit him.'

'So would I, sweetheart, but we can't go to Heaven until we die.'

'We can see Daddy when we die?'

'Yes.'

'That's good. We'll see him one day. Can I go and play with Mrs Hunter's kitten now?'

'Yes, if you like. I have to telephone Granny Marsden and tell her.'

'Daddy was Granny Marsden's little boy a long time ago, wasn't he?'

'Yes, that's right, so Granny Marsden will be very sad, too.'

'I'll give her a kiss next time I go and I'll take her an egg from our hens. That will make her better.'

'Of course it will,' replied Lucy, only wishing it were so easy.

'So, can I go to Mrs Hunter's?'

'Yes, I'll walk round with you.'

'Mummy, I'm five and a half. I can walk on my own now.'

'Yes, you are. Off you go then, but if Mrs Hunter is busy, you must come home again.'

Grace didn't come home immediately, so Lucy picked up the telephone to ring Mrs Marsden, but then thought better of it. It would come better in person than a telephone message. Lucy slipped round to Liz's house and asked her to keep Grace until she returned, then got in the car and drove to Clitheroe.

Mrs Marsden was distraught, but more concerned about Lucy and Grace. Lucy managed to make her laugh when she told her what Grace had said would cheer her up. Mrs Marsden also didn't understand how Harry could have died, when he was in the medical corps, and that brought fresh anxieties for her son-in-law, who was serving in France also.

On arriving home, Lucy rang all her family before collecting Grace. She tried to stay as normal as she could for Grace, even though her heart was breaking. Just after tea, Laura turned up and hugged Lucy.

'I had to come over. You sounded so bleak on the telephone.'

'I can't think straight, and my mind won't believe it yet. I keep thinking it must be a mistake.'

'Shall I telephone William and see if he can find anything out for you?'

'No, don't put him to any trouble. Liz, my neighbour, said that she received a letter a few days after her son died, explaining what had happened. I'll wait for that.'

They chatted for a long time and then Laura put Grace to bed, who thought that was a real treat to have Aunty Laura read her bedtime story and say her prayers. Grace was soon off to sleep, as children can do, even when everyone around them is falling apart.

'Who's looking after the children?' Lucy suddenly asked.

'My mum. She's staying the night in case you wanted me to stay.'

'Shouldn't you be resting? What about your baby?' Lucy suddenly remembered.

'I'm fine. The doctor says I can get up and about now, as I'm five months and there's been no sign of further trouble.

'Good.'

'Do you want another cup of tea?' asked Laura.

'No thanks, I'm drowning in tea.'

'Would you like me to stay the night?'

'No, I'd prefer to be on my own tonight, with Grace of course.'

'If you are sure, I'll be getting home then. Relieve my mum of the children!'

'Thank you for coming, Laura. I really appreciate that.'

'Goodbye, and telephone me anytime, promise?'

'Promise. Goodbye,'

The door shut and Lucy locked up for the night, then banked the fire down so that it would still be lit tomorrow morning. So far, she had managed to stay strong and hadn't cried properly, but as soon as she got into bed and felt Harry's side of the bed, the tears started and wouldn't stop. She tried to smell him on the sheets but they had been washed far too many times for there to be any trace of him now. The thought of never seeing him again totally overwhelmed her and she started to get angry at God and railed at him. 'Why God? Why did you let him die? How could you do this to me? I can't manage without him.'

Eventually, she fell asleep but had tormented dreams where Harry was just in front of her and she kept reaching out but couldn't quite catch him. She woke exhausted, with a bad headache, but when Grace came into the bedroom, she had to make an effort.

'Hello, Grace. Come and give mummy a cuddle. I'm going to need lots of cuddles now.'

'Yes, I've been thinking. Now Daddy's gone to Heaven, you will miss his cuddles, as you liked Daddy's cuddles, didn't you? Well, I'll just have to give you lots of cuddles instead, and Granny Marsden, of course.'

'That's right, Grace,' said Lucy, trying not to cry. 'Shall we see if the hens have laid?'

'No, Mummy, that's my job. You make the porridge.'

'All right, bossy boots. I'll just have a bath first, is that all right?'

'Yes, but hurry up or we'll be late for church.'

'I'm not going to church this morning, Grace.'

'Why not? I want to go. Can I go?'

'Yes, if you like. You can sit with Mrs Hunter.'

'Must I? I want to sit with Harriet Fallon. She's my best friend.'

'All right, then, as long as Mrs Fallon doesn't mind.'

When it was time for church, Lucy watched Grace as she crossed over the road and then went back inside. She couldn't face going to church; she was too mad at God for letting this happen. She hadn't read her Bible or prayed last night. She didn't want to pray to a God who could ruin her life. So, she sat in a chair, thinking about Harry and how she would cope without him, but she didn't come up with any answers.

Chapter 27

Grace was soon back and full of what she had learned in Sunday School, showing her mother the pictures she had drawn. Lucy smiled at her efforts and listened to her prattle, without much enthusiasm.

Bill and Liz called round after the service to ask her for lunch. Lucy politely declined, but was pleased when Bill told her not to come into school next week. At least that would give her a breathing space.

'I've taken a leaf out of your book, Lucy,' Bill said.

'Oh? What's that?'

'I've asked Mrs Jackson to come and help me for a week or two. I've set all the work and Mrs Jackson can oversee it but come to me if she has any problems. I think she'll do well. If you want to stay off longer, I can contact the Education Board to find me a replacement.'

'Yes,' replied Lucy distractedly.

'Yes, you think Mrs Jackson will do well, or yes, you want me to find a replacement for you?'

'Whatever you think fit. I can't think straight at the moment.'

'Come round if you need us,' Liz said gently, to which Lucy nodded, so they left.

'Is it Granny Marsden's or Aunty Laura's for Sunday lunch this week?' asked Grace.

'Neither. We're staying here.'

'We always go to one of them on Sundays. Why aren't we going?'

'Because your Daddy died yesterday and I don't want to go. I feel too sad.'

'Won't you feel better if we go? Granny and Granddad Marsden will be sad, too. We would be a blessing to them if we went.'

Lucy had to smile at how old-fashioned Grace was, and thought there might be a grain of truth in what she said, but she couldn't face going yet.

'We'll go next week,' Lucy promised, knowing she couldn't put off the inevitable for too long.

'So, what are we having for Sunday lunch today?' asked Grace.

'I've no idea. Shall we have eggs on toast?'

'That's not a Sunday lunch,' pouted Grace, 'it should be meat and vegetables and roast potatoes and lovely gravy. That's what we always have.'

'Not today. I haven't got any meat to roast as I didn't know we'd be staying here. We could have a sandwich?'

'I'd prefer eggs on toast if I must,' Grace replied.

'I'll make them in a minute, I just need to sit here a little while longer.'

'Can I play out, then? In the garden?'

'Yes, off you go.'

Lucy sat dispiritedly in the chair, not having the energy or the will to get up and make a meal. She just wanted to go to bed and cry, but knew she couldn't with Grace to look after. There was a knock on the door, and Lucy wondered who was coming round now to pester her. She thought about not answering the door, but the door opened and someone was coming in.

'Lucy? It's Betsy. I've come to see how you are?'

'Hello, Betsy,' replied Lucy, not even getting up out of her chair.

'I'm so sorry about Harry. It was such a shock when Mother rang me. You must be devastated.' Lucy just nodded.

'I can't seem to get going. I've just been told off by Grace because I wasn't making a proper Sunday lunch. She was most put out.'

'I'm not surprised; it's far too early to be able to get yourself organised. That's why I've brought you both a Sunday lunch.'

Lucy managed a smile. 'Grace will love you for that!'

'It's ready plated up so you just need to pop it in your oven to warm through. Here, let me do it for you. It'll soon be ready.'

'You are so kind, Betsy. I don't know how to thank you. The thought of making a proper meal just overwhelmed me.'

'My mother says that you are welcome to go and stay at her house for a few days or weeks. You won't want to stay at my house; it's far too noisy, although you'd be welcome, if you wanted to.'

'That's kind of both of you, but I prefer to stay here.'

'I understand, but don't hesitate to ask us if we can do anything to help. What about letting Grace come round to play next Saturday? I know she loves playing with her cousins.'

'Yes, Aunty Betsy, I'd love to come round and play with my cousins next Saturday. Thank you for asking,' Grace said to Lucy's surprise as she hadn't heard her come in the house.

'Right. I'll come and pick you up next Saturday morning, Grace. It'll give your mummy some time on her own.'

'Yes, then she can cry all day,' Grace added.

Lucy and Betsy looked at each other, and Betsy whispered, 'Out of the mouths of babes and sucklings….' and Lucy nodded.

'She's so old-fashioned,' Lucy said, and Betsy agreed, then said she had to be off.

'Say thank you to Aunty Betsy for bringing us a Sunday lunch.'

'Sunday lunch? Oh, thank you, Aunty Betsy,' she said, giving her a hug. 'Mummy didn't want to make one today and it made me sad.'

'Well, you can be happy again, as it's in the oven warming. Goodbye for now,' and Betsy left.

'Shall I set the table, Mummy?'

'Yes, please,' replied Lucy.

Grace sat up to the table, her knife and fork in her hands ready, and Lucy brought both plates over to the table.

'Thank you for our food,' chanted Grace, 'and God bless Aunty Betsy for bringing us a Sunday lunch. Amen.' Grace tucked in to her lunch, but Lucy picked at hers, not feeling hungry.

'Come on, Mummy, you have to eat up your dinner so that you will be a big strong girl.'

Lucy smiled as she heard her own instructions that she'd said many times to Grace, coming back to her. She picked up her knife and fork and forced the food down, to please Grace.

'There's apple crumble and custard for afterwards,' said Lucy.

'Oh, my favourite,' said Grace, and polished off the whole dish very quickly. 'Well, that was better than eggs on toast, wasn't it, Mummy?' and Lucy had to agree.

After Grace had gone to bed, Lucy started thinking about Harry again and then suddenly realised that Betsy had been so caring and sympathetic to her, when she was in mourning for her own brother who had died. It wasn't just Lucy and Grace who were mourning, but the whole of Harry's family. Lucy started thinking how she would feel if it had been William who had died. Her heart contracted just at the thought of it, and she realised just how much Betsy must be suffering.

Picking up the telephone, Lucy asked the operator to put her through to Betsy's number. When she answered, Lucy apologised for not acknowledging that Betsy was also grieving for her brother and thanked her again for bringing the meal, which they had both enjoyed. Betsy told Lucy not to worry. She understood what Lucy was going through, as she'd seen it with many of her father's patients who were also mourning the loss of loved ones. Feeling better that she'd made the telephone call, Lucy went to bed early and only cried for a short time before she went to sleep, exhausted by too much crying.

Next morning, Lucy got up early with Grace and got her ready for school, then waved her off, watching as she crossed the street carefully, checking for horses or motor cars coming. As soon as she had tidied the breakfast things away, Lucy got the dishes that the Sunday lunch had arrived in and put them in the motor car. First, she went into Clitheroe and parked near Mitchell's Modes. Going straight to the dress department, Lucy picked out three black mourning dresses, two for everyday and one more suited to dressing up, not that she felt like going anywhere where she needed to be dressed up. The assistant offered her condolences; it was a much-used phrase at the moment, with many local families being in mourning. Lucy decided not to put Grace in mourning clothes but did buy her an armband, as she had seen many of the children wearing them.

Going to the café for a cup of chocolate, Lucy slipped into the toilets afterwards and changed into one of her new everyday black dresses. Catching a glimpse of herself in the mirror, Lucy pulled a face. She wasn't used to wearing such a severe, plain dress, but she must just put up with it for a few months. Before she went home, she stopped at the florists and bought two bunches of flowers. Calling at Mrs Marsden's on the way home, she took her a bunch of flowers and stayed for a cup of tea. Then as she returned the dishes to Betsy, she also gave her a bunch of flowers, with which Betsy was very touched.

On arriving home, Lucy tried to keep herself busy but kept being overwhelmed by tears and having to sit down. It would help if she knew just what had happened to him, but there was no letter in the post. The letter didn't come until the Friday morning. It was from Harry's commanding officer and it explained that Harry had suffered a wound in his hand during an operation, which had festered and, despite all treatment, had resulted in an overwhelming infection that had killed him. He also added that Harry had been an upright and loyal member of the unit and she should be proud of him. Then he added his condolences. Lucy suddenly thought of this man, who must be writing the same thing every day to wives, mothers, and children of soldiers who had died. It must be soul destroying, she suspected. Then she noticed there was another letter in the envelope. It was from the surgeon with whom Harry had worked closely.

My dear Mrs Marsden,

I am so sorry to be writing this letter to you. Harry became my dearest friend in the temporary theatre we were working in. He worked more like a junior doctor than a medical orderly, undertaking many of the minor procedures so that I could deal with the greater emergencies. You should be rightly proud of him. He saved many lives. It is ironic that a slip of the hand meant he got a deep cut in his own hand and, due to the nature of the wounds we are treating, it was inevitable that he would get an infection.

In our rare times of quiet, he would talk about you and Grace and how much he loved you and couldn't wait to return to you. He also talked about his work as a carpenter. He was forever making things with spare scraps of wood, using old scalpels, and giving them to the soldiers to send home to their children.

I will never forget him and I pray you will always remember, he died to save others' lives. May God bless you, my dear.

Major Arthur McGeorge

The tears came afresh when she read this second letter, and she felt that it was ironic that Harry had died almost by accident. *What a waste,* Lucy thought. *If only God had protected him.* Once her tears were spent, she decided that at least she now knew how Harry had died. It didn't make it any easier, but she had more knowledge. Before she knew it, Grace had arrived home and was excited about her school day. She had persuaded her mother that she should go to Aunty Betsy's that evening, instead of Saturday morning, so that she could have longer there. After Grace had got changed out of her school clothes, Lucy took her over to Clitheroe and left her to sleep overnight.

Lucy decided to sort Harry's clothes out that night and as she looked through the wardrobe, she held the clothes against her to smell them, loving the smell that still lingered on his clothes. Eventually, but forcibly, she put them into a pile and would take them to the Red Cross next week, as they were always wanting good clothes for poor families.

Next morning there was a knock on the door about 11am. Lucy answered it and there was Cynthia on her doorstep.

'Cynthia! Come in, how good to see you. How have you got here?' as there seemed to be no sign of a motor car outside.

'Hello, Lucy, how are you? Laura rang to tell me about Harry. I had to come and see you as I know just what you'll be going through. My sister, remember Jessie? The middle one? She's driven over with me and she's gone to Clitheroe shopping now. She's coming back in four hours.'

'Let me put the kettle on the hob. Oh, this is so good of you. You have no idea.'

'Oh, yes I have. I know that at first, I just needed someone to talk to who had been through the same as me. I told my Mother, "I'll just have to go and see Lucy" and she understood and said she'd look after the children. By the way, where's Grace?'

'Grace invited herself to her Aunty Betsy's, that's Harry's eldest sister, to sleep and play with her cousins. I'm going to pick her up at teatime. I think that's a ploy on Betsy's part so that she knows I'll be having a proper meal tonight. I'm not much up to cooking yet,' said Lucy.

'The company will be good for you, too.'

'I'm glad of your company today though, knowing you have been through the same things. Let me just make the tea and then we'll talk. Sorry there is no cake, I haven't baked lately.'

'Don't worry about cake. I'm fine with a cup of tea.'

Lucy brought the two cups of tea over and sat down.

'So, tell me what happened?' Cynthia asked.

'It wasn't heroic, like your Huw, going over the top to kill or be killed. It was an accident with a scalpel.'

'What?' asked Cynthia, disbelieving. So Lucy told her of the accident and what had happened, but that she had a lovely letter from his commanding officer and also the surgeon that he'd worked with.

'What you have to remember, Lucy, is that they gave their lives for others. That's what you have to hold on to. They followed the road that Jesus took, and what he said to His disciples, *"Greater love hath no man than this, that a man lay down his life for his friend".*'

'I know in my head that is right – other people have said that – but it's here, in my heart, that I can't quite make it work.'

'It's only been one week. Don't be too hard on yourself, Lucy. I could still cry, even now, but it does get easier. You just have to live a day at a time.'

'I'm still mad at God. There, that's shocked you, hasn't it?'

'No, Lucy, because I was the same. "Why my husband? Why didn't you protect him?", I kept asking.'

'Are you still mad at God?'

'No. I understand more now. God has a plan for everyone. We only see the small part of our own lives. We don't see the bigger picture. God would never want nations to war against nations but it happens, and people die.'

'I feel as if I'll never be right again. Sometimes this week, I've felt like I'm going mad.'

'I know, but it will pass, I promise you.'

'I'm so glad you came, Cynthia. It has really helped me. I'll make you some lunch. Will a sandwich do?'

'That will be lovely. Will you show me round the house and garden afterwards? You know I've always been nosy about other peoples' houses.'

'Of course. Ham or cheese, or both?'

'Ham, please.' Lucy made the sandwich and more cups of tea and the two ladies ate in silence for a while. Afterwards, Lucy took Cynthia round the gardens first, showing her the hen hut and her vegetable patch, and the orchard. Cynthia asked what the out-buildings were used for and Lucy said that they were Harry's workshops. Next, they went round the house, Cynthia saying how much she liked the house and thought Lucy was very fortunate, especially as she was working again, with her work right across the road. They got in to Lucy's bedroom and her heart sank. She'd forgotten that all Harry's clothes were still at the bottom of the bed.

'Have you been having a sort out?' asked Cynthia.

'Yes, sorry, I forgot they were here.'

'Are they Harry's things?'

'Yes.'

'Do you want me to take them away for you? Our church runs a clothes exchange for the poorer people of the congregation and surrounding streets. They would love these; they are of such good quality.'

'By all means, take them. I was only going to send them to the Red Cross in Clitheroe, but I'd rather they weren't in Clitheroe to be honest. I wouldn't like to see someone else in them.'

'I know just what you mean. Huw had a distinctive jacket and I kept seeing it for ages. I was glad for the poorer person, that they had a good warm jacket, but it kept upsetting me again. It'll be one less thing for you to have to think about.'

'Thanks, Cynthia.'

'When do you think you'll go back to work?'

'I hadn't even thought about it, but, do you know, I think I might be ready. I've sorted a lot of things out in my head since I got the letters from the army and with what you've said, so I think I'll go back on Monday. I was getting fed up stuck at home anyway,' Lucy admitted.

'That's good.' Soon Cynthia's sister arrived and the two friends parted again, Cynthia taking the piles of clothes with her.

'Don't hesitate to telephone me anytime or come over with Grace.'

'I won't, Cynthia, and thank you for helping me to make sense of what has happened.'

After they had gone, Lucy got ready to go and have tea at Betsy's and collect Grace. Lucy told Betsy about Cynthia's visit and how it had helped her, for which Betsy was glad.

That night, Lucy talked to God about her feelings, but also thanked Him for her friends and family. She had a better night's sleep afterwards.

Next morning, Lucy was awake early and was putting on her best black dress, ready for church. Grace was happy when Lucy said they were going to church, but asked if she could still sit with Harriet Fallon, to which Lucy agreed, with a smile.

After the service, she sought out Bill Hunter and told him that she would be back at school in the morning. He said she must only do it if she was sure, but she said that she was. Lucy was pleased that Bill had prayed in the service for all those who were bereaved due to the war, which must have been hard, Lucy thought, knowing that he himself was bereaved.

At school, Lucy was thrown into preparations for Christmas services and plays, so was soon distracted from her grief. Only in the quiet of the night did she allow her feelings full reign.

Christmas 1917 was fairly quiet, apart from when Grace opened her presents. They decided that they would spend Christmas at the Marsden's this year and stayed for three days. There was time amidst the traditions and fun to quietly reflect on Harry's life. Mrs Marsden said that it was hard when your child died before you; it wasn't the natural order of things, but a lot of other people locally were in the same boat, and you just had to get on with it. Lucy nodded her agreement. She was glad there was no Christmas Wishes tradition at the Marsden's. She couldn't have thought of anything to say this year, apart from the end of the war, which everyone was wishing for.

Coping wasn't instantly easier for Lucy. There were still bad days when all she wanted to do was to curl up in bed and cry all day, but with having a child to care for, and a class full of children to teach, she had to make a big effort to keep going. There were good days and bad days, but slowly, the good days seemed to be more than the bad days, as time went by. Despite being initially mad at God, she realised that He was indeed her help and strength, and her mind began to ease.

Chapter 28

The year 1918 started with a cold snap, with lots of snow, so Lucy hardly took the motor car out. Eventually, she sold Harry's commercial vehicle and put the money in the Marsden Building Society account for Grace, as she was managing to live on what she earned.

Some good news happened in late March as Laura gave birth to another boy. William managed to get home for his Christening service and Lucy was a godmother, as she had been for all Laura's boys. Lucy was very touched when they decided to call him George Harry and had to fight back tears when she heard the news. When she took her vows as godmother, she prayed that baby George would never have to go to war in his lifetime.

On the first week of June, it was quite hot weather and Lucy decided that it was time to stop wearing her widow's weeds. At first, she chose lilacs, purples, and grey clothes, but by the end of the year she was wearing normal clothes again. Grace noticed and said that she was glad her mummy was wearing her nice clothes again, which made Lucy smile. Gradually in fits and starts, and with support from Cynthia, Lucy returned to a more normal life. She would never forget Harry, but she was getting used to being on her own and coping. It helped that she had enough money, as she knew many widows who were struggling since being widowed due to the war.

For the summer holidays, Lucy and Grace went on holiday to Scarborough again to the same hotel as before. Laura and her children came, but this time, Cynthia and her parents came as well. All the children had a wonderful time, playing on the beach and in the parks. They all discovered a love of ice cream, which was echoed by their mothers. One day, Mr and Mrs Shaw offered to take the children out on a trip in a charabanc, so the three women went to Whitby for the day. After looking at the ruined abbey, they found a nice tearoom and enjoyed a long leisurely lunch with lots of chatting. It felt so good for all of them to be together again, without the encumbrance of children, much as they loved them.

The news from the war front was looking good now and there was hope that the war would soon be over. Everybody was longing for that.

Lucy was enjoying her work and welcomed the new children into her class at the beginning of the school year. She always loved this time of year, with the challenge of all the new little ones, who weren't sure about coming to school, but Lucy had the opportunity of instilling a love of learning in their tiny minds.

Throughout the war, the Suffragettes had stopped their disruptive practices and turned to helping the war effort in various ways, and it was thought that this work that they did went a long way towards getting votes for women. Lucy kept abreast with all their work, but as a working mother, she had no time to attend any meetings, which had been largely abandoned during the war, anyway. So, she was very pleased when it was announced that women of 30 would get the vote if they were householders. That meant that she only had another year to wait until she got the vote. It was also good that more or less all men over 21 would get the vote as well, regardless of whether they were householders or not. The world was changing, Lucy was pleased to note.

At long last, in November 1918, the war ended and the peace treaty was signed. The world gave a collective sigh of relief. Although it wouldn't bring back Huw or Harry and many others, Cynthia, Laura, and Lucy agreed that it was good news for all. William returned to his garage and took up the reins from the Captain who had kept the business ticking over safely during the war, and indeed had made a handsome profit for William, for which William rewarded him. Young Albert was making a sterling mechanic, and William and Laura's eldest two boys were regularly making visits to the garage and spending time with Freddie and Albert, looking under the bonnets of motor cars, despite their young ages. Albert's brother, Arthur, was also working at the garage now. Laura was thrilled that all her siblings were not working in the mill: such a different life from their parents.

Christmas 1918 was a joyous time for everyone. Although rationing was still in place to some extent, people made a big celebration of festivities, especially at the churches where Lucy and Laura attended. On top of celebrating the birth of Jesus, there were great celebrations that soldiers were coming back from the war and lives were being rebuilt. Matthew also returned to Betsy and the family, and Harry's younger brother, John, survived the war and decided to stay in the army as a career. Sadly, the teacher that Lucy replaced in the school did not come back from the war, so her job was secure. But all was not well, as some families were soon to find out. A new kind of war was beginning to be waged. It was a very virulent form of influenza which was nicknamed the Spanish Flu, due to its origins.

The numbers of deaths from the Spanish Flu soon outnumbered the number of people who had died in the war. Nobody seemed to be safe. It was especially virulent in Clitheroe, as family after family succumbed. Both Dr Marsden and Matthew were working all hours, trying to give succour to the families of the dying, and to the dying patients themselves.

With the strain of overwork, Dr Marsden finally succumbed to the disease himself in the first week of January 1919. He was dead within two days, shortly followed by his wife. A week later, Matthew and Betsy's youngest child also died and the whole family grieved yet again. Harry's Granny Marsden was especially distraught to have lost two generations of her family in one week, and she kept saying it should have been her not them, as she'd had her life. To have got through the war and then to have a triple disaster like this was so painful. Grace cried bitterly for her grandparents and cousin and the only way that Lucy could comfort her was to talk about them being reunited with her daddy in Heaven, which cheered Grace up a little.

A few weeks later, Lucy received a letter from Archie Alderson, saying that he had some belongings of Harry's and please could he bring them on the following Saturday? Lucy remembered the name from Harry's letters, that the two men had been friends, so she replied in the affirmative. Lucy wondered what he would be bringing, but time would soon tell. She would have to be patient, for once.

Saturday arrived at long last. Lucy looked round her living room with pride. It had been cleaned thoroughly; not that it needed it as she and Annie Jackson always kept on top of any dirt, but a special visitor was coming today. His letter said that he would arrive at Whalley station at 1pm, so she could expect him before half-past. She had got up early today, leaving Grace asleep in bed, to bake some special treats for their lunch. There were cheese and onion pasties, chicken and mushroom pies, ham and cheese sandwiches, cheese and fruit scones, a Victoria sandwich, and butterfly buns. She had baked far more than they could possibly eat at one meal, but she wanted to show her gratefulness that he was coming to visit her.

Once Grace arrived downstairs, Lucy gave her little jobs to do after her breakfast. Grace got out the best china and laid it carefully on the large table that was in the centre of the room. The starched cotton napkins were carefully folded and Lucy nodded her approval. Later on Grace asked if she could have something to eat.

'No,' replied Lucy, 'wait until Mr Alderson comes. Then we can eat. Why don't you go and play with your toys in the parlour? But don't make a mess. I've tidied up in there.'

'All right, I won't make a mess,' she replied. 'I never do.'

'You are right,' Lucy replied. 'You are Mummy's good girl.' However, before anything else could be said, there was a knock at the door and Lucy hurried to answer it.

A tall, gaunt-looking man stood on the doorstep, still wearing his army greatcoat, his patched and worn clothes hanging loosely on him as if he'd lost weight. Hanging on to his hand was a small boy about two or three years old. In his other arm was a large cardboard box and a square package wrapped in brown paper. She wondered why the man had brought his son with him but remembered her manners before she said anything.

'Welcome. It's so good of you to come. Come in out of the cold and get warm.' The man and boy stepped over the threshold and she led them to the comfy chairs by the fireplace. Lucy took their coats and put them on the hook on the back door, and the parcels on a chair near the sideboard.

'The food's ready, so unless you need to wash your hands or anything, we can make a start. Come and sit at the table.' The man and boy got up and moved towards the table. She remembered that she still had the chair with long legs that Harry had made for Grace, so she got it out of the parlour for the little boy to sit on. When the teapot was brought to the table, she said grace, and then they all tucked in to the food. The man talked about his journey and general matters, but the little boy never spoke, but just sat eating and looking warily about him.

After the food was finished, Lucy suggested that Grace took the little boy into the parlour to play with the toys, whilst more serious adult talk could take place. The little boy was a bit reluctant to go, but was soon persuaded by the man's encouragement and the mention of building bricks.

'My Daddy made these building bricks for me out of bits of wood,' she could hear Grace jabbering away. Satisfied that they could talk in more detail, she left them and returned to the man at the table.

'So, what have you got of my husband's? I got the official letter that all the soldiers were recommended to write before they went to the Front, but that's all I got, and letters from his commanding officer and a doctor he worked with.'

The man went to his coat pocket and pulled out a package and passed it over to her. On opening it, she saw a lot of her letters that she had written to Harry and her eyes filled with tears. There was also Harry's pocket watch, which was the present she had given him on their wedding day. Finally there was his tiny Bible, which just contained the Gospels and the Psalms.

'Is that all?' she asked, a little disappointed. The man swallowed and looked nervous.

'Yes, apart from the boy.'

'The boy? What do you mean? Isn't he your son?'

'No. It's your husband's son.'

'My husband's son? That's ridiculous! How can that be?' she asked, her whole world falling apart.

'With his last breath Harry asked me to bring the boy to you. He said you'd understand and forgive him.'

'I don't understand,' said a bewildered Lucy. 'How can this be my husband's son?'

'It's a long story. I'm sorry to be the bearer of it. I thought Harry had written to you about it.'

'No, he didn't. He must have forgotten that slight detail,' Lucy replied sarcastically.

'Well, there was a young French nurse in our department who worked on night duty mainly. Her name was Mimi and she'd become a nurse when her husband had joined up so that she could be serving her country, the same as him. She was already a qualified nurse, so they overlooked the fact that she was married. However, her husband died and she was very distraught and we were all worried that she would take her own life, so upset she was. So, we all took turns at talking to her and going on little walks with her. It was hard work, but we all did it and it kept her going.'

'What has this to do with Harry? I don't think I like where this story is going.'

'No, I'm afraid you won't like it, but please hear me out. One night, it was Harry's turn to take her for a walk and she was particularly distressed. So, Harry tried to comfort her and started to cuddle her and things got out of hand. Harry never went out alone with her again, but it was too late, she was expecting a child.'

'How do you know it was Harry's child? Didn't you all comfort her?' Lucy asked bitterly.

'No, nobody else. Not in that way.'

'Hmm, I'm not sure about that. The others may have lied. She may have been spreading her favours with many men.'

'She wasn't that kind of girl.'

'No? She slept with my husband, so that makes her that kind of girl to me.'

'Please believe me, she was a good upright woman, just distraught.'

'I was distraught when Harry died, but I didn't fling myself into the arms of the first man I found,' Lucy cried bitterly. 'So, what happened next? Did Harry swear undying love and promise to divorce me?'

'No, they were both mortified by the event. When her parents found out about the baby, they threw her out and wanted nothing further to do with her, and the same with her husband's parents who were even more disgusted with her. She had the baby, but there was some complication and she died three days afterwards. After her parents threw her out, she went to live with a friend who had just had a baby six months before. So as her child was ready to be weaned, she said she would nurse the boy until something permanent could be sorted out.'

'So why isn't the child there still?'

'The lady was widowed a few months after the boy was born, and she had the chance of a new start with a new husband, but he wouldn't take the little boy. We'd all been taking care of the boy on our time off, so he was familiar with us all and, as he grew, could speak French and English.'

'Why can't you keep him then if he knows you so well? Or one of the other men?'

'The other men already have children and have no blood ties to the baby. I'm a single man and I'm struggling to find work. My landlady said she would allow me to stay with the boy until I brought him here, but no longer. Also, I have to work. My money is running out. My old job in the factory is gone. Women took over our jobs in the factory whilst we were away fighting and now they're keeping the women on, because they can pay them less. I've got a four-week job starting on Monday, so I can't keep the child. Besides, I have to keep my promise to Harry. He asked me to bring the child here.'

'You could have refused.'

'I could, but Harry was pleading. He knew he was dying and didn't want his son to be brought up in a French orphanage, which is what would have happened to him. Harry said you'd understand and forgive him.'

'Forgive? I don't think so. I don't understand either; how could he put me in this position?'

'I'm really sorry, Mrs Marsden.'

'Yes, I'm sorry too, but I'm also sorry that I'm taking it out on you. It's not your fault, any of this.'

'Don't you think the boy looks like Harry?'

'I didn't really take notice; I thought he was your son.' Lucy got up to go and take another look at this little boy with blonde hair, who was only just three years old. He sat playing with Grace, his head on one side and his little hands were stroking the wooden pieces of bricks. A sudden memory of the first time she had seen Harry came into her mind. He had been stood in the hallway at her house, blonde head on one side, stroking the wood of the hall table. This boy was definitely Harry's child. Suddenly Lucy's eyes filled with tears. This was the little boy that they had planned to have together and now this was the only son left of her husband, and it was tainted. Lucy flew from the room and, leaving Mr Alderson downstairs, ran up to her bedroom and wept inconsolably. Wept for herself, wept for Harry and wept for his betrayal of her. Eventually, she remembered her manners and came back downstairs, apologising to Mr Alderson, whilst putting the kettle on for another cup of tea. She certainly needed it now.

'How am I going to cope with this little boy? I don't even know his name?'

'It's Raymond. Raymond Edward Marsden. His birth certificate is in with the bundle of letters.'

At least he hadn't called him the name we had chosen for our child if it was a boy, when Grace was born, Lucy comforted herself, *and he had given him his father's name of Edward. What a shame that his father hadn't lived to see this baby, although Harry's parents would have been less than pleased with the circumstances.*

Mr Alderson spoke again, seeing that Lucy had gone quiet. 'I've been preparing him to come and live with you for some weeks, ever since I brought him home with me. I've told him he would get a new mother and sister, and they would love him.'

Love him? thought Lucy. *That I can never do.*

'I'm going to have to go soon, to catch my train. In the package are his clothes.'

'What's in the large parcel?' Lucy asked.

Mr Alderson opened the parcel and handed over a stool. 'It's a stool that Harry made for him when he was a baby.' Lucy took the stool. It was identical to Grace's, but it had the name 'Raymond' carved into it. It seemed as if it was the final piece of evidence that this little boy was her husband's son. All she could utter was, 'Thank you.'

'I'll just tell him that I'm going now.'

'Just a minute, before you do, here's some money for all your trouble.' Lucy gave him a handful of £1 notes. 'Also here's my Father's and my Granny's places of work, both in Burnley. Tell them I sent you and I'm sure they'll give you a job.'

Mr Alderson tried to refuse the money but she was adamant, saying that he would need it until he was in a better position, so he took it. Lucy called the children out from the parlour and they returned to the kitchen, Raymond clinging to some bricks.

'I'm going now, Raymond. You are going to stay here with your new family.' A torrent of French came out of Raymond's mouth. Mr Alderson held him and calmed him down, telling him to speak English. 'This is your English Mummy and sister now.'

'Come on Raymond, you'll be all right with me and Mummy,' said Grace. 'Is that right, Mummy? Is Raymond going to stay here with us? Is he my brother?'

'Yes,' said Lucy, swallowing a lump in her throat.

'I've always wanted a brother, but I thought I'd never have one. This is such fun,' said Grace.

'May I call again in about two weeks' time?' Mr Alderson asked. 'Just to see if he's settled in?'

'Yes, I think that would be helpful,' Lucy said. 'We'll see you in two weeks then.'

'Thank you so much. I've been dreading this visit.'

'I'm not surprised,' replied Lucy. 'Goodbye.' Mr Alderson left and, although there was a little tear in his eye, Raymond said not a word.

'Mummy, Raymond likes eggs. Can I show him the hen house?'

'Yes, go on then.'

'Can we have eggs for tea?'

'Of course.' The two children toddled outside and Lucy collapsed in a chair. She couldn't believe how her life had changed in one day. Her perfect marriage was now in tatters and she was left with her husband's illegitimate child to bring up. She would never forgive Harry. Never. He had ruined her memories of their life together. Her first thought was that she would give the child to Harry's family, but with the loss of the Marsdens and Betsy grieving over her lost child, how could she give the child to them? Lizzie was too far away anyway. Also, Harry had wanted her to bring the child up with Grace, his half-sister. No, she was stuck with the child.

Chapter 29

What on earth was she going to tell everybody? Could she pretend it was just a war orphan that she had decided to adopt? Or would everybody recognise that it was Harry's son. Would people pity her? Would they call her a fool for accepting the child, not that she had much option to refuse. Her brain was aching and she couldn't think straight. The children coming in made her begin to set to and prepare tea. He was a quiet little thing and ate everything she gave to him and said thank you, but didn't offer any other conversation. When he started to yawn, Lucy realised she'd better check in his parcel to see what clothes he had with him. There was only one change of clothing, two night shirts, and one change of underwear.

'Time for bed,' Lucy said. 'I think you need an early night as well, Grace. He can sleep in your room tonight, until we can get another bedroom sorted out for him. He can sleep in the other bed next to you. We'll not bother with baths tonight. Just go to the toilet and brush your teeth. There's a new toothbrush under the sink for him.'

The two children toddled off and when Lucy went up later, Grace was in her own bed and the boy was in the other. Lucy stood at the end of the bed and said prayers with both of them and went downstairs with a heavy heart. Half an hour later, she crept upstairs to see if the boy was settled. They were both fast asleep, in Grace's bed, with their arms round each other. Lucy hadn't the heart to move him, so left them there together.

Lucy came downstairs and picked up the telephone, waiting to be connected.

'Laura, I've got something to tell you.'

'How did the visit go with Mr Alderson?'

'That's what I have to tell you about.' Lucy proceeded to tell Laura all that had happened that day, with cries of disbelief from Laura as the story progressed.

'Don't tell me any more. I'm coming over.' With that, Laura put the telephone down, leaving Lucy standing with the receiver in her hand. Laura was over within the hour, bringing William with her.

'Who's looking after the children?' asked Lucy.

'Edie. We said it was an emergency,' William answered. So Lucy had to retell her story to them both. They were both shocked at what had happened, but were ready to support Lucy in her time of need.

'Can we have a look at him?' William asked.

'Yes, he's in Grace's bed.' The pair went upstairs quietly and when they came back down, looked sympathetically at Lucy.

'There's no denying that he's Harry's child, is there?' William said.

'No, he even holds his head on one side and strokes wood, just like Harry did.'

'What are you going to tell people?' asked Laura.

'I wouldn't want to tell lies; it's not in my nature as a Christian. Besides, you always get found out. However, I think people would guess it's Harry's child anyway, so it's useless trying to deny it.'

'That's true,' said Laura. 'We need to come up with a plan.' Half an hour later, William decided that he would go home to the children but leave Laura there. Then Lucy would bring Laura back tomorrow. As he left, William gave Lucy a hug and told her not to worry. Lucy was touched as they rarely hugged. Laura and Lucy talked long into the night and then Laura ended up sleeping with Lucy in her bed, so that if she woke in the night, they could talk. By morning, they had a clear plan of action. It was going to be very hard to carry out, but Lucy knew she had to do it.

In the morning, Grace was heard explaining to Raymond that they would be going to church, as she helped him to get dressed before they came down for breakfast. Raymond was introduced to his new Aunty Laura, and they set off across the road to church. Lucy had a quick word with Bill and Liz before the service started to warn them of what was coming. Lucy also insisted that Grace and Raymond stay in the pew with them, which Grace sulked about because she wanted to be with her best friend, Harriet Fallon. When the children were dismissed to Sunday school, Lucy walked to the front of the church. She'd spoken to the minister, Reverend Buckley, the previous night to tell him what had happened. As she was walking to the front of the church, Reverend Buckley announced that, prior to his sermon, Mrs Marsden would like to say a few words.

Lucy looked out at the sea of faces and swallowed, very hard. She wasn't sure she could go through with this, but she knew she had to. This was her church family, her friends. They would wish her well, not harm. She looked at Laura, who was smiling at her, and Lucy felt encouraged. Taking a deep breath, and saying a quick prayer for strength, Lucy started to speak.

'You probably noticed that I brought a young boy into church with me today. His name is Raymond and he has been orphaned during the war. He has been brought to me to bring him up as my own child. That is the first part of what I have to say, and that is all anybody else needs to know. What I tell you now, will be in strictest confidence and I know you will honour that. It is not a nice story, but it needs to be told to you, as my church family and friends.' Lucy took another deep breath.

'You all knew my husband well. He was a caring, loving husband and father but he was away from home for three years, working in the medical corps. Sometimes, when we are away from all we love, we make rash decisions and do things that we would never do in normal circumstances. That is what happened to Harry. In wanting to support a young nursing colleague who was extremely distraught, his comfort went a stage too far with the result that the woman was with child. She died just after the child was born and he was looked after by a foster mother. When Harry lay dying, he made his friend promise that if ever the foster mother couldn't look after the child, that he would be sent back to England to me, rather than go into a French orphanage. The foster mother was remarrying and her new husband wouldn't take the child, so he was brought to me yesterday. I am still shocked by all this, but I'd rather you knew than look at Raymond and guess whose child he is. Thank you.'

There was a stunned silence in the church as Lucy walked back to her seat, not looking at anyone for fear of bursting into tears. The minister quickly stood up and spoke.

'Thank you, Mrs Marsden. I have to say that that was the bravest thing I've ever seen anyone do. We know how hard that must have been for you. Now, let us pray for Mrs Marsden that God will give her strength to cope with this new revelation and be able to give care to this poor orphan. Let us pray.' Reverend Buckley gave a heartfelt prayer, beseeching God to help Lucy and Grace in their new life with Raymond, and there was a resounding 'Amen' from the congregation at the end of it. Laura squeezed her hand as she sat down and whispered, 'Well done', to which Lucy smiled.

Lucy heard nothing of the sermon afterwards, as she kept going over what she had said, and wondering if she'd done the right thing. After the service, many people came up to Lucy. Some were fulsome in praise of her actions, others just squeezed her hand, and two ladies said that they didn't think they could have taken the child in themselves. Lucy merely smiled and thanked people for their support. When the children came out of Sunday school, Lucy and Laura beat a hasty retreat, after speaking to Bill and Liz, Lucy saying that she'd speak to them later.

'Well done, Lucy. That's part one of the plan done, which is probably the hardest. Now for part two,' said Laura. After a quick cup of tea and a piece of cake, Lucy, Laura, and the children got into Lucy's motor car and drove to the Marsden family home, now occupied by Matthew and Betsy. Laura stayed outside with the children whilst Lucy told the family about Raymond. Betsy showed surprise when Lucy appeared, as it wasn't her week for visiting, but was soon horrified at what Lucy had to say. Fortunately, Granny Marsden was visiting, so that saved another telling of the sad story. When the family had got over their shock, Lucy signalled for Laura to bring the children and Grace proudly showed off her new brother.

After another cup of tea, Laura and Lucy and the children set off to Burnley. Laura applauded Lucy in carrying out part two of the plan.

'Now for part three,' Laura said, as they drove over to Burnley.

At Laura's house, William had rallied the whole family. Mr and Mrs Coombes and Granny Wall were all present, wondering what was happening as William refused to tell them anything. When they all arrived, Laura told Samuel to take Grace and Raymond and his brothers up to the playroom in the attics, whilst the adults talked. Once the children were gone, Lucy had to tell the story all over again. They were all shocked at what she had to say and asked if the Marsden family were going to take any responsibility for him? Lucy shook her head and said she would abide by what Harry had requested in his dying wish, even though it was very painful.

Sunday lunch was very late that day as the family all tried their best to understand what had happened and how to help Lucy in the future. She told them of what she had done at church and they commended her for that and admired her bravery. After lunch, Lucy was exhausted and decided to go home early. Fortunately, it was the half-term break, so she didn't have to go to school the next day but would have two days free to sort her new life out. When they got home, Lucy called at Liz and Bill's to ask about how they would manage Raymond in school. Bill said to leave it to him and he would think about it and see her on Tuesday.

Next morning Lucy was amazed by her church community. The door knocker never stopped all morning. First to visit was Annie Jackson.

216

'I've brought some old clothes of my lads that still have some good wear in them, if you want them?'

'Thanks, Annie, that's so kind of you.'

'It's the least I can do. You've been good to me, so now I want to return the favour.' The next person brought some toy soldiers for Raymond, the next brought a cake, another brought a beef casserole. It went on all morning, people turning up bringing gifts. One lady brought flowers, squeezed Lucy's hands and said, 'God bless you, my dear. You will be rewarded.'

Lucy was overwhelmed by the kindness and generosity of the church people, who wanted to show their support for her. The final visitor was Reverend Buckley, who brought Raymond a child's Bible with pictures, in case he didn't have one. Lucy thanked him and assured him that Raymond had not brought a Bible, so it was a timely gift. His wife had also sent a batch of scones. Such manifestations of love were so helpful to Lucy's vulnerable feelings and she knew she'd made the right decision in telling everyone, however hard it had been.

After lunch, Lucy took Grace and Raymond into Clitheroe. First stop was Mitchell's Modes children's department. Lucy bought several new outfits for Raymond, letting him choose which he liked best, plus new underwear and a warm coat, rather than the thin jacket he had arrived in. Socks, gloves, a hat, and shoes were next. Lucy noticed that Grace was enjoying helping Raymond choosing his garments, without even asking for anything for herself, so in a fit of love for her daughter, she bought her a new dress, which had lots of frills, which were dear to Grace's heart. Afterwards they had a hot chocolate in the tearooms and then returned home. Raymond told Grace that he loved hot chocolate now, and Grace replied that she did too, and it was because he was her brother; they liked the same things. The words pierced through Lucy's heart, but she said nothing. Grace seemed to have accepted that Raymond was a gift from her daddy, but that now her mummy would be Raymond's mummy too. That was enough facts for both children, Lucy decided. In time, they would have to be told the whole truth, but let them remain in ignorance for as long as possible.

Tea was easy, as Lucy had left the casserole in the oven and it was cooked to perfection. She wasn't sure what she was going to do with the boy when she went back to school, but Bill came round next morning with a solution.

'I think that for the time being, Raymond should come to school with you. That way, he'll get used to being part of your family. He must have had an awful time, being passed about from pillar to post for most of his young life. Eventually, when he is feeling more secure, you may be able to get other people to help you with his care.'

'You are right, Bill, thank you. I'm grateful that I can bring him with me.'

So, on Wednesday morning, Raymond went to school along with Grace and Lucy. Lucy sat him in a corner of the classroom and gave him picture books to look at and some chalks to use on a small slate. Lucy was glad to note that he seemed happy and was listening to the lessons as well. She was surprised when she looked at his chalk slate at the end of the day. He had copied some of the letters she had been teaching the little children. He was obviously going to be a bright child, Lucy decided.

On the Sunday, they all went to Betsy's for lunch and, after they had eaten and the children had gone upstairs to play, Betsy asked how Lucy was coping with him.

'He's no trouble, Betsy. He just does what I tell him, or rather what Grace tells him, as she seems to have taken over the role of mothering him.'

'I was thinking, do you remember when you first went back to work, I used to have Grace to stay so that you could get on with teaching?'

'I do. That was so helpful.'

'Would you like me to do the same for Raymond?'

'You'd do that for me?'

'Yes. I think you've been left in a mess because of my brother's misdemeanour. You are marvellous for taking him in. I don't know whether I could have done it, if Matthew had brought a child of his home from the war.'

'I didn't get any option. Mr Alderson just left him with me. He had to go to work and his landlady wouldn't let the boy stay. I wish I'd been warned. If only Harry had told me before, then I could have got used to the idea in advance. I still wouldn't have liked it, though.'

'It was so out of character for Harry.'

'Yes. I'm still furious, I don't think I'll ever forgive him.'

'Well, in a week or two, when he's more settled, I'll start having him from Sunday evening until Tuesday night, like I did for Grace.'

'Thank you, Betsy. I really appreciate that.'

'What did you do for me, Aunty Betsy?' asked Grace, coming through the door, followed by Raymond.

'I used to have you to stay here when Mummy first went back to teach in the school.'

'Yes, you did. I remember. Are you going to do the same for my brother?'

'Er, yes,' said Betsy, a little surprised to hear Grace call him her brother. 'Will you like to stay here, Raymond?'

'With Elsie? And the fort? And the soldiers?' Raymond asked. Raymond had already taken a shine to Betsy's youngest daughter, Elsie.

'That's right.'

'And Grace stay?'

'No, Grace will be at school, but you'll go home to be with Grace after you've stayed here. Is that all right?' Raymond put his head on one side, stroking a wooden soldier, whilst he thought about that and then nodded his agreement. *Just like Harry*, thought both Lucy and Betsy together, but neither said anything.

'You could come here with Grace in the school holidays, though. Would you like that?'

'Yes.'

'Good, that's settled then.'

Lucy was grateful that she would get some relief from caring for the boy, as every time she looked at him, it reminded her again of her husband's betrayal. She was also glad that Harry's family were taking some responsibility for their relative.

On returning home, she had a telephone call from Laura and she told her what had transpired at Betsy's.

'Oh, Lucy, I never thought to offer. What a fool I am. I'll do the same as well. Do you think he will come?'

'He was happy to go to Betsy's, so perhaps you can ask him next Sunday?'

'I will. Now, what I was contacting you for was because I've managed to get hold of Cynthia. You asked me to bring her up-to-date with the events, so I have done and she said you must telephone her anytime, if you need help or just to talk.'

Thank you. I don't know what I'd have done without you and Cynthia these last few years.'

'We don't know what we'd have done without you all these years, either. It works both ways. That's what friends are for. It's just a shame that Cynthia lives so far away and we don't see her as often as we would like to.'

'We'll make an effort over the Easter holidays, then. Shall we go the first day after the children break up for the school holidays?'

'Good idea. It'll be so good to see her again.'

'I'll telephone her tomorrow unless you want to do it?'

'No thanks, Laura. Please will you do it for me? It saves me having to go over it again. It's still very raw.'

'I know. I'm not surprised; it was such a shock.'

'I don't think I can ever forgive Harry, and I don't think I can ever love the boy. He's such a reminder, but I will do my duty by him and bring him up properly.'

'A child needs love, too, Lucy. You know that.'

'He's getting plenty of that from Grace. He worships her and follows her around all the time.'

'That's because she gives him unconditional love, Lucy.'

'Well, I can't. Grace doesn't understand the full implications of his birth. Now, what time do you want us to come over on Sunday?'

Laura realised that the subject was closed as far as Lucy was concerned, so she said 'Goodbye, until Sunday,' and hung up the receiver.

On the following Sunday, Raymond said that he would like to come and stay with Samuel, Edward and George and play with their toys. Raymond was fitting in well with his extended family, Lucy noted. If only she felt the same way about him herself.

Chapter 30

A week later, a new phase began in Lucy's life, reflecting an earlier time when Grace had been small. Raymond was no trouble at either house and seemed to thrive on all the attention he was being given, and his vocabulary was increasing daily. On Wednesdays, Annie Jackson managed to look after Raymond as well as cleaning the house and making the tea, and Lucy frequently told her she was a Godsend.

The following Saturday, Mr Alderson came to visit Raymond, who ran up to him and hugged him and chattered away, telling him about all his new family. Lucy watched them together and thought it was a shame that Mr Alderson wasn't married as he would make a good father, and he could have kept Raymond himself, if he'd had a wife. Although on second thoughts, his wife probably wouldn't have wanted a stranger's child either. After lunch, Raymond insisted on taking Mr Alderson all round the garden, showing him the hen hut, the vegetable plot, and the orchard. Lucy was surprised to see him talking so volubly to an adult; usually he was only talkative to other children.

Mr Alderson said it was time to go but was pleased to see that Raymond had settled in well.

'How are you?' Lucy asked. 'Did you get a permanent job?'

'Yes, thank you. They're keeping me on now, not just for a month. Hopefully, I can rebuild my life.'

'I do hope so. May God bless you and thank you again for your part in this difficult transaction.'

'I'll keep in touch with you for a little while if you don't mind?'

'As long as you want to,' replied Lucy, and Mr Alderson left.

It was soon Easter, and Laura and Lucy took all the children over to see Cynthia. The children played out in the garden, whilst the three friends talked non-stop. Cynthia shyly admitted that she was seeing a gentleman. Lucy and Laura were all ears, wanting to know all the details.

'He's a widower, like me. His wife died in childbirth when he was in the army, serving in Belgium. The child also died.'

'Where did you meet him?' asked Laura.

'At church. He has recently moved to Bolton. He's a solicitor and his office is next door to my father's office, so he invited him for a meal and to church, as a token of friendship.'

'Has he any other children?' asked Lucy.

'No, it was their first child.'

'How sad,' said Laura.

'Yes, they had been childhood sweethearts. They'd planned to have lots of children.'

'What a shame, but at least he seems to have recovered now, if you are seeing him?'

'You'll have to keep us informed,' laughed Laura.

'I will, I promise, or my life will be worth nothing!' Cynthia said.

'I don't think I'll ever marry again,' said Lucy.

'Why not? You are too young to stay alone,' said Laura.

'I don't think I could ever trust a man enough to love again. I loved Harry unconditionally and totally and he let me down. It would always be in the back of my mind. Anyway, who would want to take on my husband's illegitimate child?'

'A lot of men would understand, I'm sure,' said Cynthia. 'I know Henry would take on my children if it comes to that.'

'I agree,' said Laura. 'A lot of attitudes have changed since the war.'

'That might be right for you, Cynthia, but not for me.' Lucy was adamant, so Laura changed the subject and talked about holidays when the peace was interrupted by a cry. Little George had fallen and hurt his knee and needed his mummy, so Laura went to the rescue, asking for warm water and a flannel to clean the wounds. Soon after that, it was time to go home, so the women all promised they would meet up again in the school holidays. Cynthia suggested that perhaps Henry could drive her over, rather than them always having to come to Bolton. They agreed to meet at Laura's house in mid-July. Then Lucy, Laura, and the children set off back home, the children worn out after their day's playing, sleeping all the way home.

During the summer school holidays, when Cynthia and children came over to Laura's, they decided to take the children to Blackpool for a few days. They persuaded Freddie to take them in the new charabanc that William had invested in. This one carried a few less people, but wasn't open-topped like the other one, so was much more comfortable to ride in, whatever the weather. They stayed at the Norbreck Hydro and had adjoining rooms. They also took Albert and Arthur with them. Some days, Albert and Arthur looked after the children so that the three friends could spend time together. Fun days were had on the beach when it was good weather, with picnics provided by the hotel, and on rainy days, they spent time on the Pier, playing on the slot machines and going to variety shows. They spent one day on the Blackpool Pleasure Beach, where the children had a riotous time, going on all the slides and roundabouts and some scary rides.

Another day, Henry managed to drive over and visit them, which pleased Cynthia, and the two friends were glad to meet him, and give him the 'once over', as Laura said to Lucy behind Cynthia's back. Fortunately both friends approved of Henry, not that it would have mattered to Cynthia what they thought, but she was glad they'd liked him, nevertheless.

All too soon, it was time for them to go home, the children declaring it was their best holiday ever. It was certainly the costliest holiday the friends had ever had, but they didn't mind, as the children were all happy.

October brought a rush of weddings. Bessie was marrying Mrs Smith's nephew, Robert Jones. He had become the traveller for the business and sold clothes, collected repairs, or sourced materials and trimmings for the shop. He also drove the women to any home fittings, so was a very useful person to the business. They were to live in the flat over the shop initially until they could find a house they liked. Aunty Brenda, as Mrs Smith now was, made Bessie's wedding dress, but it was a very busy time for her, as besides Bessie's wedding dress, Agnes was getting married the same day and also wanted a dress. Agnes was marrying an engineer who worked on the railway. They'd met when Agnes was coming home from a teaching conference and had tripped and fallen on the platform. John Yates had picked her up and insisted on strapping her ankle and helping her home, as he was at the end of his shift. He visited a few days later, just to see how she was getting on, so he said, but romance soon blossomed.

The girls were getting married the first Saturday of October at the old Mission where they'd been brought up, and where Laura and William had got married. Mr Carter looked so proud as he walked his two daughters down the aisle, one on either arm. Lucy noticed that he looked much older now and had a cough, but that was probably due to working in the mills all his life. Laura made everybody laugh as she commented that at least it saved them having to buy two new outfits in the same year, and Mr Carter said it had saved him a fortune, too, with only one wedding breakfast to provide. Laura wasn't a Dame of Honour for her sisters, but young Samuel was a ring bearer for both girls. Robert and John both had sisters, so there was no shortage of pretty bridesmaids, dressed in their finery.

At the end of October, Cynthia married Henry Pickup. It was a much quieter affair at the Methodist church they attended, as they had both been married before, but it was still moving. Cynthia was given away by her father and her children, Stephen and Elizabeth, followed her down the aisle, holding hands together. The family were to live in a detached house with large gardens, near to his office.

All too soon, it was nearly Christmas, and plans were afoot for school activities. Lucy and the children were planning on going to Betsy and Matthew's on Christmas Day and spending Boxing Day at Laura and William's.

Three weeks before Christmas, on a Saturday morning, Grace complained of feeling unwell. Lucy gave her a cooling powder and put her to bed, but she was much worse in the morning, complaining of a sore throat. When Lucy looked at her, she noticed a rash on her neck and when she checked, it was all over her chest, too. Lucy rang Matthew to come and see her.

'It's scarlet fever,' Matthew said. 'There's a bit of an epidemic going on at the moment.'

'Will she be all right? What can I do?'

'Just make sure she drinks plenty, give her cooling powders, and you can use some calamine lotion to ease her skin. Oh, and you'd better not go to school for now.'

'Of course not. Have you time for a cup of tea, Matthew?'

'No, I'd better get on. I've a lot of visits to do today. I'm so glad I've got a new partner now, otherwise I'd be run off my feet. If you're worried, call me again. Otherwise I'll pop in tomorrow.'

'Thank you, Matthew,' Lucy said as she closed the door after him. She ran back upstairs to Grace to check she was all right. She appeared restless, so Lucy gave her a drink of water, which seemed to settle her. Running downstairs, she found the bottle of calamine lotion in the medicine box, searched for some cotton wool, and then went back upstairs. Grace was sleeping, so very carefully Lucy soothed the lotion onto the rash.

Coming back downstairs, Lucy telephoned Bill Hunter to tell him she wouldn't be in school on Monday and neither would Grace.

'Oh dear, I'm so sorry for Grace. There were several children off sick on Friday, weren't there, so I suppose we are in for a bit of a run. I'll double up the classes for now. Is there anything Liz or I can do?'

'No, but thanks for offering. Goodbye.'

Suddenly she realised that Raymond wasn't around and wondered where he was. Thinking he might have gone in to see Grace, she ran upstairs to look at Grace, but there was no sign of him. Next, she looked in his own bedroom, as he had moved next door to Grace, but he wasn't there, nor in the bathroom either. Going downstairs, Lucy went outside and found Raymond talking to the hens, telling them that Grace was sick and he was looking after them today. Smiling, Lucy came back inside, without letting Raymond know that she had heard him. Lucy lost count of the times she ran up and downstairs that day and the day after. She was also in and out of Grace's bedroom most of the night.

On Monday, there were signs of improvement. Grace's temperature was down and she was able to manage a little soup that Lucy had made for her. Within the week, she was back to normal, the rash was fading, and Lucy gave a huge sigh of relief. But her relief was premature, as the next day Raymond started showing the same symptoms. It was inevitable really, Lucy thought, as they were so close together all the time. Although Lucy rang Matthew, she said that Raymond wasn't too ill, and she would follow the same regime that she had with Grace, to which Matthew agreed. As the days wore on, however, Raymond didn't get better. After a week, he got suddenly worse and began coughing. Lucy sent for Matthew.

Matthew examined Raymond and looked grave and asked Lucy to come downstairs with him.

'It's not good, Lucy. He's got inflammation on both sides of his lungs. This occasionally happens with scarlet fever.'

'What can I do?'

'Keep him sat up as much as you can to help his breathing, and carry on with what you have been doing. Give him fluids and cooling powders. If he gets any worse, I'll get him into hospital.'

'Hospital?'

'Yes, if consolidation sets in, I may have to admit him. In very severe cases, scarlet fever can affect the heart. You're going to have a busy night looking after him. Shall I take Grace home with me?'

'No, you and Betsy have enough to do. I'll send her to her friend Harriet's. She had the scarlet fever the same week as Grace, which isn't surprising as she and Harriet are inseparable. Could you just wait here a moment, and I'll nip across the road to ask her mother?'

'Of course, you go.'

Lucy grabbed her coat and ran across to the Fallons' house. She came back very quickly with Mrs Fallon, who collected Grace and took her home. Grace was ecstatic to be going to stay at Harriet's house, even though she was worried about Raymond. Matthew took his leave and Lucy went back upstairs. Raymond's breathing seemed to have got worse in those few minutes. It was going to be a long night. She pulled up a chair besides Raymond's bed.

Watching Raymond struggling to get each breath, Lucy started thinking about how he had come into hers and Grace's life. She thought about Raymond's mother. All this time she had hated her, along with Harry for what they had done, but in the long reaches of the night, Lucy started seeing it from their point of view. They had not intended having an affair, it was just a spontaneous occurrence, that was never repeated. They had repented of their sins, and kept away from each other, but it was too late; Raymond had been conceived. Lucy realised how desperate Mimi must have been when she knew she was having a baby. To make it worse, all her family and her late husband's family disowned her. Lucy idly wondered what she would have done if it was her in that situation? *I'd never have been in that situation,* Lucy thought, *but what if I were? What if someone came to comfort me when Harry died? I was so upset at first that I would have taken any comfort from anyone if it relieved the pain in my heart even for a minute.*

Suddenly, Lucy saw a clear vision of herself and didn't like what she saw. Her hatred of Harry and Mimi was selfish. They had sinned, but they had also repented, and yet Lucy couldn't forgive them. What did that say about her? Was she sinless? Certainly not. She may not have done anything so serious, but she had many sins in her life. Daily, in her prayers, she asked God to forgive her sins, unconditionally, and fully expected Him to forgive her, and yet she couldn't forgive their sins. Lucy started to weep quietly. Who did she think she was, refusing to forgive people for whom Jesus died? If Jesus could forgive them, why couldn't she? Her weeping had to be quiet, so as not to disturb Raymond as he lay struggling for every breath.

Getting on her knees, Lucy prayed a desperate prayer, asking forgiveness from God. Forgiveness for her hard heartedness, her attitude of hatred, her anger, her refusal to forgive, her bitterness of spirit, her failure to repent of her sins earlier. Eventually, her prayers spent, she looked up at Raymond, but he was still struggling to breathe, so her prayers continued. She asked forgiveness that her hardness of heart had been extended to Raymond. She had blamed him for all her ills. She had physically cared for him and provided well for him, but had never loved him, as she saw that as a betrayal of her love for Harry. But the fact was, she had never loved him as a mother – until now. Suddenly, Lucy realised that she loved this little boy. She had never treated him with love and, despite being only three years old, he seemed to know that Lucy didn't want much physical touch from him, unlike Grace. Lucy wept all over again for her wilfulness in not treating this small child with love. She'd shown more love to her pupils in school than she had shown to Raymond. It wasn't his fault that he had been born. Her prayers became more desperate as she pleaded for his life, making promises to God that she would show love towards him at all times.

The knot that had been in her heart for all these months felt to be slowly unwinding, as she was aware that God was forgiving her and giving her peace for the first time since Harry died and Raymond arrived. It felt as if the Holy Spirit was flooding through her body, heart, and soul, and she wept again, this time for happiness that she felt back on right terms with God again, after all these months. She must have dozed for a while, but woke up with a start. Raymond's breathing seemed to be getting worse.

Chapter 31

Lucy was frightened. Matthew had said that it could affect his heart. He was such an uncomplaining child. Surely he wouldn't die? Raymond was rambling in his sleep, saying French words that Lucy didn't understand. It struck her that she never acknowledged his French-ness and she vowed that in future, if he survived, she would try to find someone who was fluent in French, so that he could keep his French language alive. Probably there would be a French teacher at Clitheroe Grammar school whom she could contact. She would also take the children to France in a few years time, to see their father's grave.

Around 4am, Raymond was even sicker, his breath catching in his throat and Lucy, in desperation, rang for Matthew. He was there within minutes, still in his nightshirt, with a large coat over it.

He looked at Raymond and examined him and said, 'I think this is the crisis. There is some consolidation in his chest. The next few hours are crucial. I'll stay here with you.'

'Thank you, Matthew. You are such a comfort. I've been so scared by myself.'

'I'm not surprised. I did wonder if I should move him to hospital, but he's too sick for that now. We'll just have to wait and see and trust God. That is all we have left.'

'I've done a lot of thinking during the night,' said Lucy. 'I have never forgiven Harry for this child coming into being, or the child's mother. I have had anger, bitterness, and hatred in my heart. But I've repented of it all now and I feel at peace, for the first time since Harry died.'

'That's good. I'm glad you've come to terms with it all.'

'That's not all I've repented of. I have physically cared for Raymond, but I've never loved him, until tonight. When I thought that I might lose him, I was scared. I realised I did love him. Harry had entrusted him to me and I was letting Harry down by not loving him as I should.' Matthew nodded.

'I'll just listen to his chest again,' Matthew said, so Lucy remained silent. Matthew felt Raymond's pulse and said that it was very rapid and feeble, but there was nothing he could do to help him. Lucy's heart sank. She bathed Raymond's face and put some more cooling lotion on his body, saying, 'Come on, Raymond, get better. Mummy loves you.'

He was beyond taking sips of water now, so Lucy kissed him tenderly, her tears also falling on his brow. Lucy had brought Matthew another chair to sit in and eventually, they both dozed off around 6am.

Lucy woke first and realised that there were no noisy breathing sounds and ran to Raymond, fearing the worst, and shouting to Matthew. He was awake instantly and came to the bedside. He listened to Raymond's chest, felt his pulse and his forehead, and said, 'Thank God. He's through the crisis.' Lucy burst into tears.

'Thank you, Matthew. I'm so glad you were here.'

'He's not out of the woods yet; there may still be damage to his heart. He'll have to take things very easy for a while to come. I think I'd better be going now. I have a surgery at 9am, but call me back if you're worried.'

'I will and thank you again.'

Matthew nodded and left the house. Lucy sat staring at this little boy whom she had so resented, and now felt floods of love in her heart for him. As he seemed to be sleeping peacefully, Lucy curled up on the bed next to him and allowed herself to go to sleep, knowing that if he needed her, she would be there for him.

Lucy woke about 11am and, as Raymond was still sleeping, she went downstairs and made herself a cup of tea and some bread and jam. She'd not eaten for two days, and knew she'd be no good to Raymond if she was ill. Checking that Raymond was still all right, Lucy telephoned Laura and brought her up to date with what was happening. Fortunately, none of Laura's children had caught the disease, even though they had spent the Sunday at Laura's the week before Grace was ill.

Going back upstairs to the bedroom, Lucy saw that Raymond was still sleeping peacefully; Matthew said that this is what would probably happen after the crisis. Climbing onto the bed, Lucy felt herself dozing off again. Not only had the last few days been physically demanding, last night had also been emotionally and spiritually draining. A little voice woke her. 'Mummy?' Lucy was instantly awake. 'Thirsty.' Joy flooded through Lucy's soul.

'Are you thirsty? Here, have a sip of this water, and then Mummy will go and get you a glass of milk.'

'Milk, please,' he replied, but even before Lucy got downstairs, Raymond had fallen asleep again. When Lucy returned with the milk, she smiled down at his sleeping form. He had called her Mummy. That was the sweetest sound she had heard for some time. A little later, Raymond woke and drank the milk, but then fell asleep again. They were both asleep on the bed when Matthew let himself in at teatime, so he just examined Raymond in his sleep. Lucy woke up suddenly.

'Oh, Matthew, sorry, how long have you been here?'

'Not long. He sounds a lot better, Lucy.'

'Yes, he's managed a glass of milk, over the day.'

'Excellent. Keep him on fluids today and then see how he is tomorrow before starting any food. A little thin soup to start with, I think.'

'I will. Will his heart be all right?'

'It's too soon to say yet, but he's recovered well so far, so we'll wait and see. I'll come back tomorrow teatime again and see how he is.'

'Thank you, Matthew,' said Lucy, starting to get off the bed, but Matthew told her to stay there; he'd let himself out, but not to forget to have some food herself, as he didn't want his nurse being ill as well. Lucy smiled and said 'goodbye', and promptly went back to sleep.

Very slowly, Raymond began to recover and eventually Grace was allowed home. She had had a lovely time at Harriet's she said, but missed Raymond and her Mummy's cuddles at night.

As soon as Lucy could leave Raymond alone with Grace, she went into Harry's workshop for the first time ever. He had always kept it locked because of his tools and with it being an outside building. Lucy stood in the centre of the workshop and said 'sorry' to Harry. It seemed fitting to say it here because it was his private domain. She also said 'sorry' to Mimi. When she looked round the room, Lucy couldn't believe what she was seeing. There were toys all over the room. There was a beautiful doll's house, which he must have made for Grace, even though she was too young to use it. There was also a wooden doll's pram, with little wheels, which Grace would love now as she and Harriet played with dolls all the time.

There was also boys' toys: a fort and soldiers, a whistle, and a catapult. Lucy also found another stool, with no name engraved on it. He must have been anticipating their next child, Lucy thought tenderly, and hoping it would be a boy. 'Well, you did get a boy,' Lucy said to the empty room, 'but not in the way I expected.' Sadly, she left the room, locking the door, and knew that Raymond had inherited his father's love of wood. This would become

Raymond's room as soon as he was able to use a woodworking tool safely. The tradition would pass from father to son.

That evening, Lucy finally decided to look at the letters that had been brought by Archie Alderson. She had never looked at them before, as she had been overwhelmed by Raymond turning up and had put them at the back of her drawer. First, she looked at the letters that she had written to Harry. She could tell that every letter had been read by Harry many times and some were nearly worn through. Also, the little pictures and letters from Grace were looking fragile. At the bottom of the pile, Lucy found two letters addressed to her, that had never been posted. They were both from Harry.

The first one was a painful telling of the story of how Raymond had been conceived. In the letter, Harry begged her forgiveness and told her of the coming child. In the second letter, he told of Mimi's death and the subsequent problems of bringing up the child. He had never posted either letter. 'Oh, Harry,' cried Lucy afresh. 'Why didn't you post these letters?' It would have broken her heart at the time, but at least she would have been more resigned to it, and better prepared when Raymond arrived and perhaps would have loved him a little earlier. It was too late now, but at least he had written, even if he hadn't the courage to post them. Perhaps he had always intended to post them before he came home with Raymond, but events took their course and he didn't get the chance to come home with Raymond. Lucy put the letters carefully back with the other ones. Someday, in the long far-off future, she would show them to Raymond, but for now, she had to concentrate on getting him better and loving him as she should have done before. She must also remember to tell Archie Alderson that Harry had written to her, but never posted the letters.

Before Raymond was fully recovered, it was Christmas time. Lucy decided to decline all offers to go anywhere for Christmas dinner that year, but invited people to call in to her house, but not to stay for a meal. Lucy managed to drag them to the church service that morning, allowing them a new book each to take with them. During the prayers, Lucy felt like shouting her praises to God out loud as she was so thankful that all her prayers about Raymond had been answered, but more so, that she had been forgiven for all her wrongdoings. The best part was that she was really able to love Raymond now, like she did Grace, and he was responding to that love, like a flower opening from bud to ripe bloom.

They had a cosy Christmas meal together and the children were amazed at the presents that they received that year. Grace was even more amazed to learn that they had been made by her father, before he went to war, to give to her when she was older.

After their lunch, Laura, William, and family all came over to visit, along with Mr and Mrs Coombes, and Granny Wall. There were even more presents for everyone. Laura's boys were amazed by the fort and the soldiers, and Laura was even more surprised when Lucy told her of her find just before Christmas in Harry's workshop. Before they left, Betsy, Matthew, and the children all arrived with Granny Marsden, which was a cue for the Coombes family to leave, as the house was getting too full.

As they were leaving, Laura said, 'What's your Christmas wish for next year?'

Lucy looked over at Raymond, then Grace. 'To be the best mother I can be to both my children.'

'I'll say "Amen" to that, Lucy. In fact, I think I'll make it mine as well, to all my children, that's a good phrase, especially as I'll have four by next Christmas.'

'Four? Laura, you are not….'

'I am, but only just. All's well so far,' she whispered, but further talk was impossible as she was enveloped in a hug by Lucy.

'I'm sure 1920 will be the best year ever,' said Lucy. 'The Twenties has such a ring to it. A new decade. I wonder what will happen in this decade?'

'I'll have another child to look after!' Laura replied, laughing. 'That's what the Twenties will bring. Thank God for my mum.'

The Coombes family left, so Lucy could concentrate on the Marsden family members. More presents arrived and they all settled down to a cup of tea. Nobody could eat anything else, as they'd all had a substantial lunch. Lucy thought that Granny Marsden wasn't looking very well, but nobody said anything, so she let it pass. She looked very pale, Lucy thought. After the family had left, Lucy heaved a sigh of relief and said that it was time for Raymond to go to bed. He was looking even paler than Granny Marsden had done, and Lucy remembered that Matthew had said not to let him tire too much at first. Raymond didn't argue, so Lucy knew he must be feeling exhausted.

On Boxing Day, they went nowhere, and nobody visited, so it was a more peaceful day, to play with presents and rest. Gradually, day by day, Raymond made progress and, by the beginning of next term, Lucy was able to go back to school with Grace. Annie Jackson agreed to come in and mind Raymond each day, as they thought it might be too much effort for him going to different houses for half a week each. Also Liz came and relieved Annie if she had another job to go to. Matthew approved of this decision, and so far, there didn't seem to be any damage to Raymond's heart, for which Lucy thanked God.

As Raymond got stronger, Lucy rooted out the old three-seater bicycle and, after wrapping up Raymond warmly, they all went out for a ride, down to Whalley village and back, which brought the glow to Raymond's cheeks, she was pleased to see.

On the fourth of February it was Raymond's fourth birthday, which he shared with Laura's second child, Edward, who was seven. A joint birthday party was held at Laura's house, with an enormous cake, which had both names and ages on. After the candles were blown out, they were relit so that each child could blow them out.

Time seemed to be going fast and it was soon July, when Laura rang to say she was in labour, so to wait for news soon. It was a quick birth, and Laura had a little girl. She was ecstatic, she told Lucy, as it made a change from having boys! They were to call her Margaret Lucy.

As often happens in families, as one person arrives, another person leaves. Granny Marsden had a sudden decline with a growth in her stomach and died peacefully in the beginning of August. All her family were devastated, none more so than Grace, but had happy memories of her. Later, Lucy was surprised that she had left her estate to be divided between her four grandchildren, and Harry's share would go to her. Lucy knew that she didn't need the substantial amount of money that she received, so it went in the appropriately named Marsden Building Society, with the other money from Granny Wall. She knew that it would secure any career or plans that her children might have in the future.

A new school term loomed and it would be Raymond's first time at school. He couldn't wait to go and had learned from Grace that he had to call Mummy, Mrs Marsden at school. He adapted very well to school and was a quick learner, far quicker than Grace had been. In late October, Bill called in to see her at the end of the school day.

'I want to talk to you, Lucy.'

'Yes?'

'I've been offered another post as headmaster.'

'Where?'

'Not far from here, in Read village, on the way to Burnley.'

'Are you unhappy here?'

'Certainly not, but I've been here for 20 years and I feel ready for a change. Besides, Read school is a bigger one. We won't be too far away for you to visit though.'

'Where is it? I've not seen a school on my way through Read when I'm going to Burnley?'

'It's on East View, and you won't see it from the main road. It's called the Chapel School in the village, as there is another school called St John's, which is Church of England.'

'Well, I'll miss you. I've really enjoyed working here with you.'

'What I want to ask you, Lucy, is, would you be interested in becoming the headteacher? I could recommend you, if you wanted it?'

'No, I love my job with the little ones, but I wouldn't want to be the headteacher with having two children to bring up on my own. If they were ill, I would struggle, as it was very obvious last year when Raymond was so poorly. No, I have no higher ambitions than what I am doing now, but thank you for asking. When do you leave?'

'At Christmas. I start the new job in January.'

'So soon?'

'Yes. I didn't want to say anything until it was all confirmed.'

'When are they appointing the new headmaster?'

'The post is being advertised this week, that's why I wanted to ask you. Also, the education board have suggested that, due to the increased number of our pupils, we divide the children into three classes, so they will interview for another teacher, besides the Head. Would you want to take the middle class, or stay where you are?'

'Definitely stay where I am. I love being the first teacher that the children have.'

'Good. We'll leave it at that then. Good night. See you tomorrow.'

'Good night,' said Lucy. As she slowly collected her belongings together before going home, Lucy smiled to herself that Bill had thought her worthy of being a headteacher. She couldn't wait to ring Laura; she would never believe it.

It was a few weeks later that a young boy from Mr Hunter's class came into her classroom at the end of the school day.

'Please, Miss, Mr Hunter says he wants to speak to you and can you go to his room?'

'Thank you, Peter,' Lucy replied. She walked into Bill's classroom, noticing another man standing there looking out of the window.

'Ah, Mrs Marsden. I want to introduce you to the new headmaster. This is Mrs Marsden, who teaches the little ones, and this is....'

'Jacob Atherton!' Lucy gasped. 'How lovely to see you.'

'Lucy! You teach here?'

'I take it you two know each other,' Bill said dryly.

'Yes,' they both said together, then laughed.

'We trained together,' explained Lucy.

'Well, I want to talk about the school, so can you leave your reminiscing until later?' asked Bill, laughing.

'Jacob, I live right opposite the school, in that house there. I'll have to go now, as the children will be waiting, but come over afterwards for a cup of tea, if you have time?'

'Yes, I'd love to. See you later.'

Lucy smiled, then left the room, her day suddenly brightening at this turn of events. It wasn't long before there was a knock at the door.

'Come in,' called Lucy, 'and sit by the fire, whilst I make a cup of tea.'

'Thank you. I hope I'm not intruding on your family life?'

'Certainly not. Children, come and say "Hello" to Mr Atherton. He is to be the new headmaster at school.' Lucy introduced both the children to Jacob and then sent them off to play in the parlour, so that she and Jacob could talk in peace.

'So, tell me all about your life, Jacob. The last I heard, you had gone in the army, and David Wood had gone in the navy, but after Huw died, we didn't hear any more.

'That's right, I served in the army and harrowing it was, so I'll say no more.'

'I don't blame you. Nobody enjoyed the war that I've heard of. Did you marry the girl from the first year? I remember you being keen on her when we left.'

Jacob's face clouded over.

'No, she didn't wait for me. I wanted to get married before I joined up, but she wouldn't. Said she wanted to teach for a while first. We got engaged, but she met someone else who had a job that was exempt from war service and she married him quite quickly.'

'Jacob, I am so sorry. That must have been very painful.'

'Don't worry, I'm over it now. She wrote to me when I was in France. I got the letter just before a big offensive. I went out into battle in a terrible state and wanted to die, but somehow, God hadn't finished with me yet, because I survived.'

'I'm so glad you did.'

'What about you? The last time I heard from Huw, he said you'd married Harry, and Laura had married William, your brother, but again, I never heard any more. You've two children, I see. What's Harry doing now? Will he be home soon? I'd love to see him again. Your little boy is so like Harry.'

Lucy wasn't sure what to say. How much should she tell Jacob? In the end, she opted for the whole story.

'Harry died in the war.'

'Oh, I'm sorry Lucy. Me and my big mouth.'

'It's all right. I might as well tell you the whole story, as you're going to be the new headmaster, and most of the village people know it anyway.' Slowly and painfully, Lucy told Jacob the whole story, even to her need for learning how to forgive others and needing forgiveness herself. Jacob sat in silence throughout.

'What can I say, Lucy? You must have been through terrible struggles and pain.'

'Yes.'

'I can certainly relate to those feelings of rejection and hurt. It's amazing that you have brought Raymond up as your own. I don't know whether I could have done that if Felicity had borne another man's child out of wedlock, but still wanted to marry me.'

'I didn't have an option. Harry's friend just turned up on the doorstep and left him with me.'

'I suppose we don't know what we can cope with until we find ourselves in that position.'

'No, and without God's strength, I wouldn't have coped, even though I didn't want to cope at first.'

What changed your mind?'

'Raymond got seriously ill with scarlet fever and when I thought I would lose him, I realised just how much he'd got under my skin, and I did love him, despite my heart not wanting to, because I was still mad at Harry.'

'Lucy, I'm so glad that I applied for this job and will be working with you. We always got on so well together. How's Laura now? Did William survive the war?'

'Yes, he was most put out. When he enlisted, he told them that he was a driver and conversant with how motor cars worked, so he got picked to drive the top brass around to important meetings. He never left London! Except once when he had to take important people to Yorkshire.'

'Lucky him!'

'Yes, but he didn't think so. He and Laura now have four children. Three boys and then a girl.'

'Good. Do you hear from Cynthia now?'

'Yes, Laura and I keep in touch and meet up several times a year. Cynthia really helped me when Harry died and I was still mad at God for allowing it.'

'I remember that phase too,' said Jacob ruefully. 'So what happened after Huw died?'

'She moved in with her parents, but last year she married a solicitor who was a widower and had moved to Bolton, and they've bought a house near his business. She seems very happy.'

'I'm glad about that.'

'Did your father ever forgive you for not joining the mill?'

'Oh, yes. My sister married a mill owner's younger son, who wouldn't inherit his father's mill, so he was happy to inherit my father's mill in return for marrying my sister. A good deal all round, I think, and got me off the hook,' Jacob laughed.

'Did you go back to the school where Laura used to work?'

'No, not after the war. I wanted a change, so I worked in a school in Bury. Then I realised that I wanted to work in a school that is connected to a church, not a state school, so I applied for the headmaster's job here.'

'I'm glad you did. Do you still hear from David Wood?'

'Yes, he went into the navy and managed to survive. He married a lovely lady called Veronica and they have a girl. They live in Littleborough. David teaches in the school there.'

'Do you hear from anyone else?'

'No, but I did hear about Mary Watson.' Lucy pulled a face, but Jacob continued. 'She married The Honourable, but he was killed in the war, so she married the older cousin instead. She's Lady Mary now,' he laughed.

'Well, I hope she's happy,' said Lucy, as graciously as she could.

'I'm sure she will be, he was very rich!'

'Where are you going to live when you start as headmaster?'

'Just down the street. Mr Hunter is renting his house to me, as his son is getting married and moving to Burnley, and there is a house provided with Mr Hunter's new job. So I'm going to rent his house, until I find somewhere to buy, or I may stay there, as the Hunters don't need their house until they retire.'

'I'm so glad. I'm sure you'll love the village and the church.'

'It seems to be a real community, from what I've heard.'

'It is. They were so supportive when Harry died, but also when Raymond arrived. I stood up in church the day after and told them all who Raymond was.'

'You didn't!'

'I did. I thought it was better to let everybody know, before there was idle gossip.'

'I really admire you for that. It can't have been easy, but you were never one to hide away from a challenge. That's what I liked about you,' said Jacob smiling.

Lucy looked at this dear friend, who had been through so much himself and learned to live with it, like she had done. She felt a shiver of excitement. Suddenly, she knew that Jacob Atherton was going to be important to her in the future, not just as a work colleague. She didn't know how she knew it, but she did, deep in her heart. She tried to remember what Cynthia had said about love the second time round. Rather than a sudden flame, it's a slow burning, she had said. The way Jacob was looking at her suggested that he was thinking along the same lines, and she blushed at her thoughts. Jumping up, she said, 'I'll have to start making tea, Jacob, can I press you to stay?'

'I thought you'd never ask,' said Jacob, smiling warmly.

Yes, thought Lucy, *the Twenties are going to be a good decade. I can't wait!*

About this book

I got the idea for this book from a dream. In my dream I was at a writers' conference and we were given a task to write about. It was to make a story about someone from the past, someone from the present and someone from the future. My first thoughts were related to a nurse who was inspired by Florence Nightingale, on the eve of her own daughter's graduation as a nurse. But soon after, this story came in to my head and two hours later, I'd planned the whole book in my head! Then we went into lockdown 2021. What else was a writer to do?

About the author

Linda Sawley is a retired senior lecturer in children's nursing, having worked with children for all her career. After having to re-write a 40,000 word dissertation for a Master of Philosophy degree, Linda decided to try non-academic writing. She set up her own publishing company in 1998. A committed Christian, Linda is a member of the Association of Christian Writers and an Associate Member of NAWG (National Association of Writer's Groups.) Linda loves her friends, family, knitting, classical music, reading, talking, singing, eating out and buying shoes – not necessarily in that order! She hates cooking, cleaning and all things domestic.

Linda is a founder member of the charity 'Petal' which was formally known as Ribble Valley and White Rose Ladies Luncheon Club, which raises money for childhood cancer in the north of England. She supports the charity through a donation made from the sale of each book. Her other charity, who also receive a donation from the sale of each book, is Derian House Children's Hospice, in Lancashire.

In 2004, she was awarded two prizes at the David St John Thomas Self-Publishing Awards for her third book 'The Key'. One award was the Community Cup for self-publishing for charity, and the second award was the Overall Grand Award, for the person showing the most promise in self-publishing.

www.linricpublishing.com